three perfect liars

also by heidi perks

Her One Mistake

three
perfect
liars

a novel

HEIDI PERKS

Gallery Books

New York   London   Toronto   Sydney   New Delhi

G10

Gallery Books
An Imprint of Simon & Schuster, Inc.
1230 Avenue of the Americas
New York, NY 10020

First Gallery Books hardcover edition August 2020

GALLERY BOOKS and colophon are registered trademarks of Simon & Schuster, Inc.

For information about special discounts for bulk purchases, please contact Simon & Schuster Special Sales at 1-866-506-1949 or business@simonandschuster.com.

The Simon & Schuster Speakers Bureau can bring authors to your live event. For more information or to book an event, contact the Simon & Schuster Speakers Bureau at 1-866-248-3049 or visit our website at www.simonspeakers.com.

Interior design by Davina Mock-Maniscalco

Manufactured in the United States of America

1   3   5   7   9   10   8   6   4   2

Library of Congress Cataloging-in-Publication Data is available.

ISBN 978-1-9821-3993-3
ISBN 978-1-9821-3995-7 (ebook)

For my mum,
for being such a great one.

monday, may 13

the night of the fire

I t had taken seven minutes for the first of the fire engines to screech to a halt outside the offices of Morris and Wood, but even by then anyone could have seen it was too late. The fire had coursed through the building at an alarming rate. Red and orange flames were already obscured by a billowing cloud of dark gray smoke. The sound of breaking glass shattered the air.

She was on the quay across the river from the office, with a perfect view she no longer wanted, yet she couldn't bring herself to turn away.

To her right a few people had spilled out of the Star pub and the couple of restaurants nearby. It was a warm evening in mid-May, warm enough to be out enjoying the longer days even though it was a Monday.

Most of the onlookers had probably protested against the development of the Morris and Wood offices when plans for the building were first proposed to the council. The development had caused outrage five years ago. Ad hoc meetings set up in cafés and school halls had been attended by angry residents from Lymington and beyond who refused to allow such an eyesore to be built.

No one, they had said, *wants to look across the Lymington River from the beautiful quay and see a monstrosity of a glass office staring back at them.*

Bloody Londoners, they had murmured among themselves. *They are the problem, coming to the south coast from the city, taking over our town.*

But a few months later, Harry Wood had had them all eating out of his palm. Well, maybe not all of them, but the ones who counted.

And so the plans had been approved, the building work started. Anyone who knew the first thing about architecture should have been able to see the offices would be a thing of beauty—though too much so for an advertising agency perhaps.

Harry Wood found a way to the locals' hearts, recruiting locally and supporting charities close to them. The Lymington Care Home had never had so many minibuses and outings to the New Forest.

Yet once upon a time, some of the people now gawking at the fire as it continued to ravage the building might have joked to their friends that they'd have liked to have burned it to the ground themselves. Because even after it was built, when its tall glass front reflected the light from the water, dappled against the setting sun, it still left a bitter taste in the mouths of a few. The ones who saw through people like Harry Wood.

Possibly, she considered, over the course of the next few days the police might wonder if there was any link between those early protestors and the fire.

Her heart beat rapidly at this thought, her eyes scanning the small crowd.

Might they think that? Was it possible that the police would focus their attention on something so altogether different from the truth?

She pulled back against the wall, hoping to keep out of sight. Her pulse reverberated through her ears, deafening her to the sounds of the commotion unfurling in front of her eyes.

Three fire engines were haphazardly parked, along with at least two police cars that she could see, and now an ambulance was pulling to a halt. The scene played out like a silent movie. She could imagine it unfurling in slow motion even though the reality was frenzied.

There was a taste of salt on her lips and she licked it away, realizing tears had escaped without her knowledge. Clenching her arms across her chest, she wrapped them around herself as tightly as she could, almost folding inward. Her fingers tingled. If she brought them to her nostrils she would smell the fuel on them. She didn't think she would ever forget that stench, its potency making her want to retch.

Is this what you wanted? she asked herself.

She pulled a hand away from her chest and held it over her mouth, her mind racing. She tried to imagine what would happen in the morning. How many employees would turn up to find nothing more than a pile of rubble where their precious offices had once stood, or if they'd have already been told that they no longer had jobs to go to.

Every one of them would no doubt have to speak to the police, tell them what little they knew. She was certain the detectives would be merely scratching the surface when it came to most of the staff, led on a merry dance that took them far away from what had really happened.

There would likely be the odd comment from one or two members of the team who thought they had something of interest to say, but she doubted they'd point the detectives in the right direction.

She focused her gaze on the small gathering of uniforms that had grouped beside one of the fire engines. A fireman was gesturing, pointing fiercely toward the building while another one yelled behind him, calling others over. She hadn't imagined the fire would spread so quickly.

Suddenly it was apparent that something was happening. Something urgent, for even from here she could sense the apprehension in the air. It had darkened somehow, become thicker with foreboding.

Automatically she inched forward until she was trapped in the beam of a streetlight. Her heart pounded even more heavily against the wall of her chest as she strained to get a better view, edging closer along the narrow pathway that ran in front of the waterside houses.

Everything told her she should leave. She should be at home with her family. At some point there would be a call about what had happened, and when it came, that was where she needed to be.

And yet, she couldn't tear herself away from the scene.

One of the firemen now stood aside, allowing her a perfect view of the stretcher on the pavement. A body was being carried out of the burning building, laid upon the stretcher, and then a circle of people gathered around it and she could see no more.

Her body felt like liquid, as if at any moment she would melt away and sink into the ground.

What had she done? It had seemed such a perfect solution. But now she could see it was by no means an end. It was only the beginning. Now she could see that her actions would strip her of everything that was truly important.

Her family.

She clutched her stomach and bent double, retching on the path beside her. Her hands shook violently.

Revenge and anger had blinded her, and now she might very well lose the two most important people in her life. And it was too late to do anything about it.

Initial interviews between Detective Emily Marlow and staff of Morris and Wood following the fire at Morris and Wood offices on Monday, May 13.

<u>Bryony Knight, Account Assistant, on Tuesday, May 14, at Lymington Police Headquarters.</u>

Bryony:	Is anyone dead?
Marlow:	I'm afraid we can't answer that at this moment.
Bryony:	*Can't* answer? (pauses) Okay. Well. In answer to your question, I've worked there for eighteen months.
Marlow:	And who do you report to?
Bryony:	Well (laughs), it was Laura Denning before she went off on maternity leave. Then it was Mia, who replaced her, and now—it's both of them! It doesn't really work, but . . . do you know what's going to happen? I mean, am I going to carry on getting paid? I've got rent to pay, and if I can't work . . .
Marlow:	These are all things you'll have to ask your Human Resources department. As I'm sure you can appreciate I'm investigating the fire.
Bryony:	I know. I just—well, I can't afford to lose the money, that's all.
Marlow:	Do you like your job, Miss Knight?
Bryony:	Totally. It's an awesome place to work. The offices are—were, I mean—the offices *were* amazing. Shit. I can't believe they're actually gone. Who could have done it?
Marlow:	That's what we're trying to ascertain.
Bryony:	And you think it was someone who worked there? That's why you're interviewing us all?
Marlow:	No, I'm not saying that. I'm just trying to build a picture of what the staff thought of the company and how you all felt working for Harry Wood.
Bryony:	Well, Harry's amazing. He's a totally great boss. Everyone loves working for Harry; you won't be able to find one person who doesn't. Harry always stops and talks to you, he's (laughs) . . . I don't know. He's very good-looking.

Marlow: So in your opinion, you think everyone believes Harry Wood is a good CEO?

Bryony: Oh God, yeah. I mean, I don't really know what a CEO does or anything, but if you mean do I think everyone was happy working for him, then as I said, totally. That's why no one ever leaves.

Marlow: I see someone left very recently. Sarah Clifton?

Bryony: Oh right, Sarah. Yes, of course. I forgot about her.

Marlow: Do you know why she did?

Bryony: Well, not for sure, but I heard the rumors.

Marlow: The rumors?

Bryony: Well, yeah. She had issues with her boss, Mike Lewis. But . . . well, one day she'd just suddenly gone. She was a very quiet girl. I didn't even realize she'd left until a week later.

Marlow: Did you hear any other rumors, Miss Knight?

Bryony: Like what?

Marlow: Anything at all.

Bryony: (pauses) There are always rumors in an office that big; it just depends which ones you mean.

———————

Henrietta James, Senior Account Manager

Henrietta: Harry Wood is a good CEO, I suppose, but I didn't have much to do with him on a day-to-day basis. Of course all the young girls love him. By "young" I mean the ones in their twenties. Not that I'm old, for God's sake, I'm only forty-two, but you feel it sometimes, you know? Especially when everyone around you wasn't even born when you were leaving school. (laughs) Anyway, I think they like him because he's always very nice, and of course he is handsome. Even I can give him that, but I guess they're blinded at that age, aren't they?

Marlow: How do you mean "blinded"? Do you think you saw things they didn't?

Henrietta: I'm sure I did.

Marlow: Such as?

Henrietta: (sighs) Such as the way he only really has time for his own, I suppose. The people who work directly under him. He makes a show of speaking to us all, of course, but it always feels a little—*off*. I think he's happiest when he's around the board table with the senior directors.

Marlow: Mia Anderson is one of your directors, is that correct?

Henrietta: (nods) That's right. We have five of them now, since Harry kept Mia on. Thank God, if you ask me. It was about time we had someone like Mia.

Marlow: What do you mean, "someone like Mia"?

Henrietta: A woman at that level we could talk to. You know she's only the second woman to sit on the board?

Marlow: Mainly men were appointed?

Henrietta: Oh yes.

Marlow: Do you think this was an issue?

Henrietta: I don't know. I never really gave it much thought before. I'd always thought it was just the way it is. Women go off and have babies. That's what they say, don't they? Take me, I went part-time after having kids, so why would anyone consider me for a promotion?

Marlow: You don't think you'd get promoted because you're part-time?

Henrietta: I know I won't.

Marlow: Is that the way it is throughout the company?

Henrietta: I'm not saying there's anything wrong with the way Harry does things.

Marlow: I'm not suggesting you are.

Henrietta: I'm not trying to cause trouble or anything, I'm not saying there's some inequality issue . . . I never did buy into all the stuff that—

Marlow: Yes?

Henrietta: It doesn't matter. I'm just saying I don't want you to start thinking I had any issues. I didn't.

Marlow: I realize that isn't what you're suggesting. You say it was nice to have Mia Anderson because you could talk to her. How about Laura Denning? I believe she's the other director you referred to? The other woman who sits on the board?

Henrietta: She is, but I've never really felt comfortable talking to Laura about anything personal. Laura Denning is very— professional, I suppose you would say.

Marlow: Mia Anderson was brought in to cover Laura Denning's maternity leave, correct?

Henrietta: (nods) Laura went off for six months. She came back two months ago.

Marlow: And yet Mia Anderson is still there? Has this caused any issues, in your opinion?

Henrietta: (laughs) Oh yes, and that's a whole different story.

Marlow: In what way?

Henrietta: It didn't go down well at all. The moment Laura Denning walked back in after she'd had her baby—well, let's just say we all knew there'd be problems. Yes, I suppose after that things definitely started to change at Morris and Wood.

chapter one

eight weeks before the fire

Laura stood in the doorway to the kitchen and watched her husband, Nate, carefully stirring a wooden spoon around a pan that was balanced precariously on the edge of the stove. In his other arm, nestled into his side, was Bobby. Her son's little head lolled against his dad's shoulder, and every time Nate moved, Bobby sprung up as if he'd been jolted wide awake.

Laura tensed as she waited for her son's eyes to open. He was fast asleep, and while Nate hummed quietly, seemingly oblivious to her standing there watching, she felt her eyes moisten.

"I'm off, then." The words left her lips almost silently, but Nate turned immediately and broke into a smile.

"Hey, gorgeous, you look amazing. And see, it still fits perfectly."

"Not really." She ran her hands down the front of her shirt. The buttons tugged her blouse tightly over her breasts, so much so that she'd worn a camisole underneath, even though the offices were always too hot.

Laura had spent more time in front of the mirror in the last hour than she had the last six months. Her dark hair had been pulled into a ponytail, then let loose, and was now tied in a straggly bun at the base of her neck. She'd chipped flakes of dry mascara off its wand before applying it to her lashes and added more gray eye shadow than she'd ever worn to work previously, all in an attempt to feel more confident, and yet still she didn't know how she'd make it out the front door.

"You're nervous," Nate said. "You're bound to be, going back after all this time."

She shook her head and attempted a smile, biting her lip as she strode over to where Nate had switched off the stove. "I'm going to miss you, little man," she whispered into her son's warm hair, kissing his head, her lips lingering, too afraid to pull away.

She shouldn't be nervous. She loved her job. Morris and Wood had been her life until Bobby came along. And yet Laura thought there was every chance she was going to be sick. That it would be a whole lot easier if she called Harry and postponed her return. Just for another week. One more week and then surely she would feel better.

But they had done the math, and now that her full maternity pay had ended, they were reliant on Laura's salary to pay for the mortgage they'd excitedly stretched themselves to afford five years ago when she started working for Harry Wood. They both knew that when Bobby came along it would be Laura who'd return to work full-time, because even putting aside the fact that she outearned her husband by a significant amount, it was Laura who had the career, who had never been able to imagine her life without her job.

Nate was smiling. "You're going to knock 'em all dead. Like you always have."

"You're biased."

"I know I am, but I also know how brilliant you are. Particularly with all the work you've been doing to prepare," he added, nodding at the laptop sticking out the top of her purse. "It'll be like you haven't been away."

"Maybe," she replied, her gaze still on Bobby. It was impossible to believe it would ever feel like that. Not when she'd spent the last six months caring for another human being around the clock.

But Nate was right about one thing. She had put a lot of hours in over the last couple of weeks, preparing herself to dive straight back into her biggest accounts. She felt excited to talk to her lead client,

Coopers, about ideas for the TV advert they wanted to start work on this summer. They'd been planning to invest heavily in promotion for their new health drink brand, and she was keen to sink her teeth into the campaign. And anyway, surely the moment she stepped out of the office lift onto her floor she would stop feeling so nervous.

"Just go," Nate told her, turning back to the porridge on the stove and scooping out a spoonful, which he tipped into a small plastic bowl.

"You know that'll be too hot," she said. "You need to cool it down first. He can't eat it like—"

"I know." Nate laughed.

"Call me if anything happens."

Nate nodded as he pushed the bowl to one side and twisted around to kiss her. "Hey!" He reached out his free hand and ran a thumb across her cheek. "Why are you crying?"

"I'm not." She pulled back and laughed, swiping a hand against him. "I'm just, you know, I haven't left him in six months."

"Well, this guy and I are going to have a blast. As soon as you're gone, we're going to vacuum the house and put in a load of washing, and then—then we're off to the park."

"Nate, am I doing the right thing?"

"Yes." He took hold of her arm. "Of course you are."

Her stomach felt heavy and twisted. The decision that had always been such a simple one suddenly felt like it was swamping her. Like she had no other choice, and in that moment Laura wished that Nate's job in IT paid more than it did. Or that her husband had the same degree of ambition she had.

She quickly shook the thought from her head. Deep down there was nothing she would change about Nate. They were different, and it worked. Laura had often wanted to be more like him and happily throw dinner parties at a moment's notice or not be remotely bothered when the doorbell rang and a visitor showed up uninvited. But she wasn't that

person. She was the one who felt most content when she was con-
trolled and organized, and efficiently running the marketing for a number of clients was something Laura thrived upon. It was why she'd felt
like she was leaving a part of herself behind the day she walked out of
Morris and Wood to go on maternity leave. And deep down, when she
reminded herself of this, she thought how wonderful it would be to find
that part again.

Despite this thought, her intermittent tingles of excitement
blended with dread as she gazed at her son and told Nate she would be
home early. "Well, early enough to give him tea, do his bath . . ."

Nate grinned. "Just do whatever you have to on your first day. I
won't expect you until I see you."

"No, but I will," she said, looking up at him sharply. "I want to."

"That's cool." He continued to smile. "We'll look forward to seeing
you."

Of course he probably didn't believe her because she'd so rarely
gotten home before seven in the past, but she would prove him wrong.
She wasn't about to let her job take away her time with her precious
family. She was confident she could make both work, despite the warn-
ings she'd received from the mums in her parent group.

She had brushed off their concerns when in passing conversation
she'd told them she was returning to work. If anything, she'd wanted to
slap the look of horror off Chrissie's face. Not that she was surprised by
Chrissie, who passed judgment on everything from treating colic to
when was the right time to stop breastfeeding. But none of them were
planning to go back full-time. Even Nancy had said she would only do
three days if one of them could be working from home. And certainly
none of them had even considered the possibility of going back before
their full twelve months were up.

Laura knew what they thought of her: that she clearly didn't want
to spend time with her son. Of course, they never said as much, but

she could tell that's what they thought, just by the constant, persistent hammering of questions of whether she would miss him?

Yes, she was going to miss him. What did they think, that she was a bloody robot? Her heart was tearing in two, and she hadn't even left the house.

Laura had justified herself to the women in her group time and time again, and all the while they'd made out they weren't judging her, but of course they were. Or it had felt that way.

"As soon as you get to the office you'll be fine," Nate was saying as he reached behind and passed her a thermos. "Decaf tea."

She sighed. "You're amazing, you know that?"

"I do. Now go. You don't want to be late on your first day back. And text me and tell me how you're getting on," he called, after she'd kissed him and walked away. "We miss you already."

Laura held up a hand but she couldn't look back again.

———

The offices of Morris and Wood looked out over the Lymington River and to the quay on the other side. It was an idyllic location. Laura hadn't believed her luck when five years ago Harry Wood branched his successful advertising agency to the south coast. She had heard of the London agency long before the first plans were submitted to the council. Laura had been one of the very few who hoped the development would go ahead, because the chance of working for such a prestigious advertising company, which happened to be on her doorstep, was unbelievable. It felt like all the good jobs were in London, and Laura had been wasting away in a small family-run agency that had tried its hardest to get some exciting clients but never quite made it.

She had followed the plans with interest, and then once it was given the green light had eagerly watched the build and put in her application as soon as she caught wind that Harry was recruiting.

Laura hadn't considered what Harry's reasons were for setting up on the south coast and didn't particularly care. She just hoped she would get a job working for him. She hadn't dared consider that he would spot how talented she was so soon, and that within a year he would give her a promotion, and then another two after that that would eventually make her a director.

The last five years had been the best of her life, and being on the board meant she and Nate could finally move out of their rented flat and buy a three-bedroom detached on the outskirts of town. Harry had given her these opportunities, and she would never forget that.

The day Laura found out she was pregnant, her heart had dipped slightly. It was a feeling she'd never once admitted to anyone, especially not Nate, but as she'd driven to the office that morning with the pregnancy stick wrapped in toilet paper and buried in her purse, she'd pushed the news to the back of her mind. Laura knew how awful it was that her first thought had been that she would have to give up her job.

She kept her pregnancy hidden from her coworkers for five months. But by that point she had come to the conclusion that her career didn't need to suffer, that a short sabbatical wasn't the end of the world. And by the time she was due to leave, Laura was beyond excited to be having a baby.

Her first morning back, Laura took the lift up to the third floor, guilt flooding her body and seeping into every part of her that she'd once not been delighted at the prospect of having Bobby. Her initial reaction hadn't been utter joy, and it was something she'd never be able to change. Since her son had been born, she'd reminded herself of this time and time again, and in those times had looked at her son's gorgeous face and felt sick that she'd ever felt that way, convincing herself that one day she'd be paid back for those feelings. That maybe she didn't deserve to be a mother, and something would happen to put that right.

To say she was a mess since giving birth seemed a little of an understatement, Laura thought as she waited for the lift doors to open. When they did, she stepped out onto the floor, her stomach still bubbling. It would be so easy to turn around and go back down, drive home, scoop up her son, and tell her husband that he would have to return to work.

Yet she knew she never would.

Laura glanced across the floor nervously. It was before eight and there were only a few people in already, heads buried in concentration. No one looked up, which gave her the time to take in the changes. The wall behind the water cooler had been repainted, the configuration of desks to her right had been redesigned into star shapes at awkward angles, no longer rows looking out of the floor-to-ceiling windows that looked over the river.

She strained to see if her own desk was still in the same position, just outside Harry's glass office at the far end of the floor. Had they moved her? She couldn't see from where she was standing, but there was always the possibility someone had decided to put her somewhere else while she wasn't there to defend herself.

Laura could already feel a burn of anxiety at the thought of the conversations she'd have if that were the case, and suddenly she realized it was going to be much harder settling back in than she could ever have imagined.

It was no surprise that to her left the display boards had been refreshed with new creatives she'd not seen before, but it didn't stop her heart from sinking. Six months ago, more than half of them had been her own work, and now she didn't recognize any of them bar one in the bottom corner, which had won her and the company a prize.

She feigned confidence as she started walking across the office, willing at least one person to look up and acknowledge her so she'd be able to break the silence. It was Henrietta James who appeared first, out of the toilets, stopping short when she saw Laura.

Henrietta's face broke into a wide smile, and she glanced briefly in the direction of Laura's desk before turning to her and loudly declaring, "You're back!"

"I am," Laura replied, following the woman's gaze toward where her desk should be, but still she couldn't see it from where they stood.

"Gosh!" Henrietta declared. "I can't believe how quickly six months have flown."

"I know," Laura said as the woman continued to smile at her. She liked Henrietta well enough; she'd always done a good job, worked hard, even though there'd been many times when Laura had squirmed, irritated, as she'd waited for Henrietta to finish a conversation with someone about her weekend before returning to her desk to complete the work Laura urgently needed. Laura had needed to address the issue with her a couple of times.

"So how are you finding life as a mum?" Henrietta asked. "Is he sleeping through?"

"He was," Laura said, "but recently not so much." She smiled to convey it wasn't really an issue, though it had been taking its toll on her and Nate.

"And how was it leaving him this morning?" Henrietta went on, diving straight for the jugular.

"Oh, it was fine," Laura said, though as Henrietta's eyebrows rose, Laura wondered if this was the right thing to say. Maybe she was supposed to open up with the women in the office now. She and Henrietta were both mothers, after all. Should she tell her the truth, that leaving Bobby that morning was the hardest thing she had ever done?

But baring her soul didn't sit well, so instead Laura said, "Well, I should get to my desk."

Henrietta nodded and stepped aside, and Laura saw the disbelief in Henrietta's eyes that she had managed to cut her off so swiftly. Her thoughts quickly turned to Nate, and she decided to call him in a bit.

She had a pang of longing, more than she would have ever expected. She straightened her back and started to walk toward Harry's office and the place where, hopefully, her desk still sat.

As she neared it, she felt instant relief to see her desk in the same place it had always been—until Laura realized someone was sitting at it. Someone with a bright pink pencil pot and a Gucci handbag, a gray cardigan slung over the back of Laura's chair, and, for whatever reason, some Christmas paper chains still hanging over the top of the computer screen, even though it was the third week of March.

Even before the woman at her desk slowly turned around, Laura knew it was Mia Anderson, the person she had hastily recruited to cover her maternity leave. Her thoughts flitted back to the interview, and how Mia had nodded, answering Laura's quick-fire questions, so grateful to be given the opportunity to step into her shoes for a few months.

And yet the woman sitting in front of her today had clearly made herself at home, and while Laura should have expected her to still be here, she hadn't thought for one minute she'd find Mia sitting in her seat like it was her own.

chapter two

Laura stepped forward as Mia turned around, smiling and gesturing to her ear and the earpiece stuck in it as she carried on
chatting. "Of course, that's totally fine," she said to whoever was
on the other end of the line, her eyes still on Laura as a sheepish grin
hung off her lips. "Yep, it's really no problem, I can get on that straight-
away." She raised her eyes dramatically as if the whole conversation
was nothing more than amusing, while Laura stood stupidly beside her
own desk and waited for her to finish. Eventually Mia turned her back
to her and flipped open a notebook, rifling through it until she got to a
blank page.

Laura hot-stepped from one foot to the other, her handbag weighing heavily on her left shoulder, her jacket now making her too hot.
She didn't dare look about her; she could already sense people were
watching, and there was no sign of Mia finishing her phone conversation.

She glanced around at a few vacant desks, considering whether to
drop her things onto one of them. But no, this was her desk and Mia
was in it. Laura's notepads and pens were presumably still in its drawers, her files must surely be stacked in the lower cabinet. She couldn't
remember ever feeling so painfully embarrassed at work and was still
dithering behind Mia when Harry's voice boomed across the floor, so
loudly that even Mia looked up from her call.

Usually Laura wanted the ground to swallow her when he did that, but in that moment she was grateful for her boss coming to her rescue, giving her something to distract her from listening to Mia's conversation.

"Here she is," Harry announced as he made his way toward her, reaching out his arms and leaning forward to kiss her on the cheek. He grinned and then seemed to register why she was standing awkwardly in the middle of the floor, for he quickly added, "Come on into my office. Let's catch up."

She followed him into the office, and once they were inside and Harry had kicked the door shut behind him, he said, "God, we've missed you around here. The place has nearly fallen apart."

"Really?" she asked hopefully, despite the fact she knew this was exactly the kind of thing Harry would say whether he meant it or not.

"Please tell me you aren't going to be having any more kids," he joked.

"Harry, you can't say things like that."

"Oh, come on, you know what I mean."

"Well, after the birth, I don't think I'm going to be pushing any more out just yet."

"Okay, too much info," he said, "but seriously, it's so good to have you back." He held her at arm's length, his eyes roaming her face. "You look wonderful. Motherhood suits you."

"Thank you." She blushed and pulled away, glancing through the glass windows of his office to those sitting at their desks on the other side of it. Everyone could see into Harry's office; she had felt their eyes on her enough times over the years, most likely wondering what was being discussed between them, probably drawing their own ridiculous conclusions about why she was in there again. Rumors were as rife in Morris and Wood as they were in any other office, and Laura wasn't naive enough to think she'd escaped being the subject of gossip. But this morning no one was watching, not even Mia.

"How's the little one?" Harry asked.

"Bobby's fine. He's six months old already. I can't believe where the time's gone."

"It flies fast, I know. Ella's starting secondary this September. It makes me feel ill. Or maybe that's just the hike in fees." His mouth skewed into a lopsided smile that made Laura cringe. Harry had a habit of brazenly throwing money into the conversation, and she was still never quite sure if he did it on purpose or whether he genuinely had no idea how other people might take it.

"So anyway," he went on, "how are you feeling? Ready to get back into it?"

"Totally." Laura nodded. "Only—" She indicated out of the window. "Mia seems to be sitting at my desk."

"Oh, that's not a problem," he said. "She likely forgot you were due back this morning." His eyes lingered on Mia for a moment before he turned back to Laura. "She's done a good job. You were right on the money when you told me to hire her."

Laura glanced across at her too. Mia had finished the call and was leaning back in the chair, laughing with Bryony Knight, who was peering over the top of Laura's PC. Bryony was Laura's account assistant and yet there she was, as if she had transferred her allegiances too.

"I want to have my desk back, Harry." She turned back to her boss. "I don't want to sit anywhere else." Laura hoped her words didn't sound as childish as they suddenly felt.

"Of course not." He waved a hand through the air. "Don't worry about it. I'll have a word after the exec meeting this morning."

Laura nodded and released a breath. "I can't wait to take you through some things I've been thinking about," she said. "I have some great ideas."

"That's what I love about you, Laura," he replied. "Your dedication." Harry gestured to the leather chair and she sat down, waiting for him to head to his own on the other side of his desk as she pulled her note-book out of her purse.

"I want to talk to Coopers about the TV ad first thing, because I want to get that off the ground and hopefully start filming late summer. Honestly, I can't wait to get stuck in. I've done loads on it." She flapped her notebook in the air. "And I was thinking about sponsorship for their premium health bar range, too, and—" Laura paused. "What?" she asked, when she noticed the look on Harry's face. His eyebrows were pinched into a point, frown lines dug into his forehead.

Harry ran a hand across the stubble that neatly covered his chin. He'd had his hair cut, she noticed. Maybe a little too short. It was a mixture of light and dark gray, and in places looked white in contrast to his black-rimmed glasses. He was in his early fifties and easily still the most attractive man in the office.

He leaned back in his chair, the movement making it swivel gently to the side, and crossed a leg, flashing a bright pink sock beneath his suit trousers. Then, uncrossing it again, he shifted forward, steepling his hands on the desk in front of him. "The thing is, Laura, Coopers already commissioned the TV ads while you were away."

"Oh?"

"They wanted to move forward with them."

"But they'd *wanted* to wait," she protested. "They said they were going to hold off until I was back. Who's picked them up?" she asked, though she already had the unnerving feeling she knew exactly who had been working on them.

"Actually, Mia," he said, confirming her fears. "And I have to say, she's doing a great job . . ." Harry trailed off awkwardly when he noticed the shock on her face. "Like I said, Laura, you were right to recruit her. It was a good call. She reminds me of you, you know, five years ago when you came here. You both have the same go-getter attitude." Harry smiled, but it slid away quickly.

"I didn't recruit her," she said. "I hired her. Temporarily. She was only a replacement because—" Laura waved a hand through the air. "She doesn't have as much experience," she went on in disbelief, fragments of the interview coming back to her. It was one of the reasons she had taken Mia on. Because she wasn't a threat; she was just good enough to keep the job ticking over.

Mia had seemed nothing like Laura in the interview. She didn't have ambition or the desire for achievement that Laura had always shown. If anything, Laura had worried Mia was a little too casual about her plans for the future, because she was clearly happy hopping from one temping post to the next. She had wondered if Mia might not even hold out the six months needed, because frequently members of the Coopers team changed their minds at the last minute and had demanded Laura work weekends to turn around creatives. Laura thrived on that, but she wasn't sure Mia would, and yet she had taken the chance on her because in every other way Mia was exactly what she was looking for. All Laura needed was someone who would keep her job going, with no aspirations to get their hands on it.

Not like Patrick. Laura's colleague, another account director, had made no attempt to hide his desire to take over Coopers, and Laura had worried that if he did, she might never get it back.

"I'm sorry, Laura. I'm sure that wasn't the news you wanted to hear."

"No . . . well . . ." she stammered. "I mean, I'm just surprised they didn't wait for me to come back." She glanced over to where Mia was now standing beside her desk, one arm casually leaning on the top of the computer screen as she spoke with a woman Laura had never set eyes on before. "She seems to have made herself at home," she muttered.

Harry pulled back in his seat. "Laura, Coopers wanted to go ahead, and so of course that's what we did. I'm sorry, but that's the way it is."

Laura nodded, her eyes stinging with the unexpected pressure of tears. God, surely she wasn't going to start crying? She inhaled a tight breath and bit down on her lip and mentally tried to pull herself together. So this wasn't what she had expected, but it wasn't irretrievable. "Right, well, I'll need to have a chat with Mia."

"You will."

"It's fine. I can take everything back from her by the end of the day. I shouldn't need more than that." Laura had, after all, only had one day's handover with Mia before she'd gone into an early labor the following morning. "I don't think I'll need her after today," she said, though as she turned back to Harry she saw his face had paled.

"Actually, I've agreed with Mia that she's staying on for a bit."

"What? Why?"

"I've asked her to carry on working here. I thought it would be best to have her see the campaign through. The Coopers team is on board with it—"

"No, no, hold on." Her heart raced as she held up a hand to stop him. "What do you mean she's *seeing the campaign through*? That's not necessary, Harry. She can hand it over to me. There's no need for both of us to be on it."

Harry dipped his head.

"This is ridiculous. What's going on? She was here to cover me and now I'm back. She doesn't need to be here any longer. What is it?" she snapped. "I can tell there's something on your mind. Will you just say whatever it is?"

"You won't both be on the account while the campaign's running. Mia's going to be keeping it. For now," he added, after a beat.

"What?" Laura felt the heat creeping up her neck. "No!"

"She's done a really great job and—I feel like crap for what I'm saying. Laura, this isn't anything on you, I just think it's the right thing to do. And it means you can have the time to settle back in."

"I don't need to settle back in, Harry." Laura stared back at him as her voice rose to a high pitch. "I've only been gone for six months and I've kept up-to-date on all my clients. You know that. We've spoken about it on the phone while I've been on leave. I don't need to be babysat."

"That's not what's happening." He shook his head, the frown darkening his already deep brown eyes. "It's just, Mia's got her teeth in this and—Laura, you said yourself before you went off that we could do with an extra pair of hands on the accounts."

"To work *under* me, Harry, not to replace me." She could feel the rise of anger soaring through her body as she brushed a hand across her cheek, praying she didn't break down in front of him. Out of the corner of her eye she could see Mia swishing her arms in the air as she animatedly spoke to whoever it was still leaning over the top of the PC.

Mia had told her in the interview that she was moving on, out of the area. Six months was supposed to be perfect because she wasn't hanging around Lymington any longer. Laura hadn't dug into what Mia was moving on from; it hadn't felt relevant. But she'd been so adamant she was going. "I cannot believe she has the experience to handle this campaign," she said, shaking her head. "I mean, she came from—" Laura gestured in the air, trying to recall Mia's previous job. It had been a marketing company in Southampton, but not one she had heard of. It was a short-term contract that had conveniently just finished, because it meant Mia could start the following week.

"Are you actually telling me she's doing a good job on it?" Laura asked, though she didn't want the answer. "Better than me?" she went on. "Is she doing a better job than me, is that what it is?"

"No, Laura, it isn't. You know that's not the case—"

She could laugh at the thought that she was once so worried about Patrick Carter covering her job. At least she would have known how to get Coopers back from Patrick, but Mia? She was an unknown entity.

Harry squirmed in his leather chair. The irritating squeak sounded loud in the silence between them.

"She's not replacing you," he said at last. "That's not what this is."

"So tell me what it is, then," she said through gritted teeth. She had to keep it together. With everyone milling about outside the windows, she couldn't let herself down, though she feared she might do so. "It sounds to me like you've taken my job away from me while I haven't been here. I don't actually think you can do that, Harry." She could hear the rise in her voice again, the way it was peaking, too high.

"Okay," he said, leaning back, his face more rigid now, holding his hands up to stop her, like she had gone too far. "Let's not get carried away. You know I would never do anything like that, Laura."

"'Let's not get carried away'?" she repeated. "Are you kidding me? This is not fair. What you're doing to me isn't fair." She wiped a hand across her eyes again, once more catching Mia in her peripheral vision.

Laura would not cry. The anger was burning her from the inside, but she would not cry.

"What I mean is that I just thought it was the right thing to do for now. Mia started the campaign; she's going to complete it. No one is taking your job away from you, Laura. You still have it, nothing's changed. And listen, I wasn't going to say anything today," he went on more softly, eyeing her carefully as if worried she'd either break down or start screaming at any moment. "But there's a new opportunity on the horizon. It's a start-up. It'll be a big account, but it's not concrete yet."

Laura continued to regard him. She didn't trust herself to speak.

"Someone I used to work with," he went on, "and he wants to put a lot of money into building his new company's brand. Laura, you'd be perfect to handle it, but there's no way you could possibly do both."

She opened her mouth, but for a while no words came to her. She'd been talking to Harry about new opportunities before she had left, begging him for something else she could invest in, but she hadn't factored in giving up her most important client to do it. Eventually she said, "But this opportunity isn't even definite."

"No, not yet. But I'm going to set up some time for you to meet him in the next couple of weeks, and in the meantime you can settle back in. I thought it would help you," he said, wide eyes imploring her. "I remember when Janie went back to work after Ella was born. She felt awful every time she had to take some time off when Ella was sick, and—"

"Harry!" Laura snapped, "Nate's at home. You know that. He's given up his job so I don't have to run home every time something happens."

Harry splayed his hands wide on the desk in front of him. "I know that, I know. But please, Laura, this wasn't meant to make you feel worse. I was only trying to help." He flicked his wrist, and she caught a flash of the gold watch peeking out from his cuff.

"You couldn't make me feel any worse if you tried," she said, her voice on the edge of snapping. "I want to keep Coopers. I don't want another account."

"Okay," he said calmly. "Okay, let's have another chat about this later. My meeting starts in five, and we can't both be late for it. We'll catch up again later in the day."

Laura pushed the chair back. "I want her out of my desk."

"It's done." He nodded.

She turned and left the office, tears still pricking the corners of her eyes, though she made it to the toilets before slamming her fists down on the surface beside the basin. Tugging a paper towel out, she dabbed it roughly against her skin, the other hand still curled into a tight ball as she gripped the basin.

She wanted to scream. She wanted to call Nate. She wanted to burst into tears and flee the office, run home before she had to face anyone else. Harry had no idea what she had given up to come back to work. But she had done it because of how much her job meant to her and because she believed she would be a better mum if she still had her work.

All she wanted now was to see Bobby's face, and the thought that she was missing out on a whole day of his young life for *this* was breaking her.

Her already knotted stomach twisted itself tighter. There were telltale patches of red clinging to her neck, which wouldn't disappear before Harry's exec meeting, and she knew, she just knew, that Mia Anderson would be in that same meeting room and she would have to face her.

Already Laura's bun was looking scruffy, and in the bright light of the toilets, the eyeshadow she'd so carefully applied that morning looked smudged and heavy.

She didn't believe a word of what Harry had told her. There might well have been an old friend he was talking to, but in all likelihood he wouldn't have considered Laura for the job until five minutes ago. She certainly didn't think it was the reason he'd allowed Mia to dig her claws into the Coopers campaign.

There could only be one reason why Harry had allowed this to happen. Mia had to be better than her. That was the only thing Laura could think of—her replacement had done a better job in the last six months than Laura had in five years.

Laura's fingers clutched the edge of the basin as the door swung open behind her. A petite girl with tortoiseshell glasses paused momentarily as she stared at Laura in the mirror, a thin smile twitching on her lips before she dropped her head and scurried into one of the stalls.

What was her name? Susan? No, Sarah. That was it, Sarah Clifton. She'd joined the company a few months before Laura went on maternity leave and had always seemed petrified whenever Laura asked her to do anything. It was a surprise she was still here. Laura had never seen her fitting into Mike's graphics team.

Laura shook her head and looked back at her own reflection. Harry wouldn't have gotten away with what he'd said if she were a man. That was what galled her the most. That and the fact she hadn't pointed it out when he'd said it.

She would make sure she got her client back if it killed her. By the end of the week, Mia would be gone.

chapter three

Mia Anderson had a number of things on her mind on Monday morning that didn't involve work, and so for a moment she had forgotten that Laura was coming back. It sounded ridiculous, especially after the conversation she'd had with Harry only the week before, but that was the truth of it. The events of her weekend had taken over, and it had been a relief when she'd left the house early that morning and driven to the office.

As soon as Henrietta had trilled out that Laura was back, Mia felt her stomach lurch with apprehension, because she knew Laura would be shocked to find her still here.

Within minutes Laura was standing behind Mia's desk while she was trying to have a call with one of the marketing team at Coopers, and it was putting her off track. She needed to concentrate, but now Laura was shuffling back and forth, and Mia was torn between ignoring her and hanging up the call—something she just couldn't do. Everyone knew how important this TV ad was. She would be presenting the final outline to Coopers in less than two weeks and she had to get it perfect. This was her big chance to prove herself.

Mia had been so relieved when Harry had pulled her into his office a fortnight ago and told her the news that she was to keep Coopers. She'd worked her arse off over the last six months, and it had paid off. That night, she'd taken some of her new friends from work down to the pub and told them the good news, that she was staying on, and they'd been so happy for her. Henrietta James had insisted on buying the first round of drinks, even though she must have known Mia was paid more than she was, and Mia let her, even though she felt guilty about it. In fact, she'd been relieved. Her pockets really weren't as deep as everyone most likely thought.

On her desk her mobile began to vibrate. She pulled it toward her and checked the caller. Mum—Home. Mia briefly closed her eyes and for a second shut out the incoming call, the voice on the other end of the office line, and the fact that Harry Wood had emerged from his office. When she opened them again, the call from her mum had already stopped and Laura had disappeared.

Mia held her breath as she scribbled some notes, willing the conversation to be over soon, as she waited to see if her mum would call straight back or leave a message. Mia had only been in the office an hour. What was so important that she was calling so early?

By the time she put the phone down she noticed Patrick striding across the floor toward the boardroom and knew she didn't have time to call back. Harry's meeting was due to start, and she couldn't be late. She was up first, updating the rest of the directors on how the campaign was going, and today more than ever she needed to be on the ball, now that Laura was back. Now that there was someone, Mia felt, who was going to be watching her carefully.

The night in the pub, a few rounds down, Henrietta had grabbed Mia's arm and leaned in, slurring into her ear, presumably to be heard over the loud chatter, "I'm pleased you're staying, but I know someone who won't be."

Mia had raised her eyebrows questioningly, even though she knew to whom Henrietta was alluding.

"Laura Denning. I have to say I'm bloody surprised he's done it."

"Who's done what?" Mia had asked.

"Harry. Given you that account. Everyone knows it's Laura's baby. And Harry and Laura, you know—their past."

Mia had nodded. She'd heard the whispers, watched Henrietta's delight in telling her that something had once gone on between Harry and Laura. Mia had asked how Henrietta knew that. Someone once said, apparently. The usual. No one could really say for sure, and she wouldn't make any judgments until she saw anything for herself, though if they were as close as everyone was saying, it did make Mia wonder how it was going to pan out now that Laura was back.

Mia quickly gathered her notes and picked up her mobile, following Patrick to the boardroom. "Laura's back," she called out when she had almost caught up with him. Patrick had barely spoken about Laura in her absence; everything she had gleaned about Laura had come from the women Mia had befriended.

"Yes, I saw," Patrick said, his face shadowing briefly, making Mia wonder if he, too, couldn't imagine how this was going to work out.

"It'll be nice to get to know her," she said breezily. "I've heard so much about her."

"I'm sure," Patrick replied. He wasn't taking the bait.

"About how good she is, I mean," Mia went on, annoyed that he could put her in the same camp as the others. She might listen to the gossip, but she didn't spread it.

Patrick nodded. "So how's it going, anyway?" he asked as he held the door open for her. "Everything under control?"

"Yes, I think so." She beamed. "I'm updating you all on the ad in a bit anyway, so it'll be good to get your thoughts." Her heart skipped a beat as she said this, because even though she was confident enough, she didn't relish putting herself out there. And Patrick was such a closed book. She knew he saw himself as Harry's right-hand man, but there had been something so offish about him toward her right from the start. Mia wondered if at some point the other people around the board table were going to take sides, and if they did, she had a clear picture of where Patrick would go. Straight to Laura's. And if that happened, she feared she might be the one to lose her job, because she was the new girl.

Mia straightened as she walked into the room, dropping her notepad and phone onto the table before pouring herself a coffee from the pot that had likely been standing there for the last hour. The women on the floor, outside the glass walls of the boardroom, might have her back, but if it came to it, were they going to be enough?

Finally Harry arrived, and a couple of minutes later so did Laura. It was odd for me knowing she wasn't the only woman around this table anymore, like she had been for the past six months. There were seven men in the room—account directors, chief finance officer, chief operating officer, and her. They had danced around her like peacocks when she'd first joined. Each time she spoke, the room had descended into silence, a few of the men shifting in their seats. Apart from Patrick, that was, who had a habit of talking over her and finishing her sentences.

Laura was now the center of attention, as the men all asked after her and her baby. Mia felt uncomfortable as she stood by the coffeepot at the far side of the room, not knowing whether she should join in the chat or wait until later when they'd have a chance to speak in private.

In the end she pulled out the chair next to Harry, who was already sitting down, and waited for the meeting to begin. Probably better to remain professional at this point, especially when she had so little first-hand knowledge of what Laura Denning was like.

She had only met Laura twice, once for the interview and then a week later for her handover. The very next day Laura had had her baby, four weeks early. But Mia remembered her well. Her handover was nothing more than a brief run-through of what accounts she would be looking after and the key points of contact, and Mia quickly deduced that Laura didn't answer anything she didn't want to. She hadn't idled in gossip, had barely looked at Mia as she pulled up information on her computer screen and handed over numerous booklets about the companies she represented; she churned out figures and told Mia not to worry about anything that was too far off in the future. Making it clear, Mia presumed, that she wouldn't need to know because she wouldn't be here once Laura got back from maternity leave.

Mia had tried to take a different tack with her and had asked her about the baby. Did she know what she was having?

"A boy. Now, this account is unusual in that—"

Mia couldn't even remember what was unusual about it; she wasn't particularly listening. She pressed Laura more about the child. "It must be very exciting," she persisted, "getting the nursery sorted, buying the clothes."

Laura's responses had been curt. She made it seem as if she was pretty pissed off that she was having to take six months out of her job, as if the whole pregnancy were just one big inconvenience. She had rubbed her stomach, a frown shadowing her face, not that dissimilar to the one she wore now. But by then Mia had already decided Laura was worrying over something, because she'd had the same feeling in the interview, covering the same questions, like why was Mia only looking for a short-term placement? Was she happy that this was only for six months?

Laura, she thought, did not want to let her job go, and so Mia had assured her it wasn't what she was after, that she would be moving on, out of the area. To be fair, she hadn't been totally lying. Because she would have liked to be moving on, even if she knew deep down it was highly unlikely she'd be able to get away.

"And you can definitely start on such short notice?" Laura had asked in the interview, telling her she wanted her in five days' time.

"Of course," Mia had told her without missing a beat. She would do whatever she needed to do.

Now Mia watched Laura hover on the periphery of the boardroom before Harry finally called everyone to the table. Mia was prepared to give her a friendly smile and wave, but not once did Laura look over at her. She turned back to her notes and scanned her eyes over them, her heart fluttering as it always did when she was about to present. And then it happened again. On the table her mobile began to vibrate, and she already knew who was calling. Sliding it closer, Mia looked at the name and knew she couldn't ignore it a second time, because there was no way her mum would be calling her twice if it wasn't urgent.

"I'm sorry," she whispered to Harry, "I'm going to have to take this."

"Oh," he said, cocking his head, unsure what to do.

"I'm sorry," she repeated, pushing back her chair. "I'll be as quick as I can."

As she left the room, Mia wondered if there was ever a time Laura Denning would be so unprofessional as to leave a meeting just as she was about to present, and decided most definitely not. But then, no one around the table had any idea about the parts of Mia's life that would always take priority over work.

Initial interviews between Detective Emily Marlow and staff of Morris and Wood following the fire at Morris and Wood offices on Monday, May 13.

<u>**Patrick Carter, Account Director, on Tuesday, May 14, at Lymington Police Headquarters.**</u>

Patrick: I can't get my head around what's happened.

Marlow: I understand this is a stressful time for you, Mr. Carter.

Patrick: It is. It just doesn't feel real. The whole thing's burned to the ground, hasn't it? Was it—was it an accident, or did someone do this on purpose?

Marlow: At this moment in time we don't know exactly how the fire started.

Patrick: I know you think someone did it. Someone who worked at the office.

Marlow: Mr. Carter, I have a lot of interviews to get through, so if you wouldn't mind just answering a few questions for me?

Patrick: I know, but can you tell me the truth? Please? I heard they pulled a body out of the building last night, and now neither Harry or his wife are answering their bloody phones.

Marlow: I'm afraid we can't—

Patrick: I just want to know that they're all right. I want to know it wasn't Harry because—you must know if it was or not?

Marlow: I'm really sorry, Mr. Carter. I'm afraid I can't tell you anything at the moment.

Patrick: He's a friend, that's all. Harry Wood. He's my boss and everything, but he's a mate, too, and if anything's happened to him . . . That's what doesn't sit right. If someone did start the fire intentionally and he *was* in there, well, then I can't tell you one person who would want to do that. It makes no sense.

Marlow: Mr. Carter—

Patrick: I just don't know why he's not answering his phone.

Marlow:	Mr. Carter, please. Would you answer some questions for me and then I'll see if there is anything I can find out?
Patrick:	Fine. Okay.
Marlow:	Could you confirm your position at Morris and Wood?
Patrick:	I'm an account director. I sit on the board. I've been there since the start. Since long before Harry came to Lymington and set up an arm of the agency here. I worked with him in London.
Marlow:	Can you tell me what your role entails?
Patrick:	I manage some of our most important accounts. I'm responsible for five of them, the ones with the larger marketing budgets.
Marlow:	You're pretty high up there, then, is that what you're saying?
Patrick:	I'm a director. Yes, of course. I'm Harry's deputy.
Marlow:	Officially?
Patrick:	Not in a contract, if that's what you mean, but Harry involves me in all the decisions. When he's not around, I pick things up.
Marlow:	Were you involved in the decision to keep Mia Anderson at the firm?
Patrick:	(pauses) No.
Marlow:	So Harry didn't run that past you?
Patrick:	Not that decision. What's your point? Aren't I supposed to be here because of the fact the entire office has burned down? What does it matter whether I had any part in the decision to recruit someone?
Marlow:	I'm just trying to get some facts. That's all. You *are* helping, Mr. Carter, and I appreciate you probably have many things you need to sort out right now, but your assistance is crucial in helping us build a picture of what happened last night.
Patrick:	Fine. Fine. (pauses) No, I wasn't involved in Mia Anderson

remaining in the job. That was one Harry took on by himself. I suppose he thought she was doing a good job. I don't know, I didn't really get involved in her accounts.

Marlow: Did the decision upset anyone in the office?

Patrick: Like I said, it was nothing to do with my job, it was Laura Denning she'd taken over from.

Marlow: And how did it go down with Laura?

Patrick: (laughs) How do you expect? She was pretty pissed. Sorry, excuse my French. She was annoyed.

Marlow: Thank you, but you don't have to excuse your language for me. How was she annoyed?

Patrick: Well, she thought she'd been replaced, I guess. I suppose she had been. To tell you the truth, I thought Harry was treading muddy water. I'm pretty certain legally he shouldn't have done what he did.

Marlow: How do you mean?

Patrick: Well, he took Laura off her job. Gave the firm's biggest client to someone else who'd only been doing it five minutes.

Marlow: You didn't agree with the decision?

Patrick: I don't know *why* it was made, is what I'm saying. I couldn't actually see the reason for it, but Harry was adamant he didn't have a choice, and that was that. I felt for Laura, to tell you the truth. Anyone else wouldn't have been able to get away with it, I suppose, but Harry— (shrugs)

Marlow: What do you mean?

Patrick: Well, he clearly wanted to make sure Laura was okay. I don't know whether that's because he's worried she might leave or—you know, if it's because it's her. It's probably both. Harry has a soft spot for Laura, that's all I'm saying. You'll hear it from one of the women in the office soon enough, if you haven't already. The rumor mill is rife, but as far as I'm concerned, there's nothing more to it than that.

Marlow: So what did Harry do to make sure Laura was okay?

Patrick:	He promised her some new job, some new big client that was supposedly on the scene.
Marlow:	And did that materialize?
Patrick:	(pauses) Nothing's been signed on the dotted line. And in my experience, you don't put in the amount of work Laura has in the last few weeks without having anything signed. She's been putting more hours in than anyone lately, and—I don't know, sometimes it can all be just a huge waste of your time. Anyway, as I said, Harry's a mate, but he isn't always . . .
Marlow:	Always what?
Patrick:	He does favors for his own, you know, the men from the directors club he's a part of from his London days. This new client was one of them.
	Harry's bloody good at what he does. That's one of the reasons I followed him down here, but sometimes— oh, I hate talking out of turn about him, but I think he believes he needs to do things for certain people. Harry can't always say no. It's his weakness.
	Anyway, Laura might have been annoyed about the fact she'd lost one of her main accounts, but she didn't take it out on him. She wouldn't have started the fire.
Marlow:	How can you be so certain of that?
Patrick:	Laura's not crazy. You set fire to a building, and something has to be pretty wrong in the head, doesn't it? No. She and Harry had a good relationship. Always did. She was his golden girl.
Marlow:	But she must have felt put out?
Patrick:	Yeah. But like I said, it didn't seem to affect her relationship with him.
Marlow:	Don't you think that's odd? He was the one who made the decision, after all.
Patrick:	Only Harry could manage it. He gets away with stuff the rest of us can't. All the women think he's a god, and not just because he's CEO. Like I said, he's a mate and all, but Harry,

(shakes head) he's just on a totally other level. No, he and
Laura were as close as ever.

Marlow: How well do you know Harry's wife, Janie Wood?

Patrick: I know her well enough. She comes into the office now
and then. Not much anymore, I suppose, but of course she
throws the party every year.

Marlow: Party?

Patrick: Yeah, Harry's party happens every May in their back
garden. They open up their house to all his employees.
Every one of them is invited, even the ones right at the
bottom.

Marlow: What do you mean by *the bottom*, Mr. Carter?

Patrick: The lowest pay grade.

Marlow: How kind of him.

Patrick: I don't mean it like that, I'm just saying. He doesn't have
to do it, does he? You don't see many bosses opening
up their home to everyone. Anyway, Janie's always there.
I'm sure she's the one behind it because I can't imagine
Harry getting involved in all that stuff. (laughs) Women like
planning parties, don't they? My wife would have a field day
if I gave her that kind of money to blow on one.

Marlow: When was the last time the Woods held one of these
parties?

Patrick: (pauses) You haven't heard anything about it yet? I'm
surprised. It was Friday night. Four days ago.

Marlow: Is there something I should have heard?

Patrick: Yes, you could say that. You mix highly charged emotions
with alcohol and you're always going to get an explosion.

Marlow: There was a fight?

Patrick: (nods)

Marlow: Who was involved?

Patrick: Mia, Laura, Harry, Janie . . . The party was a disaster, really.

chapter four

eight weeks before the fire

Janie Wood's washing machine beeped at the same time that the home phone rang and the cat leapt through the cat flap with another mouse still twitching in his mouth. "Urgh!" Janie yelled. "You bloody cat. Take that thing out the house."

The cat looked up at her with soulful eyes as it dropped the mouse on the floor and patted it toward her with its paw. The mouse didn't move a limb except for its eyes, which found hers and pleaded with her to either put it out of its misery or save it.

Janie stared back at the cat. "Shoo, go on, get out of here." She waved her hands until it eventually retreated and then, with one last scowl at her, turned and disappeared.

The mouse continued to look up at her with fright before it, too, scampered away. "Oh God," she moaned. "Where the hell have you gone?" She followed it into the hallway, the cat brushing past her legs in haste, only it was nowhere in sight. "Damn it," she muttered, crouching down to search under the side table.

She would have to leave it and hope that somehow either the mouse would escape or the cat would get rid of it by the time she returned. Eventually Janie grabbed her keys, ignoring the phone as she headed for the front door. She checked her watch. She was already running late for coffee with her school-mum friends, and if she didn't get there on time they'd start without her and then she would have to ask them to repeat it all, because she wanted to know what Lucy had said to the head teacher.

Then if their coffee meeting ran over, she'd in turn be late for golf, and as much as she thought the instructor was particularly easy on the eye he did have an ugly temper, which she didn't care to be on the receiving end of.

Janie deactivated the car alarm and climbed in. The entire morning had been a game of catch-up, ever since Harry had snoozed his alarm and woken in a panic. She'd not gotten into the shower until quarter past seven, and even an extra five minutes getting out of the house meant the traffic on the school run built up and getting a parking space was nigh on impossible. It meant having to pull up on double yellows and ignore Frosty Fiona, who was ready to slap an A4 sheet of paper on the windshield full of horrifying statistics she'd googled about road accidents.

If only Lucy didn't have a doctor's appointment straight after drop-off, the four of them could have met right after, but Janie had to concur the mole had gotten bigger. And that meant Janie had too much time to kill, and so she went home first, which in hindsight was a mistake.

She switched on the engine and Radio One blasted out from the car stereo. Janie didn't know why she still listened to the station; at forty-five she was well past the outer limits of its target audience, yet for some reason she couldn't bring herself to switch. She supposed it was because it would be another part of her youth left behind, and more than anything Janie couldn't bear the thought of that. There were enough things time had stolen from her, and if she had to listen to a DJ who was young enough to be her son speaking words she only pretended to understand, then that was what she'd continue to do.

As Janie pulled out of the driveway, she wondered who had been calling. Harry, probably. Most likely he'd want to tell her he wouldn't be home for dinner, even though as he walked out the door that morning he had promised her he'd be back by six. She almost wished he wouldn't come home for dinner. Then she could put the salmon back in the freezer before it defrosted and just eat beans on toast with the kids.

Jesus, was that really what occupied her mind these days? she thought as she drove through the now much quieter streets of Beaulieu. For a moment she allowed herself to be relieved by the serenity, just as her mindfulness teacher had been instructing her to do, and for a brief five minutes she felt like it might actually work.

In the early days of moving to the New Forest, five years ago, the solitude had hit Janie hard. It was a stark contrast to the high-powered job and life in London she'd left behind, but then she'd told herself this was exactly what they needed. And yet her head was used to being busy, a multitude of things running through it at any one time, and what she had found when she first moved to the south was that the peace gave her the space to think about the things that were probably more import-ant. And if she were honest with herself, she didn't particularly want to do that.

When the girls started at the private primary school nearby, Janie had flung herself into anything she could find, regardless of whether it was entirely up her street. Over the last five years she had dedicated her time to PTA meetings and bake sales, which gradually gave way to ridiculously unfounded ideas that she should take courses in creative writing and basket weaving, before she eventually settled on coffee mornings with her friends, yoga and golf, and generally living her life through her daughters.

No one could say she didn't keep herself busy. What she didn't admit was that there was busy, and then there was *busy*, and while she might have been running around like a headless chicken, she could never say it was satisfying, because she wasn't even using a fifth of her potential.

But that had been the choice she had made. Moving south meant giving up her career and devoting her time to raising two girls, just as her mum had always told her she should.

"You're losing precious time, Janie. They won't be young for long. These years will fly, even if it doesn't feel like it now." Janie could still hear her mother's voice as if she were sitting in the passenger seat next to her.

The more her mum had protested, the more Janie had dug her heels in, ignoring the guilt that crawled through her veins. She was doing this for her girls, she told herself. Showing them that women didn't need to give up their careers.

Though quite frankly Janie had already realized that no one should have ever promised women they could have it all, because they couldn't, and the realization of it only made them feel like they were failing. The idea was laughable really, especially when she considered that some weeks her working hours combined with Harry's topped one hundred and fifty. Of course she wasn't having it all. She was losing out on being a mother, replaced by the twenty-three-year-old nanny who was living in her house and bringing up her toddlers.

"It's your choice," her mum had muttered once. "That's all it boils down to. Choices." Her mother had stayed at home to look after Janie until the day she went to university.

Janie later realized that her mum was right. It was all about making choices and accepting them. Janie had chosen a full-on career, which meant she was supposed to accept that she needed to outsource her childcare. Only she never could.

She glanced at the empty passenger seat beside her and inhaled a breath that seemed to swell in her throat. "I wish you could see me now, Mum," she said. "I finally did what you said I should." Unfortunately, her mum had died six months after Janie moved south and had never gotten to see the so-called choice Janie had made to give up her career and be a stay-at-home mum. So-called, because Janie never could reconcile that it *was* a choice. In the end, by the time they left London and she had left her role as a defense barrister, Janie didn't believe she'd had a choice at all.

But by then she had been thankful when Harry had told her about the site he had found across the water from Lymington Quay. When he was excited about the possibility of branching his already successful ad agency out to the south coast, Janie considered that maybe it was exactly what they needed. And so she listened as Harry told her that he'd been playing with the idea for a while. He already had some big clients based along the M3 corridor, and there were a number of financial companies he'd been speaking to in Southampton and Bournemouth. He could split his time between London and the south and how about, he suggested, she and the girls move down full-time?

Janie continued to let him list the pros as he sold his argument. Schooling, property prices, they could even have a pool in their back garden. He didn't need to remind her that Lymington had a place in her heart already, as she'd visited often as a child, her dad being a keen sailor.

Harry reminded her that London was not even a two-hour commute. He could work up there a couple of days a week, maybe rent a flat. He could, by all accounts, carry on living the life he wanted during the week and then have the luxury of leaving it all behind on a Friday.

Janie, however, would have to make a choice, they both silently understood. But by then, in Janie's head, it was already a done deal.

She pulled off the country lane and onto the small gravel park alongside Lucy's silver BMW. The coffee shop sat on the outskirts of Brockenhurst, a little way from the school, but she and her friends all agreed it served the best coffee around, and it was a good place to talk without the threat of being overheard by another school parent.

She could see all three of her friends gathered around the table in the window, so Janie hurried inside, banging the door wide open as she did. She didn't know when she had gotten to the stage in her life that she hated being late because of the gossip she was missing, but at some point it had happened.

"Just in time," Kristen called. "Lucy was about to tell us about the meeting with Mr. Steele."

"Oh, don't start," Janie said. "Let me grab a coffee first." She threw her purse onto the empty seat, grabbing her wallet out of it as she rushed to the counter. They were the only customers, as they often were, but there was no sign of anyone to serve them, and in her impatience Janie called out, "Hello?"

Eventually a young girl appeared, and Janie ordered a black coffee.

"I'm sorry I'm late," she said as she pulled her purse from the chair and sat down without offering an explanation. None of them cared why; they were all busy running back and forth between school and the various activities they had during the day. Not one of her small group of mum friends worked, yet each of them filled their days with so many things that they barely had time to breathe. Moments like these were precious—catching up over a coffee and sharing their news, which invariably revolved around the school and their children, and who had fallen out with whom. "So tell us, what did he say?"

Lucy rolled her eyes and waved a hand in the air. "Oh, he basically told me this was in *my* daughter's head," she said. "That they've been watching Dexter and he hasn't shown any signs of violence on the playground."

"He didn't actually say that," Janie said with a gasp, as she fiddled the clasp on her wallet shut and threw it back in her purse. "That it was in her head?"

"Not in so many words, but he might as well have."

"I can't believe they're not doing anything about it. Dexter's clearly insane. I mean, you only need to look at his mother," Kristen chimed in.

"His mother's the problem, isn't she?" Lucy said. "If they weren't donating so much bloody money to the school left, right, and center, someone might have actually opened their eyes and seen their son was a lunatic. You know they've invited Mr. Steele out on their boat this weekend?"

"That and the fact she works full-time, of course," Kristen murmured.

Janie winced. "Kris, you can't say things like that," Lucy said. "It's got nothing to do with it."

"Of course it has." Kristen shrugged. "She's never there. Dexter's left to the au pair to sort out, who I'm afraid barely speaks one word of English. He gets away with murder. I see it outside the school gate. She's just eighteen and can't control him."

"Well, you're not going to like my news, then." Anna smiled. "I'm going back to work."

"You're what?" Lucy spluttered.

"I know." Anna grinned. "Crazy, eh? But my old boss called and said they need someone urgently, and it's something I've been thinking about for a while anyway. Why are you all looking at me like that?"

"I don't know," Lucy said. "I mean, of course it's great if that's what you want to do but . . . Aren't you going to miss all this?" She waved an arm around the empty coffee shop.

Janie's stomach dipped so deep she could feel it sitting like a lump of rock inside her. She'd never regret being around for the girls the past few years, but sometimes it was hard to ignore the hole stretching and tugging inside. If things had been different . . . If she hadn't taken on that case . . .

But they weren't. And she had. And this was her life now, and as far as the girls went at least, Janie was happy with it. She turned her attention back to Anna, who was grinning and shaking her head.

"I'm still going to see you all, it's just—" She paused and shrugged. "I just have to do it. You can understand that, can't you?" she asked, and her eyes roamed to Janie, who felt immobile as she stared back at her. "What do you think?" Anna asked, reaching out to grab Janie's hand.

The others had stopped murmuring, and she realized she hadn't commented on the news. "I think it's great," she eventually got out. "I really do."

Anna nodded, smiling back at her. "I knew you'd understand, Janie. I mean, you were always such a career woman yourself. You must know what I mean when I say I need to be doing something just for me?"

"Yes." Janie smiled. "Yes, I do."

"Oh, please don't tell us you're going to get yourself a job too," Lucy said. "There'll be none of us left."

Janie continued to smile and shook her head. "No," she said. "No plans for me." She nodded at the girl bringing her coffee over to the table and pulled a packet of sugar out of a little porcelain dish, averting her eyes from her friends, whose gazes she could feel on her. "I just need a little," she said, tearing it open, already feeling a stab of regret. When was the last time she'd had sugar? She didn't even know why she was tipping it into her coffee.

They lapsed into silence before Lucy piped up. "In other good news, my mole is actually a wart, so I guess that's something to be grateful for. Everyone up for yoga tonight?"

They all agreed they were, and although Janie knew she wouldn't be able to go if Harry wasn't home in time, she didn't bother saying as much. Her friends knew the possibility well enough.

By the time she left the coffee shop and started her car, Janie realized she was jealous of Anna. And once the thought had entered her head, she feared she might not be able to get rid of it.

She played with the idea that she would miss her girlfriends and their catch-ups, but their oldest girls would be going to secondary school soon. Things were going to change. And really, what did they all talk about that was remotely important? It was so far from the evenings she used to spend with friends in a wine bar in London at the end of a heavy day. When Janie would regale them with tales of her latest cases, drip-feeding them as much information as she was allowed.

They were always keen to know the ins and outs of her job because Janie's firm had some big-time clients—but it was Janie's last-ever case that had particularly piqued their interest.

She knew how to handle questions, how to avoid getting into debate, but sometimes she would get drawn into it. Janie knew her friends were interested in what she really thought, how she could possibly detach herself. The truth was she'd learned early on to stop caring about the victims, because if she didn't, she wouldn't be able to do her job properly. She'd observed how to look at her cases as if they were pieces of fiction.

Only, that case that her friends had relentlessly questioned her over had caught her in the end. When there was no way of escaping the fact it wasn't fiction—it was reality—that was the point when Janie had to face the question that had begun searing into her every waking moment. How could she carry on doing her job?

Janie drove on, heading toward Lymington, her mind full of thoughts: she still dreaded the days she switched on the TV or opened up a newspaper and read about it again. In the last five years, thoughts of her career that had once triggered excitement had shriveled away to disgust—and, if she ever allowed the thought in, an element of self-loathing.

It was an unconscious decision to pull into the parking lot at the quay on her way to golf, and for a few seconds Janie didn't know how she had turned off the main road and headed in this direction, but now she was there and looking across the river to her husband's office.

At the edge of the quay she got a direct view of the shiny building, though she could only imagine what was happening on the other side of the glass. They could see out, but she couldn't see in. The way it had so cleverly been designed.

The building looked beautiful. The way the light reflected off the water and hit the glass. All as it was supposed to. That building had been her lifesaver five years ago. Her chance to start again; and yet some days she would look at it and feel a hatred bubbling beneath her skin. A hatred that was potentially misplaced, but which also stood for everything she had lost, and everything Harry still had.

She wondered what was going on inside its four walls right now, how her husband felt, making decisions, giving orders, pulling in another big client, or congratulating his staff on a job well done. On the whole, Harry was amazing at what he did, he always had been. His ambition was part of what Janie had fallen in love with. There was something so sexy about success, and Harry had been nothing but successful.

Janie stared at her husband's building as the light bounced off it. Today was one of the days she hated it, but not just because of her reaction to Anna's news. It was also because Laura Denning was back.

chapter five

By the time Laura had extracted herself from the toilets, she was five minutes late to Harry's meeting. The boardroom was already full. From outside the glass wall she could see the jostle for chairs, the banter by the far window. She could hear the laughter erupting through the glass.

There was a time when Laura felt a buzz upon entering the room, but now her stomach was jittering for a very different reason. She gripped her notepad more tightly as she caught sight of Mia at the far end. Laura's eyes trailed down the length of Mia's gray woolen cardigan. It hung open and unbelted, reaching her mid calves. Under it she had on an almost sheer white top that was pulled out from the waistband of slim navy jeans.

Mia's hair was cut short, tapered at the back of her neck but hanging lower at the front. It was much darker than Laura remembered. There was something so effortlessly chic about this woman that it made Laura feel dowdy by comparison. She'd been pleased with how she'd looked this morning, but now she was just unsettled. The men who stood around the long oval table were all dressed in either open-neck or polo shirts, as if it were some kind of uniform. They wouldn't even consider checking out what each other was wearing. They probably couldn't tell her what color their own shirts were if she asked them to close their eyes. And yet somehow, for some reason, the sight of Mia looking so elegant filled Laura with irritation, because more than anything it sapped away what little confidence she had left.

Mia was smiling at something Harry was saying, and eventually he glanced up and caught Laura standing on the other side of the glass. He beckoned her in. A smile was plastered across his face, leftover from whatever joke he'd just been sharing, but she could tell that beneath it there was a layer of something more. She wondered how much he was wrangling with his decision, and hoped it was enough that he would come to his senses quickly.

Laura forced a smile as she opened the door to a chorus of "Hey, you're back. Good to see you."

She answered their questions about Bobby and agreed how quickly the time had gone by, and silently thanked their financial officer for standing so close to the door that she could direct her attention on him.

Meanwhile she could sense Mia moving toward the table. As if on cue, she pulled out the seat next to Harry and sat down. Rage bubbled inside Laura. Misplaced, maybe, for how could she explain to anyone why she was so disproportionately angry that this woman had taken a seat at their boss's side, for what did it really matter? But Laura realized that it mattered a lot—because Mia was there and she shouldn't be.

As Harry called them all in, Laura dropped her notepad onto the table and took the seat nearest the door. Inside the pad were her copious notes on how she was planning to develop the Coopers campaign, a now-futile exercise that had taken up many hours of her last two weeks of maternity leave that she could have spent with her son. It both surprised and annoyed Laura that this thought brought her to the edge of tears. Never before had her emotions teetered so precariously close to their breaking point. She inhaled deeply, focusing on Harry's words as he ran through last week's top-line figures.

To everyone who worked at Morris and Wood, Harry was some kind of hero. Back in London, before he'd set up another arm of the agency in Lymington, Harry had turned the company into a multimillion-pound, award-winning agency after taking over from his father and buying out the other partner.

He rarely made decisions that anyone on the board disagreed with, which was why this latest one was so unsettling. Laura scanned the men around the table and wondered what they had thought when he told them Mia would be staying on. Did they agree with him? Had they seen her in action and understood that she was too brilliant to lose? Had one of them even suggested it? Laura clutched her hands together under the table. Never in her time at Morris and Wood had she felt so on the periphery.

Suddenly Harry's patter was broken by the vibration of Mia's phone. Mia told Harry she was going to have to take the call. Laura glanced at her boss, who nodded indifferently and picked up again as Mia left the room. Out of the corner of Laura's eye she could see Mia pacing back and forth outside the window. She wondered what was so important that it took Mia out of the Monday exec meeting.

And then, just as it seemed the meeting couldn't get any worse, Harry announced that Mia was back just in time to present her update.

"Well, we're meeting with the Coopers health-drink marketing team a week from Friday," Mia began. "I'm going to be taking them through the concepts for TV, and we hope to start shooting the ad as soon as June."

Laura squeezed her hands tighter and prayed the others would continue to look at either Mia or the table in front of them and not turn in her direction, as they must have been inclined to do. The air felt sticky and oppressive. The thought that she'd stand out as the only one not called upon for an update was mildly tempered by the idea that if she did open her mouth, no words would come out.

Her body was rigid as she listened to Mia's seemingly eternal presentation, and all Laura could conclude was that somehow, during the last six months, Mia Anderson had transformed from a laid-back temp with no ambition to a woman who had clearly earned her place around Harry's board table. The idea of it seemed so implausible that Laura wondered if she had actually read Mia completely wrong when she interviewed her last September.

She willed the next fifty minutes to pass as quickly as possible. As soon as the meeting was over she was ready to run, and thankfully, being nearest to the door, was the first one out of it. Yet as she stepped out onto the open-plan floor, she realized she had nowhere to go. Mia bloody Anderson's things were still on her desk, and as tempting as it was to hurl them off, Laura wasn't quite at that stage yet.

"Welcome back, Laura."

Laura turned.

"Sorry I didn't get a chance to say hi earlier, I was on a call and just couldn't get off the phone."

"It's really not a problem," Laura said as she faced Mia.

"How was it, leaving your baby this morning?"

"It was fine," Laura lied. No way was she going to get into a conversation about her personal life.

"I expect you'll miss him though, won't you?" Mia went on. "I mean, it must be a wrench, you know, worrying over someone who depends on you so much. It's not easy."

"He's very lucky to be with his dad," Laura replied curtly.

"Of course." Mia's gaze didn't leave Laura's face, and Laura wondered at the woman's confidence. "I'm just saying, I can understand you must be feeling a bit weird this morning." Mia paused and smiled. "I just think if it were me, I wouldn't be able to stop thinking about him and—"

"Mia, would you mind moving so I can have my desk back?" Laura interrupted before this woman went any further.

"Right, yes of course." Mia hesitated and then, "I'll do it now," she said.

As soon as Mia disappeared, Laura headed straight for the lift and rode it down to the ground floor, where she pulled out her mobile and phoned Nate. "How is he?" she asked breathlessly, as soon as her husband picked up.

"Hey! Everything okay?"

"Yes, how's Bobby?"

"He's great. He's having his nap."

"That's good. Did he eat all his porridge?"

"Most of it, greedy little man." Nate laughed.

"He is." She smiled, closing her eyes and pressing her fingertips against them.

"Laura, are you okay? You sound upset."

"No, I'm fine."

"Bobby's all right, you know. I've been looking after him for the last hour and fifty minutes," Nate joked.

"I know."

"Seriously, has something happened?"

"Oh God, Nate. I don't know what to do," she began, before filling him in.

"What did Harry actually say was the reason?" Nate asked.

"That she'd started, so she might as well see it through. He said something about easing me back in and that there was something else in the pipeline."

"Okay."

"But it's all crap," she cried.

"What is? The thing in the pipeline?"

"All of it. What's she done that's so special, Nate? She's clearly done a better job in six months than I have in the last five years."

"That can't be true."

"It must be. I can't think of any other reason why she'd be kept on."

"But maybe there is something else Harry wants you to work on?"

"Of course there isn't," Laura protested, as she paced to the front door of the empty foyer and then back again to the lift. Her head was spinning, and she couldn't clear it. Her stomach was a jumbled mess of knots at the thought of stepping back in that lift and having to face Mia again, because right then she would like nothing more than to run out the door and not come back.

"Well, maybe he's right," Nate was saying, "and it'll be good to ease yourself back in."

"I don't need to do that, Nate," she said, her voice rising. "Harry knows what I'm like; he would never have thought I needed time to get back into it. No. I'm telling you, she's clearly better than I am, and so I'm just going to have to accept that, aren't I?" she said, knowing there'd never be a day that would happen.

"Laura, you're getting yourself worked up."

"Of course I am," she cried, splaying her other hand against her head. "She's a bloody temp, Nate. And she's stolen my job."

"No she hasn't, love. By the sound of it, she's doing this one thing and—"

"Oh my God, Nate, will you stop doing that."

"Doing what?" he said. "I'm only trying to help you."

"I know you are trying, but you aren't helping. I just want you to be on my side and not keep telling me it's okay, because it actually isn't."

"I'm sorry." Nate paused. "Of course I'm on your side, but I don't know what else to say. It's probably only temporary, and whatever Harry's got in mind might be better. Laura, I don't get what else I can say," he repeated.

And that was the problem. Nate didn't understand because his job in IT was so different from hers. He had tasks to complete and he got on and did them and then passed them back to his supervisor. She admired his skills, she really did. She certainly couldn't find her way around a computer like he did, but he didn't understand the complexities of her career. And while she could never expect him to, it meant that sometimes she knew she would never get any useful advice out of him. And right now that just made her feel worse.

"Why don't you speak to one of the team at Coopers?" he suggested. "Who do you know best?"

Laura shook her head. She couldn't imagine putting herself on the line like that. "Listen, I need to go back to work," she said eventually. "I'll talk to you tonight. And I'm sorry I shouted."

———————

Laura thought about Mia as she took the lift back up to the third floor, and the way she'd been in the interview, perching on the edge of the chair, her eyes intently focused on Laura. Every so often Mia's gaze had flicked out of the small meeting-room window to the offices beyond, and on a couple of occasions Laura had wondered, frustrated, what she was looking at.

In answer to every one of Laura's questions, Mia had given a textbook response, nodding enthusiastically. Laura had put her behavior down to nerves. No one liked being interviewed for a job, though it had been a surprise when, right at the end, Mia had given a little reassuring speech as they left the room about how much she would relish looking after Laura's position while she was on maternity leave.

Ironically, it had been those final words that sealed the deal, only now Laura considered that Mia had actually been very determined she was going to get her job. And the idea that she wasn't just after it temporarily now made those words feel more sinister than comforting.

Laura saw Mia as soon as she stepped out of the lift, hovering by the water cooler, chatting to Henrietta James. Mia's head was bouncing up and down with laughter as she wiped a hand across her face. Had Henrietta actually brought Mia to tears with whatever they were talking about? Laura couldn't remember a time when she had shared a joke with Henrietta, certainly not to that extent, and she realized she felt a ripple of jealousy at the sight of the two women, so close.

She glanced around the floor and considered there was not one woman in the office she could call a good friend. There had been once. Saskia. But Laura's fingers had been burned by that friendship, when the line between work and her social life blurred, and after that she knew it was advisable to keep the women who worked for her at arm's length.

Yet it meant there wasn't anyone else she felt she could confide in in the office about what was happening, while there was every possibility Mia already could. And that thought suddenly made Laura feel so alone.

She still stood by the lifts, this realization dawning on her, when Mia finished her conversation and then turned to have a new one with the quiet woman Laura had earlier seen in the toilets. Sarah Clifton had been hovering nearby, and now that Henrietta had gone, Mia's attention was solely on her instead, but there was a very different dynamic between these two women. The way Mia hung her head, her brow furrowed, one hand lightly touching Sarah's arm, rubbing it gently as she finished talking to her before her gaze drifted over Sarah's shoulder to Laura.

Laura inhaled a tight breath as Sarah left the water cooler and Mia started walking toward her. Whether she was prepared for it or not, they were about to talk, and Laura knew she was going to have to play this carefully.

Initial interviews between Detective Emily Marlow and staff of Morris and Wood following the fire at Morris and Wood offices on Monday, May 13.

<u>Henrietta James, Senior Account Manager, on Tuesday, May 14, at Lymington Police Headquarters.</u>

Marlow: You said things started to change at Morris and Wood when Laura Denning came back from maternity leave. What did you mean by that?

Henrietta: I mean everyone was on edge. There was a tension in the air, and we didn't know what to do for the best.

Marlow: Tension between Laura and Mia?

Henrietta: Yes. Mainly.

Marlow: What happened between them?

Henrietta: Well, they both tried to hide it in the office, but then Laura got it into her head that Mia was somehow out to get her. Like she had come for her job on purpose, or something.

Marlow: Do you believe that was the case?

Henrietta: Of course not. Laura was trying to blame her because she wanted her account back. Why on earth would Mia do that?

Marlow: I don't know.

Henrietta: Well, she wouldn't. It makes no sense.

Marlow: Yet Laura thought she had. How do you know this—did Laura tell you?

Henrietta: (laughs) No. No, she wouldn't have told me. I overheard her speaking to Harry. She said she had evidence but—well, I didn't hear the rest of it. All I know is that Harry seemed to get annoyed with her. He ushered her into his office pretty quick.

Marlow: Harry got annoyed? Did this cause tension between them, then?

Henrietta: Laura tried to maintain everything was all right between her and Harry, but after that I didn't think it was. I didn't see how it could be. You see, Laura always had Harry's ear, and now suddenly he wasn't listening to her. I think we all expected that as soon as Laura returned she'd somehow manage to talk him round, and Mia would be gone. None of us wanted that, of course. Everyone likes Mia, but all the same, I could see where Laura would be coming from if she had started demanding her job back.

It's not that I don't like her, you know. I hope that's not how it's coming across. It's just that Laura is—she's just not as easygoing as Mia to get along with. Mia's so much easier to work for. She doesn't mind stopping and chatting for a start, not like Laura, who's always checking her watch if she wants something from you—

Marlow: You were saying about Laura and Harry?

Henrietta: Sorry? Oh right, yes. The point is, Laura never did get her way with Harry, did she? Because Mia is still working there.

Marlow: Did you notice any other changes around Laura in the last two months?

Henrietta: Apart from the fact she's always working, even though she has that young baby at home? Mind you, that's no different from the way she always was, but with a child—you know? You'd have thought she would have cut back. I feel sorry for her husband.

Marlow: Nathan Denning?

Henrietta: That's right. I thought we might see him at Harry's party last week, but that was another odd thing. He didn't show.

I did say to someone at the party that I was worried about Laura. I remember doing that. Before everything kicked off, I mean. I said I hope she's okay, because she certainly wasn't looking it by then.

chapter six

eight weeks before the fire

Mia knew this was not going to be an easy conversation, but it was one she had to get out of the way. Yet as Laura's eyes bored through her, she began to wonder whether it would be easier to sidestep the woman and pretend she was heading for the lift. Any earlier confidence was rapidly evaporating.

"Hi again, Laura. I've moved my things." Mia gestured a hand in the direction of the desk she had just vacated.

"Okay. Great. Thanks," Laura said awkwardly, and then, appearing to pull herself together, she added, "I hear you're continuing to run with the TV campaign for the time being."

"Yes. That's right." Mia smiled at her, as warmly as she could muster when the anger bubbling off Laura was almost palpable. Of course Laura was angry, she must have clearly wanted to run the campaign herself. It was, after all, bringing in a large sum of money for the company. So Mia understood how Laura must be feeling right now, but at the same time they were going to have to find a way to get on with it.

"I could do with your input actually," Mia said, watching Laura stiffen as she plowed on. "I'd appreciate your thoughts on what I'm presenting. You've known the brand for so long, after all . . ." She was waffling, but Laura wasn't answering as she sucked in a short breath. "It would be good to see if you spot anything I've missed."

"You want me to help you out so that *you* can present the work to the client?" Laura's eyebrows rose and she gestured to a small meeting room to the side of them. Mia followed her in. When Laura had closed the door behind them she said, "Mia, I have to be honest. I'm a little shocked you're still here. You were only supposed to be covering for my maternity leave."

Mia had known this was coming, and yet now that they were here, pressed into the smallest of rooms, she didn't know how to respond.

Laura pursed her lips. "I'm grateful you've been keeping my accounts running, but I've been managing Coopers for the last five years. I know it back to front. Harry knows I'm ready to take it back again, and while I'm sure you've made a great start on the TV campaign, I'll want it handed back to me as soon as possible."

Mia watched as Laura straightened her back. This was completely patronizing—did Laura really have no idea how capable she was?

Maybe it was her own doing, Mia understood that. In the interview she had told Laura what she wanted to hear because she needed this job and she'd had to get it. What she had quickly deciphered was that Laura didn't want someone who was a threat, she wanted an assistant. Someone who could keep things going for her so Laura could walk back in and pick up where she'd left off. So it wasn't Laura's fault that she didn't know how easily Mia could run a campaign like this, but that didn't mean she wasn't pissed off with the way she was talking to her. Especially after she'd already snapped her fingers to get her out of her desk.

Mia wondered what she could possibly say right now when it appeared Harry had told Laura the bare minimum, and if that were the case, then Laura was going to keep pestering her. But at the same time, Mia was also wary of Laura and Harry's close relationship, and above anything she could not lose this job.

"So I'm sorry, Mia, but I won't be helping you run this campaign just so you can take the credit for it."

"I realize you've been doing this job for a long time—"

"Except *you* are now."

Mia held a tight breath. "Yes," she said. "Now I am. And I want to continue doing a good job. Which is why I thought you might help me, but obviously I was wrong."

"Do you know, I don't actually remember you having that much account director experience," Laura said sharply.

Mia could feel the bite on Laura's tongue and the sneer in her voice. So that was the game she was going to play. Make out Mia didn't deserve to be in this role, as if she hadn't been putting everything into it over the last six months, proving her worth.

Clearly Harry hadn't told Laura the reasons he wasn't readily handing the Coopers account back to her, but Mia wished he would, so she could get this woman off her back.

"You wanted a temporary role," Laura persisted. "You told me that yourself in the interview. You said you didn't want to stay in Lymington. That was why you were coming to cover me. So what's happened?"

Mia thought for a moment. "Things have changed," she said eventually. "And I'm enjoying working at Morris and Wood. I love the people, it's great experience . . ." She trailed off. She didn't need to answer to Laura Denning anymore. She wasn't being interviewed. She certainly didn't work for Laura, as much as Laura might like to think she did. They were on the same level.

"Laura, this is the way it is, and I'm sorry you're not happy about it, but I'm running the Coopers campaign. I understand if you don't want to help me, I just thought I'd ask," Mia said, and righting herself she moved past Laura and opened the door.

Outside, she caught sight of Sarah Clifton hovering nearby again, and while she knew she shouldn't add fuel to the fire, Mia called out. "Hey, Sarah, do you mind if we catch up on the creatives you're working on for me?"

Mia didn't look back as Sarah nodded, albeit a little confusedly. She took Sarah's arm and led her toward another meeting room, where she'd brush off what she'd just said and turn the conversation to Sarah instead, who'd been wanting to talk to her privately all morning. Behind her, she felt Laura's wrath seeping out of the doorway.

Mia was drained when she pulled up to the bungalow that night. One day of Laura being back and Mia was not only managing the TV campaign workload, she now had to manage Laura's resentment of her too. On top of that, she'd had to carve out time for Sarah Clifton, who was increasingly reaching the point where she wanted to make a formal complaint about Mike Lewis's harassment, and Mia needed to be there for her. As the only one who knew what was going on, she'd promised she'd be by Sarah's side every step, but right now juggling all three things wasn't easy.

Clutching her Gucci bag to her chest, she checked the road with the broken streetlamps before stepping out of the car and up to the front door. It was the smartest door on the street. The only one that had been freshly painted and cared for, and the pale green stood out among the others, just like the neatly mown small patch of lawn beside the driveway did.

Sticking her key in the lock, Mia took a deep breath and held it for a moment before turning the key and pushing the door open. She never knew what was awaiting her on the other side of it, and she always entered with a sense of apprehension.

But tonight the TV was humming in the background and the smell of roast chicken drifted from the kitchen and there was nothing that raised an alarm. Her pulse was already starting to slow as she stepped in and called out with feigned joviality, "Hi, Mum, I'm home."

In the kitchen her mum turned and smiled at her, wiping a hand across the plastic *Bistro* apron she'd had since Mia was a child. "Long day, was it?"

Mia nodded and gave her mum a kiss on the cheek. Today had been busy, but there were some days when she lingered in the office later than she needed to. She would never dare tell her mum that, however. Even though her mum would likely understand that being anywhere but inside these four walls was a breath of fresh air.

Mia wondered whether she'd continue to feel that way now that Laura was back. She'd enjoyed the last six months. Morris and Wood had felt like a comfort blanket in some ways. It was a shame things had to change, but change they must, and at least Mia had the Woods' party in her sights.

"I do so wish it wasn't there you were working, though," her mum sighed.

"I know you do, Mum."

Mia's mother had once protested about the development of the offices and still considered Harry Wood to be the enemy. When Mia had gotten the job, she'd warily told her mum where she would be working, but by then the money was so desperately needed that she thought her mum wouldn't have minded if she went to work for the Conservatives.

"And there really isn't anything else out there you could be going for?"

"No, there isn't. Besides, I like it." She wrapped an arm around her mum's bony waist and gave it a squeeze. Every time she did so she felt her mum getting a little thinner. And every time that happened, Mia felt an even greater weight pressing down on her shoulders.

chapter seven

On Friday morning Janie pulled a pair of black capri trousers and a white shirt out of the wardrobe. It didn't escape her that making an effort for a child's assembly was ludicrous, but if she didn't she would stand out. The girls were already waiting by the front door when she descended the stairs, their blazers on, their hats slightly askew. She straightened Lottie's and reached for Ella, who pulled out of her way, making hers slip even farther to one side.

"We're going to be late," Ella moaned.

"We're not. It's not even ten to."

"You won't get a good seat. Don't you want to be at the front?"

"Of course I do, but wherever I sit I'll be able to see you. Are you nervous?" Janie asked her oldest.

"No."

"You shouldn't be. You've practiced so hard. You were playing beautifully last night."

"OhmyGod, I just said I wasn't nervous!" Ella shouted.

"Fine," Janie held up her hands in surrender and ushered them through the door toward the car.

"Lacey's dad's coming," Ella muttered when she climbed into the back.

"You know Dad would have liked to come," Janie said as she slid into the driver's seat and looked at her daughter in the rearview mirror. "It's just today he has something important to do at work and—"

"I'm not even saying anything about Dad, I just told you Lacey's is coming. Are you not even listening to me?"

Janie ignored her daughter's tone as she started the engine. Ella wasn't usually remotely bothered if Harry was there or not, but then the evening before Janie'd overheard her asking him if he was coming, in a way that suggested she was. He'd told Ella he couldn't this time, and then Janie had waited to see if he would bring up the piano recital before they went to bed, because the truth of it was that she couldn't remember if she'd even told him about it in the first place. She didn't actually think she had.

But Harry didn't ask. He must have thought he'd forgotten all about it, and Janie decided to let him think that. There was no point admitting it might be her mistake, but she felt guilty that Ella quite clearly wished her father was there.

She knew she was about to make it worse, but she couldn't help herself when she said, "Honestly, Daddy really wanted to be at the recital—"

"Mum!" Ella yelled. "I told you I don't care."

"Okay. I'm sorry," she said, and they fell into silence. Janie wondered if hormones kicked in again at eleven, or whether they had even stopped from the last surge.

Once they had reached the school playground, Janie kissed Ella hurriedly on the top of her head and waited with Lottie for the bell to ring.

"You know you won't get a seat at the front if you don't go in," Lottie warned her.

"I know, poppet, but I'll be fine."

"Mummy, why doesn't Daddy ever come to see our shows?"

"Lottie, he does," Janie said. "That's not true, he always comes if he can make it." But even as she said it she tried to think back to the last time Harry had accompanied her to a school event. Even on open-school nights he had rarely been home in time, but always the teachers had brushed it off, because everyone knew how busy and important Harry Wood was, and everyone was more than happy to excuse his absence.

Just like Janie had always been too. Over time, she realized, there had been many occasions when she felt like a single parent. Perhaps that was why she had inadvertently stopped telling her husband about the girls' events. Maybe she found it easier to support them on her own.

There would come a day when Janie would leave Harry. She had known this for some time now but had always assumed it wouldn't be until the girls were older. When they left home themselves, she wouldn't need to worry about what they thought as much as she did now.

She often wondered what everyone would say when she told them, how surprised they would be. Even her own sister wouldn't foresee it. If Janie were being honest, thoughts of both their families were another reason that made the idea of leaving him seem impossible. From the outside, Janie and Harry were still the golden couple they always had been, their marriage the one everyone else supposedly craved. They'd both always attracted people like honeypots.

On the surface, their relationship *was* still the same. They rarely argued, they still had fun with friends, they continued to do things as a family on weekends. It was the layer below where there were cracks. They didn't argue because they didn't have enough meaningful conversations anymore, or perhaps because they didn't care enough to get heated about them.

And then there was another layer way below that. The one that had hardened just over five years ago, the root of all their issues that was never spoken of. Janie didn't speak to anyone about it, not to her sister, not even to her best friend, Sophie, with whom she'd always been so close. Maybe at the time she could have handled things differently and not believed that moving to the New Forest was enough.

A house move and a change of scenery went some way toward plastering over what had happened, but the problem with putting a Band-Aid on was peeling it off. And so sometimes it was so much easier to just carry on.

Next to her, Lottie's head was nestled into Janie's side, and as she reminded herself she wouldn't leave Harry until the girls were older, she also wondered if it would really be that bad. Once the girls had gotten used to the idea, would they actually miss him?

She kissed Lottie as the school bell rang before wandering into the hall and finding a seat in the fourth row. Something would happen if it were meant to.

Janie craned her neck to get a better view around Lacey's large grandfather, who was blocking the view in front of her. It appeared Lacey hadn't just brought Mum and Dad—both sets of grandparents were here too—and therefore was it any wonder she'd never be able to get a seat at the front unless she'd started lining up at eight?

"Mind if I squeeze in?"

Janie looked up and nodded as a mum she didn't recognize gestured to the chair on the other side of her. "Let me move along," Janie said, and shuffled onto the next seat, where she had an even worse view of the stage.

"Thanks. I was told to get here early, but I didn't realize it would be this busy."

"Yep, it's pretty popular. Who are you here to watch?"

"My daughter, Amelie. She's playing the cello, of all things." The woman screwed up her nose, and Janie smiled.

"It's bloody awful," the mum went on. "She can't play it. You'll hear for yourself soon enough."

Janie laughed. This woman seemed like a breath of fresh air among so many stuck-up parents. "Janie," she said, holding out a hand. "I don't think we've met."

"Marcia. We're new. We only started this term."

"Well, welcome," Janie said, and wondered whether she should invite Marcia along to their next coffee. There was, after all, an opening going in their small group once Anna started working again. "I have Ella playing the piano and my younger daughter, Lottie, is at the school too."

"I've also got a son here," she said. "Year two. Miles."

Miles.

Janie continued to smile, but the hairs on her arms had pricked up, and for a moment she couldn't find the words to respond.

Marcia continued to talk to her, but Janie's mind had gone to other places. Marcia's son was just a little boy, of course, but that name . . . that name had frozen her.

Of course it had entered her head plenty of times, though less so in recent years. But just the sound of it being spoken aloud—she had no idea her body would react like it had, and it was a relief when the children started filing into the hall. Marcia eventually stopped talking, and Janie turned her concentration to the child who had taken a seat at the piano and was trying his hardest to thump out a tune.

Marcia nudged her when her daughter stood up, and Janie couldn't help but smile. But her thoughts kept straying, and it took all her effort to pull herself back to the present. When Ella took the stage, Janie shifted in her seat to get the clearest view she could, tears springing to her eyes when her daughter eventually finished playing her piece beautifully. Ella remained at the piano for a moment longer, as she looked over to the crowd of parents clapping, her eyes scanning them until she eventually found Janie. When she did her face broke into a smile, and it melted Janie's heart that her gorgeous and talented, if slightly angry, daughter was so clearly pleased to see her.

For the rest of the morning Janie tried to shake away thoughts of the man who now would not leave her head. Miles Morgan. She could picture his face as if he stood in front of her, even though it had been five years since she had last seen him in the flesh, or even in a photo. His dark hair, only a few flecks of gray; the light coating of stubble on his chin; bright blue eyes; his height—he was at least a head taller than Harry, which made his presence in any room so overpowering. Harry was a man who everyone admitted was good-looking, but Miles was one who made you stop and turn.

Janie had always resisted the urge to look him up. To see what he was doing now. Miles was a part of her life she had needed to leave behind, but that day, when she got home from the assembly, she couldn't stop herself from opening up her laptop and googling his name just to see where he was, whether he was still working at the same company.

It didn't take long to find him, and as soon as Janie saw his picture she took a deep breath, sitting back in her chair, her fingers tapping through images, her breaths short and ragged.

Janie pulled her mobile toward her and scrolled through her contacts. She had a sudden urge to call Sophie, although she could never tell her the reason. She could never admit to her best friend that she had been thinking of Miles, that she'd searched for him online, had seen his face.

"Hey you," Sophie answered. "How's things in the deep south?"

Janie laughed, her heart still beating a little too fast. "Good. All good," she said.

"How are my goddaughters?"

Janie told her about Ella's assembly and Lottie's ballet classes, and Sophie listened with interest about the children she loved. She would never have her own now. By Sophie's own admission that time had passed, but it didn't stop Janie from thinking she would have made a great mum.

"Harry?" she asked.

"Yep, all good."

There was a beat of silence before Sophie ventured, "Sure?"

Janie laughed. "Yes, of course," she said. "Life's busy, you know, Harry's working a lot, and I'm on the go . . ." Her words fizzled out; there was no convincing Sophie, as much as Janie had always tried, that this was the life she was cut out for. That there wasn't something missing from what should be an idyllic existence.

Janie had always been closer to Sophie than she had her own sister. As far as her sister was concerned, there wasn't anything Janie could possibly have to complain about when she had a huge house with a pool and, in her own words, a husband who looked like Harry. But then her sister had always been jealous, and Sophie never had. Not even when their lives couldn't have been more different.

Their paths had set off in opposing directions the day they left school. Sophie had balanced a string of jobs and was now living in a small flat with a struggling artist for a boyfriend, who, at forty, was five years her junior. But Sophie had never envied Janie's wealth. If anything, she was more concerned that Janie had given up her career, because she wasn't the type of person who wanted to be living off her husband.

"I know you're at work, I won't keep you," Janie said. "I just haven't spoken to you in a while." *I just wanted to hear your voice,* Janie thought. *I wanted to check you're doing all right.*

Their conversations always skirted the subjects that were important to them now, the ones they'd have once dissected over a bottle of wine and tapas. They'd never dived into the depths of Janie's choice five years ago because they didn't have to. They both knew the real reason behind her giving up her career and moving to the south coast, even if neither of them had ever voiced it out loud.

Even when her own husband had buried his head in the sand and lied to himself that his wife was happy to give everything up, it was Sophie who would have understood. But then Sophie was also aware of the part she had played in it.

Initial interviews between Detective Emily Marlow and staff of Morris and Wood following the fire at Morris and Wood offices on Monday, May 13.

<u>**Bryony Knight, Account Assistant, on Tuesday, May 14, at Lymington Police Headquarters.**</u>

Marlow:	You said you worked with Laura Denning before she went on maternity leave?
Bryony:	I did. I work with all the account directors. I'm there to assist them.
Marlow:	And you carried on working with her when she came back?
Bryony:	Yes. But it was different.
Marlow:	In what way?
Bryony:	Well, at first she didn't ask me to do much. But then as the weeks passed, she threw more and more at me.
Marlow:	And you carried on working for Mia Anderson, too?
Bryony:	Yes, as much as I could, really.
Marlow:	Did you notice Laura Denning was upset when she returned from her maternity leave?
Bryony:	Laura? No. Laura Denning doesn't do "upset," not like that. I mean, she doesn't cry or anything. She just gets tougher. Like, bossier. But then that's how she got to where she is, I suppose.
Marlow:	How do you mean?
Bryony:	Well, so successful. On the same level as all those men.
Marlow:	Did you think Laura seemed bothered by the fact the main part of her job had been given to her replacement?
Bryony:	Of course she was. She was angry. I saw her in Harry's office a few times; voices were raised, though you couldn't hear what they were saying. You know it's very clever, those glass offices, you can see everything inside of them but you can't hear a thing. They're soundproof. Quite annoying, really.

Marlow: Do you think she was angry with him?

Bryony: I don't know whether it was him in particular, but you could tell she was annoyed by the way she would throw her arms around when she spoke. But then from what I hear, Harry didn't have much choice. Mia is so amazing at the job. And she's such a lovely person. Everyone likes her, you know? And Coopers loves her. That was the point.

Marlow: What was the point?

Bryony: They wanted her to stay on their account. They didn't want Laura back.

Marlow: Laura's main client asked for her to be taken off the account?

Bryony: That's right. They told Harry Wood as much. That's why he had to ask Mia to stay on. I don't know, maybe he would have anyway.

Marlow: Why?

Bryony: (shrugs)

Marlow: Did Laura know this?

Bryony: I'm not sure.

Marlow: How do you know?

Bryony: I heard on the grapevine.

Marlow: Is it usual for clients to make demands about who they want working for them?

Bryony: I don't know of anyone else at work who's been taken off an account. But then I guess no one else at Laura's level has ever gone off on maternity leave. The rest of us get our old jobs back, more or less, though a lot of them job share. Laura would never have done that, though. (laughs) She loves her job too much. You know her husband is a stay-at-home dad? He's a nice guy. I've met him a few times. I mean, it's an amazing thing to do, isn't it?

Marlow: What? Stay at home to look after your own children?

Bryony: Yeah.

Marlow: You think it's an unusual choice to make?

Bryony: No, I mean, I don't—well, not all men would do it, would they? I know for a fact my Carl never would.

Marlow: Well, putting aside the fact that Laura Denning made the brave decision to return to work full-time, is there anything at all you've noticed about her behavior since she's been back that has seemed a little—different?

Bryony: Plenty, but—

Marlow: Yes?

Bryony: Well, it's like—I mean—is this going on record? Because this is only gossip. I mean, she's not a suspect or anything, is she?

chapter eight

Laura didn't sleep well again. She hadn't been sleeping well over the past few nights since she had gone back to work on Monday, and by the end of the week the tiredness was catching up with her.

It didn't help that Bobby was waking frequently, and the last night he had reached an impressive milestone of crying out nearly every hour. Nate had been the one to get up for all bar one occasion. It was part of their agreement. On weekdays he would see to Bobby during the night as much as he could—but then, the agreement had been made when Bobby had been blissfully sleeping through.

"He's teething," she had said blearily, at one in the morning. "You'll need to get some more gel. I can feel the teeth under his gum."

Nate hadn't answered. She didn't know if he'd heard, so she wrote it down on a piece of paper and left it on his bedside table in case she forgot to remind him in the morning.

It had felt like only minutes that she'd been asleep when her alarm blasted. Nate didn't stir, and Laura felt it cruel to wake him, so she got up to change Bobby and get his breakfast ready, and then eventually had to rouse her husband as she needed to get out the door.

"I'm sorry, but I really need to go," she said. "I didn't want to wake you."

"No, of course you have to. Sorry, I didn't realize the time."

"You're shattered. Are you going to be okay?" Laura asked.

"Course I am." Nate laughed. "Come here."

She bent over and gave him a kiss, all the time willing him to just get out of bed so she could leave the house. She was already ten minutes later than she wanted to be.

"He's still downstairs in his highchair," she said, pulling away. "I've made breakfast, you just need to give it to him."

"No worries."

"Nate!" She lingered. "I can't leave him there until you're downstairs." She told herself the traffic would be bad if she didn't go then, convinced herself that was the only reason she was agitated to get away.

"Okay," he mumbled, "I'm getting up."

When he still didn't move, she pulled the covers back. "Will you just do it, then?" she said. "I have to go."

"Okay, okay!" He held his hands up and swung his legs over the bed.

Laura watched him for a moment and then, satisfied he meant it, left him to it. By the time she got in the car it was seven thirty; she'd be in the office fifteen minutes later, but she already knew she'd be too late. And when Laura stepped out of the lift, her fears were confirmed. Mia Anderson was sitting at her desk, laughing and joking with Bryony Knight, who as far as Laura could recall had never been in before eight.

Mia had ended up at a desk near the lift, which meant she was the first person Laura saw every morning as she walked onto the floor. Somehow, whatever Laura did to get to work early, Mia was already there. And at the end of each day, when Laura was ready to leave, she was still there. And even though Laura tried to tell herself that Mia surely wasn't doing it for her benefit, she couldn't help but think that maybe she was. That possibly Mia was drawing her into a game that she couldn't afford to play when she had a husband and baby at home.

"Morning," Mia called as Laura began walking across the floor. "How are things? How's Bobby?"

"He's fine," Laura said, mustering a smile. Concept boards were piled at the side of Mia's desk, and Laura couldn't help but glance at them. Coopers' health-drink brand logo was splashed across the top.

"I bet you're pleased it's the weekend tomorrow, so you can see him again."

Laura felt her stomach churn as she dragged her gaze from the boards and back to Mia. What she really wanted to do was pick them up and look through them. See what ideas Mia was proposing to run with. Part of her wanted to make sure they were good enough, because eventually, she reassured herself, she would be taking her account back. But there was another part that wanted to hate them. So she could tear them apart in front of Harry and say, *See, she can't do this*.

"I do see my son every day," Laura replied, turning her attention back to Mia.

"Oh yes, I know"—Mia waved a hand in the air—"I didn't mean—I just meant it'll be nice to have two days off." She paused and then added with a laugh, "God, I know I can't wait for it."

Laura stared back at Mia's blank face and thought there was something so insincere about her, and yet she couldn't put her finger on what. Aside from the fact Mia had lied in her interview about not wanting to stay on, though no one else appeared to think this an issue.

Harry had spent most of his week in London, but Laura had caught up with him the previous day and voiced her unhappiness again. "I still don't see any reason why she's here," Laura had said. "It makes no sense. She never wanted to be; she said clear as anything she only wanted a six-month contract."

"What she wanted six months ago is irrelevant. She's doing a good job; she enjoys it," he'd replied.

Laura had watched Harry flicking through his filing cabinet as he spoke to her, his attention elsewhere. Any moment he would change the subject as his mind juggled a number of things, so she plowed on.

"But we don't need her. I can manage the work, you know I can. I did it before and I can do it now."

"Laura." He turned and threw some papers onto his desk, where they landed with a thud. She cocked her head, goading him to respond. She knew she was the only one who could talk to Harry the way she did. Even Patrick stopped short of contradicting their boss when he knew he was on a losing streak, but Laura had always held her ground.

"You get away with it because you're the golden girl," Patrick would often joke. If Patrick was annoyed by this, he didn't particularly show it. Patrick was confident enough that he didn't play petty office games with Laura. He might want to get his hands on the Coopers account, but who wouldn't? By virtue of the fact they brought in the most money, they were Morris and Wood's most important client.

Only now Laura could see a flare in Harry's eyes, showing he'd had enough, and he went on to say, "I've made my decision. This is the way it's going to be, and you're going to have to find a way to deal with it."

He continued to hold her gaze before eventually turning back to his cabinet. Laura's blood pumped furiously through her veins. She could feel the tips of her fingers tingle as if they were no longer attached to the rest of her.

Before, she would have told Harry she didn't care if he'd made a decision, he was going to have to change it. But then *before*, this particular problem wouldn't have happened. And *before*, Laura wouldn't have felt the prick of tears jabbing at the corners of her eyes.

She hated that she wanted to flee Harry's office and keep running. For every time she convinced herself she would get back what was rightly hers, a curveball like emotion would come and knock her off her feet so quickly she didn't even realize what was happening.

Maybe the sleepless nights weren't helping. Nate had suggested she sleep in the spare room, which seemed a rocky path to tread, but she couldn't keep coming into work an emotional wreck.

"Seriously, Laura, it would be great if you could just work with her on this," Harry had said.

———————

That night Laura called her friend Deborah, who worked in HR for a financial-services company in Reading. "Can he do this to me?" she'd asked.

"It's a difficult situation," Deborah had told her. "There are no material changes to your role or your pay. Your status is still the same. To be honest, I don't think you'd have a case if that's what you're after."

"That's what I thought."

"I thought you had a great relationship with your boss?" Deborah went on. "I can't believe he's doing this to you."

"Neither can I," she'd murmured. In the five years she'd been working for Harry, he'd never once treated her like this. Even when things with Saskia got bad, Harry had always stood by her, and Laura knew well enough that he needn't have put his neck out for her.

Saskia, her once-friend, had tried to destroy Laura's career, though not everyone saw it that way. Even Laura could now admit she'd reacted too quickly, too defensively. But still, Harry had taken her side.

As far as Laura was concerned, nothing had changed between them apart from one thing: Mia. And now she had no idea how to get Harry to listen to her anymore. But by the following morning, when Laura walked into the office and saw Mia's shiny young face smiling back at her, she'd already decided she wasn't going to take this. Somehow, and whatever it took, she was getting her account back.

Laura held her gaze for a moment longer, wondering if Mia was looking forward to the weekend as much as she was making out. "Bryony," she said as she started walking toward her desk, "have you got the direct-mail packs back from the studio yet?"

"No." Bryony shook her head and started to follow Laura across the floor.

Laura glanced in the direction of the studio as they passed, where their creative director, Mike Lewis, was hunched over his oversized screen, a large mug of coffee gripped in one hand. He got in early because he always left by four, but he couldn't make it through the morning without at least five cups of coffee. She watched him push his thick black glasses up his nose and squint at whatever he was poring over. Mike had a mop of dark hair that sprang from the top of his head, and combined with his wrinkled shirts and rolled-up sleeves, it meant he never looked remotely neat.

"They were due back yesterday. Have you chased it?" Laura asked her.

"Yes, I spoke to Mike this morning," Bryony said. "He told me he'd look at it next week."

"Next week?" Laura stopped, the muscles in her shoulders tightening. "So he hasn't even started it?"

"No." Bryony paused. "I didn't think it was that urgent?" she went on, wide-eyed, probably wondering if she'd missed a deadline.

She hadn't, but that wasn't the point. Laura's name was on it, and in the past Mike would have always gotten to it by now. "Did he say why?"

"Well, yeah, it's the TV campaign pitch," Bryony answered, as if everyone knew that. Which of course they did. And of course everyone also understood that its work was to take precedence, and if Laura was running it she would have happily shifted the direct-mail packs for the local estate agency that brought in less than 10 percent of her own targets to next week.

But she wasn't running it.

"That's not good enough," Laura snapped, and even though her anger was directed at Mike, she knew it might have sounded like she was taking it out on Bryony. But in that moment she didn't particularly care.

"Mike, I need a word with you," she called as she left Bryony and paced over to him. Mike was an irritatingly stubborn man; Laura knew if she pushed him he would retract even further. Her eye caught his screen, and a visual of Coopers' health drinks stared back at her.

"Can I ask you when you're going to get to my brief?" she asked, tearing her eyes away from it.

Mike sighed. "Which ones?"

"The direct mail for the estate agents," she snapped back.

"When do you need it by?"

"I was expecting to see something last night."

Mike shook his head. "No can do now. We're all stacked."

"What do you mean 'no can do'?"

"I mean there's no way I'll be able to get it done today. Not with this," he said flatly, his head nodding toward his screen.

Laura screwed her eyes up, swallowing loudly as she assessed her options. She knew she should walk away and not turn this into an issue, but at the same time she didn't know what to do with the ball of rage rapidly building inside her.

Mike had already moved back to his project, rolling his mouse over the desk as he worked his way around the creative.

The fact was she had no option. There was nothing she could do but wait until Mike had time to get to her work.

"I'll send it to Sam, he can do it if you need it today," Mike said eventually.

"Who the hell is Sam?"

"My intern." He nodded in the direction of an empty desk.

"Forget it," Laura snapped. "It can wait until Monday."

Mike didn't bother responding as she charged back to her desk, her blood bubbling beneath her skin. Never had her work been passed to an intern unless she'd come up with the idea herself.

She pulled out her chair and sat down, steepling her hands on the desk in front of her as she leaned forward, resting her chin against them, blowing out short puffs of breath. Beside her a photo of Bobby smiled back. She reached out and pulled the photo closer, tracing her finger over his happy face.

He was wearing the blue-and-white-striped top that she and Nate had bought on a weekend in Cornwall. Five minutes after the photo had been taken, a seagull had landed on their table and frightened the life out of her, but Bobby had giggled, reaching his chubby fingers out as he tried to grab the bird.

What was she doing here? The question swept through her so suddenly. She had given up being with her son so soon, and for what? They didn't have to carry on living in their house, they could downsize. Move out of the area. Lymington was so expensive, they could move to Wales, be nearer Nate's parents.

Laura tapped on her mobile and opened up Rightmove. House prices were so much more affordable there, they didn't have to be right on her in-laws' doorstep, and Nate could find work anywhere.

She scrolled through the houses for sale, ignoring the feeling that Bridgend was so not what she wanted.

"Moving house?"

Laura jumped and closed down the app, tossing her mobile across the desk. "No," she said.

"I was going to say, not that bad, is it?" Patrick asked.

Laura smiled thinly and shrugged. She hadn't caught up with Patrick properly all week. He hadn't been in since Monday.

"Yeah," he went on. "I can imagine it probably is."

Laura felt herself turning in the direction of Mia's desk. She had no idea what Patrick thought of Mia but didn't dare ask when everyone else in the office appeared to love her. There were a couple of women hovering near her desk, listening to Mia as she gestured her arms dramatically. Even from the other side of the floor Laura heard one of them laughing.

"Well, it's short-term," Laura said. "As soon as the TV ad's up and running, there'll be no need to keep her contract on."

Patrick frowned uneasily and cocked his head as he looked at Laura.

"What?" she asked.

"Harry didn't tell you, did he? He made Mia permanent. A week before you came back." Patrick paused and glanced over his shoulder in Mia's direction. "I'm afraid she's here to stay."

chapter nine

Mia sat beside Mike Lewis, who was leaning back in his chair, arms folded across his chest, both of them staring at his screen.

"I don't know," she muttered. "I don't even know which ones look better anymore."

For God's sake, help me, Mike, she thought. He was the creative director, the one who should be pointing her in the right direction instead of just sitting there. Waiting for her. She'd been thrown into the deep end with Coopers. It wasn't that she couldn't do it, but she didn't have history with them, not enough experience with the team to read between the lines of their briefs and work out what it was they really wanted.

"You're going to have to help me out," she said with a laugh. "I'll go with whatever you say."

He shook his head and carried on staring at the screen. "They're both what you asked for. It's your call what you give them."

"I could show them both," she murmured, though she doubted they'd like that. They wanted to be shown one clear direction, and yet here she was, staring at two completely different ways to sell their health drinks, which she'd been pretending were delicious since she'd first tried one six months ago.

The truth was Mia didn't like anything that tasted too healthy, but she wasn't about to tell them that. The Coopers account was critical to

Morris and Wood, and if she wanted to keep her job, she needed to do whatever it took to keep them in favor. If it meant gulping down a cold-pressed green juice with a shot of cayenne pepper once a week, then that was the least she could do.

"Fine. Okay," she said. "That one. The outdoor campaign. Let's go with that." She waited for Mike to tell her she'd made the right decision, or even the wrong one, but he did neither. Instead, he expelled a puff of air as he leaned forward and started fiddling with the borders, and eventually Mia pushed her chair back and stood up.

Mike Lewis was a difficult man to work with, by virtue of the fact he never looked anyone in the eye. His thick-lensed glasses didn't help, but still, behind them, his eyes would desperately avoid contact with hers. She had come across people like Mike before. In her previous company there were a few like him, harmless enough but they didn't make the day go any more smoothly.

Mike was a prickly character, yet still Mia had been shocked when Sarah Clifton first opened up to her in the toilets about her boss. Mia could see Sarah now, waiting by Mia's desk for her. She waved a hand and Sarah immediately sprang to life and hot-stepped toward her.

"Can we talk?"

"Of course."

When Sarah didn't move or speak, Mia gestured to the nearest vacant meeting room and ushered her inside.

"I've been thinking about what you said," Sarah spoke quietly.

Mia nodded, her mind stretching back to the conversation they'd had the week before.

"I know you're right, but I don't think I can say anything."

"Oh." Mia was taken aback as she pulled out a seat at the small round meeting table and sat down. Sarah followed suit. "I thought we talked it through. I thought you were happy about taking it forward?" She'd been expecting Sarah to tell her she was ready, not that she was backing out. "You know, if Mike is treating you badly and making you feel unhappy, you can't sit back and not speak up."

"I know, it's just . . ." Sarah's voice drifted away. "I really appreciate you supporting me and everything, but I spoke to my boyfriend last night, and we agreed it would be better not to rock the boat."

"'Not to rock the boat'?" Mia stifled a short laugh as she leaned forward. "Sarah, Mike is bullying you," she urged. "I want to help, I really do, but I can't do anything unless you're prepared to take this further."

"I wouldn't have said he was bullying me . . ."

Mia shifted uncomfortably on the chair. She didn't like the way this was going. "But that *is* what you said." She smiled, her voice softening. "That's what you told me. Bullying comes in many guises, and what you told me Mike was doing"—Mia paused and cocked her head—"is definitely bullying."

Sarah didn't respond, though her lips parted into a small O.

"You said he makes you feel undervalued when you speak," Mia pressed. "You know you should be able to voice your opinions without him shouting them down."

"I know, I know, but . . ." Her words once again trailed away.

"And he cuts you off when you're talking in meetings?"

Sarah nodded, almost looking ashamed.

"He doesn't ask you to do anything, just leaves you orders on your desk. And you say he hasn't given you any feedback since you started, and then gave you an underperform measure in your last appraisal?" Mia reached over and took hold of Sarah's arm. "This isn't your fault," she went on, gently but firmly. "But if we let people like Mike get away with what he's doing, he'll never stop."

Sarah slowly nodded.

She was right to use the word "we," to make sure Sarah knew they were in this together. "He'll carry on bullying other people too, and that's not right, is it?"

"It's just that 'bullying' seems such a strong word."

"Well, we can use another," Mia said, maybe a little too sharply, before adding, "I'm here for you. I have your back. I totally think you can do this, and what's more, I think you should." She was trying to strike the right balance. Because there was every chance Sarah was going to bail out.

"Yes. I suppose you're right. It's just that I feel like he hasn't been that bad—"

"Don't," Mia said. "You mustn't start making excuses for him. He *is* that bad and he's doing it because of who you are."

"What do you mean?"

"You know he wouldn't treat any of the male account directors the way he does me. He can barely look at me. Of course, he knows he needs to do as I ask—" Mia broke off and waved a hand. "But I still notice it."

"Yeah, maybe you're right."

"I am," Mia said definitely. "I am right. And I promise you we're going to be in this together." She squeezed Sarah's arm. "If you want, I can talk to Harry on Monday morning."

"Oh, I don't know."

No, Mia thought, *and your boyfriend will probably talk you out of that over the weekend, anyway.* "Well, it's just a thought," she said as her mobile beeped with a text. She pulled it out of her pocket and glanced at the screen. Her mum, asking her to pick up some food on her way home. Mia sighed. She'd agreed to go for drinks at the pub after work. It was Friday evening and the thought of heading straight home was unbearable. Not when they had no plans for the weekend. The idea of having a few gin and tonics more than she should was the one thing Mia was looking forward to.

"I better get back to work," she sighed, then stood up and opened the door. The text made her feel an inordinate amount of annoyance that she had nothing exciting ahead of her, and Sarah's reluctance to address what was happening in the company was another irritation.

———————

Henrietta James was already at the bar when Mia walked in. "I insist on getting this," Mia told her. There had been too many times when Henrietta already had a card proffered to the bartender by the time Mia had reached for her wallet, and it was beginning to get awkward. Her salary was higher than any of the other staff members' who were gathered in a huddle in the corner of the pub, and yet she'd never be able to explain to them that she couldn't afford to get them drinks.

"I'm only staying for this one," Mia said as Henrietta turned back to her conversation with Bryony, and Mia already wondered how easily she would be swayed. The food on her mum's shopping list was bought and stashed in the boot of her car. She just needed to remember to swing past the car on her way home if she did end up calling a taxi.

As she waited for the barman, Bryony's voice drifted along the bar.

". . . trying to do it all. Have you seen the way she's thrown herself back into work this week?"

"Who are you talking about?" Mia asked.

Henrietta screwed up her nose. "Laura Denning. Of course, you never knew her before. She's always been like this, but I really thought she'd cut back a bit now that she has a child."

Henrietta was eyeing her, waiting for a reaction.

"Maybe she has a lot of work to do," Mia said. "Gin and slimline, please," she added to the barman.

Henrietta leaned in. "Well, she won't like the fact you're doing so well. Do you think she knows yet? About Coopers not wanting her back?"

Mia glanced at Bryony. "No, I don't think she does," she said quietly, though the way gossip spread she was sure it wouldn't be long.

"She'll be hoping it goes badly, I'm sure of it."

Mia really didn't have a response to that. Or rather she did, but she wasn't going to say anything. Especially not to Henrietta. "I certainly hope that's not the case," Mia said, as Henrietta raised her eyebrows.

———————

It was ten p.m. by the time Mia eventually got home. The house was in darkness except for a bedroom light at the far end. She was glad she'd remembered to stop by the car but even more pleased she'd gone to the pub, because it was nicer walking into the bungalow with the buzz of alcohol fizzing around her body.

Twisting her key in the lock, Mia nudged the front door open and immediately heard raised voices from the far end of the hallway.

She switched on the table lamp and closed the door behind her. No natural light reached the hall, which made it oppressive, and it didn't help that her mum had a patterned carpet and dark-green walls that were cluttered with photos from over the years. Mia no longer looked at any of them as she walked past and down to the bedroom at the far end.

The door was wide open, and she could see her mum in her faded purple dressing gown that frayed at the hem and cuffs. Her hands were gripped tightly together in front of her. Even from here Mia could see her knuckles forming white circles under the pressure.

"Mum?"

"Oh, Mia," she said with relief when she looked up. Mia took a step into the room. Her sister was lying on the single bed, facing the wall. "She won't talk to me."

"Then leave her," Mia urged.

"I can't," her mum mouthed. The words were uttered so quietly that Mia wasn't sure she'd actually said them aloud. Her eyes were rimmed with tears that threatened to roll down her cheeks, and her thin gray hair was pushed back off her face with an Alice band, which meant she'd been either in bed or about to get into it.

"Jess?" Mia said to her sister. "Do you want to talk to me?"

When her sister didn't respond or move, Mia took her mum's arm and steered her out of the room. "Come on," she said, "I'll make us all some tea."

A tear escaped her mum's eye. She watched her grab a tissue from her dressing-gown pocket and dab at her skin so gently that it tore Mia's heart in two.

"You shouldn't have to do this," she said, following Mia down the hallway. "You shouldn't have to keep solving everyone else's problems."

"You're not everyone else. You're my mum."

"You know what I mean," she answered quietly. "You shouldn't be living like this."

"Nor should you," Mia said as she reached the kitchen door and turned around. Her mum's face was blotched red, the skin under her eyes nearly transparent it was so thin. Her arms hung limply by her side, her hands fiddling with the ball of tissue. This was the time her mum should be relaxing and going on cruises with what little money she had saved over the years, not frantically worrying about her oldest daughter.

And suddenly Mia felt an unbelievable sense of guilt that she hadn't come straight home from work—accompanied by a tidal wave of anger that their lives had come to this.

Initial interviews between Detective Emily Marlow and staff of Morris and Wood following the fire at Morris and Wood offices on Monday, May 13.

<u>**Mia Anderson, Account Director, on Tuesday, May 14, at Lymington Police Headquarters.**</u>

Marlow:	Can you tell me where you were last night between the hours of seven p.m. and nine p.m.?
Mia:	I was at home. My mum's house, I mean.
Marlow:	For the whole time?
Mia:	(pauses) No. Not all of it.
Marlow:	So where else did you go?
Mia:	I went for a drive. On my own.
Marlow:	Anywhere particular?
Mia:	Not specifically, just around the roads.
Marlow:	Is that something you often do? Go out for a drive on your own?
Mia:	Occasionally. It helps clear my head.
Marlow:	So you needed to clear your head last night?
Mia:	I was just worn out.
Marlow:	Was this because of anything to do with work?
Mia:	No. Work is fine. It wasn't important, I just—
Marlow:	Yes?
Mia:	Sometimes I need to get out of the house. Sometimes it gets too much and I just need to breathe.
Marlow:	So there was nothing at work troubling you?
Mia:	No.
Marlow:	It's just that no one saw you in the office all day yesterday. Were you at work on Monday, May 13?
Mia:	(shakes head)
Marlow:	For the tape recorder, please.

Mia: I didn't go in yesterday, no. I had an appointment I'd forgotten to tell anyone about.

Marlow: So nothing had upset you?

Mia: Why do you keep asking me that? What would have upset me?

Marlow: Well for a start, there was the incident at Harry Wood's party four nights ago. I assume yesterday would have been the first time you'd seen Laura Denning again after what happened?

Mia: (laughs) I wasn't upset about that. At least not enough to not go into work.

Marlow: And there's the ongoing issue with Laura.

Mia: *I* don't have any issue with Laura.

Marlow: So it was just an appointment? That you forgot? Nothing else deterred you from going to the office? Only from what I hear, it's unusual for you. I believe it's the only day you haven't gone in since you started eight months ago.

Mia: There was nothing else.

Marlow: It's just that someone did actually see you in the office late that morning. You apparently stepped out of the lift onto your floor and then vanished again pretty quickly. Is that right?

Mia: (pauses) Yes, I had forgotten my appointment. Like I told you.

Marlow: And you didn't think to tell anyone when you were there?

Mia: Is any of this relevant?

Marlow: I don't know. That's what I'm trying to find out. I've been wondering whether something did happen in the short time you went into the Morris and Wood offices yesterday that you aren't telling me? The same offices that are now nothing more than a pile of ashes.

Mia: I told you. Nothing happened.

Marlow: Okay. So let's go back to last night. You were driving around the roads? Did you stop anywhere?

Mia: Not that I recall.

Marlow: Did you drive to the offices?

Mia: No.

Marlow: Or anywhere near them? Somewhere you might have been able to see the fire?

Mia: No.

Marlow: How about the other side of the river? There's a very clear view of Morris and Wood from there. Did you go to the quay last night?

Mia: No.

Marlow: Are you sure about that, Ms. Anderson?

chapter ten

seven weeks before the fire

S he's here to stay." Laura repeated Patrick's words to Nate, not for the first time that weekend. "Now she's permanent, Nate, and he can't just get rid of her. Why the hell has he done that?"

Nate shook his head. "I don't know," he said, following her into the kitchen, a bundle of washing stacked in his arms.

"Let me do that." She reached out to take it from him. "You know I don't expect you to pick up everything."

"It's fine. Go and be with Bobby." He nodded toward their son, who was wobbling precariously on his playmat before toppling onto his back, which made Nate laugh.

Laura didn't move for a moment as she watched Nate load the bedding into the washing machine. Something felt so wrong about him picking up all the jobs around the house even though it was what she had done for the last six months.

She turned and crouched down beside Bobby, picking him up and snuggling into him. Laying a kiss on his head, she lingered as she thought about going back to the office the next day, and it was a thought that filled her with dread.

"You've still not spoken to Harry about it, then?" Nate asked.

"I don't want to call him on the weekend."

"So you'll speak to him tomorrow?"

Laura nodded.

"And then you'll know." He straightened up, rubbing the base of his spine. "What do you want to do for lunch?" he asked, as if that were the end of the conversation, because in Nate's simplistic world, as soon as Laura had spoken to her boss she'd be able to move on.

"It's humiliating, Nate," she said, willing him to understand. "Getting pushed to the bottom of the pile like I was with the creative studio. I hired her to cover my job, and now it's like she's more senior than me."

Laura had always known that if you wanted to stay at the top of your game you couldn't afford to take time out. She'd proven herself right, unfortunately at her own expense. While she was bringing a child into the world, another woman had slipped into her place and stolen her job from her.

"Yeah, I can imagine," he said as he came over and ruffled the top of her head. "We need to think about lunch. It's already one."

Laura shrugged. She didn't give a toss about lunch; she wasn't particularly hungry. Her precious weekend at home with her family, and she'd spent most of it going over and over her job in her head. And as much as she wanted to make the most of their Sunday afternoon, there was a part of her that couldn't, because she knew she wouldn't settle until she was back in the office and face-to-face with Harry.

"Laura?" Nate pressed. "How about we go out, grab a pub lunch?"

"We won't get in anywhere now."

"Then please, just help me out and tell me what you want."

"It's fine," she snapped as she pulled herself up. "I'll sort it." She walked to the fridge and peered inside, her gaze drifting over what little food they had as her stomach churned, over and over.

The truth was she was worried about speaking to Harry because she hated the thought of him selling her out. And if he told her that the reason he'd made Mia permanent was because she was doing such a fantastic bloody job, then where did that leave her?

Laura closed the fridge door and pressed her head against it, closing her eyes. "I'm sorry, Nate," she called. "I'm so bloody sorry. This wasn't what it was supposed to be like."

"Hey, it's okay," he said.

"No, it's not. I don't want to spend my time with you and Bobby thinking about her, but that's all I'm doing. Why the hell does she want my job, Nate?" she said, banging a hand against the door and knocking a magnet to the floor. "I don't trust her," she said, airing the thought that had been plaguing her all week. "I don't trust Mia Anderson one bit."

On Monday morning, as she walked in, Laura bypassed Mia, who was yet again already at her desk, and headed straight to Harry's office.

"Morning, morning," he said, and beckoned her in cheerily. "Good weekend?"

"Yes, great, thanks."

"And how's the little man?"

"Bobby?" she prompted. "He's doing good, I just—"

"Is he sleeping through? God, the girls didn't sleep through until they were one, as far as I remember. Neither of them. Of course, we had the nanny then, so Janie didn't have to worry about getting up in the middle of the night." He shook his head and laughed. "I wouldn't want to go through that again," he said, though Laura wondered how much it had actually affected him personally anyway. "How was the first week back?"

"Well, actually, Harry, that's what I want to talk to you about."

He nodded, straightening his chair, and leaned back, crossing his legs. Now that Laura was in front of him, the words she had earlier prepared had dried in her mouth, leaving her with a bitter taste and an inability to find them. For the first time since she'd started working for

Harry, she felt the need to tread carefully, because she no longer understood what was going on.

She pulled out a chair on the other side of his desk and sat down, inhaling a deep breath. "I hear that Mia's been made permanent. You didn't tell me."

"Right." He shifted slightly, his eyes flickering, enough to tell her that he wasn't comfortable. "I'm sorry I didn't, I just wanted you to settle back in last week."

"I'm just having a hard time getting my head around it," Laura said. "I don't understand why."

"Well, it's like I said. She's done a great job . . ." His words fizzled out as he shook his head. "I just didn't think we should lose her."

Laura took in his words. The way he skirted around, not telling her outright it was him who didn't want to lose Mia. She wondered how sure he was of the decision, or whether it was simply that he didn't want any conflict. There had been a few times when she'd seen Harry back away from it in the past, and it was interesting that he might be doing it now.

"But you've basically given her my job," Laura persisted.

Harry gave a short, nervous laugh as he shuffled again in his chair. "I haven't at all."

"You've given her my biggest account," she said, feeling the heat rising inside her.

"Because I want you to start up something new." His eyes widened as he pressed forward over the desk as if he expected her to be excited about that. "I told you this. I want you to meet the guy in charge soon, in the next week or so. This comes off like I hope it's going to, and I promise you, you won't have time for Coopers."

"But you didn't ask me, Harry." Laura heard the slight crack in her words, a hint of a whine, but she continued regardless. "Why can't *Mia* have this new opportunity?"

"Because—" Harry gave another shake of his head as he settled back in his chair, and she wondered if his pause was because he was trying to find a reason. "Because I need someone I can trust on this one, and that's you. I know how you work, Laura; I know you'll be able to crack it."

Laura released a breath, her heart thumping as she considered what he was telling her and whether or not she believed him.

"I need my best person, and that's you," Harry continued, smiling. He was on a roll now, though Laura knew well enough Harry had mastered the ability to say what people wanted to hear. And he must have known how desperately she wanted to hear this.

"Has Mia done a better job than me?"

"What?" Harry laughed. "That's not what this is about. Laura, is that what you think? You think I'm trying to get rid of you or something? The company would collapse if I didn't have you, you know that. You're my best." His smile had spread into a broad beam now, as if he felt he'd reached safer ground.

Despite this, Laura nodded, her pulse slowing, because whatever was behind them the words were still comforting. "So that's the only reason she's looking after the account for now?"

There was a beat before Harry answered, "Of course it is."

Laura knew there was no point pressing him further. They'd only go round and round in circles. She left his office with a slight sense of optimism that she was still needed, but one tempered by the niggling suspicion that he wasn't telling her the whole truth. And Laura knew it was time to finally make the call to Coopers.

She felt nervous as she dialed the number she'd once rung so often and waited for the voice on the other end of the line. "Tess is on holiday," an assistant told her. "Can I take a message and get her to call you back?"

Laura left her name, but the days passed and she didn't hear back, and neither did she hear anything about Harry's new opportunity. And the thought that there was more to it than Harry tried to make out continued to swell.

————————

On Friday, when Mia was due to present her campaign concept to the Coopers team, Laura couldn't get away from the fact, with Mia buzzing around the office like it was the only thing everyone wanted to talk about. "I'm so nervous." Laura overheard her laughing to Bryony. "It takes me back to when I was at school."

Laura didn't think Mia sounded remotely nervous as Bryony gushed that she was going to be amazing.

Her fists were clenched as she hammered away on her keyboard, wishing she could block out the noise and stop her mind from wondering what the creatives looked like. She still hadn't seen them. She had no idea what Mia had up her sleeve but hadn't the guts to ask. Instead Laura had tried keeping her head down, focusing on the clients she had left, none of which excited her much, while hoping that any day soon either Harry would announce they were meeting the new potential client or Mia would royally screw up.

Her dream career had become nothing more than a job that was paying the bills and keeping her away from her son, and as much as Laura was looking forward to the weekend ahead, she felt a considerable sense of lacking any purpose other than being a mother. And she knew she wasn't doing a particularly good job of that.

Laura still hadn't spoken to anyone from the Coopers team since she had been back, which was why, at two o'clock, wandering past the boardroom, she stopped short, her heart sinking to the depths of her stomach. She hadn't for one minute expected that Mia had invited them to the offices. Always Laura would present to them at theirs, and yet here they were—the entire marketing team sitting together on the other side of the glass.

A flash of heat spread up her neck as she scanned the familiar group of four, jostling in their chairs, swiveling toward Bryony, who had been disproportionately dividing her time between her and Mia the last fortnight.

Her legs felt like jelly as she ducked back, out of their sight, but still she didn't return to her desk. She hadn't seen any of them in over six months. There had been some contact since she'd left—they'd sent her a gorgeous bundle of baby clothes wrapped up in a blue bouquet. And in return she'd sent them a thank-you card with a picture of Bobby. But other than that? No communication. No return call from Tess Wills, who was sitting at the far end of the table, having clearly returned from holiday.

Laura had worked for Coopers from the outset, spent so many nights poring over their briefs, working with the creative studio, giving up weekends when they needed revisions made by the following Monday. She hadn't minded. In many ways she felt like she was a part of their company, like she worked for them. They had told her that. *What would we do without you, Laura?*

She wouldn't be able to walk past the boardroom now without being seen. Her only option was to slip back the way she'd come, hide, wait for them to disappear, and hope to God they didn't walk out and see her and feel the need to come over and speak to her.

Laura closed her eyes and leaned her head back against the wall. Of course, she had another option. She could pull herself together, plaster on a smile, and walk into the boardroom as if she wasn't remotely fazed by what was happening. Even as if she were completely on board with it. She could pretend it was under her control, though she had no idea how she could pull off that particular act when her breath was so tightly wedged in her throat. Laura had never been able to hide her emotions easily, but this was ridiculous. This was her domain. She needed to start fighting back.

Inhaling deeply, Laura walked to the doorway and stuck her head into the room. "Hi, guys, lovely to see you." The words tumbled out; she wasn't even sure if they'd come in the right order, but all four members of the marketing team were now standing and telling her it was lovely to see her too.

"Laura, oh my God, hi," they chorused, approaching her one by one. "How are you?" "How's the baby?"

"Bobby's great."

"I didn't even realize you were back," one said before the room fell into a momentary awkward silence.

"Yes, I've been back for two weeks." Laura smiled. "Thank you all again for your gift," she added quickly. "It was gorgeous."

"Oh, a pleasure." "God, of course." They murmured with relief and continued to regard her with wide smiles on their faces.

"I can't believe Bobby is six months already," she said, when they lapsed into silence.

"No!"

"I can't believe it, either."

"Where does the time go?"

Laura couldn't differentiate one voice from the other as they all continued to gape and nod, staring at her and looking vaguely surprised and a little apprehensive.

Her gaze wandered over their shoulders to Bryony, who had stopped pouring tea and was now chewing the side of her thumb.

"Have you got any photos?" one asked.

"Oh yes. Of course." She reached for her phone and scrolled through a few until she came to one of Bobby lying on his back on a playmat, chubby little fists clenched, his mouth open as he giggled at the funny faces Nate was pulling behind her back. Laura stared at it for a moment before handing it over.

"Oh my God, he's so cute."

"He's adorable."

"Doesn't he look like you?"

Laura nodded, and once the phone had been passed along the line she took it back.

"You must miss him."

She looked up, still clutching the phone in one hand. "Of course."

"I don't know how you do it, you know, being away from him all the time. I only went back two and a half days a week, and even that was too much."

"It's not all the time, just while I'm at work," she joked halfheartedly.

The other woman blushed and laughed too, and suddenly they were thrown into another awkward silence that Laura couldn't ever remember having with any of the team before. Her eyes panned the room. Usually she'd sit at the head of the table, concept boards stacked high, buzzing to talk through her ideas, and now—

"Laura!"

She turned to see Mia, who had just entered the room.

"So sorry I'm a little late, everyone; just getting the final touches done," Mia gushed as she waltzed in. She was glistening like a bauble in her shiny bright-pink shirt, which she'd tucked into one side of the waistband of slim black trousers. Laura tried to think if she had been wearing that outfit earlier. She couldn't recall it.

Laura's eyes drifted to the portfolio case tucked under Mia's arms while the team assured her that her lateness was nothing to worry about.

Mia hung her head to one side and smiled at Laura, and she knew this was her cue to leave. Her heart hammered at the thought of retreating, being dismissed again. She suddenly couldn't bear the thought of returning to her desk, all the while imagining what was going on behind the closed doors of the boardroom.

Wouldn't it be better to know what Mia was doing rather than remain in the dark? she thought. If she were in the meeting too she'd at least be able to see it all play out.

"Is it okay if I stay?" Laura asked, without giving the idea more thought.

Mia's mouth hung open before she quickly said, "Yes. Yes, of course." A smile fixed firmly on her face.

"If that's okay with everyone?" Laura went on, hoping her heart couldn't be heard as it banged against the wall of her chest.

"You're welcome to stay, Laura." Tess smiled. "And I'm sorry I never called you back; I was only back in the office today."

"No problem." She returned Tess's smile, pulling out a chair as she caught Mia's head pinging up to look across at her.

"So I'm really excited to share these ideas with you," Mia said as she passed around handouts. "I'm sorry I don't have enough copies, Laura."

"That's fine," Laura replied as breezily as she could muster, before she shuffled closer to Bryony so she could share hers, then waited for Mia to hold up the first creative. She wondered what the Coopers team was going to think of the ideas. She'd sat in front of so many clients in her time and knew every one of their reactions and what they were really thinking. She knew when they didn't like what they were being shown or didn't agree with the concept she had decided on, even when they tried to cover it up. Mostly it took a while for the ideas to sink in. The good marketeers would eventually see what Laura was suggesting, and even if they didn't wholly agree, they could reach a compromise.

Today heads were nodding, and though experience told Laura this was nothing to go on, her stomach still twisted itself into knots.

Mia hadn't once looked in her direction, her focus solely on the clients—as well she supposed it should be, but still Laura was beginning to feel like a spare part. Casually she beckoned to the handout in front of Bryony, gesturing for a closer look. Bryony nodded and pushed it toward her.

She smiled her thanks and flicked through the pack, zoning in on the budgets at the back. As she ran her finger down the numbers, Laura suddenly paused, turned back the sheet and looked through them again.

When she looked up, the room had descended into silence. Laura glanced around the table as everyone gathered their thoughts, waiting for one of them to start the conversation. She knew how awkward this moment was for Mia. She had been in it enough times herself, but she ignored the silence as she turned back to the pack, just to double-check that there definitely was a mistake.

Eventually the team began to murmur appreciative thoughts and ask questions, and for a moment Laura couldn't keep up with whether or not they actually liked what they'd seen.

"Well that's amazing, everyone," Mia was saying. "I'm so thrilled you all love it and I'm really excited to get started on the filming."

Laura glanced up as everyone appeared to be shuffling papers together, tidying phones away. That was it? No one had even asked for her opinion? Had she actually been passed over like she wasn't even sitting there?

Laura cleared her throat, because she was going to speak anyway. "You know, I can see what you're suggesting here, Mia, and I like how brave you're being."

Mia smiled back at her. "Thanks, Laura," she said as she got up.

Laura's pulse raced. She could point out the mistake in private so as not to embarrass Mia, but the fact was she herself was embarrassed. All the hard work she'd put into growing this client, and no one gave a shit about what she thought of their biggest campaign yet.

"But to be totally honest, I'm unsure how this will actually work on TV." She raised her voice a little. "It could be advertising anyone. The viewer might remember the products, but I don't see how they'll recall the brand."

"It's a fair point," Tess chimed in. "But I think it's fine; it can be worked in."

Mia smiled her thanks at Tess.

"And the actual filming of the ad," Laura went on, because she was not going to be passed off so easily. "Of course it will be a lot cheaper filming it outdoors and out of season, as you say."

Mia nodded. "That's why I went with this idea."

"Only I don't see where you've accounted for weather. I mean if it rains, which of course it could—I assume you've factored in weather insurance somewhere?"

Mia froze as she stared at Laura, her mouth parting as if she were about to speak but didn't know what to say.

Of course she hadn't factored any in, because it would have been in the budgets. Now members of the team had begun murmuring, and while Laura was certain that Mia had never run a TV campaign before, she began to wonder why exactly Harry thought Mia was more suitable to looking after the campaign than she was. It really wouldn't hurt one bit, she decided, to let Harry know of his error when she next saw him.

Mia's lips moved but no words came out, and Bryony was furiously flicking through her notes, but Laura knew she wouldn't find the answer.

She decided to put her out of her misery as Tess asked, "So how much would this cost?"

"Well," Laura said, "you'll need to add another twenty percent to your budget."

Ouch. She could hear a collective intake of breath around the table and she knew then that the whole plan and its budget had been shot to pieces with that one figure. And while she hated the thought that she was taking any pleasure in this rather big omission, Laura couldn't help but feel a little bit satisfied.

chapter eleven

Mia hadn't been looking for another job when she'd come across the advert for the maternity cover at Morris and Wood. But the moment she saw it she stopped abruptly, her fingers caught in midair above the keypad of her laptop. It was too good to be true, she'd thought as she'd scanned the advert, her gaze settling on the email address of Laura Denning, the woman whose role she would be covering. She was to contact her personally if she wanted to apply, an irregularity that she didn't stop to consider in her haste to send her résumé.

The first time Mia met the Coopers team she'd hit it off with all of them. Only a couple of months in and Tess Wills had told her, "It's fab having someone so fun around, Mia. Laura rarely invited us out for drinks, or if she did she always stayed sober, even before she was pregnant."

Mia liked Tess. A few glasses of wine was all the Coopers' marketing director needed to confide in her about all sorts of things, like the fact her husband of ten years had run off with his secretary a year ago. By all accounts, Tess was very quick to proclaim she would never forgive him.

It hadn't been a surprise when Harry asked her to take over the account. By then she already knew they wanted to keep her, but it was a relief to hear it. And then when he confirmed her permanent position, it was another reason to celebrate.

Mia needed this job. More than any one of them sitting around the board table would ever understand.

Twelve months ago she'd had no choice but to move in with her mum, into the small three-bedroom bungalow she'd moved to when Mia had finally left home at twenty-three. Over eight years Mia had enjoyed setting up her own future, living her life, but now here she was, back at square one.

Jess had been gone awhile before Mia had first left home. Five years older than Mia, Jess was the one who went to university, who knew what she wanted to do with her life. Not like Mia, who had drifted in and out of jobs until she finally found her niche in marketing.

Those eight years now felt like they weren't part of her life at all but belonged to someone else. Even the woman who lived in the flat above her—who kept her awake at night shouting at her boyfriend—even that felt like it had never happened. Those years had held freedom, the promise of excitement, the ability to walk in and out of the shared front door of the flats without having to feel guilt and anger and disappointment.

The job at Morris and Wood gave her a flicker of opportunity—the chance to take back some control again. Once she got it, she knew she had to keep it.

Mia wished she felt more confident about what she was about to present to the Coopers team. The contents of her stomach were doing a merry dance, but she knew once she started talking she would be all right. Or she would have been if Laura hadn't joined them. Now all Mia could feel was her intent stare, waiting for her to cock up. She knew Laura Denning was here for a fight, and that made Mia feel the pressure even more.

The reason Laura had bypassed Human Resources when recruiting for her cover had later become so obvious to Mia. This was a woman who wanted to control, and her return was always going to pose a threat. Mia often wondered what Laura was like out of the office. When you stripped away her hard shell, who was she underneath?

Harry Wood, on the other hand, was as transparent as anyone could be. On the surface he ran his company well, but he wavered over the intricate issues, always deflecting to being one of the boys, careful not to upset the apple cart. He'd been so pliable when Coopers requested Mia stay on, so ready to relent—an interesting weakness for a CEO.

His wife interested Mia. Janie Wood was an enigma. Whenever she came into the office she was always in a rush, avoiding anyone else who would probably love the chance to talk to her. Mia wondered what a clever, good-looking woman like Janie was doing with a man like Harry. Because strip away his looks and his money and there really wasn't much else to him.

Mia had read about the Woods in a local magazine after she'd come back to Lymington. Janie, who had once been a successful barrister, was photographed by an AGA in her bespoke kitchen and was quoted speaking about her husband's success and the wonderful things he did for the local community. Yet there was something about her that had made Mia wonder if she was really the type of woman to be sucked in by wealth and her husband's power.

Mia turned to her notes and started to tell the team how excited she was, before plowing through the presentation she had spent the last week rehearsing on the single bed in the box room at her mum's bungalow.

She felt like she were in a prison living in that place, but at least she escaped to work five days a week. Not like her sister, Jess, who co-cooned herself within that bungalow like there was no life outside its four walls.

By the end of the presentation it was clear how fired up the team was feeling. The fact that they loved her ideas flooded her with a warm flush. Finally she could relax, though she didn't dare look in Laura's direction. Just for that moment she didn't want anything to take away her relief.

She wasn't particularly surprised when Laura had something to add at the end of the meeting, but still Mia wanted it to be quick so she could get out of the room on a high. She even expected some sort of put-down—she knew she'd be able to handle it—but she was unprepared for the bombshell about weather insurance.

Mia thanked her lucky stars that she rarely blushed outwardly, because inside she was dying. Budget was a high priority on the brief, and this curveball was going to destroy it. But of course she hadn't thought of insurance, because she hadn't actually run a sodding TV ad before. Why hadn't anyone else in the office thought to mention this to her? What about Bryony, who was now avoiding eye contact, rustling through her papers as if she were looking for the figure somewhere in there?

You're not going to find it, Bry, Mia screamed in her head. *Because you never told me we needed any.*

Her heart hammered as she wrestled with an appropriate response. Not including insurance was such a stupid mistake, and it was one that was going to cost them dearly. "I'm just waiting for some quotes to come in," Mia lied.

As Tess stared back at her, it was clear she didn't believe her. And anyway, what use was it waiting for quotes to come in when she hadn't even factored in a figure in the first place? There was only one person who could dig her out of this hole, and that was the person who'd thrown her into it.

Mia didn't have any other choice. She turned to Laura, who seemed faintly amused by Bryony's frantic actions. Their assistant was diving into pieces of paper like a lunatic, when Laura's voice suddenly boomed across the room. "Twenty percent."

Mia wanted to shut her eyes and close herself off from the open mouths that were hanging wide around her. She didn't want to look at the face of the woman who had just thrown her to the wolves so publicly.

Outside the boardroom, Mia's discomfort started to grow into anger.

What was it with some women that made them turn on each other so readily?

Didn't they have enough to deal with without stabbing each other in the back when they should be on the same side?

Laura might not be happy that Mia was working here, but she should take that up with Harry. And yet, all too often, women like Laura never did. Mia had seen it happen before. It was, after all, what had brought her to Morris and Wood in the first place. And she was not going to let it continue.

Initial interview between Detective Emily Marlow and Janie Wood following the fire at Morris and Wood offices on Monday, May 13.

<u>**Janie Wood, on Tuesday, May 14, at Lymington Police Headquarters.**</u>

Marlow:	I know this is a horrible time for you and I appreciate you helping us.
Janie:	Thank you.
Marlow:	I'm very sorry about your husband's building. It must be upsetting to see what happened. On top of everything else, of course.
Janie:	(pauses) It is.
Marlow:	I hope not to take up too much of your time—
Janie:	I do need to get back to my girls.
Marlow:	I understand.
Janie:	They haven't gone into school today with everything, you know—with what's happened to their dad . . .
Marlow:	I understand.
Janie:	I don't want to leave them for long.
Marlow:	I'll be as quick as I can. I just have a few questions. Mrs. Wood, have there been any problems between you and your husband recently?
Janie:	Problems?
Marlow:	Yes.
Janie:	You mean in my marriage?
Marlow:	I mean anything at all.
Janie:	What are you suggesting? That I set fire to the building? I didn't.
Marlow:	I'm not saying that at all.
Janie:	I would never . . . I would never do that.
Marlow:	I'm not suggesting you did, Mrs. Wood. Was it your idea to

purchase the site for the Morris and Wood offices five years ago?

Janie: It was Harry's.

Marlow: It caused quite a stir at the time. As I recall, a lot of people were opposed to the development.

Janie: People didn't want something so big being built there. They thought it would affect the landscape, the view—you know, from the quay.

Marlow: Could you see it from their side?

Janie: Yes I could.

Marlow: Did you ever want to rethink?

Janie: I take it from your questioning you were opposed to it?

Marlow: I didn't have an opinion.

Janie: Right. (laughs) Every local had an opinion. I used to think many got involved just because they liked the drama. Because we came from London.

Marlow: But it upset a lot of people. Didn't that ever make you want to pull out?

Janie: No.

Marlow: Yet the plans were withdrawn at one point, weren't they?

Janie: Yes. Briefly.

Marlow: And wasn't that because of you?

Janie: (pauses) No, actually, it was because of my husband. He had a change of heart. He thought it wasn't worth the effort fighting. I was the one who persuaded him it was.

Marlow: Oh?

Janie: That clearly surprises you.

Marlow: It does, actually. Why were you so passionate about it?

Janie: Because . . . because I was scared that if we didn't carry on, then Harry would give up on the idea of moving south.

Marlow:	And you really wanted to?
Janie:	Yes. I really did.
Marlow:	Mrs. Wood, can I get you a tissue?
Janie:	No. I'm fine. It's just everything that's happened in the last twenty-four hours. It's a lot to take in.
Marlow:	(nods) Can you tell me why were you so keen to move?
Janie:	From London? What does that have to do with anything? It's not relevant.
Marlow:	If you could just answer the question for me.
Janie:	I just wanted to get away, that's all. Make a new start.
Marlow:	You had a good job there. You were a defense barrister? You gave that up when you moved, is that right?
Janie:	I did, yes, but really, I have no idea why this has anything to do with the fire.
Marlow:	I'm just interested in why you were so keen for the plans to go through.
Janie:	It was a good business opportunity. It meant we could relocate. It *meant* we could live the life we're lucky enough to have. That was all it was.
Marlow:	Right.
Janie:	You said you were going to be as quick as you could. Why are we talking about the build of the office unless you think it was some revenge arson? Is that what you're thinking? Someone who didn't want us building it decided to burn it down?
Marlow:	No, that's not really what I'm thinking at all.
Janie:	Then what—
Marlow:	I believe you recently met up with one of the employees from Morris and Wood outside of the office, is that right?
Janie:	Yes. Once.
Marlow:	Is that usual for you?

Janie: No. It isn't.

Marlow: And do you have a friendship?

Janie: With Mia? No. I wouldn't say that.

Marlow: Yet you went out for lunch?

Janie: Like I said, only the once.

Marlow: Who pursued the lunch date?

Janie: She did.

Marlow: Mia Anderson invited you?

Janie: Yes. Honestly, where are you going with this? My girls—

Marlow: I'm sorry, we're nearly done. For the record, could you just tell me where you were last night?

Janie: I don't understand—why do you need to know all this? I can't be a suspect, surely?

Marlow: Like I said, it's purely for the record.

Janie: I have yoga every Monday.

Marlow: And where is that?

Janie: In the village hall in Beaulieu. I had to call a friend over to babysit—Anna. She can tell you. I can get you her phone number if you need it.

Marlow: That's no problem for now, thank you. So you went to yoga last night?

Janie: (nods) Yes.

Marlow: What time was this?

Janie: Seven p.m. For two hours. Then I went home, as Anna will tell you.

Marlow: Anna tried to get hold of you last night, didn't she? She said she needed to call your husband because you weren't answering your phone.

Janie: I didn't hear it. Like I said, I was in my class and—please. Are we done?

Marlow: (pauses) Yes, we're done, Mrs. Wood. Thank you for your time this afternoon.

Janie: Okay. Thanks.

Marlow: Oh, actually, one more thing before you go. You never did say if you and your husband have been having any problems?

chapter twelve

Janie placed the casserole in the center of the dining table and sat down in her usual seat, next to Lottie and opposite Ella. She watched her oldest daughter frown as she lifted the lid of the pot. "Is that chicken?"

"It is. Why are you turning your nose up? You like chicken."

"I thought you said we could have takeout on a Friday night."

"Well, Ella, you've watched me making this for the last hour, so surely by now you've realized we weren't having takeout."

"Don't be like that, honey," Harry said, playfully elbowing Ella. "Your mum's gone to a lot of trouble making this for us. It looks lovely." He smiled at his wife.

She smiled back, then turned to Lottie. "Tell me about your day, darling. How was netball?"

"Okay. We lost. Twenty to one."

"Oh dear." Harry laughed. "That's quite a difference."

Lottie shrugged as Janie spooned casserole onto her plate.

"And what about you, Ell bell, how was your day?" he asked.

"Fine."

"That's it, just 'fine'?" he said.

Janie watched her pick up her fork and swirl her meal around the plate.

"You're not hungry?" Janie asked.

"Not really."

"Is something wrong?"

"The train was packed tonight," Harry said, completely oblivious to the fact that his daughter wasn't touching her food.

Janie kept her eyes on Ella.

"I had to stand until I got to Basingstoke. Bloody nightmare. I really shouldn't go up on a Friday again."

Eventually Ella scooped up a forkful of peas and tipped them into her mouth. Janie turned to her own meal and started eating, and with relief let Lottie ask her dad about his day. She wished he wasn't sitting at the table with them, because if that were the case, she could have asked Ella what had happened, as clearly something had. But Ella wouldn't tell her while Harry was nattering on, nor would he let the subject go if he thought Ella was holding back on them.

She let his conversation drift over her head, intermittently watching her elder daughter, who finally put her fork down, leaving half the food untouched.

"Eat up," Harry said.

"I don't feel like it."

"Come on. You've hardly had anything."

"I'm not hungry."

"Don't be ridiculous, your mum—"

"Don't force her if she doesn't want it," Janie interrupted.

Harry looked up at her questioningly. "She's hardly had a thing."

"I know, but—" Janie waved a hand in the air, trying to defuse the conversation.

"Just another few mouthfuls," Harry said, turning to Ella.

"For God's sake, she doesn't want it," Janie snapped. "You can't force her to eat when she's clearly not hungry." She turned to Ella. "If you don't feel well, you can go and have a lie down," she told her.

"You're pandering to her again," Harry said as he chewed on a mouthful of chicken. He had a piece hanging on the edge of his lips that she couldn't help but stare at.

"I'm not pandering. I can just see she's not right."

"I'm right here," Ella cried. "You're both talking about me like I'm not even in the room."

Janie took a deep breath as her mobile started to ring. "You're right. I'm sorry." If she were a single parent, then at least there'd be no one to contradict her every five minutes.

She took the call from Anna, wandering out of the kitchen to speak to her, and by the time she returned, the plates had been stacked in the sink and the back door was wide open. She glanced out of the kitchen window and saw all three members of her family jumping up and down on the trampoline, and for a moment Janie couldn't take her eyes off them. They looked so happy. Even Ella was smiling and laughing as her feet landed on either side of Harry, who was curled into a ball, his hands wrapped protectively around his head.

Janie pressed her hands against the granite work surface and felt tears filling her eyes, though she didn't even know what it was that was making her upset. Possibly the thought that she couldn't break them up. Possibly the knowledge that however much she might have wanted to, she wasn't going to be able to do it.

"We're having a movie night," Harry announced when they came in forty minutes later. "Your choice."

Janie shook her head. "I don't mind what we watch."

"In that case, the girls want *Aladdin* again."

"Fine by me," she said, as Harry wavered in the doorway.

"You are joining us?" he asked.

"Of course I am." She screwed her eyes up at him, matching the way he was looking at her. What else did he think she was going to do? She would never not sit with them if they were watching a film together. "I'll make some popcorn."

Harry nodded. "Ella's obviously feeling better."

"Good," she said, as they heard her laughter ringing from the living room. "I'm glad."

As Harry left the kitchen, she watched her husband and considered how he could be so present at times and so absent at others, and wondered which way she actually preferred it.

———————————

It was late by the time the girls eventually went to bed. Harry had retreated to the kitchen and set up his laptop. She picked up a bottle of Chablis and took it through to the living room, where she flicked on an episode of *Luther*.

Now there was a man who was never home either, a man also more dedicated to his job than his family, yet watching him gave her some pleasure: pleasure she no longer got when Harry appeared in the doorway five minutes later.

"Sorry about that. I just had something I needed to finish. What are we watching?"

"*Luther*."

"Do you want to watch a film?"

No, she thought, *I want to watch* Luther. "Can do," she replied.

Harry sat beside her on the sofa and shuffled closer until she could feel his leg alongside her own. In the early days of their relationship her skin had tingled at his slightest touch in a way she'd never felt before. She was thirty when they met, already worried she might not meet someone to settle down with, which fifteen years later seemed a ridiculous notion. But all her friends had been getting married, some starting to have kids, and Janie had felt like she was being left behind.

Harry had walked into the bar where she was sitting with her girl-friends, celebrating her birthday. He looked nothing like the other men in there, making them look like boys in comparison, dressed in an open-necked pale-pink shirt and black suit trousers. Janie had watched him from the table as he crossed to the bar and leaned across it, a twenty-pound note clutched in his hand. When he looked over his shoulder and caught her gaze, she felt as if time had stopped and every-one else in the bar had disappeared.

They became inseparable. Six months later Harry proposed, and a year after that they were married, and all throughout that time Janie never had any doubts about their relationship because they were two similar people, driven by ambition, headstrong but so in love. There was a time when Janie out earned Harry, but he'd never seemed to mind. There was no competition between them, or at least none that she felt until Ella came along.

Having Ella threw Janie's life into instant turmoil. Now they both had to make some changes, allowances, yet it was quickly apparent that the thought hadn't crossed Harry's mind that he might have to do so. Janie sat him down, said they needed to figure this out, decide be-tween them how they could work around it when neither of them wanted to give up their careers. Harry had been quick to tell her that of course he would support whatever decision she made. If Janie wanted to return to work full-time, they could afford a live-in nanny. Janie didn't have to worry about a thing.

So it was her decision, she realized. Not theirs. Not a joint one. It was up to her if she wanted to stay at home or go back to work and, regardless of her choice, her husband's life would not change.

Maybe it was her competitive streak that drove her to decide she wasn't going to give up her career, either. Though every day she was the one with the burning hole inside her telling her she was giving up something—being with her girls. Janie never had been able to reconcile with that, yet they still hadn't been the main reason she'd given up her job in the end.

Unwanted thoughts flittered into her head. Thoughts of Miles Morgan. Thoughts of Sophie.

That time five years ago was as clear as crystal. Thinking about it still made her feel sick to her core. The part she had played in cracking apart her best friend's life.

Miles Morgan had been entering her head a lot since the new mum at school, Marcia, had put the name in there at the assembly, and she desperately wished it would stop.

Harry inched closer to her on the sofa. She felt nothing like she once had, with his leg pressing into hers. Now her feelings were consumed by tiredness. She didn't actually think she'd be able to stay up for another two hours to watch a film because it was already past nine.

"Love, is everything all right?" he asked.

Janie blinked and turned to him.

"I mean, at home . . . everything?"

"Of course it is."

Harry ran a finger across his bottom lip as he continued to study her, and she felt herself squirm under his scrutiny. It felt like he had caught her out, yet there was nothing he could bring up that she had done. She hadn't done a thing. That was the bloody problem.

She waited for him to pursue it, but he didn't. Instead he said, "Getting a bit tricky at work at the moment. Laura's not happy, bless her."

Bless her? Did he really just say that? She shifted her body to face him, but he was oblivious as he rattled on.

"I try to convince her I don't want to lose her but . . ." His voice drifted off, and he shook his head.

No, I bet you don't want to lose her, she thought. Her body was rigid, and she tried edging away from him, but he was squeezed against her so tightly that it was hard to move.

Janie had always had her suspicions about them. Right from the start, when Harry couldn't stop talking about her prospects, how he

wanted to give her a chance. She had watched them both at Harry's an-
nual parties, clocked the way her husband's gaze lingered on Laura as
she spoke, how he trailed after her when she walked out of the room.

Laura was pretty and ten years younger than Janie. Her long dark
hair was often loosely pulled back, and she had a smattering of light
freckles on her face that made her look even younger. She always
brought her husband, Nate, to Harry's parties—a nice man who by all
accounts had properly supported his wife in what she wanted to do
after having a baby by actually giving up his job. Not just paying for a
nanny.

Surely Laura wouldn't give up someone like him for Janie's husband, she wondered, as Harry went on. But then, would she be that
upset if Harry did run off with Laura Denning? At least then she
wouldn't have to make the choice.

"I don't know," he was muttering, and she realized she'd zoned out
for a moment. All Janie wanted was to not be made a fool. "Maybe I
shouldn't have kept Mia on, but my hands were tied. I just need to
make sure Laura has enough—"

"I'm sure she'll be fine," Janie interrupted, though she actually
thought Harry was completely in the wrong. His hands weren't tied,
he'd just taken what he'd thought was the easy option. Over the years
she'd seen glimpses of Harry's weaknesses that others likely didn't recognize. She'd always thought they were rooted in his earlier need to impress his father. Harry had never wanted to take on his dad's advertising
agency, he'd wanted to be an artist. A fact he'd once confided to Janie
when drunk. But she saw a flicker of that need in Harry at times, never
more so than when her life came tumbling down around her five years
before. Harry hadn't taken her side then. He'd taken Miles Morgan's.
As if somehow Harry had thought that was the easier thing to do.

Janie sighed as her thoughts returned to Laura. She was certain the
woman would have a case if she ever wanted to take it further. It would

THREE PERFECT LIARS   123

be something that would interest Janie to take on if she didn't suspect the person in question may have had an affair with her husband.

"Were you at the quay today?" Harry suddenly asked.

Janie felt herself blush.

"It doesn't matter if you were, it's just someone saw you, that's all."

"Laura?" Janie spat out the name before she had the chance to stop herself. She pulled herself away from him and off the sofa.

"No. Not Laura." He looked at her quizzically. "It was Mia, actually."

"Oh."

Mia. Nicely dressed. Stylishly short haircut. Apart from Laura, Mia stuck out like a sore thumb from the rest of the women in Harry's office, who often looked like they'd worn the same cardigan for weeks on end. The new girl. Though Janie supposed she wasn't that new anymore. Maybe, Janie considered, it could be good to meet Mia, finally have a "friend" on the inside. The woman certainly had something about her if she'd managed to push Laura to one side.

"Do you want coffee or more wine?" she asked.

"Wine, please," he said as she left the living room and went up to her bedroom to get a cardigan. Grabbing it from the bed, she pulled it on and went to the window to draw the curtains closed, but when she got there something caught her attention. Fingers curling around the edges of the fabric, she peered closer at first, then quickly pulled back. Her hands fluttered against the curtains as she stood aside, her breaths short and fast.

There was someone in the bushes. She would have passed it off as an animal if it hadn't been for the fact Janie had also felt someone watching her when she left yoga that Monday.

When she stepped forward again there was no longer any movement, and she swiftly pulled the curtains together, propelling the room into darkness.

For a moment Janie didn't move. She considered telling Harry, getting him to check outside, but at the same time she knew she wouldn't, because maybe it was just her mind playing tricks on her. Maybe it was only her head being filled with thoughts of Miles Morgan that brought back memories of the last time someone was watching her.

chapter thirteen

six weeks before the fire

It still made Laura pause, every morning when she stepped out of the lift, to immediately see Mia chattering away to one of the other women in the office like they were the best of friends. Monday had come around again, and on this particular occasion it was Bryony Knight hanging over Mia's computer screen in what seemed a bizarrely awkward position.

Laura's fingers found the hem of her jacket and played with its seam. She should just turn in the opposite direction and weave around the desks, but she was too fascinated by the interaction between the two women.

Laura couldn't fathom how anyone in Mia's position could be so brazenly open with the people who worked for her. Immaturity and inexperience made her act like this.

She didn't trust Mia, whose hand was now patting Bryony on the arm like she were some kind of dog, and who was screeching that she was going to *"take her up on that."*

"This Friday." Mia laughed loudly as Bryony retreated from the desk with a smile that reached her ears. "Straight after work."

Laura wondered what they'd arranged. She also knew that whatever it was she'd likely not get an invitation, and even though she would never join them anyway, it still hurt.

Maybe she had brought it on herself, holding them at arm's length. But as she stood and watched the familiarity bubbling between Mia and Bryony, Laura found herself wishing she could have what seemed to come so easily to Mia.

Eventually Laura released the hem of her jacket that was now scrunched into a ball and flattened it down, hovering on the edges of the office floor, watching this woman with ease and charm oozing out of her.

Bryony had turned away, and Mia's smile faded and she shook her head, only slightly, but enough for Laura to catch Mia rolling her eyes and letting out a puff of breath as she turned back to her desk.

Laura glanced around her, looking for anyone else who might have caught this small gesture, but the few other staff around were all pre-occupied.

It was all so fake. Everything about Mia was an act, including her supposed friendships, and yet no one else appeared to see it except Laura. And as she stood there, still watching this stranger who had come in and stolen her job, she felt an unease washing over her that made her shudder. She had no idea who this person was that she was unwittingly up against.

"Laura, how are you?" Harry stepped out of the lift that had just opened onto the third floor. "I've barely seen you in the last week," he added. "You look good."

Laura clenched her jaw and glanced across the floor, embarrassed, but when she saw Mia look over, she wondered if it wouldn't hurt to let her know that she was still close to the boss.

"Thanks." She self-consciously reached for the ponytail loosely tying her hair up that morning. She hadn't had time to wash it. She'd barely managed to streak some mascara onto her eyelashes in her haste.

She knew she didn't look good, but Harry was watching her with a sheepish grin, and she felt the rush of heat to her cheeks. "You've barely been here, that's why you haven't seen me," she said hastily. She was never going to be good at pretending to enjoy his attention.

"I know. Lot going on up in London." He rolled his eyes.

"Actually, I'm glad I've seen you," Laura said. "Can we have a chat?"

"'Course," he said and stepped back, gesturing for her to lead the way across the floor to his office.

Once inside, when he'd shut the door behind them, Harry retreated to the other side of his desk, glancing at Laura, who was still hovering by the door. "Everything all right?" he asked, his head cocked as if he'd already guessed she wanted to talk about Mia again.

She did, of course, but this time she was armed with facts he couldn't ignore. "I attended the Coopers pitch last Friday," Laura started. She watched his eyes dip away briefly as he pulled out his chair and sank onto it. She thought she saw a small exhalation of breath, but she went on anyway. "I'm not here to criticize Mia's ideas or what work she's put into her presentation," Laura said. "But she made a big mistake. She left out important things from the budget that she should have considered, things that are going to add at least twenty percent to their spend. I'm surprised Tess hasn't mentioned it—"

Harry held up a hand to stop her.

"Harry, this is critical."

"I know. And Mia's already told me."

"Oh?" Laura said, deflated that her big buildup had been flattened so easily.

"She was upset with herself and wanted me to know what had happened. She called me on Friday night, she was in such a state."

Laura shuffled on the spot as annoyance built inside her. "Well, the fact is she *shouldn't* be making mistakes like that," she said, trying to keep her voice calm. "It was easy for me to notice it was missing. It's going to cost Coopers—"

"Laura," he sighed, "Mia knows all this. She's been working on it over the weekend. I'm not worried about it, and you certainly don't need to be either."

Laura went quiet. Any thoughts she had of how the conversation might go had been shot to pieces. *What was the point?* What was actually stopping her from telling Harry what he could do with his job? She didn't know if she had the energy to fight.

She imagined what Nate would say if she went home and told him she'd quit. Would he be horrified or would he understand that not only would he need to go straight back to work, they'd have to put their house on the market, downsize, and potentially move out of the area? They wouldn't be able to go to Crete in September anymore. They'd have to make adjustments. But maybe it wouldn't be too bad.

Laura watched Harry frown, waiting for her to say something, and she felt sick that she could be pushed out so easily. She could imagine Mia's face if she knew Laura had quit, and realized it would be exactly what Mia wanted.

Laura shifted on her spot. It would be her family that suffered again if she gave in, and why the hell should they have to because of Mia?

The truth was she had no idea what to do, constantly oscillating between giving up and taking Mia on, and all the time she just wished Harry would listen to her like he always used to.

"I don't believe you can do what you've done," Laura said suddenly. "I have rights—to come back to my old job. Legally, you can't do it."

"Laura, let's not go down that road. Please."

"But it's true." She waited, her heart thumping harder now. This was so not how she wanted their conversation to go, especially since her friend Deborah had told her she didn't really have a case. She hated begging for what was rightfully hers, but then maybe the threat would be enough for him to see sense. Nothing else was working.

"You still have your same job," he said. "You're on the same level, making the same salary—"

"You think that's all that matters?" Laura cried. "Harry, you've taken my most important client away from me. I'm left with *crap!*" She shouted the last word, watching his eyes flicker to his glass walls. But in that moment she didn't care who heard.

"It's not crap," he said softly, but with a firm tone she'd rarely heard before, as if he was admonishing her, like she were a child. "And as I told you when you came back, I have a new opportunity. I was going to speak to you about it this morning," he said. "The initial meeting's set up for next week. I want you to be there. I'm excited about this."

He looked excited, she thought, as she watched him shift in his seat, nodding, holding his head on his steepled hands and looking at her expectantly. "I'll get the details sent to you. You're going to need to clear your calendar for it."

When Laura still didn't respond he said, "Clearly this is between you and me, but Coopers—" He hesitated, possibly for emphasis, she thought. "They won't be the biggest client when we win this, Laura."

When she didn't answer he went on, "We get this and you can shake off all your other crap." Harry winked at her and grinned.

Despite what she'd set out to gain, Laura found herself relenting.

"By the way, did you get the invite to my party?" Harry asked as she opened the door to leave.

"I did."

"Friday, May tenth." He clicked a button on his mobile. "God, just over five weeks. Better get myself sorted," he laughed.

Laura doubted there was much he had to sort. His wife, Janie, appeared to do most of it. Laura often wondered how much Janie enjoyed these parties, how she could when she barely knew most of Harry's staff.

"I hope you and Nate will be there?"

"I don't know, I mean, we've not used a babysitter yet." Right now, Harry and Janie's party was the last place she wanted to be.

"You have to attend," he said, his face dropping. "If you can't get a babysitter you'll have to come on your own."

Laura shook her head. "No. I'd want Nate to be there."

"Of course." He smiled. "Well, do whatever you can," he added, as if his party could in any way be the most important factor in their conversations today.

"When is this meeting with the mystery client?" she asked.

"Oh yeah. Right." He scrolled though his mobile. "Next Monday. Eleven. We're going to meet at the quay. Maybe have some lunch if we run on that long."

"Okay."

"His name's Miles Morgan," Harry went on. "He runs a financial-services company. I've known him a long time. I hope you'll like him."

———

Bobby was already in bed by the time Laura got home that night. She had tried to get back earlier, but even her so-called crap accounts had taken up too much of her time that day. As soon as she walked in the house she crept into her son's room and tiptoed up to the crib. Now she had to make do with staring at his sleeping body, wrapped up in his sleep sack, flat out, arms splayed at his sides. Laura hovered over him, breathing in his smell, longing to reach down and pull him out, hold him against her, feel his warmth and his tiny head of soft, downy hair pressing against her face.

It was funny, she realized, she had never thought she would feel like this—so desperate to be with her baby son, so guilty she wasn't.

Laura gripped the sides of the crib as she watched him, her eyes filling with tears as his eyelids fluttered, and wondered what was going through his mind. What dreams he could be having. She mustn't lean too close in case he woke. Nate had told her he hadn't settled for a while, that he'd had to sit with him in the rocking chair until he did.

She'd known something would give when she went back to work.

She'd had the discussion with her parent-group friends months back when Laura told them that she felt like a part of her was lost without work. She understood that working full-time meant there would be times when she wouldn't see Bobby before he went to bed, or when she'd be out the house before he woke, and at the time she was okay with that. It was a sacrifice she was prepared to make because Laura would come home satisfied, buzzing, able to throw herself into the time she did have with her family.

She had never expected to feel so desperate and vulnerable, and as she peered at her beautiful son, she hated that Chrissie and the other parent-group mums were right. She couldn't have everything, and she no longer knew what to sacrifice. All she did know was that she definitely wasn't happy.

With a deep sigh Laura eventually retreated and went downstairs, wiping a hand across her face before Nate noticed she was upset. They were seeing the other couples and their babies this weekend, and Laura didn't particularly want to face it, yet it had been in the calendar for weeks. There was no good way of escaping it. She had known for a long time she'd never be true friends with this group of women. Their hearts were often in the right places, but they didn't understand her one bit, and she certainly couldn't talk to them about how awful her first weeks at work had been.

Nate handed her a glass of wine as soon as she reached the bottom of the stairs.

"Thank you."

"You look like you need it," he said. "I haven't had a chance to think of tea, with Bobby not getting off to sleep."

"Oh, don't worry about that. Let's get takeout," she suggested, following him into the living room, where she sunk onto the sofa and stretched her legs out. "I'm so done in." Laura closed her eyes and leaned her head back.

"How was it today?" he asked. When she looked up he was flicking through his phone. "What do you fancy? Pizza?"

"Anything. I spoke to Harry today," she added.

"Oh?" He passed her his phone. "Do you want to choose what you want first?"

Laura sucked in a breath as she took the phone. Nate's mind was clearly on food as he peered over her shoulder, waiting for her to select from the menu. She quickly pointed to the twelve-inch vegetarian pizza she chose every time and passed it back to him and waited for what seemed like an eternity for him to make his choice and place the order.

All the time she sipped at her wine, studying her husband, and by the time he eventually put his phone down and asked how it went, she couldn't actually be bothered to tell him.

"Did you say anything about her mistake?" he asked.

"Of course."

"So what did he say?"

"Mia had already told him," Laura said blankly. "He didn't seem to think it was a big deal."

Nate nodded, stretching his legs out next to hers.

"He keeps telling me about this new client, Miles Morgan. Apparently there's a meeting with him next week, but I don't know, Nate," she went on. "I don't know if Harry's just telling me what I want to hear."

"Maybe you just need to see what happens with this Miles guy?"

"I will, but that's not the point, is it? The fact is she's still there, lording it around the office, and I'm left to hover about, waiting to see if something comes from a mate of Harry's. She's gotten away with that bloody mistake, that's what so infuriating. She's working everyone in the office, and they're all falling for it."

"I don't get why you have it in for Mia," he said.

Laura's head snapped round to look at him. "Are you kidding?"

"Surely it's Harry you should be pissed off with. He's the one that's made this decision, not her."

"Haven't you been listening to me, Nate? I told you from the start there's something about her; she's not the same person who came for the interview."

Nate gave a short laugh that he turned into a cough.

"Are you shaking your head?" she said. "You think I'm making it up?"

"No, I don't think that at all. I just have no idea why you're so intent on getting at her and not Harry."

Laura's pulse was racing as she looked at her husband. She knew what he thought of her boss. He'd always said he never trusted him, and yet he trusted her implicitly. He knew she would never so much as flirt with Harry Wood. So why did she feel now like he was accusing her of something?

"I've known him for years. He's always looked out for me, you know that," she told him defiantly. "We wouldn't even be in this house if it wasn't for Harry taking a chance on me. I believe him," she said, because even though she wasn't entirely convinced by her own words, it was what she desperately wanted.

Nate nodded. "Okay."

"What, you don't?"

"I'm not saying that at all. I'm sure he's telling the truth. But you don't owe him everything, Laura, just because he gave you the job."

"I think this is down to her," Laura said, ignoring him and willing him to understand where she was coming from. The fact was she needed to believe Harry, because she *needed* him. All she needed from Mia was for her to leave the company. "And somehow I'm going to prove it."

"Oh, Laura," he groaned. "Don't go down that road."

"What?" she cried, pushing him in the arm when he didn't respond. "What do you mean?"

He shook his head. "You don't need this right now, do you? You've only just gone back after having Bobby. Don't you just need to—I don't know, keep things plain sailing for a while?"

"'Plain sailing'? What are you saying? That I should just accept everything that's happened?"

"Well, yeah. For now, anyway. I think you've probably got enough other things going on in your head." He waved a hand about the room. "And you're not getting enough sleep. You're probably exhausted."

Laura screwed her eyes up at him. "You think I'm not up to dealing with it? Because I've had a baby?"

"No. That's not what I mean."

"So what do you mean by I'm not getting enough sleep?"

"I'm just saying, Laura . . . Christ, I don't know, you're taking this the wrong way."

"Because I'm, what, too emotional?" she asked.

"Oh for God's sake." Nate rolled his eyes and sunk back on the sofa.

Laura shook her head as a tear escaped and rolled down her face. She wiped it away quickly before it could prove his point. Eventually she sunk back too, and after a moment Nate reached out and squeezed her leg.

"I mean, just be careful," he said. "That's all."

"I don't think that's all, though, is it?" she said. "You mean something more than that. Just tell me."

"I mean this happened before, Laura. And I don't want you starting a witch hunt, because it won't turn out well."

"Nate," Laura gasped. "I can't believe you even said that. This is nothing like it was with Saskia."

Initial interview between Detective Emily Marlow and Nathan Denning following the fire at Morris and Wood offices on Monday, May 13.

<u>Nathan (Nate) Denning, on Tuesday, May 14, at Lymington Police Headquarters.</u>

Marlow:	You say your wife texted you to say she was going to be home late last night?
Nate:	She did. That's not unusual, though.
Marlow:	What was her reason?
Nate:	She said she was held up at work.
Marlow:	And how often is she held up and late back?
Nate:	Most nights now.
Marlow:	Do you know what time she supposedly left the office?
Nate:	I don't. She texted me at about six p.m., I think.
Marlow:	So three hours before the building burned down she told you she was still in it?
Nate:	Yes. But she wouldn't have been the only one. There would have been other staff still there at six. It's not that late, really, is it?
Marlow:	And what was her reason for staying on?
Nate:	She said she was meeting the Coopers team members. They're her main account. They *were* her main account, rather.
Marlow:	Only we now know she didn't actually meet any of the team from Coopers.
Nate:	So I hear.
Marlow:	Mr. Denning, I'm sorry to ask you this—
Nate:	Please call me Nate.
Marlow:	Nate. Have you any idea why your wife might have told you she was meeting up with staff from her old account when it's apparent there was never any such meeting scheduled?
Nate:	I don't. You'll have to ask her that.

Marlow: For some reason your wife isn't telling us anything. Either she's covering up for herself or for someone else.

Nate: (sighs) I wish I could tell you more, I really do.

Marlow: What time did she get home last night?

Nate: It was late; it wasn't until about ten o'clock, I think.

Marlow: And how did she seem?

Nate: I was already in bed. We didn't speak. We haven't been— we haven't been speaking much lately. After the weekend I wasn't in the mood to talk to her last night, so I didn't acknowledge her when she came home.

Marlow: Had something in particular happened over the weekend?

Nate: Yes, the party happened. Harry Wood's party.

Marlow: And did you attend it?

Nate: No. I didn't. My wife went on her own.

Marlow: Had everything been okay between you and your wife until the party?

Nate: (pauses) Not really. She's been getting—I've been worried about her.

Marlow: Worried? In what way?

Nate: That she's been— (shakes head) Oh, I don't know, I suppose that she's been getting too involved with someone at work.

Marlow: "Involved"? You mean she's been having a relationship with someone in the office?

Nate: (laughs) That's not what I mean. "Obsessed," then, if you want. She's been getting obsessed. The thing is, it's not the first time it's happened, so . . .

Marlow: So who is it that Laura is obsessed with right now?

Nate: Her name's Mia. But this has absolutely nothing to do with the fire, you know that, don't you? I mean, what I'm telling you—there's no way Laura had anything to do with the fire last night.

Marlow: Your disagreement over the weekend, was it because of your wife's argument with Mia Anderson at the party?

Nate: What? No. No, I don't know anything about any argument. No, I was pissed off about what happened with Harry Wood.

chapter fourteen

six weeks before the fire

Mia poked her head around Harry's office door. "Have you got five minutes?"

"I have." Harry beckoned her in. "I hope you bring me good news, though." He gestured to the seat. "How's everything going?"

"All good, thanks."

"The TV ad coming on well?"

"Really well."

Harry nodded and smiled, though his eyes didn't light up the way they usually did. Mia wondered what was on his mind. She had seen Laura in his office earlier, her arms flailing around as she spoke to him. The woman clearly had something to discuss, and Mia had no doubt it was probably her. In contrast to Laura's frantic movements, Harry had been immobile at his desk.

Mia wondered how he put up with it. He was the boss, and yet, from where Mia had watched, outside the glass wall, Laura had been the one in control. How she wished she'd been able to hear what was being said.

The rumors about Harry and Laura were partially true, from Mia's point of view. The way he pawed at Laura's shoulder outside the lift, hovering over her just a little too close. It was an unnecessary display from the CEO in such a public space. No wonder the gossip had spread, when it was clearly apparent he fancied her.

But what did Laura make of it? This intrigued Mia because as far as she could see there was no reciprocation, yet Laura hadn't told him he was too close, or even pulled away.

If it had happened to her, Mia would have turned around and slapped him across the face. Everyone else in the office might think he was hot, but Mia didn't get it. She didn't particularly think he had many attractive qualities.

Of course she had never said as much to anyone, especially not the likes of Henrietta or Bryony, because there was no way she would chance it getting back to him. Or Laura. The thought of that—Laura would have a field day if she could report back to Harry that Mia didn't like him.

He was waiting for her to tell him what she wanted. She'd always been grateful that he didn't dally in small talk; he hadn't once asked about her personal life.

"It doesn't look like you're bringing the good news I was hoping for," he said now, raising his eyebrows.

"Not really, I'm afraid."

"But you're not here to talk about Coopers?"

"No, that's all going fine. This is a more personal issue I need to discuss with you."

"Okay," he said cautiously.

Mia straightened herself in the chair. "I think you need to know there's a lot of concern among the women in the office."

Harry screwed his eyes up at her and leaned his head to one side. He had no idea what she was talking about, but then of course he wouldn't. He could sit in his office with the door closed and have no idea what went on outside its glass walls. "How do you mean?"

"Bullying," Mia went on. "I'm afraid someone has confessed to me that she is being bullied, and I feel it right to come to you with this."

"Bullied? Who?"

"Sarah Clifton, but she's not the only one concerned."

"Who's she complaining about?" he asked.

"Mike Lewis."

"Mike?" Harry gave a short laugh. "You're not serious?"

"I am," Mia replied, confused by his reaction and a little angry that he could think this was anything to laugh about.

"But Mike's, you know what Mike's like, he's—Christ, what's he actually supposed to have done?"

"He undermines his staff," Mia said. "He doesn't listen to what they have to say. He makes them feel like they aren't important."

"Oh, right."

God, Mia thought, he wasn't taking her seriously.

"It's the women he does this to, Harry. I'm just pleased they feel they can finally share their concerns with someone."

Damn you, Harry Wood, she thought, as she watched his expression change from shock to confusion to a mild irritation that she had brought this issue to him.

"Why hasn't Sarah spoken to me herself?" he asked.

Ah, that was the problem. Sarah didn't actually know that Mia was here. As Mia had predicted, Sarah had spoken to her boyfriend again over the weekend and had come in that morning and told Mia she didn't want to take it any further.

"I'm doing it on her behalf," Mia told him.

Harry raised his eyebrows. "Okay, I'll speak to Mike." He waved a hand in the air as he shook his head. Was he dismissing her?

Mia could feel the anger burning in the pit of her stomach.

"Anything else, because I really need to make a call—"

"No," she said, very faintly but through gritted teeth. "No, there's nothing else."

Initial interviews between Detective Emily Marlow and staff of Morris and Wood following the fire at Morris and Wood offices on Monday, May 13.

Michael (Mike) Lewis, Head of Creative, on Tuesday, May 14, at Lymington Police Headquarters.

Mike:	You still don't know anything more? Staff are talking, asking questions no one can answer. I hear there were people in the building?
Marlow:	I'm sorry. I can't confirm anything at the moment.
Mike:	It's just that I have a friend who knows someone in the police. He said they pulled two people out but—
Marlow:	As I said, I'm really sorry, but right now we can't confirm any details.
Mike:	(nods) That's okay. I understand.
Marlow:	Mr. Lewis, I believe you were accused of bullying someone who worked on your team. A Sarah Clifton?
Mike:	What? Why are you asking—that was nothing more than office gossip.
Marlow:	So you're denying she accused you of harassment?
Mike:	She might have said something, but it was ridiculous. I wasn't bullying anyone. I thought I was here about the fire? Why are you asking me about a girl who doesn't even work for the company anymore?
Marlow:	Oh, this is about the fire, but I'm trying to understand exactly what was happening inside Morris and Wood prior to last night.
Mike:	That isn't relevant.
Marlow:	Maybe not. But all the same, I'd appreciate if you'd allow me to—
Mike:	You're thinking someone who worked at the company did it, then? Set fire to the place, I mean? Who?
Marlow:	It's early in the investigation, and right now we're talking to everyone who worked there.

Mike: Well, it has nothing to do with me. And whatever the girl said about me . . . it was all fabricated. I've never heard anything so— (breaks off) It can destroy people, you know, lies like that.

Marlow: How do you mean?

Mike: I'm just saying, people start accusing you of things and it sticks. Whether or not it's true, it gets round and then (shakes head) I don't know . . .

Marlow: Could you speak up please, for the tape.

Mike: I just said I don't know; I don't know what started it and I don't know why it was all blown out of proportion. But it was. By Mia Anderson.

Marlow: I was under the impression that an official complaint was made against you and taken to Harry Wood. Is that true?

Mike: No. There was nothing official.

Marlow: You mentioned Mia Anderson. Wasn't she the one who spoke to Harry Wood about it?

Mike: Yes. That's the point. It was nothing to do with her. Only she started it, and it snowballed, and she wouldn't let it go. I was going to give Harry this, you know. (shows letter)

Marlow: What is this?

Mike: My resignation. I've been carrying it around with me for the last two weeks. To be honest, I don't really want to go.

Marlow: Can you think of any reason why Mia Anderson was so keen to complain if you believe you did nothing wrong?

Mike: (shrugs) None at all. She was nice as anything to my face. But there was something about her. This fiery spark. I saw it at Harry's party Friday night, the way she blew.
         I don't know, I didn't really know her at all, not like some of those girls in the office do, but there was something I couldn't quite put my finger on.

———————

Bryony Knight, Account Assistant

Marlow: By your own words, Mia Anderson was amazing at her job.

Bryony: (nods) She was.

Marlow: But wasn't there an issue with a TV advertising budget?

Bryony: Yes, but that was an understandable mistake. Anyone could have made it.

Marlow: Even someone who had experience in TV advertising?

Bryony: I don't know for sure, but yes, I would have thought so.

Marlow: Did Mia Anderson lead you to believe she had that kind of experience?

Bryony: Of course she had. She had tons of it. Has Mia done something wrong? It sounds like you think she has, by the questions you're asking me. She didn't—she wouldn't have—I mean, no way it was her. She wouldn't have started the fire.

Marlow: What makes you so sure of that, Miss Knight?

Bryony: Well—I just know she wouldn't. She's a lovely person.

Marlow: How well do you know her?

Bryony: I know her really well. I mean, I report to her and everything, but we're friends too.

Marlow: Tell me about your friendship. What do you do together?

Bryony: Well, you know, we go out for drinks after work, that sort of thing.

Marlow: Anything else?

Bryony: She's more of a friend at work.

Marlow: So other than a few drinks after work, have you met up with Mia on any other occasion?

Bryony: No, but we've been out a lot of times. Most Friday nights we go down to the pub.

Marlow: What do you know about Mia's home life?

Bryony: Like what?

Marlow: I don't know, you tell me. Anything at all you know about Mia Anderson's personal life. Who does she live with?

Bryony: Well, I know for sure she lives on her own.

Marlow: Oh?

Bryony: In a flat. She has her own place, she laughs about the woman who lives above her who's always shouting at her boyfriend.

Marlow: Okay, Miss Knight, I think we're done here for now.

chapter fifteen

five weeks before the fire

On Saturday morning Mia's mother stood at the kitchen sink, her hands plunged into the water as she scrubbed hard on a pan. "You'll wear your fingers away," Mia told her.

"Well, these pans won't wash themselves, will they?" her mum answered, feigning brightness in the way she always did when there was something on her mind.

Mia looked at her, hunched over, shoulders taut. She could almost see the cogs inside her brain working overtime. "Here, let me help," she said, reaching for the sponge.

"No, no." Her mum brushed her away. "I'm perfectly capable of doing a few dishes. I'm not dead yet."

"Mum—don't talk like that."

Her mother stopped, shoulders heaving upward. She rolled her head from side to side but didn't speak.

"Your neck's hurting again." Mia knew what that meant. Her mum had been doing too much, putting too much pressure on herself. It scared Mia to see her like this, because she didn't know how far her mum would stretch before she broke altogether. "And besides, I want to help," she muttered, grabbing a tea towel from the side and picking up a dish from the draining board. "You can at least let me dry."

Her mum gave her a thin smile before turning back to the pan and plunging it into the soapy water again.

They fell into silence as they stood side by side. Mia looked out to the yard at the back, where a few large tubs took pride of place next to a bistro table covered in rust. They really could do with another set, but there wasn't enough money left that month.

"Maybe we could go out this afternoon," Mia suggested. "Do you fancy a pub lunch?"

"That would be lovely." Her mum nodded enthusiastically but she wasn't smiling. "Yes. That does sound nice. But I don't think—I don't know if Jess will come."

"I'll ask her," Mia said.

"Yes . . ."

Mia clocked the pause, the deep intake of breath. They both knew her older sister wouldn't want to go anywhere, but it didn't mean they would ever stop trying to persuade her to.

Time had softened their mother. She'd once been so determined, so unwilling to accept a fuss, yet now she was more than willing to cave in to Jess, not to push her. Mia knew this was possibly the worst thing she could be doing for her, but at the same time she couldn't blame her mum. With her ailing health, Jess was too much for her to cope with.

Mia understood that some days it was easier for her mum to let Jess sit in the house all day because the argument and the fallout was too much to take. There were enough times when Mia wanted to do the same, so she didn't blame her mum for giving in. But she also thought she'd been relenting too much lately, giving in to her oldest daughter's behavior, and it was a downward spiral. Anyone could see that. Even their mum must.

"It's like she's a child again," she had told Mia once. "It's hard enough to deal with a three-year-old when she won't do what's best for her, but at least then you can pick her up and strap her into the car when you need to go out. How am I supposed to do that with Jess? She's an adult now. She's thirty-five."

"Of course Jess wasn't ever that bad as a little one," she had gone on, and Mia knew what was coming. "You were the rascal. The one who refused to go to bed, who would lie on the floor of the supermarket kicking and screaming. Look at us now," she had said, her words fading to a whisper. "You don't expect this."

Mia hated that her mum was living this life. She was sixty-eight. She had been about to give up her part-time job at Sainsbury's a year ago; she'd wanted to take a pottery course. The flyer had been pinned to the fridge for as long as Mia had been back at home. But everything had been put on hold. For Jess.

"I'm going to try my best, Mum," Mia said as she folded the tea towel and laid it carefully on the draining board. "It's such a gorgeous day, and we don't have to go anywhere too crowded."

"No, no, of course, but don't . . ." Her mum paused again.

"I won't push it," Mia said, biting her tongue. As she wandered out of the kitchen and toward Jess's bedroom at the far end of the hall in the bungalow, she also knew that if she couldn't get her sister to agree to go to the pub for lunch, then their mum wouldn't go either. She wouldn't want to leave Jess on her own, not on a day like this. Sunny Saturdays were always so much worse. And yet the thought of them all sitting inside made Mia's fingers curl as she rapped on the closed door and gently pushed it open.

Jess was facing away from her, her own finger outstretched, running along the line of her heaving bookcase until she stopped at one and tugged it out. Mia peered closer. *Wuthering Heights.* Such a depressing book, in Mia's mind, yet Jess was drawn to reading it time and time again.

Mia sat on the edge of her sister's bed and waited for her to turn around. "You look tired," Jess said eventually, when she locked eyes with her sister. "Are you sleeping?"

Mia shrugged. "I had a late night. I woke early. But yeah, apart from that I'm sleeping okay."

"You're working too hard."

Mia shook her head. "I enjoy it."

Jess stared at her, her gaze intense, her mind whirring with something. "Do you really?" she asked. It unnerved Mia when her sister studied her the way she did, like she knew there was more going on than Mia could ever tell her. Jess had always had an uncanny ability to sense the things left unsaid, but that ability had intensified in the last year.

"I do," Mia told her.

"I still don't understand what you see in that place," Jess muttered, still watching her intently. "You know how Mum felt about the building when it was being developed. She used to rally up signatures to petition against it being built in the first place. You working there is like you're going against her."

"Mum doesn't mind one bit," Mia said. There were plenty of things she could have said to Jess. Her working at Morris and Wood was surely the least of their mum's worries. Mia's salary had relieved the three of them as much as it could, even if it wasn't stretching far enough.

"You didn't see her at the time. She hated it. She thought it was disgusting that someone like Harry Wood could waltz down here and take over. It's like he was building a bloody shrine to himself."

Mia shook her head and turned away.

"I'm sorry. I know you're doing this for us."

You have no idea, Mia thought, but she couldn't say this to Jess.

"Is he still a good boss to work for?"

"Yes," she said, her voice clipped. She always tried to avoid getting into a conversation with Jess about work or Harry Wood, but sometimes Jess pushed her. "He's fine as bosses go. And I don't know why you try to make me feel guilty about working there," she added, opening her mouth to carry on, but clamping it shut at the last minute.

Mia sighed. It was a constant seesaw of anger that Jess didn't always appreciate what she was doing, and then guilt for feeling that way.

Mia had often wondered what Jess would say if she told her the truth. How the fact that her mum had battled against the development of the office had briefly tainted her view on taking the job, but an over-powering sense had overtaken her, that this was the one opportunity she could not afford to miss.

When she'd seen the ad, her breath had been momentarily trapped as she'd read and reread Laura Denning's job description. It was per-fect. Too perfect to be true, really. The opportunity had practically fallen into her lap; now all she had to do was ensure she got the job. She had six months of Laura not being there to get her feet under the table.

Neither her mum nor Jess knew the whole truth. She could imagine what they would say to her if they did. They would tell her to get out.

"How did that pitch go that you were worrying about?" Jess asked.

Mia didn't mention that the pitch was a week ago now, it was nice that Jess had remembered it at all. "It was fine to a point," Mia told her, "and then I cocked it up. I forgot something major, but I think I've gotten past it."

"You always do." The corners of Jess's mouth twitched. "My little sister always has a knack of making sure things go her way."

"Here's hoping." Mia smiled. She reached a hand out and touched Jess's. "Come to the pub with us for lunch? We can go locally; we don't have to get in the car and we can sit outside. You don't have to go in."

Jess pulled away.

"I know you don't want to, but I'm thinking of Mum. She won't leave you, Jess, you know that."

"Don't put that on me."

"I'm not. I don't mean to. But she looks done in. Honestly, she could do with this. The three of us girls together. Please."

Jess turned and looked out the window that faced the road. It wasn't a pleasant view, and Mia often wished Jess had something better to look at, given the amount of time she spent in her room, but then she'd been the one to stop her mum from trying to give up her own bedroom at the back. As far as Mia was concerned, that was one thing she shouldn't have to do for her daughter.

"I know how hard this feels for you, but it doesn't have to be," Mia went on. "Please just try. If it gets too much, we'll turn around and come straight home. I promise."

"Okay," Jess said eventually.

"Really?"

"I'll try, but—"

"I know, I know." Mia stood up and kissed her sister on the top of her head, closing her eyes and lingering for a moment as she breathed in the faint scent of coconut shampoo.

It would seem such a small step for most people, but it was a victory for them, and Mia tried to focus on that rather than the thoughts that often invaded her head: the events twelve months earlier that had turned their world on its axis. The reason they were all living in this prison.

Mia eventually pulled away and whispered to her sister, "I love you, you know."

Initial interviews between Detective Emily Marlow and staff of Morris and Wood following the fire at Morris and Wood offices on Monday, May 13.

<u>Henrietta James, Senior Account Manager, on Tuesday, May 14, at Lymington Police Headquarters.</u>

Henrietta: I suppose they kept it pretty professional in the office, their mutual dislike for each other, that is, though you could tell there were things going on behind the scenes.

Marlow: What kind of things do you mean?

Henrietta: Well, they clearly didn't trust each other's motives. That's why it all blew up at the party. One of them had found something out. I wasn't trying to eavesdrop, of course. But you just couldn't help it. They were so loud.

Marlow: Who found out what, do you have any idea?

Henrietta: I can't say for sure, but what started it was when Laura went running over the lawn yelling at Mia that she was a liar. She was shouting that she knew. That's what she kept saying, *I know about you.*
    But like I said, I couldn't hear all of it.

Marlow: What did Mia do when Laura was yelling at her?

Henrietta: She looked—well, she was furious, to be honest. I mean, you can't blame her, can you? It was embarrassing for everyone, but it must have been horrific for her.

Marlow: You think she looked more cross than embarrassed?

Henrietta: Oh, I really can't say; I mean, I might be twisting everything all around here . . .

Marlow: Your loyalties appear to lie with Mia Anderson.

Henrietta: Of course. Well, I don't mean I was taking sides or anything. I really wasn't. But Mia, well, it was all just so out of the blue.

Marlow: Did you speak to either of them after their argument?

Henrietta: No. I went to look for Mia, but when I found her she was with Janie Wood and—well, I didn't want to interrupt that.

But I still don't see what the argument at the party has to do with the offices being set on fire?

Marlow: Maybe it doesn't. Did you happen to notice how much both women had been drinking that night?

Henrietta: (laughs) Well, Laura, yes; I mean, you couldn't help but notice how much she'd put away. And with a baby at home and everything. It wasn't right. She was in such a state. To be honest, I was surprised to see her in the office yesterday. I thought she might have been too embarrassed. Though she did come in *very* late.

Marlow: How did the argument end?

Henrietta: Well, eventually Harry had to break it up, but by then everything had gone wrong, hadn't it? You know, I felt so sorry for Janie Wood after all the trouble she went to. She'd laid out such a wonderful spread, lots of hors d'oeuvres. Have I said that right?

Anyway, she'd gone to so much effort—but then she always does. And she looked stunning too. She's a very beautiful woman, Janie Wood. She must have been furious.

You know, at first it was strange because I remember her standing behind me, just watching the argument, and she didn't look remotely bothered that they were making such a scene. It looked like she almost found the whole thing amusing. Though of course ten minutes later her smile had been wiped straight off her face. Poor woman. And then there was the whole issue with Harry and . . . oh, it was all such a shame. It was supposed to be a lovely night, but after that—you know, I didn't actually see Janie again? That was a funny thing too.

Marlow: Ms. James, do you have any idea why Laura accused Mia of lying?

Henrietta: No. But what I do recall is that at one point she said she knew Mia wasn't who said she said was, and she was demanding to know why the hell Mia had come for her job.

chapter sixteen

five weeks before the fire

J anie was sitting at her laptop, trying to focus on preparations for her husband's staff party, but she couldn't clear her head. She sighed as she sat back in her chair and gazed out the window, her hand cradled around a mug of coffee.

Maybe she should take a break from party planning. Do some yoga in the garden. A headstand might help the unwanted thoughts to drop out of her head. Searching through Pinterest for pretty platters of food and decorations was certainly not doing it for her, and she was beginning to wish she'd told Harry that she didn't want to host another sodding party ever again. They were nothing more than a chore. In fact, Janie had lost any interest in them the moment the first was over, when she was left with an untidy house, bin bags stacked high in the garden, and the feeling that she was the caterer rather than the wife.

Janie wasn't a woman who felt a sense of achievement from throwing a bloody party. She had achieved much greater things than that. She was once a woman who made the difference between people walking free or being convicted.

Janie closed her Pinterest board, her fingers hovering over the computer's keypad. What she really wanted was to dive into something she had forbidden herself to do, but parties, and Harry, and a long stretch of the day ahead before she had to pick up the girls left her feeling low. And what better place to go to when you're already feeling like life can't get worse, she thought sarcastically, than Facebook?

The site pinged to life and Janie typed his name into the search bar, her gaze drifting down the profiles until she came to the third Miles Morgan. She felt the same twinge she had the last time she'd looked at his face. He hadn't changed one bit.

Clicking on his page, Janie took in the information, looking for what, she wasn't quite sure. A wife? Kids? What he was doing now? That he was still safely tucked away in London?

There were no signs of children in any of his pictures, most of which were of him in various luxurious locations, some with a group of men, others with a woman. Janie zoomed in closer on a photo of her. Pretty, long dark hair, deep brown eyes, and a figure to die for in her tight tops and skinny jeans or shorts. She could easily have been twenty years younger than Miles.

She wondered what version of Miles this woman saw, and whether any of it was the truth. Had he told her what he'd done? Somehow Janie doubted it.

Holding a hand over her knotted stomach, Janie tried to make sense of what she was feeling. But as Miles Morgan stared back from her computer screen, nothing came to her, and eventually she deleted her search so no one could find it and closed down the laptop.

Miles wasn't in her life anymore. She didn't need to ever see him again. And as she reminded herself of this fact she felt some relief, because it was one thing to look at him on her screen, but the thought of coming face-to-face with him sent a shiver down Janie's spine.

———————

When Harry got home from the gym, Janie could tell he was wrestling with something. She could see it in the way he rubbed at his chin, his attention only half on the girls as they talked about going to the cinema that afternoon and the film they particularly wanted to see. It still surprised her how keen Ella, in particular, always was to share everything with her father, while Janie got little more than a grunt from her when she tried asking questions.

Now, as she watched their interchange, she wondered if the girls found him attentive, because she could tell his answers were vague, his eyes blank. As soon as there was a pause in the conversation he picked up his mobile, and eventually the girls got up to watch TV in the living room.

"Anything on your mind?" she asked dryly.

"Yeah." He screwed up his eyes, wrinkling his nose. "Yeah, there is actually. I've got a bloody complaint on my hands to deal with."

"Oh?"

"One of the women in the office," he went on. "Harassment."

Janie paused, midway through pouring beans into the coffee machine, and turned to look at the back of her husband's head. "Harassment?" she repeated.

He glanced over his shoulder. "Not me," he said. "It wasn't me. Is that what you thought?"

Janie shook her head. "No. Of course not." Though the thought *had* been there, if only for a moment. She let out her breath and wondered why her husband had chosen a Saturday morning to bring it up with her, when it must have been playing on his mind through the week.

Harry continued to regard her curiously, until she looked away.

"No," he said firmly, "it's Mike Lewis."

"*Mike's* harassing someone?" Janie asked. "What's he done?"

"*Supposedly* done," Harry said, as if she of all people should know there were two sides to every story.

Yes, she had wanted to reply, *but there's no smoke without fire*. She of all people knew that, too.

"Anyway." He pulled himself up, as if he realized himself he had sounded like an arse. "It's nothing sexual, as far as I'm aware. He's just treating this particular girl as if she's—" Harry waved an arm in the air as he searched for the right word. "I don't know, not worthy of being there or something, apparently. Thing is, I have to do something about it now, don't I?"

"Woman," Janie corrected. "She's a woman, not a girl. And yes. Of course you do."

"But it's Mike. We all know what Mike's like. He doesn't mean anything by it. He's just direct, old-school."

"'Old-school'? You mean he doesn't know how to talk to women," she replied. "He's rude," Janie went on. "I talk to him, and he responds to you."

"He's shy, awkward, I don't know," Harry argued. "But he's not a bully."

"So what is she saying Mike's actually done?"

Harry shrugged. "I thought it was all going to go away when Mia mentioned it earlier in the week," he started, making Janie clench that he could think that was the right outcome. "I've asked Mia to get the girl to write down some specifics, which it seems she now wants to talk about next week." He held up his phone as if it were evidence of the fact. "It all seems so bloody vague to me." He bowed his head in his hands, then ruffled them through his hair. "I think I'll go and have a shower. This is the last thing I need right now."

Janie shook her head, biting her lip as she handed him an espresso, which he downed in one gulp. To Harry, brushing over the fact that Mike could be a little bit odd and in some ways completely out of order was easier than having to have a conversation with the guy who'd been working with him for the last five years.

"I don't know what to do about it," he admitted as he dropped his cup into the sink. "I have the feeling Mia Anderson isn't going to let up."

"Why don't you know what to do about it?" Janie asked. "Surely you need to address whatever the woman is saying."

"That's the point, really," he said. "She doesn't seem to be too—" He broke off. "I called her into my office to talk, and she just clammed up."

"Probably because she's scared," Janie said. "Imagine what it must be like being pulled into the chief exec's office, regardless of what it's about. Add on top of that it's something personal—you're asking her about someone she probably thinks you're mates with."

"I'm not mates with Mike." He looked up at her. "Mike's a fool. You know what I think of him."

Yes, she did. Mike Lewis would never be one of Harry's boys. "I know that, but she's not going to."

"You think that's what it is—she's scared?"

"I'm sure of it."

"God." He rubbed his hands over his eyes. "This could turn into a right mess. Mia mentioned a 'bullying culture,'" he said, forming his fingers into quotation marks. "I mean, seriously, I've never had anything like this; there's no *bullying culture* in the company." He spat the words almost sarcastically.

Janie stiffened. She didn't like where this was going. She had seen it time and time again. It's what had brought people to her, to defend them when ultimately things had gone too far.

During her career, Janie had defended men in court who had been accused of harassment or worse. There were often blurred lines, one person's word against another, little evidence. Sometimes it made her job easy. She could get them off on a technicality when there was no hard evidence. But a bullying culture? When more than one person was on the attack? That could destroy Harry.

"Janie, I need your help, love. You need to tell me what to do."

Oh no, she thought. *No, no, no.* She had done her fair share of standing up for the big boys, helping them get away with whatever they'd been accused of. Ultimately it meant someone who'd been hurt hadn't seen justice.

She could give Harry plenty of advice, but if there were an issue in his company, he couldn't ignore it, could he?

Damn you, Harry, she thought as she watched him leave the kitchen for his shower, no doubt content that when he came back she'd help him gloss over his problem. He really did have no idea how her last case had broken her, but at the same time she couldn't stand by and watch her husband ruined.

Janie knew what was likely to happen. The woman who had made the complaint would likely be gone in the next few weeks, but it didn't mean the problem would go away.

She wondered whether Mia Anderson was the type of person who wouldn't let up, as Harry had suggested, and Janie made a decision. She was going to ask Mia out to lunch.

chapter seventeen

It was a sunny Saturday when Laura's parent group of five couples and their young babies met for a picnic. Nancy had been the one to set up the meet, had chosen a spot in Brockenhurst, by the river where they could park nearby and go for a walk. It was organized to perfection, but that was Nancy, she never left anything to chance.

For the next two days Laura had Bobby and Nate to herself, and she was going to make the most of this precious family time. "We could stop at a pub for dinner on the way home," she suggested as Nate drove through the New Forest. "We haven't been out to eat for so long." Laura couldn't even remember the last time they hadn't sat on the sofa and eaten in front of the TV. The thought of ordering off a menu and having a large glass of chilled white wine at the end of the day already felt exciting.

"Let's just see how it goes, shall we?" Nate murmured. "Bobby's got a cold, and I'm shattered, Laura."

She flipped her head back against the seat rest and turned to look out the window. "We won't be late. I meant we can go at five-ish, on the way home."

"We're out for lunch already."

Laura sighed.

"Look, I'm just saying let's see, that's all. We don't have to plan the whole day."

I do, she wanted to say. Because the thought of going home after the picnic that she wasn't particularly bothered about going to depressed her for some reason. "I'm working all week and I just want a treat," she muttered. She didn't want the weekend to pass and for Monday to come around and for them not to have done as much as they could. "I thought you'd be happy to get out of the house."

Nate glanced at her out of the corner of his eye.

"What?"

"Nothing," he muttered. "It's fine. If you really want to go out, we'll go out."

"I do, Nate. I'm sorry, I just want to forget about this shitty week. Oh look, there they are." She pointed at the group gathered between the parking lot and the river. "How come they're set up already, what time did Nancy say to arrive?"

Laura glanced at her watch. They weren't late, but still she wondered how the rest of them managed to have gotten there and laid out their checked rugs, coolers placed strategically on the corners to stop the babies from crawling too far or just to keep the rugs held down. For a moment she wondered if she'd gotten the time wrong. All the women were sitting in a huddle, chatting, the men standing. Dave had popped open a can of beer; likely he had another cooler full of them. In the time she'd known them all, Dave had never once assumed anything other than the fact his wife, Chrissie, would be driving him home.

Nate pulled into a space in the gravel parking lot beside Nancy's Audi, and Laura took a deep breath. "This actually feels a bit weird," she admitted. "I haven't seen any of them in ages." She waved back at Nancy, whose arms swung wildly in the air.

"They're your friends," Nate said. "This shouldn't be weird."

They weren't particularly her friends, but she didn't say as much as she stepped out of the car. They had been good to have around in the late months of pregnancy and in the early weeks after birth, but they were more like acquaintances now, their varied views on parenting having driven an unspoken wedge between them. Ever since she'd told them she was returning to Morris and Wood, she'd felt herself edging farther apart from this group of mothers, who'd always managed to make her feel like they were doing a better job than she was.

She stood by Nate as he reached into the back for their sleeping son and asked Nancy as she came over, "Are we late?"

"Oh, not at all. You're right on time." Nancy gave them both a kiss on the cheek, stroking Bobby gently on the head. "We just said at Baby Swim yesterday that if it was a nice morning we'd come down earlier, you know, make the most of the lovely weather."

And there it was. The first reminder that the other four women still met every week when Laura was at work. Even though she knew Nancy wasn't the type to do it intentionally, Laura felt a pang of estrangement. Of being an outsider.

"Do you want me to get the buggy out?" Laura asked Nate. "He could probably do with the sleep."

"Oh, what a shame," Kay called out from the rug from which she hadn't moved. "Joe's looking forward to playing with Bobby. Him being the only other man here." She laughed.

Of course he isn't looking forward to doing anything of the sort, Laura thought. *Because he's only seven months old.* But she smiled and said, "Yes, boys have to stick together." She didn't bother getting the buggy out and instead ushered Nate toward the mat, where he put Bobby down and watched him sit unsteadily on his plump nappy before toppling onto his side.

"Oh, bless him!" Chrissie said. "He's still not sitting yet? Little poppet."

"Not yet," Laura said through gritted teeth, as she resisted the urge to reach out a fist and punch Chrissie in the face. Out of all of them, she was the one Laura no longer liked. Chrissie managed to get a jab in at every opportunity, and it amazed Laura how the others put up with it.

Laura had passed a comment to Nancy once, asking if she'd noticed the way Chrissie was always so competitive, but even Nancy brushed it off and said Chrissie didn't mean anything by it, it was just the way she was.

That was the trouble with this group. She didn't know any of them well enough to be honest. Even Nancy. She didn't feel like she could take her to one side and open up to her. And it was only going to get worse now that she had returned to work. The others would continue to meet, their lives would go on without her. She could see that soon she and Nate would only be invited to these gatherings out of politeness.

Laura watched Nate wander over to the group of men and take a beer, laughing and slapping Dave on the back as if they were the oldest of mates. She turned back to the four women, who were discussing feeding and how the pouches of baby food were completely necessary for when you were on the go, though of course nothing could compare to making your own.

Laura didn't agree with this one bit. Bobby had only been weaned a month earlier and he was a fussy eater, and if they could avoid having to fill multiple containers with mushed-up vegetables that invariably ended up in the food waste, then all the better. She knew Nancy didn't agree, either, because on the few occasions Laura had been to her house when they had begun weaning, Nancy had been shoving Ella's Kitchen pouches into baby Lily as quick as she would take them.

But it seemed even Nancy had taken the side of the home-cooked brigade as she reached into her insulated travel bag and produced a pot of green slush, whose wholesome ingredients she reeled off for the group.

Laura's mind drifted. She hadn't had anything to do with the picnic. Nate had been in charge of pulling it together because he'd been the one to go shopping yesterday. Instead she found herself listening in to the men's chatter, which involved nothing to do with weaning or crawling or growth percentile charts, and began to wish they hadn't bothered coming in the first place.

It was some time after they'd all eaten, when Dave had drunk at least seven cans of beer (Laura hadn't intended to count them, but his intake had captured her interest), that the men and women eventually started mixing up, and she found herself talking to Nancy and her husband. For a while Laura enjoyed the conversation that centered around things other than babies, but every so often her ears would prick up at something one of the other mums was saying to Nate.

"You're doing so well," Chrissie was saying. "Honestly, Laura mentioned that you'd put the picnic together, too."

She heard Nate laugh, as her insides knotted. For God's sake, why was it so hard to contemplate him making a bloody picnic?

"Oh, you really are." Kay had joined in. "And Bobby looks so happy. Do you not want to go back to work at all, then, Nate?"

"I'm good with what we've arranged," Laura heard him say. "But yeah, I guess I'm missing it a bit. My boss emailed this week and asked if I wanted to pick up some part-time work at home, so you know . . ." Laura turned and watched him shrug. This was news to her. He hadn't mentioned any work, or the fact he was missing it.

"Well, I think you're an absolute star. I mean, what a godsend for Laura to come home and have her dinner cooked every night, too."

She heard him chuckle again, and her insides clenched tighter. What the hell? Wasn't that all they did for their own husbands? It was only what had been expected of all of them since their babies were two weeks old and paternity leaves finished.

When she and Nate got into the car to drive home, she turned to him. "You're an absolute star," she said, cocking her head, rolling her eyes. "Can you believe she actually said that?"

"Well, I am." He grinned.

"Obviously, but I mean, why does she think it's so bloody impossible for you to do exactly what she does every day?"

"Maybe she just thinks men are lesser beings, so she's surprised I'm able to do more than one task in a day."

"That's not what she meant, and you know it," Laura muttered. "She was having a dig. Again."

"I don't think she was," he sighed. "You're imagining things that aren't there."

"I'm not, Nate. Everyone is judging us. Judging *me*, more to the point."

"You know it isn't just you," he said, perhaps a little more harshly than he intended, since he looked a bit sheepish as he turned to her. "I get judged, too. You don't think the men question me about when I'm going to go back to work, because surely I'm only doing this for a few weeks as I can't want to do it forever. I know what they think, Laura. That being a stay-at-home dad is second to going out and earning the money, because that's what men should be doing. I get judged as well, I just don't let it get to me all the time like you do."

"You never said anything."

"I know. Because I don't let it bother me. Because all that's important is you, me, and Bobby, and doing what's right for us as a family."

"And this is what's right?"

"Of course." He gave a sideways glance. "Don't you think so?"

Laura shrugged. "You didn't tell me your boss had been in touch."

"It was nothing. He just called earlier this week and ran an idea by me. Asked if I'd consider doing some work from home. We didn't agree to anything."

"And? Do you want to?"

"I don't know. I mean, we'd need to make sure it fits in with taking care of Bobby, but I guess it could be good."

Laura sighed and turned to look out the passenger window.

"What is it?" Nate asked.

"Nothing's as I expected it would be," she admitted, willing the tears not to spring to her eyes as they threatened to do. "I thought going back to Morris and Wood would feel the same as before, but it doesn't. I don't feel like I have a place there."

"Laura, it's bound to feel odd. You have a baby, you're a mum. Life's changed."

She shook her head. "It's not that," she said in a tight whisper. "It's not got anything to do with being a mum. I feel like . . ."

"Like what?" Nate prompted.

"Like I've been replaced. By someone younger, who's not doing the job any better than I am, except that everyone else thinks she is."

"Laura, you need to let this go," Nate said.

She turned to him sharply.

"You've still got a massive job that's taking up most hours of the day as it is," he went on. "We barely see you all week. Maybe Harry's done the right thing and given you some space. I can't even imagine when you'll get home if you get Coopers back. Laura, maybe you just need to accept that this is the way it should be for now."

"Nate, I can't even believe you're saying that. You *know* what this means to me. You know how much I put into that account."

"I do know that, I do. But you have to step back and look at the wider picture. If you start fighting this, then are things really going to be any better? Sure, you might get your account back, but then what? How many extra hours will you have to put in?"

"I can do it," she said, though her words came out in a whisper.

"I think something else would have to give, and—"

"Something *else*?" she asked. "You think something already has?"

"I'm just saying I honestly don't know how you'd be able to do it. I don't begrudge you working, Laura, you know that. I've *never* stopped you. But I don't want you missing out on Bobby, either. It would just be nice to see a bit more of you in the evenings."

Laura looked away. It was impossible. She was in a no-win situation. "I know I could make it work," she persisted. "I just want to be given the chance to prove it."

"I don't know why you're getting so worked up about it," Nate snapped.

"Argh! I know you don't!" she cried. "I know you don't understand, even though I'm trying to get you to, but don't worry about it. It's fine. I'll work it through on my own." She flung her hands in the air in surrender.

Nate let out a short laugh and shook his head as he turned toward his window.

"You've no idea how much she's affecting me, Nate," Laura went on, wiping her hand across her eyes. "She makes me feel *useless*." She stared at her husband, waiting for him to respond until it became clear he wasn't going to.

Laura folded her arms and scrunched herself up as she turned her head away from him and closed her eyes. Something had to give. And if she were going to carry on working, which she couldn't feasibly see a way out of, then she wasn't going to sit back and let Mia keep doing her job.

The more Laura wound herself into knots about Mia, the more she had the unnerving feeling that there was much more to the woman than she realized. And in that moment she became resolute that in the morning she was going to start finding out who she was and where she had come from. And she wasn't going to stop until she did, because Laura didn't trust one word that came out of Mia Anderson's mouth.

"You still want to go out later?" Nate asked eventually.

She shook her head. "No."

"Come on, let's not ruin our day." He reached over and squeezed her hand. "We can do whatever you fancy."

"It's fine," she said. "Really. You're right, Bobby could do with going home; he doesn't sound well." She glanced over at her son in the back and reached out for his chubby arm.

"Maybe we should look into babysitters again soon," he said. "Go out on our own instead?"

"We'll need one for Harry's party," Laura muttered. "He mentioned it during the week. It's five weeks away now."

"How about asking Louise's daughter across the road?" Nate asked. "She's about fifteen. Wouldn't she do it?"

"We don't know her," Laura said. "I don't want just anyone looking after him."

"She isn't just anyone." Nate laughed. "She's a neighbor. Anyway, no point worrying about it, if it's going to be a problem you can always go on your own," he went on. "Though it would be nice to come out with you."

"No. I want you there," Laura said. "I'm definitely not going to go on my own. We've got a few weeks to sort something out. Hopefully by then some amazing Mary Poppins of a babysitter will fly into the area, but if she doesn't, I won't go. I'm not actually that fussed about it anyway."

"You're a wonderful mummy, you know that? And the most amazing wife. Me and that little man in the back would be lost without you."

Her eyes welled with tears again. "I know," she sighed. "And I'm sorry for getting annoyed. I really don't know what I'd do without either of you."

chapter eighteen

On Monday morning Laura opened up her PC and found the number for a woman called Katie Burton. She tapped it into her mobile and strolled over to a spare meeting room, where she closed the door behind her so she wouldn't be overheard.

It didn't take long for her to answer. "Hello? Katie speaking."

"Hi, Katie," Laura started. "My name is Laura Denning and I work at Morris and Wood. I'm hoping you can help me. I'm calling about someone who used to work for you."

"Oh?"

"You gave me a reference for her a few months ago. I was wondering if you might be able to give me a bit more insight."

"Okay. Well, I'll see what I can do. I mean, this isn't the channel we'd usually adopt."

"Yes, I realize, and thank you. I'd just like a bit more information."

"Who are you calling about?"

"Her name's Mia Anderson. I believe she temped for you. She left seven months ago now, so you might not remember—"

"I remember Mia."

"Oh, okay, great. Then—"

"But she wasn't a temp," Katie said. "I don't know what gave you that impression; I'm sure it wouldn't have been anything in the reference?"

"I assumed she was," Laura replied. "Because she was coming for a temporary role here. I thought she'd said as much in her interview too," she went on, though now she couldn't actually recall if Mia had or not. Whether she'd just been led to think it, and even if she had, did it make a difference?

"No. Mia was permanent. Can I ask why you're calling me? What it is you actually want to know?"

"I just—" Laura broke off. "I suppose I was wondering if there was anything more you could tell me about her."

"Has something happened?" Katie asked.

"No. Not specifically."

"Then I'm sorry, this isn't protocol. I don't know what you're fishing for, but I gave Mia's reference—"

"I know, I know that," Laura said, desperate for Katie not to cut her off. "And I also know I shouldn't be calling you, but I wanted to do this off the record. I wouldn't be phoning if I didn't think there was an issue, and I'm sorry I can't tell you more, but please, can you tell me if there's anything at all I should be worried about?"

There was a beat before Katie answered. "Her leaving," she said.

"What?" It was the last thing Laura expected to hear.

"Her leaving you high and dry like she did us. Mia had just received a promotion. A good one, by all accounts, that I'd let six other applicants down on, and then one day she just called in sick and never came back."

As Laura listened, she could tell how much Katie was still annoyed by this.

"She didn't end up working her four weeks' notice because of it, and I had wondered at the time if it was because she'd found another job. But then when I didn't get asked for a reference—or at least not until at least two months later—I didn't think she had."

Laura shook her head, trying to think back. Katie was right, they hadn't asked for a reference for ages because Laura'd suddenly gone on maternity leave and Rebecca from HR had left and everything was so up in the air. It *was* a good two months before anyone had gotten around to sorting it.

"I was worried about her." Katie let out a small laugh. "But then when I knew she'd gotten another job, I guess I thought no more of it, I just . . . I don't know what I thought, really. I was too caught up in recruiting our role again, I suppose."

"It doesn't make sense," Laura said. "Why would she give up a good promotion, a permanent role, for a temporary job?"

Katie didn't respond.

"Don't you think it's odd?" Laura persisted. "It doesn't make sense, does it?" she repeated. Though of course there was one explanation. Mia had her sights set on something else. Something in particular. Laura's job. And for some reason she was willing to risk her career because she wanted Laura's.

"You're right, it doesn't," Katie said eventually.

Laura hung up the call and wandered out into the office, scanning the floor until she found Mia lingering by the far window, her hand resting on Henrietta James's arm. Her loud bursts of laughter rang out sharply above the murmured conversations, until everything around Laura muffled into one blurred buzzing that rang through her ears.

Mia was befriending these women as if she were making herself indispensable, and it was all Laura could do to stop herself from running across the office and demanding to know why she was there, because she didn't like it. She didn't like it one bit.

"There you are."

Laura turned sharply as Harry walked toward her, his jacket on, one hand tucked in his jeans pocket.

"You ready?"

"Ready?"

He hung his head questioningly, flicking up his wrist, which in turn made his gold Rolex flash in the light. "It's quarter to eleven, Laura. We need to get going if we want to walk to the quay."

"But I thought—" Laura pressed the button on her phone to check the time. "I thought we were meeting at eleven thirty."

Harry shook his head. "Eleven." He nodded toward her desk. "You better grab your stuff. Don't want to leave Miles waiting."

"Shit, okay, give me a minute," she said, as Harry jostled anxiously from one foot to the other. He was clearly keen to make a good impression on this old friend of his.

"Baby brain!" Harry joked as she walked away, making a few of the nearby staff chuckle and Laura shudder. She glared at them and then back at him and wondered how she was going to focus on impressing Miles Morgan when she was so wrapped up in Mia and what the hell she was doing here.

Initial Interview between Detective Emily Marlow and Nathan Denning following the fire at Morris and Wood offices on Monday, May 13.

<u>Nathan (Nate) Denning, on Tuesday, May 14, at Lymington Police Headquarters.</u>

Marlow: Nate, I know you say you and your wife didn't speak when she finally came home last night, but did she tell you anything about the fire at the Morris and Wood offices?

Nate: No! Of course not. You're saying that like you think she knew about it. How would she?

Marlow: She didn't say that she'd seen it?

Nate: No! She got a call this morning.

Marlow: Were you there when she received the call?

Nate: Yes. I was with her in the kitchen.

Marlow: And you believe that was the first she had heard of it?

Nate: Of course—yes. Of course it was. I don't understand. What is this about?

Marlow: How was your wife when she heard the news?

Nate: Well, I don't know—she was shocked. Sorry, I really don't get what you're suggesting. Are you saying Laura was lying? That the phone call was all one big act or something?

Marlow: We both know it wouldn't be the first time she's lied to you in the last twenty-four hours.

Nate: She wasn't *lying* about the fire.

Marlow: Can you tell me what her relationship is like with Janie Wood? Are they friends?

Nate: Janie? Harry's wife? No, not especially. I don't think Laura has any relationship with her, why?

Marlow: What's Laura like with her friends, do you know? Is she a very loyal person? The type who would do anything for them?

Nate: Her friends? I don't understand. I mean, she's got a few close ones from school and university that she still sees, but—sorry, what's this got to do with anything?

Marlow: Nate, we have reason to believe your wife knows a lot more about the fire last night than she's letting on. And the best thing she can do for herself is to start talking, because I have a feeling she might be covering up for someone.

Nate: No way. My wife wouldn't do that. She wouldn't risk that, she—Christ! Listen, she barely has anything to do with anyone in that office. She's not *friends* with them.

Marlow: Right. But you said earlier she was "obsessed" with someone in the office once—before Mia, that is. Tell me about this person.

Nate: Saskia? (shakes head) This was two, maybe three years ago. A long time. Laura and she were good friends, but then they had a falling out. Really, what's that got to do with any of this?

Marlow: Humor me. What happened to Saskia?

Nate: (sighs) Saskia's boyfriend worked at Morris and Wood, too, but Laura found out he was being laid off. She didn't tell Saskia it was happening. That was all. Laura was more senior than Saskia, I think Saskia even reported to her. It was confidential information, and Laura decided she couldn't say anything.

Marlow: By the sounds of it, Laura did the right thing.

Nate: She did. Only Saskia didn't see it that way, and they fell out. And then things took a turn for the worse, and Laura was convinced Saskia was out to get her.

Marlow: Out to get her in what way?

Nate: She thought she was trying to destroy her career, spreading gossip about . . . I don't recall all the ins and outs of it, but Laura was certain Saskia was setting her up. But like I keep telling you, whatever's happened with Mia, it has absolutely nothing to do with the fire. My wife's not capable of anything like that.

Marlow: You said Laura isn't friends with anyone in the office anymore.

Nate: That's right, as far as I know. After Saskia, Laura found it hard to trust anyone for a while, and certainly at work she didn't—I don't know, she doesn't talk about it, but I don't think she has any real friends there. I don't think she wants to get too close to anyone.

Marlow: That's also the impression I get from talking to her and the other staff. But for me that leaves only one other option. If she's not covering up for anyone for the fire, then—

Nate: Then what, Detective?

Marlow: Then did she do it herself?

chapter nineteen

It was only half an hour after Harry and Laura had left the office when Mia saw Janie Wood appear on the floor. She was immaculately dressed in beige tailored trousers, cropped to skim her ankles, a long-sleeved white shirt, and an oversized purse weighing down her shoulder. Large sunglasses were pushed to the top of her head, and she looked like she'd stepped out of a magazine rather than the office lift.

Mia paused what she was doing and watched Janie out of the corner of her eye. Janie rarely came to the office, and whenever she did she'd head straight for Harry's office and briefly speak to her husband behind his closed door before walking straight back out again. She obviously didn't know he wasn't here, and yet today Janie was lingering by the lift as if she were looking for someone else instead.

Janie Wood. The woman had made her life so public with her magazine appearances, and yet even in the articles, Mia could see she didn't look comfortable with it. She didn't have the look of someone who was happy the cameras were snapping the inside of their house, with its glossy cream kitchen and plump, oversized sofas, draped in throws.

Mia had pored over those pictures as she'd sat at the small round table in her mother's kitchen, with its deep-red beetroot stain ingrained into the cheap wood, and thought how their lives were a million miles apart, and yet there Mia was, working like a dog with nothing to show for it, while Janie swanned around, spending her husband's wealth, no doubt his Black card cushioned in a designer wallet somewhere in that purse of hers. The disparity was almost immeasurable.

Janie was walking toward her, and Mia felt herself stiffen. They had spoken on a few occasions, but it was always stilted and clumsy, or at least on Mia's part, because she'd never been prepared to see her or known what to say.

"Mia?" Janie's soft voice had a slight lilt to it. "Have you got a moment?"

"Of course." Mia beamed back at her, running her hands down the front of her jeans.

"I just wondered if you had time for a quick lunch? On me, of course," she added.

"Erm . . ." The invitation took her by surprise, and Mia was immediately flustered, because why on earth would Janie Wood want to take her to lunch, unless there was a specific reason, and if there was—

"We don't have to be long," she was saying. "I'm sure you're very busy."

"I, er . . ." *Come on, Mia, say something*, she berated herself, because on one hand it felt like all her Christmases had come at once that she could be lunching with Janie Wood, but on the other—why was she?

"I just thought we could have a chat. I feel bad I haven't done it before. You've been here months already," Janie said.

She sounded genuine enough, but it didn't feel like a strong enough reason to want to take her out to lunch, and if that was the case, then Mia wondered what Janie's ulterior motive was. When she replied, "That sounds lovely, and you don't have to feel bad," she felt uneasy.

They agreed to meet at a sandwich bar on Lymington High Street in half an hour. Somewhere away from the quay, Mia realized. As if there was every likelihood Janie wanted to keep Harry in the dark about what was beginning to feel like a clandestine meeting.

"Harry doesn't know I'm here," Janie said, confirming Mia's suspicions as they ordered their sandwiches and sat down. She shrugged sheepishly like it was no big deal, though Mia wondered whether it was.

"Do you think he'd mind?" Mia asked.

"Oh no—" Janie waved her hand through the air, and Mia shifted in her seat as she waited to find out the purpose of their lunch.

Janie was asking her how she was getting on, what she thought of the job, and so Mia told her she liked it as she picked the cress out of her egg sandwich. She noticed Janie hadn't touched the wrap that sat intact on her plate.

"How do you find everyone?"

The sudden thought crossed Mia's mind that Janie could be here to ask about her husband and Laura Denning, and it was such a relief that the reason could be something that didn't involve her that she let out a deep breath before plunging the sandwich into her mouth. She had no idea how she'd answer if Janie did ask outright, although the woman was already moving on.

"So where do you come from?" Janie asked, squinting her eyes as if she were trying to place her.

"Lymington, actually," she said. "I was born here. I grew up here."

"Oh really?"

Mia nodded.

"It's such a beautiful place, isn't it? Do you have a family?"

Mia assumed she meant children and so shook her head.

"No one nearby?" Janie asked.

Mia put her sandwich back on the plate and swallowed the mouthful. "Just my mum," she told her, the omission weighing heavily. It wasn't the first time she'd dismissed her sister as if she didn't even exist.

"You must know all about the development of the offices, then?" Janie asked. "If you've both always lived here?"

"My mum told me bits about it when it was being built." Mia hadn't show any interest in the building of the offices at the time. She had wondered why her mum had been so interested in it when there were clearly more pressing issues their family should be focusing on. Maybe it had been nothing more than a distraction.

But it seemed Janie wasn't remotely bothered about Mia's opinion on the office build and instead plowed on with questions about her personal life. Where did she work before she joined Morris and Wood? Had she always been in marketing?

Mia's responses were short and flat. She knew how she must be coming across, but what did it matter? They were never going to be friends. Their lunch date felt like an interview, and she was still trying to fathom what she was doing there when Janie insisted she would pick up the bill as promised and began pushing herself out of her seat to leave.

It was as they were walking to the door that Janie suddenly paused and said, "Harry tells me there's an issue with Mike Lewis."

Mia could have laughed. So that was it. Janie wanted to find out what was happening so she could tell her husband how to handle it. So she could find a loophole for him to worm his way out of the issues he didn't want to face. Mia had guessed Harry would use his wife to help him, but she was determined to create such a watertight case that even someone like Janie Wood wouldn't be able break it.

"There is, but I'm not comfortable discussing it. It's not about me," Mia told her.

She waited, but Janie merely nodded and said, "Well, Mia, I hope you do the right thing."

Then Janie kissed her on the cheek and told her it was lovely to see her and that she hoped Mia was coming to her party.

Mia watched Janie walk off down the street, her relief that Janie wanted to discuss the issue of Mike with her already dissipating, usurped by something else entirely, and as she closed her eyes and inhaled a deep breath, Mia realized it was fear. Janie had left her on edge. The questioning by a clever woman with Janie Wood's background. How long would it be until someone found out exactly what Mia was doing at Morris and Wood?

––––––––––

Janie walked down the street to where she had parked her car and went over the strange conversation in her head. She had wanted to meet with Mia because of what Harry had told her. Yet for some reason she'd felt drawn to the younger woman, and she sensed that she could do with someone inside the company who could tell her what it was really like in Harry's castle.

Mia seemed to have her head screwed on the right way. She'd always appeared so much more open and friendly than Laura Denning. Janie had noticed it when she'd been in the office before. She had watched Mia from inside of Harry's glass office and seen her laughing and joking with the other women.

And yet their brief lunch had surprised Janie. Mia was nothing at all what she had expected. Janie had always prided herself on seeing people, on cutting through the thick outer layers that sometimes cloaked the reality beneath. It was what had made her good at her job. She rarely misread anyone—Miles Morgan had been an exception.

Anyone with Janie's knowledge of fashion would see immediately that Mia's Gucci was a fake, and that the rose-gold bangles that hung around her wrist were the same ones Ella had recently bought from a cheap accessory shop.

In contrast to the bubbly woman she had previously witnessed, today Mia was reserved, to the point of being on edge. And when Janie had asked her about her family life, nothing more than anyone would do when trying to get to know someone, she got one distinct impression: Mia Anderson was holding something back.

chapter twenty

Laura and Harry were meeting Miles in the Star pub, which had pride of place on Lymington Quay. As soon as they walked in he stood up and held up a hand in greeting, and Laura had to force herself to keep walking. Miles had to be at least six foot two. He was wearing a gray woolen jacket, with a gray V-necked sweater and open-necked shirt under that. Out of his jacket pocket peeked a blue silk handkerchief. His whole look was mesmerizing, and yet he managed not to look overdressed for the pub.

Like Harry, Miles had dark gray hair that was styled into a quiff, and a closely cropped beard, and Laura couldn't take her eyes off him. She followed Harry, who was clasping the man's hand with both of his own. From the beginning it was apparent the two men went way back, but she guessed they hadn't seen each other in a while, since they told each other how good it was to finally catch up again. Eventually Harry stepped to the side and introduced her.

Laura reached out to shake Miles's hand as he leaned forward and kissed her cheek, and despite herself, she was pleased that she'd added another dab of Chanel before leaving the office.

"Laura. It's good to meet you," Miles said. His steely blue eyes didn't leave hers. They seemed to twinkle as he smiled, and it was only after he finally pulled away that she told herself to get it together.

He offered to get them both a drink, but Harry insisted drinks were on him, and she watched her boss walk to the bar. He was a good three inches shorter than Miles and next to him looked slight, so different from his usual presence that filled a room. Put them both together and you would automatically look past. Harry, and Laura considered that Harry must know this. She wondered how he felt about it.

"Have a seat." Miles smiled and pulled one out for Laura, his hand lingering on the back of it as she sat down. As soon as Harry came back to the table, the two men began chatting easily, names thrown back and forth, some she thought she might have heard, others she hadn't a clue about, and at no point had she been able to do much more than sit there cradling her lemonade, listening to the conversation like a spare part they'd both forgotten about.

"I'm so sorry, Laura," Miles eventually said, breaking off. "You must think we're rude. I always hate it when my girlfriend gets together with her old friends from school and I can't join in the conversation."

Laura noticed the way he said, "girlfriend" like he was proud of the fact he wasn't married, even though she figured he was easily in his late forties.

"Harry and I haven't seen each other in, what—how long has it been, Harry?" he continued.

"Five and a half years," Harry said without missing a beat, raising his eyebrows as he did, which made Laura wonder if there was a partic- ular reason why Harry knew it was exactly five and a half years since they'd last met.

Miles nodded. "Doesn't time go?" His lips were pursed, his expres- sion more somber than it had been. Laura was desperate to ask what memory had flashed into both their heads, stopping them in their tracks, taking them back to a time she wasn't sure either of them were keen to go to.

"So you're looking for someone to launch your new brand," Harry said, pulling himself together, leaning back in his chair and crossing one leg over the other. He ran his fingers up and down the seam of his suit trousers, a habit of old that Laura knew from the number of times she'd watched him do it.

"That's right, and so of course I thought of you."

"Miles here has broken out on his own." Harry turned to Laura. "Banking, financial products."

"And about time too." Miles laughed, causing Harry to laugh along with him, only she was more intrigued by their interchange now, and suddenly wondered how easy Harry actually felt in his company.

Harry was pressing forward in his seat again. "Well, I can't say how pleased I was to hear from you again. You know I'd be thrilled for the two of us to work together."

"I'm glad to hear it, Harry." Miles beamed. Then he turned toward Laura. "And I believe you're the woman for the job." Miles put his beer down, carefully squaring the coaster beneath it as he leaned her way. "I'm looking for someone who can put her heart and soul into it, Laura. We're talking budgets in excess of three million for TV alone."

She held her breath. This was three times the amount Coopers was spending on their TV campaign. Harry was right. If they won this pitch and Miles's business, it would be huge. She had little experience in financial services, and none in start-up banking, but she could learn.

"So what do you think, Laura? I take it Harry's told you all about the business."

"He has. And I can do whatever it takes," she replied.

Miles nodded. "We have tight deadlines. For a start, we want our first TV ad to air sometime in September."

"That soon?" she asked.

Miles nodded. "Think you can do it?"

"I mean, it's a very tight time frame," she said. "I don't—" She paused, glancing at Harry, who was looking at her encouragingly.

"Of course we can," he finished for her.

"Yes, of course." She smiled, though a number of things flashed through her head: concepts, plans, actors—there was a lot to put together in a short space of time, and that was before they even started filming and talking to the media buyers. She could already picture herself working around the clock through the long days of summer to get it done. What the hell would Nate say? How did *she* actually feel about it?

An image of Bobby sprang into her head; a flash of guilt. There was no way she could take it on, she thought, flexing her hands that were beginning to numb. But at the same time she couldn't ignore the fizz of excitement in the pit of her stomach. She hadn't experienced that feeling in a very long time.

"Of course I need you to tender for the business first. Have to do everything by the book."

There was a pause before Harry readily agreed. "Completely. Of course." She wondered if Harry hadn't been expecting this, because they both knew what it meant. Spending the next few weeks working her arse off to put together a tender that might not even get accepted. But if she didn't put in the work, they wouldn't get it. Laura hated tendering for business. It was a thin line between proving you deserved the job and working for free.

———

"See, I told you I had something up my sleeve," Harry said as they left Miles at the pub. "You think you can do it?" he asked as they walked in the direction of the office. She hadn't seen him this fired up about a new business opportunity in a long time.

Laura knew she had to tell Harry she needed time to think about it. She had to talk to Nate first, make sure he was on board with what it meant in terms of the extra work. She needed to make sure she was on board with it too. Turning down the opportunity meant she was effectively writing herself out of the game, but at the same time she didn't see enough of her son as it was. "His timescales are pretty unrealistic," she eventually said.

"Yeah. That's the problem with Miles . . ." Harry trailed off until he finally added, "He won't budge. And if it isn't us, he'll take his money elsewhere. Quite frankly, it's too much to lose." He stopped and turned to Laura. "I don't need to tell you how good it would be for you to take it on. But I mean it when I say if you don't think you can handle this right now I completely understand. You've got enough on your plate, and I've got other people I can ask who don't have babies they need to think of—"

"No," she interrupted, knowing exactly who he'd have in mind. There was no way she was going to give this opportunity over to Mia Anderson. "I'll do it."

"That's my girl." He grinned, and as they carried on walking back to the office, Laura tried to shut out the voices in her head that were screaming at her she'd done the wrong thing. That were asking her how the hell she thought she'd be able to break this to Nate.

chapter twenty-one

On Thursday night, with no school clubs to attend, Janie made the last-minute decision to take the girls to the quay for hot chocolates on the way home. Now she was watching as they dropped crab lines, bacon clinging to the ends of them, over the side and into the water. They hadn't meant to stay long, but when they had passed the gift shop Lottie had seen the crab nets and begged her to buy them.

Janie had been surprised to see Ella almost as excited as her sister. It was the first time in weeks she'd reverted to the little girl Janie feared she was losing. It wasn't long until Ella would finish primary school, and what was going to happen beyond that didn't bear thinking about. Phones, WhatsApp groups, retreating into her bedroom every evening . . . Janie wanted to hang on to their childhood days for as long as she could, and if it meant crabbing with her girls instead of arguing with them over homework, then that was what she would do.

Ella was bouncing from foot to foot, screeching at Lottie to pull her net up. In turn her younger sister stepped back, laughing as she pointed out a tiny crab, which Ella helped her upturn into the bucket with a plop, making them both laugh harder. Janie smiled and stroked Lottie's dark-brown hair that hung down her back in a long plait. The sun had warmed it and it felt comforting to the touch. She could feel her youngest pressing into her hand, the way she always did when Janie played with her hair.

Lottie was nothing like Ella. Ella had outgrown the desire to be touched in any way since she was five. Even in reception Janie had barely set foot on the playground when already Ella had run off to chat to her teachers or join a group of older girls. Lottie was the one who had continued to stay by her side, holding on to her top, not wanting her to go.

"Are we going to throw the crabs back in at the end?" Lottie asked.

"Of course we are," Ella told her. "What do you think we're going to do, take them home and eat them?"

"You can eat crab," Lottie replied. "Daddy does, doesn't he, Mummy?"

"He does, darling, but Mummy won't be taking any crabs home to cook tonight." Or any other night, she thought, grimacing at the bucket.

"You could call Daddy," Ella said, helping her sister dip the line over the edge of the quay again. "You could ask him to come and meet us."

Janie glanced up at the office building, squinting against the reflection of the sun on its windows, already low in the sky. Her husband was inside, oblivious to the fact that his family was on the other side of the water. If she called him would he come to the window and look out at them, like he'd said Mia had done a few weeks back?

Ever since their brief meet-up, Janie had been wondering about Mia and her closed behavior, and she considered how many more women there were in Harry's office that she needed to be worried about.

"Mum?" Ella had stopped and was facing her, a line dangling from one hand.

"I'll ask him," she murmured, taking her phone out of her pocket and pressing Harry's number. "He might be in a meeting," she added as the call connected, preparing her daughter for whatever excuse he'd come up with, because she knew Harry wouldn't leave work to come crabbing.

When there was no answer, she didn't leave a message. He would see he had a missed call and maybe call her back. "Sorry, girls, he must be busy." She put the phone on the wall beside her with a surprising feeling of disappointment and realized that after seeing him so engaged with the girls the other week, she'd hoped he might carve out more time to be with them. They should be his priority, like they were hers. He could be spending the evening with his family having fun that cost less than ten pounds.

Janie shifted position on the uncomfortable concrete. Maybe both their priorities were wrong, she wondered. Maybe every decision they continued to make was about money and having the best of everything. The biggest house, the most expensive swimming pool, the best education. The most spectacular office for the business.

Janie continued to look across the Lymington River at Morris and Wood. The glass windows sparkled back at her, an image of her husband behind them filling her head.

Over the years she'd wondered whether Harry realized their marriage had all gone so wrong, because after they had moved to the south coast, they hadn't discussed what had happened. Possibly he thought he'd fixed it by moving, keeping Janie in a comfortable life where she didn't need to think about going back to her job if she didn't want to. Ignoring the part he'd played in it, probably not even realizing he'd played one at all.

No, Janie didn't believe that. Harry knew, he'd just pushed it out of his head so he didn't have to confront it. He knew because she'd told him clearly enough, but all he'd said in response was, *What did you expect, Janie? What did you expect?*

She'd expected her husband to understand. To offer his support in any way, but he hadn't. He had been more invested in ensuring there was no blame laid at his door.

She was a defense lawyer, after all, so what *did* she expect? That was what Harry had meant. And in a way he was right.

Maybe if Miles Morgan hadn't ever walked through her door she wouldn't be sitting on the quay now, staring at her husband's office, wishing she was no longer married to Harry. But he had, and she had fallen for his charm and readily snapped up his case. And so what use was it to deliberate over the what-ifs? There was nothing she could do to change the past. Because that was the only place Miles was now—in her past.

Janie leaned back and sighed. Maybe she should talk to Harry. Surely he had the right to know how she felt; that one day they would not be married to each other. She continued to stare at the twinkling light of the water reflecting off the glass building and wondered what it would be like to tell her husband that she wanted a divorce.

When she looked back at the girls, the cold realization hit her that she didn't think she could do it. *But I don't love him,* she wanted to say to them. *I don't love your father.* The guilt of it made her sick. Not because of him, she realized, but because of them. Because if she ever did leave him, it would break their tiny hearts.

"Girls, let's go and get some fish and chips," she said, feigning brightness as she grabbed their hands to help them return the crabs to the water. It was six-fifteen already and she didn't want to linger any longer.

She pulled herself up, flinging her phone in her bag, and turned toward the car as a shadow flitted out of sight behind it. A shiver ran down the length of Janie's spine, and for a moment the sound of the girls behind her, chattering and gathering their buckets together, became a muffled blur.

"Mummy!" Lottie screeched, tugging her sleeve and banging the bucket into her thigh. "Can you take it for me?"

Janie turned back to them and shook her head. She was imagining it. Nothing more. No one was watching her.

Initial interview between Detective Emily Marlow and Anna Halshaw following the fire at Morris and Wood offices on Monday, May 13.

<u>**Anna Halshaw, on Thursday, May 16, at Lymington Police Headquarters.**</u>

Marlow:	Did Janie tell you she was being followed?
Anna:	(pauses) Janie was? No. God, no, not at all.
Marlow:	She tells us she had been, though it appears no one else knew about it. She hadn't told a soul.
Anna:	Who was following her?
Marlow:	We don't know for sure.
Anna:	I'm—I mean, I'm—
Marlow:	Shocked?
Anna:	Well, yes, totally. I mean, something like that—she must have been terrified. I can't believe she didn't tell me.
Marlow:	That's the thing. Don't you think it's strange that she didn't?
Anna:	I don't know what you mean.
Marlow:	Well, something as important as believing you're being watched . . . it seems odd she's only brought this up now.
Anna:	You think she's lying about it?
Marlow:	I'm asking what you think.
Anna:	No. (shakes head) No. Janie wouldn't do that. There must be a reason she kept it to herself. Janie doesn't lie.
Marlow:	Didn't she lie about where she was on Monday night, Anna? When you were babysitting for her?
Anna:	I'm sure that was a misunderstanding. I thought she'd said yoga but . . .
Marlow:	And didn't you try to get hold of her at—7:05 p.m.?
Anna:	I did, yes. Like you know.
Marlow:	And in the end you had to call Janie's husband, Harry?
Anna:	One of the children wasn't well. And it doesn't pass me by

that I might have been one of the last people to speak to him before—before . . .

Marlow: Anna, when you phoned him, you said you knew someone else was in the office with him?

Anna: That's what I told the other officer. Because I heard Harry say, *Excuse me a minute*, when he picked up. He told whoever it was that he'd take the call outside his office. I assume it was Miles Morgan. Isn't that the name of the man?

Marlow: It is. And was it just the one person with him that you know of?

Anna: (shakes head) I don't know. Why, are you—do you think Janie might have been there too?

Marlow: Anna, had Janie ever mentioned the name Miles Morgan to you before Monday night?

Anna: No. Never. Why? Did she know him?

Marlow: She did know him, yes. So she's never talked about him?

Anna: No. Who is he? Is he the person who was following her? Do you think *that* has something to do with the fire?

Marlow: That's what we are trying to ascertain. But like I said, we don't actually know what happened because it appears no one knew Janie was worried about anyone watching her.

chapter twenty-two

four weeks before the fire

C ome out for a drink with me." Harry was hovering in his doorway. Laura looked around at the empty office, glancing at the clock. Six-fifteen, she realized, her stomach dipping. It was Thursday evening, she'd been late home every night this week so far and had promised Nate she'd definitely be home by six tonight.

But Laura had been engrossed in Google. Firstly she had been looking into Miles's company, setting out thoughts to help her with the tender. At some point her search had blended into another around Mia, and for the last fifteen minutes she had been scouring Mia's sparse Facebook account as far back as 2009, when she had first joined.

It told Laura little. There was no job history, no relationship status, and recently a lack of photos altogether. In fact, in the last twelve months, Mia hadn't posted or shared a single thing.

Before that there had been a few pictures of her with friends, but nothing that gave Laura much background on her. One woman appeared more than others, a girl called Jessica Louise, a middle name used for reasons Laura couldn't fathom, unless she didn't want anyone to track her down, or possibly because of her work.

There was something about Jessica that looked vaguely familiar, something in her eyes, though Laura doubted they'd ever met, for surely that would be too much of a coincidence.

She had been so engrossed that she hadn't noticed the time or registered the office emptying. For the past four nights, since meeting Miles, Laura had been working flat out and every evening.

She sighed as she shut down the website, the one behind it appearing like a flash. The Venue. The company where Mia used to work. Laura had been looking into what jobs they'd been recruiting for in the hope she would find the one that Mia was supposed to be promoted into before she suddenly left. Only one seemed plausible: an account director with a salary twenty thousand pounds higher than Laura was being paid. And if this was the job, then it made even less sense that Mia would give it up to cover Laura's, though by now Laura was pretty certain that Mia's purpose for being here was neither the money nor the career opportunity.

Harry hovered nearby as Laura closed down her computer and turned to face him. Maybe she should tell him here and now what she'd discovered from Katie Burton, but then she could imagine his reaction. He would make her feel like she had a vendetta against Mia for no other reason than she was jealous.

No, what Laura needed was more proof, something concrete. She needed to figure out *why* Mia could be out for her.

"I really can't," she told Harry. "I didn't realize how late it is. I'm sorry, I need to get home." She'd told Nate to hold off bathing Bobby because she'd wanted to do it herself. Before she had left that morning she'd looked in on her son, listening to his sleepy murmurs, and her heart had ached to hold him close to her. She had fought tears as she stepped out of his room.

Now she was angry with herself for forgetting the time again. She'd texted Nate at six to say she would be a little late, but his response had been a curt, *Okay.* No kisses. No *I love you.* She knew he was pissed off that he barely saw her, and she also knew he thought she should be spending more time with Bobby. Which was why she still hadn't told him about the tender and the possible new account.

Laura quite literally felt like two different women—Laura the account director and Laura the mother—and she didn't know how it was possible to merge them together.

There wasn't even any room to consider Laura the wife. She had thought as much that morning when she'd slipped back into the bedroom and watched Nate roll over. She hadn't woken him, there was no need so early, especially when she'd heard him get up in the night again and go to a crying Bobby. She couldn't even say how long he'd been out of bed; she had fallen asleep again before he came back, exhausted from such long hours in the office.

Less than a month and they were becoming more like housemates than husband and wife, except for the fact they still shared a bed. Though that had been used for nothing more than sleeping in the last few weeks.

"I want to talk to you." Harry smiled at her, carrying on as if he hadn't heard her or wasn't prepared to accept no as an answer. "Just a quick one down at the quay."

"I don't know. I really need to get home."

Harry nodded, perching on the corner of her desk. "How's Nate coping without you? I've seen you working very long hours. He must miss you."

"He's coping fine," she said, maybe a little too abruptly.

"He's a good man," Harry went on. "What he's doing at home and—"

"It's no different than what Janie does," Laura said sharply. Too late she realized how it must appear that she didn't appreciate everything Nate had given up for her.

She opened her mouth again to tell Harry how much she valued Nate, but already he was speaking.

"Just one drink, Laura. Please. I need to talk to you about a few things and I promise I won't keep you late." His eyes sparkled as if he somehow already knew he would get his way.

Laura pursed her lips. Nate would not be happy one bit. She didn't want to go for a drink, she wanted to go home.

Mia's tinkling laugh rang out from the far end of the office and Harry looked over at her, shuffling off the edge of Laura's desk to stand, and suddenly Laura thought, *What if I don't go with him and he asks her instead?*

Even then it felt like a ridiculous notion, something two teenagers would worry over when they were after the same boy, but Laura also knew how much she needed to keep Harry close right now. And she could do with making sure Mia wasn't.

"Just a quick one," she said, glancing at the clock again. "I really can't be long."

She didn't miss his lopsided smile before he turned to get his jacket, and even though this was all her doing, it irritated her he'd gotten his way.

———

Harry wanted to talk about the new account. He wanted to run some ideas past her and see what she thought she could do on the tender. He suggested they have a drink at Le Bateau, a small wine bar off the cobbled path that led down to the quay. Laura asked for a lemonade, but Harry came back to the table with two glasses of Sancerre. She screwed up her nose at him but took a sip anyway.

"You can't come to a place like this and not have wine," he said, and leaned forward as he started talking business.

"You sound like you want to impress Miles," Laura told him, fingering the stem of her wineglass. She got the impression Harry would do anything to make sure they didn't lose this opportunity, and wondered if there was more to it than just money.

"This is an important deal for me," he told her. "Miles is trusting me with a lot here; he doesn't have to put all his money in one agency. And no, I'm not trying to impress him," he said. "Not in the way you think. Not like I *owe him* or anything. We just—" He waved a hand in the air. "We do things for each other. You make mistakes . . ." He trailed off. "Well, you just do it."

Laura nodded. She didn't really understand what Harry meant, but she had seen him doing jobs before for so-called old mates.

"There's something else I need to tell you," he said.

Laura peered over the rim of her glass as she finished her wine.

"Can I get you another?" he asked, as she placed it back on the table.

"Definitely not, thanks. Go on, what do you need to tell me?"

"I've had a complaint about Mike Lewis," he said, pausing briefly. "That he's been bullying someone."

"Who?"

"Sarah Clifton."

"The quiet woman? She works for him, doesn't she?"

Harry nodded. "You haven't heard anything about it, then?"

"No." Laura shook her head. "Not a thing. Why? Should I have?"

"Apparently it's the talk of the office," he said, looking at her steadily as if expecting her to admit she had known about it.

"Harry, I promise you, I haven't heard anything," she said. It didn't pass her by that she was likely the only one who hadn't heard the rumors. "If I had, I would have come to you."

He paused before admitting, "Yeah, I know."

"So what's she said Mike's done?" Laura asked.

"Undermining her, making her feel worthless, speaking rudely to her," he listed. "I asked for examples and that's what I got back."

"So now what?" Laura asked. "You have to talk to Mike?" She couldn't believe anyone had made any complaint about him, let alone the timid girl Laura recalled hovering in the toilets on her first day back. "Has anyone else complained about him or was it just Sarah?"

"Well, that's the thing, I'm hearing that a few other women are coming forward and saying they feel undervalued. I'm *hearing*—" He paused. "I'm hearing that this is how our culture is perceived. I can't believe you haven't heard any of it."

She shook her head, her mouth agape. "Nor can I. So who else has spoken to you about him?"

"No one," he said.

"I don't understand. You said others have come forward."

"No one's complained to *me* about him. They're speaking to Mia."

"Mia?" she repeated, and let out a laugh, shaking her head.

"That's right. And to tell you the truth, Laura, I don't really know what to do," he said, ignoring her reaction.

"You don't do anything for now," Laura replied firmly.

"What?"

"Don't do anything." She threw her hands up and shrugged. "We both know what Mike's like, and that it's just the way he is. He isn't a bully, Harry. You know that. This is something that's just escalated and gotten out of hand, and I know she's behind it."

Harry raised his eyes.

"Mia," Laura confirmed. "She's doing this. She's trying to cause trouble. I don't know why she's focusing on Mike, but—"

"Laura, don't," he said, stopping her. "You can't make this about your desire to get back at Mia."

"I'm not trying to get back at anyone," she said through gritted teeth. "But you know that Mike's—Mike's just . . ." She trailed off, waving her hand. "Harry, why are you looking at me like that?"

"No reason."

Laura glanced down and twisted her fingers around the stem of her empty glass.

"It's just that I don't want to see you getting so wrapped up in Mia. I don't want you to make yourself ill—"

"Harry," Laura snapped. "This is so completely different, and if you just listened to me you'd realize that I honestly believe Mia is out for me. For some reason. I have no clue why, but I know she is."

Harry pursed his lips, releasing his breath slowly. "Let me get us another drink."

Laura opened her mouth to speak but closed it again sharply, sinking back in the seat. What was the point of going over the same ground with Harry when every time he'd shift the conversation? The thought had been crossing Laura's mind lately that if she wanted to get a proper answer as to why she'd been so easily shifted off the Coopers account, then there was only one person she could ask. But the thought of addressing Tess Wills was too humiliating.

"Laura? Another drink?" Harry said again.

Laura glanced at her mobile, her heart plummeting when she saw the time. It was eight o'clock, and she had forgotten to take her phone off silent after a meeting she'd had earlier that afternoon. She'd missed another text from Nate half an hour ago.

"Shit," she muttered. "I can't. I really have to go." She texted back a quick reply. So sorry. Am on way now xx

"Come on, then," Harry said, and they left the bar, walking back to the offices where their cars were parked. "Miles is doing me a big favor putting this opportunity my way," Harry went on. It was his way of letting her know she couldn't cock this up. That if she didn't think she could do it, she should say so now so he could get someone else in on the job. Someone like Mia, most likely. He took her arm and pulled her out of the way of a couple walking in the opposite direction on the thin path by the river as Laura's phone started ringing.

She stared at the screen. Nate.

"You going to answer that?"

Laura nodded uncertainly and eventually picked up. "Hi."

"Are you in the car?"

"Nearly," she said.

"I thought you said you were on your way back."

"I am. I'm literally at my car," she lied. It was at least another five minutes before they reached the office.

"Say hi to Nate for me," Harry said from beside her.

Laura felt herself tense as Nate went silent on the other end of the line. "Nate, I'll be ten minutes," she said as she hung up, her pulse quickening, picking up her steps as Harry raced to keep up with her.

———————

Eighteen minutes later Laura pulled into the driveway and hurriedly scrambled out of the car. Nate wouldn't be happy, and she couldn't blame him. He had never liked her boss, had always said he didn't trust him, insinuating that Harry's intentions crossed a boundary. Tonight would only add fuel to his argument that Harry was seeing more of Laura than he was. What made it worse was that she hadn't even wanted to go out for a sodding drink with her boss in the first place, and he hadn't spoken to her about anything that couldn't have been said in the office.

"Then why the hell did you?" Nate snapped when she told him.

"Because he's my boss, Nate," she cried. "He asked me to; he told me he needed to talk about work and, I don't know, you know what he's like—he's persuasive. I didn't have a choice."

"You did have a choice," he snapped. "And you chose him over me. You know how I feel, Laura, you knew I'd be pissed off, and yet you still went out with him."

"I didn't *go out* with him, stop saying it like this was anything more than work, when you know it wasn't."

"Do I?"

"God, Nate, yes!" she cried again. "Don't even go there."

He looked away, having the decency, she thought, to look admonished. "You really don't see it, do you, Laura?" he said.

"See what? What are you getting at?" She grabbed his arm and swung him round. "What are you saying, Nate?"

"Why do you actually think Harry wants to go out for a drink with you? It isn't to talk about work."

"Oh my God, are you serious? Did you really just say that?"

"Laura, I trust you, you know I do," he said. "But I don't trust him one bit."

"Nate, he has never so much as tried anything on with me."

"But you know he would if you gave him the chance," he said. "Don't you?"

Laura shook her head. "I'm not having this conversation."

"Then how about the one where you're still prioritizing work over me and Bobby," he said.

Laura slumped on the sofa next to him. "Nate, don't make me feel bad about this. I don't know what else to do. I have work I need to do, I can't just walk away from it; it's too important."

"And you think this isn't?" he said, waving an arm around him.

"No, that's not what I'm saying. You don't understand," she replied. "Ever since I walked back in and found that Mia had taken over my job—"

"Oh please," Nate interrupted, hanging his head in his hands. "Please don't bring Mia into this again."

Laura pulled back, annoyed. It was true, Nate didn't understand, but he wasn't trying to.

"I know you're busy; I know you want to prove you can do it all, I get that," he went on. "But something's got to give, and at the moment, all that's giving is me and Bobby. This isn't fair, Laura. Not to me or to him. I am shattered. I am so tired and I don't mind doing any of it but sometimes I just want to see you in an evening, to remind me that I've got something to look forward to."

Laura noticed the wetness in his eyes before he swiftly wiped a hand over them.

"Is this actually what you want? To be working all the time?" he asked.

"No," she shook her head emphatically, tears pricking her own eyes now. "No, it's not what I want."

"So why are you? You've been there long enough that you can tell Harry if it's too much."

"It's not too much," she said, her throat tightening at the thought that it soon would be even more. If they won Miles's account, like she was doing everything to ensure, it was going to get worse. "You make it sound like I'm not coping," she went on, ignoring this thought.

"I'm not saying that," he sighed. "I just don't get that if you haven't got Coopers anymore, then what's keeping you so bloody busy?"

"It's just—" She broke off. "My other accounts are demanding," she lied. "It's not like Coopers was the only one."

"That's not what you've said in the past," he retorted, holding her gaze.

She looked away. She'd put more effort into what accounts she had left than she'd ever done before Bobby, but even they'd slipped to the wayside since Monday. Part of her already thought it would be a good thing if they didn't win Miles's account, but at the same time she knew she wouldn't be able to let that happen. She would have to do as much as she could to ensure they secured it, because otherwise she'd feel like she'd failed herself.

But the truth was that in the last four weeks, Laura could have spent fewer hours at work if she hadn't tied herself into knots about proving her worth, or about outstaying Mia.

"I can make it better," she said. "I think I know how. You just have to trust me."

"What are you talking about?" he asked, resigned.

"I spoke this week with someone where Mia used to work," she started. Perhaps when Laura could prove Mia wasn't who she said she was, then she'd get Coopers back. And if that happened, she wouldn't worry about this new account. Someone else could have it. Patrick could do it. "And she said that—"

"Stop, Laura." Nate's words were so quiet she wasn't sure she'd heard them. "Just stop," he said again.

She looked at him, her mouth agape.

"You're obsessing over Mia," he said, turning on the sofa until he was facing her. "This is Saskia all over again."

Laura reeled back. "No." She shook her head. "I *know* Mia's taken my job for a reason. I know she has, Nate. She wanted my job and she made sure she got it."

She wiped the arm of her sleeve across her face, collecting the tears that were sliding down her cheeks. She didn't want to think about what had happened after Saskia's boyfriend had left. How things had gotten so much worse for her in the months to follow. How she'd wound up making herself ill. "This is not the same thing. I want you to trust me on that," she said.

"All I want is for us all to be happy," Nate replied softly. "And I don't think any of us are at the moment. I want you home more, Laura."

She didn't answer as he carried on staring at her.

"I want you to come home earlier. I need you to. From now on, at least three times a week, I want you to commit to leaving at five. That's not unreasonable," he added.

She continued to stare at him.

"I'm not asking much. I just need to know that you're still a part of this family. I want you to come back and be here for tea and bathtime sometimes."

"But I can't—" she muttered. "I can't promise I can do that three times a week." She knew it was impossible. Not now that she had the tender hanging over her. The only way she could do what he was asking was to admit to Harry that she couldn't take on this new project. And if she did that, there was no way he'd risk losing Mia.

Nate let out a laugh, but it was one that suggested he was anything but happy. "Are you serious?"

"I am—I just, I just can't commit to doing that, Nate. I'm not saying I won't try, because I will, but you can't force this on me. You know what my work's like. You know I have to work around the clock when the clients demand it. That's the way it's always been."

"No," he said, "it's not the way it's always been. Because everything's different now. We have a baby. *You* have a baby. And besides, you're working *more*, Laura. More than you ever did before."

"I'm not. I—"

"You are," he snapped. "And you know it. Shit, Laura, if you can't even accept it, we've got no bloody hope." He pulled himself off the sofa and stormed out of the room. Laura sank back against the cushion, inhaling a deep breath that caught in her throat.

"Okay," she cried, calling after him. "Okay, Nate, I'll come home early, three times a week. I'll do it," she sobbed.

Nate appeared in the doorway again, leaning against the frame as he watched her carefully. "That's all I want," he said. "I just want you to try."

Initial interviews between Detective Emily Marlow and staff of Morris and Wood following the fire at Morris and Wood offices on Monday, May 13.

<u>**Laura Denning, Account Director, on Tuesday, May 14, at Lymington Police Headquarters.**</u>

Marlow:	Okay, let's go over yesterday again. You didn't get to the office until around midday, is that correct?
Laura:	Yes.
Marlow:	And when you came in you were searching for Mia Anderson.
Laura:	I just wanted to speak to her.
Marlow:	Your husband was worried about your relationship with Mia, wasn't he? He thought you were getting obsessed with her?
Laura:	No, he didn't think that. He was a little worried, maybe, but that was only because he could see how upset I was.
Marlow:	But something like this had happened before at work with a woman you were friends with.
Laura:	What happened with Saskia was different. It was . . .
Marlow:	Go on.
Laura:	It was just different. Saskia set me up, and my husband knows that, so I have no idea why he's worrying about me now.
Marlow:	How did Saskia set you up?
Laura:	She made it look like I was making mistakes. On one occasion she altered a brief from a major client before it got to me so I worked on something altogether different and—
Marlow:	I can see this is distressing for you.
Laura:	I just don't know why you're talking to me about her.
Marlow:	But when you returned from maternity leave you thought Mia Anderson was doing the same thing?

Laura: I've already gone through all this with you.

Marlow: After the issue with Saskia, you were advised to take some time off from work, weren't you, Ms. Denning?

Laura: I wasn't *advised* to.

Marlow: It wasn't a suggestion from your boss, Harry Wood, then?

Laura: He asked if I wanted to and I agreed I could do with a break.

Marlow: And did you end up being prescribed any medication at this time?

Laura: You told me I was here to help you investigate the fire. I don't see what my past medical history has to do with it. I don't want to answer any more of these questions. I assume I don't have to, do I? I'm not under arrest? I can leave at any time, isn't that what you said?

Marlow: You can, Ms. Denning, and that's fine. Let's go back to the night of the fire instead. You texted your husband at six p.m. on Monday evening to say you were still in the office, and that you were meeting with your old account team from Coopers, so you would be late. Is that right?

Laura: (pauses)

Marlow: Laura?

Laura: Yes.

Marlow: Was it true?

Laura: (shakes head) No.

Marlow: Why did you lie to your husband about why you were still at the office?

Laura: Because I was working on something he didn't know about and so—I don't know, maybe—maybe I just felt guilty about being late again. Everyone was making me feel guilty, especially my husband.

Marlow: Guilty about what?

Laura: About working too much. Do you have children, Detective?

Marlow: I do.

Laura: Then you might know what I mean. I can't do anything right. I feel like all the time I'm at work I should be at home and whenever I'm at home my workload creeps up to some unmanageable peak. So yes, maybe I lied to him because I thought he was more likely to accept me meeting the Coopers team.

Marlow: Ms. Denning, other than Harry Wood, you were the last member of staff in the building on Monday night, weren't you?

Laura: As far as I know.

Marlow: And a few hours after you left, that same building was burned to the ground. (pauses) Do you know who set fire to the Morris and Wood offices, Ms. Denning?

Laura: (pauses) No.

Marlow: Are you sure about that?

chapter twenty-three

four weeks before the fire

Janie walked back from the fish-and-chip shop to the parking lot with the girls, down the cobbled lane, their crabbing buckets still swinging in their hands. Both of them were laughing over a joke that Ella had heard at school, heads dipped toward their packets of chips.

This was what happiness felt like.

She looked up briefly. She didn't know why or what caught her attention, but something made her glance toward the wine bar, tucked almost out of sight on the cobbled street leading down to the quay. Her husband was walking inside.

Janie stopped in her tracks, her heart tapping out a rapid beat. The girls carried on obliviously, walking a few steps ahead until they too stopped and turned around to see what was keeping her.

"What are you doing, Mummy?" Lottie called.

She shook her head, gazing at the door that had now closed behind her husband, and eventually pulled herself away and caught up with her daughters. "Nothing." She smiled. "Just thought I saw someone I knew."

"Who?" Lottie asked.

"No one," she replied at once, and pierced her fork into another chip, forcing it into her mouth, past her lack of appetite, resisting the urge to spit it out on the ground in front of them.

He was with a woman. She'd seen her walk in front of him, and even though Janie hadn't gotten a clear view, she would have sworn it was Laura Denning from the way she walked, the way she wore her hair, scraped back into a low bun.

As the girls started chattering again, Janie's mind whirled, her heartbeat still erratic as she tried to reason with herself that what she had seen was nothing. Harry often went for a drink after work; he had always done business in wine bars or pubs or the Directors Clubs he belonged to in London. She knew that better than anyone. They were the places he would meet people like Miles Morgan.

She knew that if she later asked Harry if he'd been out for a drink, he'd tell her he had, and would no doubt admit who he was with, and it would then be up to her to believe him or not when he said it was nothing more than work.

As these thoughts fizzed around her head, it didn't matter that she no longer loved her husband, so then why did she suddenly feel so empty? So betrayed?

She smiled at the girls again as they turned around to catch her attention. He should have been with them. They had wanted their dad to meet them crabbing, and he hadn't even returned her call.

Janie tossed the rest of her dinner into a bin.

Don't make a fool of me, Harry.

That was one thing she would not tolerate. She might not love him any longer, but she would not allow her husband to humiliate her.

chapter twenty-four

It was Friday night, and by the time Mia got home and crashed into the house, she expected her mum and Jess to both be in bed. She'd agreed to go to the pub with Bryony and a few other people from work and had drunk more gin and tonics than she had in a long while. Already she cursed the morning, when she'd have a hangover, but at the time it had seemed like a good idea.

Pausing in the hallway, she listened. The blissful sound of silence. She went into the kitchen and filled a pint glass with water. There was no alcohol in the house anymore. She was the only one in her family who still drank. Her mum used to enjoy a glass of rosé, but not any longer, and maybe this was one of the reasons Mia enjoyed her after-work drinks so much. They were the only time she could forget, even if only temporarily.

Mia pulled a chair up to the small kitchen table and gulped back the water, sighing as she drained the glass and slammed it down on the kitchen table. She didn't want to live here, but she had no choice. She hadn't even wanted to move back to the New Forest, and certainly not anywhere near Lymington again. All three of them were suffocating in this tiny bungalow.

Suddenly a loud crash from the far end of the hallway made Mia push back her chair with a screech across the linoleum. She froze, only briefly, before running to Jess's room. When she got there she flung the door open, her heart beating fast as she scanned the dark bedroom, feeling for the light switch and flicking it on.

"Jess, what the hell happened?"

Her sister was the other side of the room in front of a broken mirror. Shards of glass lay around her, one of her hands was clutching a sharp piece, pressing it into her fingertip.

"Seven years' bad luck," her sister murmured, so softly she was barely audible, before letting out a chuckle. "How ironic would that be, to have seven more?"

"Jess?" Mia stepped toward her carefully. "What happened?" she asked again. When she was at her sister's side, she reached out for the piece of glass still pressing into Jess's flesh and gently pried her fingers apart until she could take it.

"It was an accident," Jess said sharply. "I didn't—I wasn't doing it on purpose," she snapped. "I knocked the damn radio into the mirror. I didn't even want it here. It was you that put the thing on the dressing table."

Mia ignored her. "You're bleeding," she said. "I'll get you a bandage."

Jess lowered her head and gazed at the drop of bright red blood that appeared like a tear on the end of her finger. Slowly she lifted it to her lips and held it in there. "It's not that bad, I don't need one."

Mia sunk down onto the end of the bed and slowly she turned her sister to face her.

"Talk to me," Mia said softly, but Jess shook her head.

"No. Tell me something about your life instead," Jess replied. "Talk to me about something else. Something from the outside world." Tears had filled her sister's eyes, and Mia fought hard not to reach out and wipe them away.

Mia laughed. "I have nothing to talk about other than work."

"Then tell me about that."

That was the one thing she really didn't want to talk to Jess about, but her sister was searching her eyes, pleading with her to take her out of whatever moment she was currently in, and so she had to say something.

"It's fine," she shrugged eventually. "Some of the women are a laugh."

"And you're still glad they made you permanent?"

Mia nodded. Yes, she had definitely been pleased about that.

"So you're happy, then? Because you don't need to stay here, you know. It was never supposed to be this long."

Mia didn't know how to answer, because what could she tell her sister? That of course she didn't want to be at Morris and Wood for much longer, that this wasn't her dream job, that she didn't care about selling health drinks.

Before she'd had to move back to Lymington she'd had a job that meant something. What she'd once done had made a difference, working for a charity—helping people. Then she'd had to give it up and move back to Lymington, back to her childhood home.

"Of course I'm happy." Mia smiled.

Jess nodded slowly. She didn't believe her, of course. Her sister could see through her. "Do you remember when you were little you wanted to be a pilot?" Jess asked.

"Yes! And then I went on my first flight and threw up."

"I wouldn't get in a plane you were flying." Jess laughed.

"I don't blame you. And you wanted—" Mia stopped suddenly, cursing herself that she could be so stupid.

"It's okay, you can say it."

Jess's eyes were drawn and heavy and didn't mask the sadness that hid behind them. There were too many dark memories and shadows that were now cast over their lives to give either of them much to be happy about when they were together. Even when they were having a laugh, there would always be a reminder.

Sometimes, when she saw her sister like this, remembering a time before, Mia's heart fractured into even more pieces. She wanted to take Jess into her arms and take away everything that had made her into this.

There were other times when she wanted to scream at Jess that she could do something about it. That she didn't need to live in such misery, she could pull herself out of the dark depths to which she'd descended.

Mia knew that wasn't wholly fair and often asked herself what she would have done. If what had happened to Jess had happened to her? Of course she would never know for sure, when she hadn't had everything taken away from her like Jess had.

"I *want* you to say it," Jess was urging her now, like it was some kind of challenge.

"You wanted to be a runner," Mia replied.

Jess was always running. Almost as soon as Jess was walking, their mum used to joke that she was trying to get everywhere quicker. At fifteen, she was school sports captain and ran cross-country for Hampshire. Throughout her teens she'd be up every morning before Mia had even opened her eyes and would be out of the house, in her trainers, pounding the pavements and the country lanes.

In those days, no one used to worry about kids running on their own down practically deserted pathways, alongside rivers, or around the streets before the sun had even come up. Her mum hadn't blinked an eyelid that Jess wasn't in her bed when she got up in the morning, she just used to hope she'd be home before the school bus left.

She always was. Because that was Jess—dedicated to her schoolwork too. She was promising in every way imaginable, all her reports foretold she could achieve anything she put her mind to.

So why *would* their mother have worried about her? Jess wasn't the one who caused her concern. If anyone it was Mia, the daughter who had to be dragged out of bed, the one who would bunk off school to smoke up in the field with the boys.

"Yes, I wanted to be a runner." Jess laughed, but it wasn't remotely funny.

Mia's gaze traveled down to her sister's useless legs and the faded blue pajama bottoms limply hugging the frail bones beneath. She saw her sister naked every morning when she helped her shower and dress, and every day it still sickened her that those once athletic legs had withered to nothing.

Jess couldn't run anymore. She couldn't even walk. And every day it angered Mia that someone had been responsible for doing this to her sister. And no one had paid.

Mia felt that anger now bubbling inside her.

It was this that always usurped the pity and guilt and sadness. It was anger that drove Mia on, and if she ever stopped, she might agree it was unhealthy. But she wasn't stopping. Not yet.

Inhaling a large breath, she reached across and took hold of her sister's hands and held them in her own. "I love you, you know that, don't you?"

"Of course I know that." Jess's eyes filled up again, and she pulled away one of her hands so she could wipe it across her face. "And I love you. And I'm so proud of you."

"For what?" Mia asked, screwing her eyes up.

"For doing what you're doing."

For a moment Mia held back, studying her sister, wondering what Jess actually knew.

"For giving up everything and living back here, I mean," Jess said.

"Oh yeah, right." Mia let out a breath and smiled.

Sometimes Mia would think God had gotten it the wrong way

round. It shouldn't have happened to Jess. Mia was the lazy one, the one who used to sit around all day in her pajamas, whiling away the hours doing nothing.

Mia often wondered if the same thoughts had crossed their mum's mind too. The first time she had considered it was one year ago when they'd both been standing in Southampton hospital, staring at her sister through the glass, hooked up to machines, her life hanging by a thread, neither of them knowing if she would make it or not.

Mia recalled the words the doctor had uttered to her as she stood next to her mum. "Your sister is very lucky to be alive," he'd told her. Mia had looked through the window, past the tubes and the beeping monitors and the nurses bustling about the seemingly lifeless body beyond that was supposedly her sister. "But," he had gone on, "if she does pull through, there is every chance she won't walk again. Her legs were crushed by the weight of the car."

He had carried on talking at them, but his words had started to fizzle and pop in bursts, and she could only grab at some of them: "*An accident on the road toward Lymington . . . Jess's car veered off the road and wrapped itself around a tree . . . Believe the accident might have been caused by drunk driving.*"

All their worlds had crumbled in that moment. Mia had seen a flash of her sister's future, but still she could never have foreseen how much it was going to affect all of them. How only a week later she would be packing up her old life and moving back to her mum's house because there was no way her mum and Jess would cope without her.

But it wasn't going to end like this. Mia was certain of that. Someone needed to pay for what had been done to her sister.

Initial interviews between Detective Emily Marlow and staff of Morris and Wood following the fire at Morris and Wood offices on Monday, May 13.

<u>**Patrick Carter, Account Director, on Tuesday, May 14, at Lymington Police Headquarters.**</u>

Patrick:	I could tell there was an atmosphere as soon as I arrived at the party.
Marlow:	What kind of atmosphere?
Patrick:	Janie—she seemed a little—she wasn't her usual self. She's usually so attentive, a great hostess, but last Friday something wasn't right.
Marlow:	Can you tell me more specifically what you mean?
Patrick:	I got there late and Janie answered the door, but her mind was elsewhere. I asked her where Harry was and she just stared at me and then eventually smiled and said, "If you find him, you'll have to tell me." She was trying to make it sound jokey, but I didn't get the sense she was happy.
Marlow:	And did you find Harry?
Patrick:	Oh yeah, he was only out in the garden talking to some of the IT guys.
Marlow:	You said earlier the party was a disaster.
Patrick:	Well, it was. Because of the argument. At least that was what started it.
Marlow:	For clarification, you mean the one between Laura Denning and Mia Anderson?
Patrick:	(nods) You could see it was going to come to a head at some point. It was one as much as the other by then; they were both worked up. I suppose it's inevitable when you mix office politics with alcohol that something's going to go wrong. I'm not sure if Harry's party came at the right time or the wrong one.
Marlow:	Did you hear the argument between Mia and Laura?

Patrick: Yes. Well, I overheard the start of it, before Mia walked off across the lawn and Laura stormed after her. That part I just watched with horror. They were standing precariously close to the swimming pool. I knew someone was going to end up in it.

Marlow: What did you overhear?

Patrick: Laura yelling at Mia that she knew what she had done.

Marlow: Where were you at this point?

Patrick: I was heading down to Harry's pool house for a cigarette. The party had spread out a bit, but there weren't many people down the end of the garden. It was a chance to get a bit of peace from my staff either asking me when they were getting a pay raise or telling me they didn't agree with this, that, or whatever else I'd lately said. It always happens on a night out, doesn't it? Like they really think it's the right time to tell the boss what they think just because they've had one too many glasses of champagne.

Marlow: And where were Mia and Laura?

Patrick: Already down there, though I didn't see them at first, I just heard the shouting.

Marlow: And did Laura say what it was that Mia had done?

Patrick: She said, and I can pretty much quote this bit, "I've spoken to Tess, Mia. I know how you managed to get your hands on my job."

    She meant Tess Wills, the marketing director at Coopers.

Marlow: And then?

Patrick: And then Laura said, "I know you're lying."

    I wanted to go and check she was okay, but at the same time I didn't know whether to interfere.

Marlow: Did Laura say what Mia had lied about?

Patrick: No.

Marlow: So what happened after that?

Patrick: Mia told Laura to get away from her. She kept saying,
"You're drunk, Laura. I think it's time you called yourself
a taxi." In hindsight it would have been better if she
had called a taxi, of course. But that was a whole other
nightmare.

chapter twenty-five

two weeks before the fire

Laura's days were merging into long weeks, filled with work and not getting home in time to see her son before he was already in bed. Laura was making every effort to rectify that, or at least she was trying to, promising Nate it was a temporary issue. "Something has come up at work," she had said. "It just needs more attention for the next couple of weeks."

"Not Coopers?" he had asked, one eye on the TV as she crashed down on the sofa next to him with a large bar of Dairy Milk she had bought as a peace offering.

"No. Something for a new client Harry has asked me to do. It's good," she said. "It's exciting."

She didn't tell him more, and Nate had nodded and eventually dragged his attention from the TV, breaking off a line of chocolate and putting it in his mouth. "So you're, you know—you're okay with not working on Coopers?"

"I am," Laura had lied. It was easier that way. Nate didn't probe any further into the work she was doing for this new client, and she didn't tell him that she was either spending these few weeks working her arse off for nothing or, more likely given the effort she had put into it, carrying on at this level for the foreseeable future.

Nate didn't ask because why would he? He had no idea what pitching and tenders involved. She might have once shared with him these excruciating parts of her job, but he wouldn't have taken on board what it meant.

And so Laura didn't reveal that if she won the tender, then the next few weeks would actually turn into months of getting home late and of pouring everything into the tight timescales Miles Morgan insisted upon.

Besides, Laura was still telling herself that it wouldn't come to that. Because once she could prove Mia Anderson was lying, she would ensure she got Coopers back, and then she could tell Harry she didn't have the time for Miles's company.

Then she could get her life back. And so Nate didn't need to know the detail.

Nate turned back to the TV, happy his wife had seemingly moved on and was no longer interested in the woman who had taken her job, leaving Laura wondering how he could possibly think it was that easy for her. Did he just want to believe that she was relaxed and confident enough to accept the fact that she'd been pushed out of her job on purpose, or did he really not know her at all?

She wondered what Nate would make of the file she had on Mia tucked at the bottom of her wardrobe. In it she had been compiling what little evidence she had. The notes she had made following the call to Katie Burton, pages from Mia's Facebook page printed off, a picture of Jessica Louise, whoever she was. And now there was the complaint about Mike Lewis to add into the mix. Laura still hadn't plucked up the courage to pick up the phone and call Tess Wills, but as time passed she was becoming more and more certain that she might just have to ask Tess the mortifying question as to why she didn't want Laura working with her anymore.

She shuddered at the thought as Nate began yawning, stretching along the sofa as he tucked his feet onto her lap.

"What shall we watch?" Laura asked.

He shrugged, his eyes already flickering shut. She glanced at her watch. Eight thirty. She'd been back for forty-five minutes and in that time she had crept up to Bobby's room, watched her son sleeping, crept out with a heavier heart, and then she and Nate had eaten pasta in almost silence.

"I don't mind. You choose."

She gave him a playful nudge on the leg, but he reacted by moving his foot out of the way, and in less than ten minutes he had fallen asleep.

The following morning the alarm went off at six a.m. Laura rolled over to switch it off as beside her Nate pulled the duvet tighter around his body. "Hey, sleepy head," she whispered gently. "Do you want a coffee before I leave?"

Nate grunted and shook his head.

"Okay." She sat and watched him for a moment before eventually swinging her legs over the side of the bed and creeping into Bobby's room. They had both been up with their son in the night. She continued to tell herself it would stop soon, the nights would get better, but it was taking its toll on both of them, especially Nate, who had never been one to do well on little sleep. On top of the stresses work was causing, it wasn't helping the obvious tensions between them.

By seven thirty Laura was in the office. She sidestepped Mia, whose head was down as she busied herself with something at her desk, and headed straight for her own, where she opened up the PC and pulled up the presentation she was working on for Miles.

Two hours had passed when she heard the ping of a text alert and, grabbing it, she saw Nate had sent her a video.

Look what our clever son is doing, it read. Laura clicked on the link and watched Bobby wobbling on his bottom and then eventually throwing himself forward and beginning to crawl.

"Oh my God!" she cried out loud, holding a hand over her mouth, smiling between her fingers as she watched the full three minutes and then immediately pressed play again. Running her thumb down the screen, Laura blinked back her tears. "You clever boy," she murmured, so full of pride for her baby.

She wanted to be with him. To be the one sitting on the sofa encouraging him toward her, clapping and cheering like she could hear Nate doing in the background. By the time Laura had watched the video three times, she could barely see through her tears and was picking up the phone to call Nate when Patrick appeared at her desk and asked if she had a minute to help him with something.

Laura dropped the phone back and told him she did, though one minute turned into forty-five, and back at her desk a myriad of emails were clogging her inbox. By this time she'd been distracted and never did call or even text Nate back to thank him for sending her the video, or even acknowledge how much she loved it.

And Laura knew later, when she did make the effort to leave work on time, how bad that looked.

chapter twenty-six

Mia had barely stepped from the lift when, out of nowhere, Henrietta James appeared, her cheeks flushed red with a cluster of broken veins. Her hair seemed particularly uncared for this morning, or maybe she had been running her hands through it. Clearly she had something to tell Mia, and Mia had come to expect it would involve Laura. Which was why it was a surprise when Henrietta said, "Have you heard Sarah Clifton has left the company?"

Henrietta wobbled from one too-high heel to the other, bug-eyed as she waited for Mia's response.

No, she hadn't heard this news. The girl had gone. What the hell?

"I was just wondering—" Henrietta leaned in. "Do you think they got rid of her?" she said in a loud whisper.

Mia glanced to the far end of the floor. From here she could make out Harry in his office as he prowled from one side to the other, no doubt on his phone. What she couldn't see was Mike Lewis's desk. "Surely not," Mia murmured.

But what if they had? Was that good news or bad? If they had dismissed her, then Sarah would have a case for unfair dismissal. It would be huge. She would need to get in touch with her.

Mia pretended she hadn't heard the news when she rapped on Harry's door and waited for him to beckon her in. His face was a mixture of calm and apprehension. "How's it going?" he asked, gesturing to a chair, his mind on something else, by the look of it, as he barely glanced up at Mia.

"Good, thank you."

He raised his eyebrows, peering up as he fussed with a stack of papers on his desk.

"Actually, I wanted to update you on the issue with Mike Lewis," Mia said boldly. In truth, she had little to update him on. The previous Friday night Mia had sounded out some of the other women in the office, none of whom had had many positive encounters with Mike, but neither did they feel either harassed or undermined by him. At least not enough to join in the formal complaint she was hoping for.

Mia had even broached the subject that she had found out Patrick Carter had taken some male clients to a strip club in Southampton, which had stirred more interest among the women.

And then one of them told her she begrudged the fact that she'd been bypassed for a promotion because she didn't want to work more than three days a week.

These were all things Mia was hoping to use.

"Actually, Sarah Clifton has left the company," Harry told her.

"Yes, I did hear. She's gone very suddenly."

Harry shrugged as if this were no big deal. "She handed her notice in last week; we agreed she didn't need to work her notice."

"Oh." Mia's mouth hung open in a wide O. It was Sarah's decision. She must have given up, and now here was Mia looking stupid, unaware, left to pick up the pieces.

Her fingers reached for the desk in front of her and curled around its edge. She felt the anger beginning to rise within her, which to Harry and most likely anyone else in the office would appear irrational.

"But this doesn't mean you're just going to drop the complaint," Mia went on, tightening her grip on the polished oak between her fingers.

"Well, of course I'm still looking into it." He waved a hand in the air, brushing off her concerns.

Mia could hear her sister's voice as if she were standing next to her. *Just forget it, Sis, this isn't your battle.*

No. Maybe it wasn't her battle. Maybe none of it was, but time had made them into two very different sisters now, and Mia wasn't going to stand by and refuse to fight.

She was angry with Sarah for giving up, but she was also angry with Harry for turning his back on her as he rifled through the drawers that sat behind his desk, and it took every ounce of determination not to thump her hands down and yell at him not to ignore her.

From the corner of her eye Mia caught sight of Laura shuffling into the chair at her desk, booting up her computer, and she wondered whether she should be more worried about what Laura was up to than confronting Harry.

She'd had a text the night before from someone she used to work with. Katie Burton. Telling her that she'd been contacted by someone asking questions about her previous employment with them. Katie wanted to know if everything was all right.

It didn't take a genius to guess it must have been Laura who'd been in touch. If she carried on running around like some sort of amateur Nancy Drew, then everything Mia had worked toward could be taken away in an instant.

Mia exhaled a tight breath and turned her attention back to Harry. She had to be careful. She also wondered if Harry actually knew that she'd met his wife for lunch, because despite Janie alluding to the fact she had set it up of her own accord, surely Harry had sent her?

I hope you do the right thing, Janie had said, and even though her tone hadn't been menacing, it must have been intended as a threat.

And now Mia didn't know whether she was getting out of her depth and if she should walk away before things went too far. But what would that achieve? She had never been someone who gave up easily.

chapter twenty-seven

Laura hesitated before closing down her PC and throwing her mobile in her bag. The clock had only just ticked past five. A stack of unread emails and an incomplete document left her with butterflies fluttering in her stomach, but when there had been little more than a minimal exchange of words with Nate and hastily devoured dinners, something had to give. The only thing that was keeping her from leaving was the fact she had finally called Tess Wills that day, and now that she had, Laura's need to speak to her was verging on obsessive. Only, six hours later and she was still waiting for the woman to call her back.

Finally she gave up and left the office. Nate was in the garden when she arrived. He was carting Bobby along on his hip as he walked alongside the thin border of plants that ran beside the fence. Every so often he would stop and point at a bush or a flower and whisper words in their son's ear that Laura couldn't hear.

She stood by the kitchen window, holding up her hand and pressing her palm against the pane as she watched her precious family. The way Bobby nestled into the crook of Nate's body, like he was attached there. She couldn't make out where one person stopped and the other started, and the sight of them both melted her heart and stabbed it at the same time. How she loved them. More than anything. But how she felt she was losing them too.

The urge to join both her boys and announce her arrival at home was superceded by a strange anxiety, which she couldn't just put down to the work she knew was waiting for her. That hovered on the periphery of her mind like a black cloud that wouldn't go away until she attended to it, but this was something so much more.

It was that Laura didn't know where her place was with her boys anymore. She didn't know where she fit in.

She could count on both hands the waking hours she spent with Bobby in a working week. The once bright smile that had lit up his face when she'd walked in the door at night had been replaced by a new hesitation before he would come to her.

Laura knew this was her making and that she had no one else to blame but herself. And although she longed to drag herself out of the hole she had dug, she didn't see a way to.

Not yet anyway. Not until she got rid of Mia. Then she would make it work. Then she would find the balance she needed to reconnect with her family, she thought resolutely, her hand pressing harder against the pane.

Nate turned around at the bottom of the garden and gave Laura a surprised wave when he caught her standing at the window. She released her hand as he pointed and whispered more words into Bobby's ear, but their son was more intent on pulling the collar of Nate's polo shirt to his mouth.

"I didn't know you were back," he said, coming into the kitchen. "How long have you been standing there?"

"Just long enough to watch you giving our son a gardening lesson." Laura smiled, holding out her hands for Nate to pass her a wriggling Bobby.

"He's hungry. I was just about to come in to get his tea."

"I can do that," she told him, pressing her mouth against Bobby's cheek and blowing a raspberry against his soft skin until he giggled.

"No, it's all right; I've got it ready." Nate was already at the fridge, pulling out a container of yesterday's shepherd's pie that he would whizz up in a blender.

She snuggled against her son, the memory of the video Nate had sent her that morning rushing back to her, along with the thought that she hadn't responded to it. "And I can't believe how clever you are," she said, pulling back and smiling at Bobby, trying to ignore the flash of guilt that ballooned inside her. "Crawling like a big boy. Mummy's so proud of you." She laughed as her son beamed back at her, and she turned to Nate. "I'm so sorry. It was a gorgeous video. I wanted to call you, but something came up and . . . " Her words trailed off. None of them were adequate.

Nate nodded, his back to her as he gave a small, strangled sound that sounded like a laugh. She chose to ignore it as she pressed her lips against Bobby's cheek. "Are you pleased to see me?" she said to Nate.

"Of course," he said flatly. "I just didn't expect you yet."

"I wanted to surprise you."

Nate nodded.

"You don't *seem* pleased."

He let out a deep breath. "It's five thirty, Laura. You left on time, you hardly left early. Don't make out you're doing me a favor." He rubbed his eyes with the back of his hand, and even though his words had jarred her, she brushed them off, telling herself her husband was exhausted and probably annoyed with her over the video. Surely it wasn't anything they couldn't easily get through.

"I'm not," she said. "I just—I'm just trying to make an effort, Nate. Can you meet me in the middle here?"

He put the container on the worktop and looked up at her. "Meet you in the middle? Laura, what world are you living in? I've been so far over the middle I'm practically on *your* side. You come home one night before Bobby's had his tea and expect me to jump up and down with joy?"

"I'm not saying that—"

"Good. Because I really don't feel like doing it, I'm afraid. God, Laura, you have no idea, do you?"

"Okay," she cried. "I'm sorry, Nate, I get it. You're pissed off with me." Laura waited for him to respond, tell her he was sorry, that he was in fact just tired and wasn't really that annoyed with her at all, because he understood her day was busy.

Instead he glanced at Bobby and then glared at her.

"He doesn't know what the word means," she hissed. "Jesus, I really didn't think this was how the evening would pan out."

"No," he muttered. "Neither did I."

———————

An hour later Laura's mobile rang. She paused before answering as Tess Wills's name flashed on her screen. Eventually she picked up. "Hello, Tess," she said. "Thanks for getting back to me."

"Sorry it's late. I hope this isn't a bad time?"

Laura stepped out of the living room and started up the stairs. "No," she said. "It's fine."

"What can I do for you?" Tess asked breezily, making Laura's breath catch in her throat.

"This isn't—" She broke off, starting again. "I need you to be honest with me," she said. "Please."

"Okay." The word was slightly drawn out, as if Tess might have some idea about what was coming.

"I need to know why I didn't stay on your account." As soon as the words were out of Laura's mouth she felt relieved, and even before she'd heard Tess's answer, she wondered why it had taken her almost two months to have this conversation.

When it was finished, Laura hung up. Her jaw was set in a tense line, and as she stared at her reflection in the bathroom mirror, she considered calling Mia Anderson right then. Get this done, once and for all.

But it was clear the woman was a liar and if they spoke in private, then Laura didn't trust what might come of it. Better, surely, that she at least wait until they were face-to-face. And maybe until there were other people around who would hear that Laura was right. That for some reason, Mia really *had* come to steal her job.

Initial interviews between Detective Emily Marlow and staff of Morris and Wood following the fire at the Morris and Wood offices on Monday, May 13.

Patrick Carter, Account Director, on Tuesday, May 14, at Lymington Police Headquarters.

Marlow:	What happened at the party when the two women walked away from the pool house? You said you watched it with horror. Did you overhear any more of their argument?
Patrick:	No. Not from where I stood. When Mia walked off, Laura turned and saw me briefly. She almost looked through me; I could tell she'd had far too much to drink. I don't think she even saw me. I've never seen Laura like that before. I held out my hand and told her to come back to the house with me, but she just stared right through me with these glassy eyes and then stormed off after Mia. I didn't follow. I went to try and find Harry but I couldn't, and by the time he did appear, all hell had broken loose by the pool. And later when I eventually caught up with him in the house, there was that whole other situation going on.
Marlow:	With Harry and his wife?
Patrick:	Yes. They were arguing. Just before he left his own party.
Marlow:	Did you speak to Janie Wood after that?
Patrick:	No. She was having this conversation with Mia in the hallway, which sounded weird from the little I could garner, and then—she disappeared. I didn't see her again, and by the time Harry returned I'd already called my own taxi. I didn't want to hang around much longer, even though a lot of the staff were happy to carry on drinking his champagne. You see, this is what I mean when I say the whole night was a disaster. Janie and Harry are friends of mine, but . . . You know, all morning, ever since I heard about the fire, all I keep wondering is whether it had something to do with that night.

chapter twenty-eight

one week before the fire

Janie stood in the doorway to Ella's bedroom, pausing for a moment before she woke her. Ella was eleven, still her baby, and yet she filled the length of her single bed, which remained stuffed with teddies and cushions. When had her daughter grown up to the point Janie could get so little out of her anymore? And yet all she had to do was look at her little girl's room and she felt the tug on her heartstrings that they were caught in this trap between child and teenager, and she hadn't even started the dreaded secondary-school years. How the hell was she going to get through them?

Janie sighed as she crept over to her daughter's bed and gently shook her awake. Ella snatched the duvet and wound it around herself tighter, and eventually Janie said softly that she was going downstairs to make breakfast and could she please start getting up. Some days all she wanted was to yell at her daughter that she didn't want to get out of bed either. But she also knew that was never a good way to start the day. And then there were days like today when she wondered if the only thing she had to worry about was her girls, how easy her days would be.

Janie's stomach was unsettled, her mind flittering with thoughts of the past and more recent, all of which she'd kept pushing to the back of her mind while knowing it wasn't going to take much for any of them to start unravelling her if she gave them space to breathe.

She knew it might help to talk to someone, however, and part of her wondered if she'd open up to her friends when she met them for coffee later that morning. The bigger part knew she likely wouldn't.

At the café, after ordering an Americano, Janie joined them at the window table. She lifted the cup to her lips and blew, peering over the rim as the group waited for Lucy to relay her latest story about her youngest.

"So she came home last night with a bite mark on her arm." Lucy raised her eyes and placed her own mug carefully on the table between them.

"You are kidding," Kristen cried. "An actual bite? Well, the school has to do something, surely?"

"You'd think," Lucy said. "Only when I told the teacher this morning he said he was sorry but he hadn't seen anything happen."

"This is outrageous, isn't it?" Kristen gasped, her voice rising as she looked around at the other two, who nodded their agreement.

"It is. Something has to be done about that kid," Anna said. "Before it's too late. I mean, can you imagine what he'll be like when he's in secondary school?"

"Surely they grow out if it," Lucy added.

"I don't know." Anna shrugged. "Show me the boy at seven and I'll show you the man. That's what they say, isn't it? A seven-year-old's brain is already ninety percent developed by that time. I think you can tell exactly what type of adult darling Dexter is going to be."

"Once a bully, always a bully," Kristen chipped in. "We'll read about him in the papers one day. He'll have beaten someone up outside a convenience store because they looked at him the wrong way. That happened to someone I went to school with. My mum said she could have told anyone his future was going to be doomed."

Janie silently sipped at her coffee as she listened to the interchange. It was so nice not to have to think about anything other than everyone else's problems for an hour, but then Anna reached out and took hold of her arm. "You're quiet this morning. Everything all right?"

Janie nodded. Out of all of them, it was always Anna who noticed when there was something on her mind. She was going to miss her friend when Anna started her job. But right then she wished she hadn't asked, because now they were all looking at her expectantly and waiting for her to contribute something to the conversation. Janie knew she had to give them something.

In the end the only thing she could think of to come up with was, "Harry's got a problem with bullying in his office." The words left her lips before she could stop them.

Her mind drifted back to the conversation she'd had with her husband when Harry came home and told her the girl had left.

"Sarah's gone," he'd said, pouring himself a large glass of Malbec that he'd picked up on their last trip to France. He'd studied the glass as he swirled the wine, letting it swish to the top as if he were prepared to let it slosh over the edge and onto the oak table.

"Sarah?" Janie had asked.

"The girl who said she was being bullied."

"Woman," Janie corrected. "She's a woman, Harry. You need to stop referring to her as a girl."

He had continued to swish his wine as he raised his eyebrows questioningly.

"Any female over the age of eighteen is a woman. You wouldn't refer to the men as boys."

"What difference does it make?" he had asked, seemingly baffled.

"It makes her sound like a schoolchild. It undermines the issue."

"I really don't think it does," he'd said, taking a sip. "Anyway, the fact is, she handed her notice in today. She left this afternoon after Mike agreed to it."

"Right." Janie rolled her eyes.

"It's a good thing."

"Because it means you can forget about it?" she'd asked.

"Well, there's no case to follow up now, is there?"

"Other than the fact Mike is still working for you? No, I suppose not."

"Janie?" Harry hung his head. "You make it sound like you're not on my side."

"I just don't think you should paper over it."

"But Mike—seriously? You know he's just an awkward fellow. He can barely look at me half the time when he's talking to me. He talks over *me*, for Christ's sake. I don't believe there's a problem." He'd put his glass down and looked away.

Janie had turned back to the oven and wondered whether Mia Anderson saw it that way. Someone should be fighting. She really did wonder if she should try to have another lunch with Mia soon, but then their last meet-up had been awkward, and Janie wasn't particularly sure about her after that.

Now Lucy was asking what the problem was, and Janie wondered why she had suddenly blurted out the news about the bullying at Harry's office and wondered if it was maybe her little way of getting back at him for the fact that she'd seen him taking Laura Denning to a wine bar—something neither of them had mentioned.

And then she wondered if it wasn't just that that had made her spill the gossip. Maybe she was simply sick of her husband avoiding responsibility.

"A woman at the office has reported a man for bullying her," Janie told her friends. "I don't know much about it."

"It goes on through life," Anna said. "I bet that man, whoever he is, was a bully at school too."

"To be honest, I doubt he was," Janie admitted. She had known Mike a long time. "If anything, he was probably the kid being picked on."

"But it doesn't mean they don't have to do something about it."

"No. No it doesn't mean that," Janie said.

"He has to," Lucy went on. "This happened to my friend's husband once. By his own admission he didn't handle it well, and then the woman left the company so he pretty much thought that was that. Next thing, she went public. His reputation was ruined."

"Well, that's not going to happen to Harry." Kristen laughed. "He has the shiniest reputation in Lymington."

"Until the day he doesn't," Lucy said.

Janie frowned.

"I'm just saying," Lucy told her, "that you have to be careful. This woman at my friend's husband's company—well, you never know what anyone's capable of until you push them too far."

"You must have seen some stuff like that when you were a barrister?" Anna was asking, and Janie snapped her head around to look at her friend. "Cases where things in the office got out of hand?"

"And tell us about your job?" Lucy was asking at the same time. "When do you go back, Anna?"

Janie felt relief ride through her as the conversation shifted to Anna, who proceeded to tell them she was starting in a fortnight, but it wasn't long before she turned back to Janie again. "Come on, did you have any interesting ones?" she asked. "When you were working?"

Janie's head flooded with images of the case she had spent the last five-odd years pushing to the far corners of her mind. But she shook her head. She'd become good at keeping her mouth shut about that. About all the things that had happened back then. Miles Morgan. Sophie. The unease rippled inside her, making her feel like she was on a fairground ride.

———

She knew she was being watched again. She might have been able to pass off the shadow in the parking lot at the quay a couple of weeks back, but she definitely couldn't ignore the fact someone was lurking near the house when she got home the previous night. She'd turned onto their quiet lane, practically on autopilot and had done a double take when she saw it.

The last time she had been stalked was when she was involved in that last case, which had become high-profile, and she understood why someone might want something from her. But it didn't explain why it was happening again now.

Last night, as she'd looked a second time, her stomach jolted and her fingers twitched against the steering wheel. As quickly as the figure had appeared in her line of sight it went away again, and by the time Janie reached their gate there was no sign of an intruder.

She'd glanced in the rearview mirror. The girls were oblivious in the backseat, Ella's head down as she flicked through photos on her phone, Lottie chewing the end of a pencil as she studied her spelling words.

Turning off the engine, Janie had stretched her gaze farther, to the bushes that provided a boundary between her long driveway and the road beyond. Someone had been watching her house, and now she wondered if they'd recognized her car. Eventually Janie climbed out and waited for the girls to do the same, all the time glancing around them. Anyone could be lingering in a number of places.

The girls were hovering by the front door as Janie had shut the car door and turned off the alarm in the house, and then, with one last glance behind her, she'd let them all inside.

There had never been any danger in the past. No threats. There was absolutely no reason to think someone was watching her again. Why would they be?

Probably, she'd thought, as she'd flicked on the lights and had a near miss with the girls' schoolbags that had been dropped in the middle of the hallway, it was in her head. It was just because she had been thinking too much lately. Her Facebook search for Miles had planted pictures in her head—she had even dreamed of him the night before.

Now Janie's phone was ringing in her bag, and yet it had taken Anna to point it out to her before she realized. "Oh," she murmured. She hadn't even heard it. Dipping a hand into her bag, she pulled it out and saw Sophie's name on the screen.

"I better take this," she said to her friends as she picked up the call. "Hey, Soph, everything all right?" she asked on instinct, but immediately she could tell it wasn't, when the sound of sobbing filled the line.

Janie scrambled out of her seat and went outside the café, pressing her phone to ear as she said, "Sophie, what the hell is wrong?"

She remembered the last time she'd received a call like this from her best friend. Five years ago she'd had to leave the house one evening and look for Sophie, whom she'd found soaking wet and sheltering from the rain in a shop doorway, her bright pink scarf tightly wrapped around her. That night she hadn't managed to get her friend to tell her what had happened, but Janie had known. When Sophie eventually opened up twenty-fours later, Janie had expected the story, but still she had been shocked by the entirety of it. What it meant.

"Sophie, please, will you tell me what's happened?" Janie begged now.

"Mark's dumped me," she wailed. "And he's taken five hundred pounds out my bloody wallet and . . ." Her words gave way to more sobs.

"Mark?" The artist boyfriend. Again no shock, only this time Janie felt some relief. Mark was manageable. They could get through this one.

"I love him," Sophie said. Janie couldn't see anything remotely attractive in the man, but regardless, she listened and told her friend she'd come up and be with her that weekend if she wanted.

When the call ended, Janie leaned back against the wall of the café and took a deep breath. Holding a hand over her mouth she shook her head. Maybe it would be good to get away to London for a night. She could take the girls, get some space.

After the night before, she might have assured herself there was nothing to worry about, that it was just her mind playing tricks on her, but it wasn't just her to think about anymore. It was the girls too. Her precious daughters could be in danger, and they were everything to her. And she would do whatever was necessary to protect them.

Initial Interview between Detective Emily Marlow and Anna Halshaw following the fire at Morris and Wood offices on Monday, May 13.

<u>**Anna Halshaw, on Thursday, May 16, at Lymington Police Headquarters.**</u>

Marlow:	Can you describe your friendship with Janie Wood?
Anna:	We're very close. We've been friends since our oldest girls were in year one. They're in year six now, so I've known Janie for five years.
Marlow:	And how often do you see each other?
Anna:	Every day, more or less, at the school gate, either at drop-off or pickup. And then we meet for coffee once a week. There's four of us that get together. We're all good friends.
Marlow:	So you would say you know her pretty well?
Anna:	Of course, which is why what you told me about this person following her is so shocking.
Marlow:	And of course the fact she never mentioned the name Miles Morgan to you before.
Anna:	Yes, but there could be many reasons for that. I mean, he probably wasn't significant.
Marlow:	He was significant, Anna—but how about her husband? Did Janie confide anything to you lately about him?
Anna:	Janie and Harry? You mean their marriage? No. They were as happy as they've always been. What is this—
Marlow:	Or anything to do with his work?
Anna:	Oh, well, yes, yes. She told us someone at Harry's office was being bullied. Is that what this is about? Because she didn't tell me much. I didn't get the impression it was a major deal, but God, you never know, do you?
Marlow:	One last thing, Anna—did she mention any of the women who worked for her husband?

Anna: (shakes head) Not by name.

Marlow: None that she may have been close to?

Anna: No, I don't think so.

Marlow: Mia Anderson or Laura Denning? You've never heard Janie talking about either of them?

chapter twenty-nine

the woods' party
three days before the fire

Mia stood in front of the only full-length mirror in the bunga-low. It was propped against the wall in her mum's bedroom, positioned so awkwardly that she was always afraid it might fall and break. As she stared at her reflection, her mind was on some-thing completely different from the party that night. It was on Sarah Clifton and what her sudden departure from Morris and Wood meant. It was on Harry Wood and his sparklingly clean reputation. But most of it was on the fact she still hadn't achieved what she'd wanted. That almost eight months later and the reason she had given up her promising career at the Venue was slipping out of her reach and she was no longer sure what to do about it.

Mia hadn't noticed Jess appearing in her bedroom doorway until she caught a glimpse of her sister in the far edge of the mirror.

"You look nice," Jess told her.

"Thank you." Mia screwed her nose up and finally took in her appearance. "I'm not sure, though." She was wearing a long pleated leopard-print skirt that skimmed her ankles and a black chiffon tank top that she nervously tugged out from her waistband. Her glittery sandals sparkled on her feet, and a pretty gold chain hung around her ankle. "I don't know whether it's supposed to be dressy or casual," she said. "Harry's invitation didn't say."

"What are the other women in the office wearing?" Jess asked.

Mia shrugged as she turned from side to side, letting her skirt swish against her legs, wondering if she was going to be warm enough. She had been told that often the Woods' parties spread to the garden beside the pool, with its neat border of shrubbery.

"Well I think you look lovely," Jess said, and when Mia caught her sister's reflection in the mirror behind her, she saw the glimmer of a smile on her lips, even though her eyes were sunken and rimmed with black shadows.

Mia wondered what was really running through Jess's head right now. Maybe it was nothing more than her little sister looking pretty and dressed up for a party at Harry Wood's house. The man that their mum still talked about as if he'd opened a drug den next door, rather than built offices on Lymington Quay.

Maybe Jess was looking at her and thinking none of this was fair when she was sat in faded navy jogging bottoms and an oversized sweatshirt, with nothing lined up for the evening except an ITV crime drama.

"Are you getting a taxi?" Jess asked.

"You sound like Mum," Mia replied, then frowned and added, "Of course I am." They both knew Mia would never get behind the wheel if she'd been drinking. They both knew all too well the heartbreak and devastation that could cause.

"Is the woman going? The one whose job you have?"

Mia laughed off the comment. "Yes, I'm sure Laura will be there."

"Is she still angry with you?"

"Yes," Mia said. "I think she's still out to get me," she added, a little more quietly.

"And who are you out to get, little sister?" Jess asked.

Mia's smile dropped and she cocked her head, her gaze falling on Jess, who was looking at her intently. But by the time she eventually went to ask Jess what she meant by that, her sister had left the room.

It was just past seven thirty by the time Mia's taxi pulled up into Harry Wood's sweeping driveway. Other staff from the office were already there. She could hear the murmur of conversation and laughter, a hint of music drifting from the back garden. Glancing at the side gate she wondered if she should go straight through, before thinking better of it and walking up to the double wooden door at the front.

It really was a luxurious home. The topiary bushes that lined the driveway were manicured to perfection. Automatic lights flooded the way as the cab pulled up. Even the driver whistled as he drove in.

Janie Wood answered the door and let Mia inside. A smile was plastered onto her face, which was naked apart from black mascara and maybe a bit of bronzer. Janie was naturally attractive, but her smile did nothing to hide the anguish behind it. Mia assumed these parties were not high on her list of things she enjoyed, though she was clearly trying to give the impression she was happy to have her house invaded by her husband's employees. She probably had other things she could be doing with her evening, friends she would rather be spending time with.

Janie pointed Mia toward the kitchen and asked if she wouldn't mind helping herself to a drink. She just had to get something from the dining room, she said.

Of course she didn't mind helping herself, Mia insisted, but she hovered in the hallway as Janie slipped away into the room on their left. The sound of an engine pulling up outside caught Mia's attention. She almost expected to hear the screech of brakes the way it hurtled up the drive. She peered through the thin slit of window that ran beside the length of the front door and watched as a gray Qashqai pulled up at the side of the drive and Laura stepped from the driver's door, banging it shut behind her and stopping to peer up at the house.

Mia drew back. No husband, she noticed. It seemed that Laura had driven herself to the party on her own. Presumably she was intending to stay sober.

Reaching up a hand, she fingered the thin veil of curtain that hung loosely by the window and then eventually let it fall. As she backed into the hallway and turned toward the kitchen, Mia considered her sister's words. *Who are you out to get, little sister?*

If Jess knew what she was doing, then why hadn't she said anything? Why wasn't she trying to stop her?

They'd had a conversation once, maybe a month after Jess's world had come crashing down, sweeping along with it Mia's and their mother's too.

"What are you going to do?" Mia had asked her.

Jess had looked up slowly, her brown eyes ovals, as deep as the earth, and in them Mia tried to read what her sister was thinking. But she found it too hard to know by then.

"Forget," Jess said eventually. "I'm going to do everything I can to forget."

Mia had shaken her head. She wanted to tell her sister she couldn't do that, because if she forgot, then someone was getting away with what they had done to her.

And yet she'd seen the sadness in those brown eyes, and Mia knew it wasn't her place to tell her sister that forgetting was not the solution. In that moment Mia swore that she *would* let Jess forget. But she also knew that she herself never would.

chapter thirty

J anie had been ready since six p.m. Her hair had been washed and styled at the salon and was hanging in soft curls that fell just below her shoulders. She'd chosen a long kaftan in rich purple that fell open at the knees, and had even had her toenails painted to match while her hair was being blow-dried. All this effort for a party she didn't want to throw, but at least it gave her the confidence to open the door to a bunch of semi-strangers she only saw once a year and welcome them into her home.

The other thing that gave her some Dutch courage was the glass of champagne she held in her hand as she opened the door to one guest after another. But Janie knew better than to drink too much too early. At least one of the guests did that every year, and she doubted this year would be any different. There were plenty who liked to make the most of the free alcohol supplied at their boss's expense.

Janie had let Mia Anderson into the house and directed her toward the kitchen. She would search her out later, when she got the chance, but for now she had no choice but to leave her stranded in the hallway. Ella had texted from Anna's house, where both girls were having a sleepover, to say Lottie had been crying for the last half hour because she couldn't find her favorite teddy, Blue Ted.

Janie dipped into the dining room and went over to the sofa in the corner where the girls had been watching TV before school that morning, and sure enough there he was, balancing precariously on one arm.

She positioned him in front of the cushions, took a photo, and sent it to Ella with a message that read, Blue Ted's perfectly happy watching TV. Love you and miss you both xx.

She waited to check it was sent, hovering over the phone until a message came back from Ella to say thanks and that they loved her too. Janie smiled as she read it, looking up sharply as a car came up the driveway far more quickly than she thought appropriate, and as she moved toward the window, she pinched back the curtains with one finger. It was Laura Denning's car, now pulling to a halt by the fence, the door swinging wide open as the engine was switched off. Laura climbed out, wearing dark jeans and a gray blazer. As smart as she looked, she was underdressed for the party in comparison to the other guests.

Janie let the curtain flutter back into place but could just about see Laura still as she closed the car door and then stood rooted to the spot in the middle of their driveway, staring at the house. Laura's eyes drifted up to Janie and Harry's bedroom above before dropping down again and finally landing on the front door.

Janie waited for Nate to join her. She peered into the car as best she could from her vantage point, but there was no sign of Laura's husband. She couldn't think of a time that Laura hadn't brought him, though perhaps there was a problem with childcare. Maybe Janie should have gone to the effort of telling Laura she could have brought the baby.

She moved away from the window as Laura disappeared from sight and the doorbell rang, though by the time Janie reached the doorway to the hall, Harry had beaten her to it. The one time her husband had appeared to greet a guest and, though she was sure he couldn't have had any idea it was Laura, it felt a little too convenient.

Janie slunk behind the dining-room door as he let her in and listened to his overenthusiastic welcome as he ushered her inside. "No Nate tonight?" he asked.

"No." A pause and then another, "No. We couldn't get anyone to babysit, so . . ." She let the end of the sentence hang.

"Oh. Shame," Harry said, in a manner that didn't sound remotely genuine to Janie as he went on, more enthusiastically, "but at least you're here. Come on through, let me get you a drink."

"Thanks. White wine, please," Laura replied. Janie glanced back at the car parked haphazardly on their driveway and wondered if Laura had already had one.

"How are you getting on with the pitch?" Harry asked her.

"I'm getting on well," Laura replied with a modesty that grated on Janie, though she detected something else in Laura's voice too, which made her think things might not be going quite that smoothly.

"That's great, really great. See, I knew you could do it."

"I just hope he likes my ideas," Laura said. "If he doesn't—" Again the sentence was cut short. "Miles Morgan seems like a hard man to please," Laura went on, her voice fading.

Janie's heart stopped beating. Just for a moment. Her breath caught in her throat before she released it in a sharp puff, poking her head around the doorway in time to see her husband and Laura disappearing into the kitchen.

Miles Morgan. Laura had spoken those words so casually. She'd have no idea that the mere sound of that man's name could have just tipped Janie's world on its axis.

She pulled out of her hiding place and followed the wake of her husband's footsteps. So Harry had brought that man into her life again. Did he really have no clue what it would do to her? And not only that, he was doing work for Miles. The man must have been in Lymington. She shuddered at the thought, her mind whirling.

Was Harry planning to bring him to the house?

Janie scanned the kitchen, catching a fleeting glimpse of her husband in the garden, guests milling around him, blurring into one. She clutched onto the counter beside her, fingers gripping it tightly as she felt the air leave her body. She wanted to cut through the guests to get to her husband and demand he tell her what was going on. Did he really think so little of Janie that he could do this to her?

Second interview between Detective Emily Marlow and Janie Wood following the fire at Morris and Wood offices on Monday, May 13.

<u>**Janie Wood, on Thursday, May 16, at Lymington Police Headquarters.**</u>

Marlow:	What I can't get my head around is that you didn't tell anyone else you thought someone was watching you. Not even your husband?
Janie:	No. I told you. I didn't tell anyone.
Marlow:	Why was that?
Janie:	Because—I don't know, I think I just wanted to pretend it wasn't happening. I didn't want to admit it was.
Marlow:	Not because you didn't think your husband would believe you?
Janie:	No. That's not it.
Marlow:	But you have children in the house. Didn't their safety cross your mind?
Janie:	Of course it did. Of course. My children mean everything to me.
Marlow:	Mrs. Wood, you'll need to calm down.
Janie:	(pauses) My children are my world, but in this case—I guess I didn't think there was anything to worry about. I didn't feel threatened. Not at the time, anyway.
Marlow:	And you didn't think about why you were being watched?
Janie:	No. I had no clue.
Marlow:	Tell me about your relationship with Miles Morgan.
Janie:	(pauses) There's little to tell.
Marlow:	But he came back into your life very recently. In fact—only on Monday. The day of the fire.
Janie:	Yes.
Marlow:	Do you think this is a coincidence?

Janie: Are you asking me if I think it was him who followed me? Maybe, yes. Maybe it was.

Marlow: You don't sound particularly sure.

Janie: Like I've told you, I didn't ever get the chance to see whoever it was.

Marlow: Janie, there are too many things that just don't add up for me.

Janie: I didn't set fire to that building. I wouldn't have done that. You need to believe me.

Marlow: Yet you were there. You admit you were at the quay on Monday night, though you can't give me any explanation other than that you were looking at the building.

Janie: I know. I just don't know what else to say because that's all I was doing.

Marlow: And then there are the other people who were also there with you that night, aren't there?

I need you to tell me. What on earth were you doing there with them? Mia Anderson? Laura Denning? Why were the three of you at Lymington Quay on Monday evening while your husband's offices were burning to the ground?

chapter thirty-one

the woods' party
three days before the fire

Laura gripped the thin stem of the wineglass between her fingers as she stumbled on a patch of grass. She had spent the last two hours making small talk, loitering on the edge of conversations, and accepting refills whenever someone appeared with a bottle. All the while she'd been keeping an eye on Mia, waiting for the right chance to talk to her.

Mia had been moving seamlessly from one person to another, clinking glasses, throwing her head back in laughter. Right now she was talking to Mike Lewis earnestly, leaning toward him, surely closer than Mike would like. Laura held her glass to her lips as she studied the woman in front of her, wondering what she was playing at.

"Penny for them."

"Huh?"

"Your thoughts." Patrick was standing beside her, she hadn't even heard him approach.

Laura shrugged.

"No Nate tonight?"

"No, he couldn't—we couldn't get a babysitter."

"That's a shame. My daughter can always come over if you ever need."

Laura nodded and finished the last of her wine, still holding the empty glass against her lips as she turned back to Mia. It wasn't a shame in the end, Nate had clearly been in no mood for the party, and if he were here he'd only be tracking her, making sure she didn't cause a fuss.

Did she intend to? In truth, Laura had no idea what she wanted the end result to be. What she didn't want was for all the attention to be on her, for everyone to be talking about her long after the party had finished, but then she also *did* want those same people to know exactly the type of person Mia Anderson was. And surely Harry's party, when each and every one of them were here, was the best place for Laura to unmask her.

Patrick was nattering on, but Laura wasn't listening, and now all she wanted was for him to leave her alone so she could go and get Mia. And another drink. She wanted a refill first. Shaking her empty glass she excused herself, and when she emerged from the kitchen Mia was alone.

Laura drew a breath and took another large gulp of the sauvignon blanc that really was going down extremely easily and, gripping the fragile stem of the glass firmly between her fingers, she strode across the decking.

"I know you're lying." Laura spoke to Mia's back, her words hushed so no one nearby could hear.

"Sorry?" Mia swung around, her eyes screwed up questioningly. "What did you say?"

"You heard me," Laura said plainly. "I said I know you're lying."

"I don't want to have this conversation here." Mia's eyes darted around them at the people standing only feet away. None of them had turned around yet, but they soon would, Laura assumed.

"*I* want to," Laura said defiantly.

Mia pursed her lips and started walking away, down the lawn toward Harry's dimly lit pool house, presumably knowing that Laura would follow.

Laura blinked. It was hard to focus when it was so much darker down that end of the garden. When she caught up with Mia, she reached out with the hand that clutched the glass and pointed it at Mia. "I know you're lying," she repeated. "I know you're not who you say you are."

Mia bit her bottom lip as she continued to watch Laura, but she didn't respond.

"I spoke to Tess. I should have done that a long while ago, shouldn't I?"

Mia gave a small flick of her head.

"So you know why I didn't? Because I was so worried about what I would hear."

Still Mia didn't speak.

"She told me they'd already started talking to other agencies. To keep costs down. They only kept the TV campaign at Morris and Wood because they thought we had much better experience at producing ads than anyone else local, and then apparently they're planning to move on with some agency near Bournemouth.

"I told her I would have done a good job for her, that I would have kept it competitive. I said if she'd told me they were worried about budgets she could have spoken to me, that she could have trusted me. But do you know what she said?" Laura paused. "Of course you do, because you put the words right in her mouth, Mia. She said she didn't know that she could trust me any longer. She didn't think I had her best interests at heart when I was having an affair with the boss."

Laura glared at Mia, who reluctantly held her gaze.

"I mean, even if I was, which I'm not," she screamed, "what would that matter? How would that ever affect my work? Except you knew it mattered to her, didn't you?" she went on, pointing at Mia. "Because Tess had confided in you that her husband had left her for his secretary.

And so you *knew* that if you wanted to get your hands on my job, then that was a safe little trick to play."

Mia glanced over Laura's shoulder. Laura didn't need to turn to sense the hush that had descended on the people nearest to them. "People are looking," Mia said through gritted teeth.

"Why did you lie about me?" Laura continued.

Mia shook her head and turned away.

"Tell me!" Laura yelled, lunging forward with her hand outstretched again as Mia dodged out of her way. "Why make that up? What have I done to *you*, Mia?"

"You're making a scene," Mia hissed. "You've had too much to drink. This isn't the time or place to—"

"Don't you dare tell me I've had too much to drink!" Laura cried. A sound rose from someone near them, a gasp or a laugh, something indecipherable. "Who the hell do you think you are? You've come into my life and stolen my job from under me and you stand there all high-and-mighty telling me this isn't the time. It *is* the time, Mia. It's precisely the time. I want to know what I've done to you that—"

"Don't you walk away from me!" Laura yelled, as Mia turned her back and began to walk across the garden. She could feel the muscles in her body clench. There were maybe half a dozen people standing around watching with horror or amusement, Laura couldn't tell which, but all she could see was that Mia was desperately trying to get away from them as she strode toward the pool.

Laura's breaths were coming short and fast and she knew that if she followed Mia, everyone else would likely see them too, but right then she couldn't give a shit.

chapter thirty-two

It was almost ten p.m. when Janie caught sight of Mia and Laura standing in the middle of her lawn. A glass of wine hung loosely from Laura's hand as she jabbed a finger at Mia. Weirdly, Janie's first thought was whether it was one of her Dartington crystal glasses, because she wouldn't have been surprised if Harry had given Laura that. Her second was that Laura clearly looked as if she hadn't stopped at the one glass of wine she'd mentioned having at the start of the night, and she certainly didn't look as if she should be driving home. Did she actually plan to leave her car here? Was she going to be back in the morning to collect it?

Laura's body swayed softly, her feet shuffling as she struggled to regain her balance. At some point in the evening she had shed her shoes and was standing barefoot, her toes curling into Janie's neatly trimmed grass.

By now all the guests had stopped their conversations, distracted by the spectacle unfurling by the swimming pool. At first Janie hadn't realized the two women were arguing, but as soon as she had woven through those who were gawping on the decking, she had a much clearer view.

Mia was standing ramrod straight, her eyes flared wide as she stared daggers at Laura. A champagne flute was clutched by her side, and Janie imagined the hand drawing up and swiping the side of Laura's face. She rather hoped it might. Mia certainly looked like she could.

Laura's arms, in contrast, were flailing everywhere, and her face was bright red. She was wobbling precariously close to the pool, which Janie noticed was still uncovered, even though Harry had promised he'd do it before the party. She glanced desperately around the garden in the hope he might come and break up the argument before it got out of hand. But there was no sign of him, and so Janie wavered between leaving the scene to find him and going over herself.

She was mid-thought when Laura's hand with the wineglass clutched within it rose again, and then suddenly, through some brute force, the woman managed to snap its stem in two.

Mia's gaze dropped to the ground beneath them as she stepped back. Janie's followed, but when she looked up, Laura appeared to not have even noticed she might be stepping on broken glass.

Still Harry was nowhere to be found, and with audible gasps arising from the excited crowd behind her, Janie stormed across the lawn to the two women. She reached out to take the remainder of her precious glass from Laura's hand, who hadn't even noticed Janie approaching.

"That *is* my Dartington," Janie muttered, as Laura pulled back in surprise. The glasses had been a wedding present from her mother—the reason she had set out the cheap ones in bulk, and yet Harry must have bypassed them as he sought out this one for Laura from the cabinet. "Give me that glass," Janie said as she made another lunge for it, and still Laura pulled back again, opening up the space between her and Mia.

Janie felt her ankle twist beneath her. The pain shot up the outside of her right calf as she tried to rebalance on the paving stones that edged the pool, but already she feared it was too late. She felt herself tipping forward, unable to stop her fall as she plunged headlong into the swimming pool.

The air was still when she eventually resurfaced. The momentary silence deafening before shrieks filled her ears, and in the distance a vision of Harry running across the lawn came to view. As she pulled herself to the side of the pool, all Janie could think was that she was sure the hand that had reached out for her as she was falling hadn't actually helped as it pressed against her back.

Someone had kindly brought Janie a towel from the pool house. She thought it might have been Patrick but she couldn't have been sure, as the crowd of guests parted and she made her way through them.

Janie had ignored both women gasping at her, asking if she was all right as she climbed out, but she had known they weren't far behind her. Neither was her husband, who, once he'd checked that she hadn't hurt anything but her pride, had jokingly called out that the show was over and told everyone to refill their glasses. *Ever the host*, she thought through gritted teeth as she approached the back door, though by then conversations had started again and at least she didn't feel everyone's eyes still on her.

Janie quickly changed and came back to the kitchen, desperate to find out what the hell had started the argument that in turn had caused her to end up in the pool. When she walked into the room she stopped short. Her husband had one hand gripped on Laura's arm and was fishing in the bowl for his car keys with the other.

"What are you doing?" She glanced at Harry and then at Laura, who was leaning against the doorframe to the hallway, her head back, her eyes semi-closed.

"I'm taking her home," he replied without looking up, as he continued to rifle through the bowl, although he did let go of Laura. Finally he picked out his keys, the *I Love Daddy* key ring playfully swinging from them.

"*Laura?*" Janie asked, stunned.

"Yes." He jangled the keys in one hand and eventually turned to her.

His face was expressionless. It was almost like he had no clue that walking away from his own party to drive home this other woman could in any way be out of order. Or maybe he just didn't care.

"Why?" she asked him, her teeth clenched, her wet hair soaking through her top and onto her back.

"Because she can hardly drive, can she?" Harry said quietly, leaning in, nodding in Laura's direction. "I take it you're okay, love?" he added as an afterthought.

Janie shook her head in disbelief. "Then call her a taxi," she said slowly.

Harry parted his lips then clamped his mouth shut, his face softening as he gave a small shrug. "It's fine," he said, pressing his mouth into a flat smile. "I don't mind."

She cocked her head. Did he actually think this was what she was worrying about? The fact he was putting himself out? "This is your party, Harry," she said slowly. "You cannot leave it to drive her home. Call her a taxi." Her words were drawn out as if she were talking to a child who didn't understand her.

"I've only had two bottles of beer," he said. "And I won't be long. No one will even realize I'm missing."

"I will realize," she said.

"Seriously, Janie?" He touched her arm. "It's fine. I promise you I won't be long." The keys continued to jangle in his hand. She held her own arm down by her side as she fought the urge to reach up and swipe them out of his grip. She could imagine the satisfaction she would get from watching them spin across the room.

Her blood was burning through her veins. *If you go, Harry Wood . . . if you dare go.* She opened her mouth to tell him how furious she would be if he left this house, but already he had leaned forward, given her a swift peck on the cheek, and she realized that if she really had to tell him this, then what was the point anyway?

If they had reached the stage that her own husband's priority was no longer Janie, then why stop him? Clearly it was too late.

Janie stepped out into the hallway as he grabbed Laura's arm again and hauled her to the front door, and disappeared. Eventually the sound of his car engine tumbled over the beat of music.

"I agree."

Janie swung around and saw Mia in the kitchen doorway. She let go of the clutches of skirt that she had been balling and smoothed them down her thighs. The heat on her neck was making her itch, and she resisted scratching what she knew must be patches of red crawling over her skin.

"Sorry?" Janie said.

"I agree," Mia replied. "He shouldn't have done that. That's what you must be thinking."

Janie went to speak, though no words came out. She hadn't known anyone else was listening to her and Harry.

"I mean, Laura is clearly drunk, but she could have gotten a taxi home," Mia went on, her eyes seemingly penetrating Janie's. "After all, that's what I'll be doing," she said, as if driving home the point that Harry's favoritism was clear for all to see. "I'm so sorry about what happened, by the way. I hope you're okay?"

Janie shrugged.

Mia nodded as she looked toward the front drive. "She has him wrapped around her finger, doesn't she?"

"What?" Janie blurted, incredulous.

"Laura? I mean, it's hardly Harry's fault."

Janie shook her head, her gaze trailing over Mia's face that was full of composure yet couldn't completely hide something dark lurking behind her eyes. "What are you saying?" she asked uncertainly.

"I'm saying we shouldn't always blame the man. If they are led on to believe that a woman is interested in them—" Mia paused and shrugged, holding her palms up flat.

Janie cocked her head, fury raging through her but at the same time battling with a need to know what Mia was getting at. "What are you talking about?"

"I'm sorry." Mia set her mouth into a flat line. It looked as if she were trying for a smile, though Janie wasn't sure. Everything about the evening was surreal, and all she wanted now was for Mia to leave her alone so she could head straight for the champagne, which until now she'd been drinking in moderate proportions.

Janie needed to bolster herself with alcohol before any of it started to feel real and she needed to face the likelihood that her husband was sleeping with the woman he had just driven home.

"Oh right," Janie said suddenly, as the idea dawned on her. "You're just pissed off with Laura. Well, whatever the hell is going on between the two of you, it has nothing to do with me or my husband."

"There's nothing going on between me and Laura," Mia said firmly. "Oh, I'm so sorry. Of course I never wanted to overstep the line when you've invited me into your lovely home," she went on. "Although I have a feeling I may have already done that. All I was trying to rather carelessly say was that I think it's often so easy to blame the man, when a lot of the time it's—"

"Not their fault?" Janie interrupted. "Is that what you're saying?"

Mia smiled thinly again.

"You think that if my husband is having an affair with someone from his office, then he shouldn't be held responsible?" Janie spat out with a bitter laugh.

"No, actually, I don't think that at all," Mia replied, her expression now so deadly serious that Janie wondered if she'd caught the right end of the conversation. "*I* think men should be held responsible for every one of their actions." Mia held her gaze, and Janie stared back at her blankly. If she'd been confused moments ago, she was even more so now.

Mia's penetrating glare was beginning to unnerve her.

"And I suppose as women we should stand by each other, shouldn't we?" Mia went on. "Only sometimes that doesn't happen either. They can be the ones to blame, can't they?"

Janie's mouth hung open. "Is this all to do with Laura?"

Mia shook her head. "Not at all, actually. Anyway, thank you for a lovely evening. I think it's probably time for me to go home too."

"Yes, I think it probably is," Janie said.

Mia nodded. "Maybe I'm just not as good as you are at putting my point across," she said as a taxi beeped from the driveway, simultaneously sending a text to Mia's phone. "Better go," she added cheerily.

"Wait!" Janie called as Mia walked out the front door, heading for the waiting car. "What do you mean not as good as I am?" Her eyes flitted back and forth as Mia climbed into the car and pulled the door shut behind her. Her mind tried to catch up, racing through their odd conversation, trying to patch together Mia's words, which were clearly intentional. Did she know her?

———————

As the car pulled away, Janie retreated to the kitchen, where a text pinging loudly from her phone on the counter startled her. She reached for it, and on the screen flashed a photo from Ella of her and her little sister, clad in pajamas. The message read, We're still up!!!

Janie's eyes filled with tears. She wanted her girls home. She wanted these intruders out of her house.

Mia's words only served to prove the idea that every one of the guests here tonight knew her husband was up to something behind her back.

She supressed the scream rising inside her.

Their laughter was grating. The clinking of their glasses sent shivers down her spine. Precariously balanced plates were tipping crumbs onto her floor.

Her daughters weren't upstairs in their own beds because of this crowd of unwanted guests, and all she wanted to do was scream, *Get out of my house!*

She wanted her husband to still be here to deal with them.

At the same time, she wanted him never to walk back in their front door ever again.

She wanted, above all, for him not to have brought Miles Morgan back into their lives.

Third Interview between Detective Emily Marlow and Janie Wood following the fire at Morris and Wood offices on Monday, May 13.

Janie Wood, on Friday, May 17, at Lymington Police Headquarters.

Marlow: Mrs. Wood, did you intend to kill your husband on Monday evening?

Janie: No. Of course I didn't.

Marlow: Did you set fire to the offices of Morris and Wood?

Janie: No.

Marlow: Did you know your husband was in the building when you went there?

Janie: Please. I didn't do it.

Marlow: But you and Harry hadn't been getting on well, had you? And you were seen at the quay at the time of the fire—

Janie: I didn't—I haven't done anything wrong. I'm begging you, I just want to go and see my girls. They're on their own. They're frightened. This is ridiculous. You must know that. It wasn't me.

Marlow: Did you know Miles Morgan was also in the office at the time of the fire?

Janie: No. I didn't know anyone was in there. I didn't even—

Marlow: So you're telling me you weren't aware either Miles or your husband was in the office? Where was Harry supposed to be on Monday evening?

Janie: I have no idea. I don't know. We weren't—we weren't talking.

Marlow: Because of his alleged affair with Laura Denning?

Janie: No! I don't know if he was having an affair with her or not. You *know* why we weren't talking. We've been over this already. I was just annoyed with him after the party. You can ask him that. Things weren't that bad between us. Ask him yourself. He may be in the hospital, but he's talking now.

Marlow:	We know he's talking now, Mrs. Wood, and you can rest assured we will be speaking to your husband.
Janie:	Good. Good, because he knew everything was all right between us. Harry knows I would never have done what you're saying I've done. Please. Please, I just want to make sure my girls are okay.
Marlow:	Mrs. Wood, I need to remind you that this is now a murder investigation—
Janie:	I know that. God, help me, I know that.
Marlow:	—and that Miles Morgan is dead.
Janie:	I know.
Marlow:	Then you need to start talking to me.
Janie:	(silence)
Marlow:	You know, I can place all three of you at the quay Monday night, and yet I can't actually figure out what any of you were really doing there. Laura Denning was the last person to leave the office unharmed that night, wasn't she? So, Mrs. Wood, if you're telling me you had nothing to do with the fire, then you must at least be able to tell me what she was doing there?
Janie:	I already have. I honestly don't know.
Marlow:	Why she didn't go straight home after she left. Why, an hour and a quarter later, she was still at the quay. And *why* she didn't tell her husband that night that she knew there was a fire. You know what I'm wondering, Mrs. Wood? I'm thinking something might have happened in that office before she left.
Janie:	If something did, I don't—
Marlow:	You don't know. Yeah, I get it. And then we have Mia Anderson too. Whom you met for lunch a couple of weeks ago, although it wasn't her who asked you out, was it, Janie? Like you told me before.
Janie:	No. I think maybe it was me.

Marlow: Because you wanted to find out what she was doing at your husband's office?

Janie: No! Honestly, I promise you, that wasn't it at all. My lunch with Mia was completely genuine.

Marlow: You didn't recognize the name—Anderson?

Janie: No—I mean, it's not an uncommon name. No, I didn't have a clue then.

Marlow: But you do now. Why don't you tell me how you knew Mia Anderson before she came to work at Morris and Wood? Mrs. Wood? Did you not think we would find out?

chapter thirty-three

the woods' party
three days before the fire

Laura didn't think she'd had that many glasses of wine at the party, though she did know it was too many to drive home. She was twisted to her left, staring out of the passenger window so she didn't have to look at Harry.

Perhaps she'd had a few more than she'd realized. At several points her glass had been refilled before she could stop it. Maybe it was four or five. And she hadn't eaten anything since lunch, so the wine had gone straight to her head, and now the motion of the car was making her feel sleepy and a tiny bit nauseated, and the blurry memories of the night were swishing about in her head, sharp-daggered reminders of how she'd embarrassed herself.

Laura hiccuped and held a hand over her mouth, feeling the burn of alcohol repeating. She should never have gone to the party. She should have stayed at home with Nate and tried to make some move toward fixing the cracks in her marriage that had spread all too quickly in the last eight weeks.

She certainly shouldn't have shouted at Mia in the middle of the back garden. Had everyone been watching? She had sensed pairs of eyes on her, but she didn't know if they'd heard. She hadn't been that loud. Or she hadn't intended to be.

Laura had told Mia she knew she was lying. *Liar*, she had called her. She might have said it more than once. She might have even prodded her in the chest as she did it, Laura couldn't really remember. All she knew was that suddenly Janie Wood was by their side and the next minute she was in the pool. And Laura hadn't even tried to stop her fall.

She had been mortified when Janie climbed out, her beautiful kaftan drenched as she'd shrugged off her husband, who had tried to help. Harry had in turn pulled Laura into the house instead.

She closed her eyes and let out a soft groan. Did everyone in the company really think she and Harry were having an affair? If they did, she could only imagine what they'd be saying now.

"Are you going to be sick? Open the window if you are," Harry ordered.

Why had he urged her into his car? Janie had seen them. Laura knew they'd been talking about her in the kitchen, though their conversation was fuzzy. She should never have agreed, but it was a ride home and he was quick to open the passenger door and nudge her into the seat.

"I'm not going to be sick," she said quietly.

She wanted to scrub out the night, go back to the start of it, do everything differently. She wanted to cry, goddamn it. That's what she wanted. She wanted to cry great racking sobs, like a baby. Tears began to fall down her cheeks, and she gulped more back.

"It's all right," Harry murmured from beside her. "We all screw up from time to time."

"I've just ruined your party," she said. "You don't have to be so kind to me."

"Stop it, Laura."

She winced at the touch of his hand on her leg.

"Don't beat yourself up about it," he said. His hand lingered on her thigh as he gently squeezed it.

"I should send flowers to Janie." She moved her leg away from him forcefully, though now she was crushed against the passenger door. "To apologize."

"That's not necessary."

"Everyone will be talking about me," Laura cried.

"Yeah. But only for a day or two. It will all blow over."

She was relieved to see that he had turned the car onto her road and was parking up on the left, outside her house. Harry turned off the engine.

Laura glanced up at the curtained windows and prayed Nate didn't look out and see her. Opening the door quickly, she swung her legs out. "Thank you for bringing me home, you didn't have to," she said hurriedly.

"Laura," Harry called, too loudly, as he gripped her arm, making her stomach twist into knots. She wanted to hiss at him to keep his voice down, but at the same time she couldn't be rude to the one person who was being kind to her.

"You two will work it out," he said. "Don't worry about it."

"What?" she said, turning back to him, screwing up her nose. When had she told him about Nate? *What* had she told him?

"Just talk to Mia on Monday and you can sort out whatever it was."

"Oh, Mia. Right."

"Who did you think I meant?" he asked. "Is everything all right at home?" He nodded toward her house.

"Everything's totally fine, and I'm not sorry about what I said to Mia." She pulled out of his reach as she sidled off the seat. "I meant it. She's lying about what she's doing at the company. She's out for my job for a reason." Even Laura could hear the whine in her drunken voice.

She thought she saw him shake his head, but it was such a slight movement she couldn't be sure. "I know you don't believe me but I'm right," she said, and slammed the door, stumbling on the pavement as she turned toward the house and up the path where Nate stood in the open doorway, arms folded tightly across his chest.

"Oh God." She swallowed down the trepidation that clung in a ball to her throat but couldn't budge it. Slowly Laura tried walking in a straight line up the path and hoped Nate couldn't tell how drunk she was. The outside light caught him in its beam, and she watched as his stare left her and traveled to Harry, still sitting in his goddamn car. Not going anywhere.

Laura looked over her shoulder. "Just piss off," she muttered at her boss under her breath.

"He brought you home?" Nate said. "From his own party?" His eyes flicked over her again. "What kind of state have you got yourself into, Laura, that your boss needs to drive you home?"

"I'm sorry— I—"

"How much have you had to drink? You drove the bloody car there. Why bother if you knew you were going to get yourself into this mess?"

"I'm not a mess," she objected, straightening up. "I just had too much to drive home."

Nate pulled her into the kitchen and filled a glass of water that he thrust into her hand. She didn't want it. She thought she was definitely going to be sick now, but she held on to it anyway, making every effort to steady herself.

He shook his head as he regarded her, and she felt the bitterness dripping off him. She wanted to roll into bed and fall into a sleep that would, at least temporarily, take away the memories of this awful evening, but she also knew how much bigger they would be when they came searing back in the morning.

"Why did he bring you home?"

"I don't know." She shrugged. "I was going to get a taxi, but he was there, insisting he'd drive, and—"

"And he just left his own party?"

"I know. I didn't want to him to, Nate, he was offering and I just wanted to get out of there and—"

"Christ." He shook his head and laughed bitterly, running his hands through his hair. "This is unbelievable. *You* are unbelievable."

"Nothing's going on," Laura cried. "If that's what you're thinking, you couldn't be more wrong. I wouldn't. I would never—"

"Go to bed," he spat. "I'll be in the spare room. Your son isn't well, by the way, he's been sick," Nate added as he started to walk out of the kitchen. "If you care."

"Oh my God, of course I care," she said, running after him. "Nate!" She grabbed his arm, tugging at the sleeve of his T-shirt, slopping water over the carpet as she did so. "Don't say that," she sobbed. "Don't ever say to that to me, you know I care about Bobby. What's wrong with him?"

He stood and watched her for a moment before eventually shaking his arm free, but when he spoke his voice was gentler. "He's just been sick," he said. "But he doesn't have a temperature. I'm sure it's nothing to worry about. Get some sleep."

"You should have called me," she said, her voice quiet.

"Why?" He paused and looked at her. "What would you have done?"

Laura opened her mouth to protest, but she knew the answer to his question. Nothing. There was nothing she could have done, because as always, Nate was here, and she wasn't. Nate could cope, and it was becoming clear that she couldn't.

Third interview between Detective Emily Marlow and Janie Wood following the fire at Morris and Wood offices on Monday, May 13.

Janie Wood, on Friday, May 17, at Lymington Police Headquarters.

Janie: When can I go?

Marlow: You've been arrested for murder. The best thing you can do right now is start talking.

Janie: I don't know what else I can tell you. Please. My girls— I need to be with them.

Marlow: Your daughters are both being cared for. Like I've said, if you're thinking of them, you need to begin telling me the whole story.

Janie: I *have* told you.

Marlow: I don't think you have, Janie. (sighs) Right now, I can only think that if Miles Morgan hadn't appeared back in your life on Monday, none of us would be sitting here. (pauses) Tell me what happened when you saw him in your husband's office. You went out for lunch with him, is that right?

Janie: (shakes head) No. I didn't go. I stupidly found myself walking to the quay with them but stopped before I actually had lunch. I made my excuses, said I really needed to take Ella's sports bag to school, which was what I'd gone there for in the first place.

Marlow: How did you feel seeing him again after such a long time?

Janie: I felt so—wrong-footed again. It was everything: his gait, the way he strode across the office like he owned it. I wanted to run at him and punch him in the face. I didn't though, of course. It's been five years. If I'd really wanted to hurt him I would have done it back then. I wouldn't have burned my husband's building to the ground.

Marlow: You were angry with your husband for working with Miles Morgan though.

Janie: Yes. Of course I was. Because Harry knew. He knew what Miles had done to Sophie. He knew how guilty I had felt afterward, and yet he was still *mates* with him. He prioritized someone who was good for business over me and my best friend.

Marlow: Tell me what happened with Sophie.

Janie: (pauses)

Marlow: Janie?

Janie: We've been best friends since we were eleven. We sat next to each other on the first day of secondary school and became inseparable. After A-levels our lives took very different paths though. I studied law, Sophie started working for an estate agent. She gave that up when she began waitressing in high-end clubs because the money was better. I mean, our lives were unrecognizable to each other at a point. I was married to a successful advertising exec, two daughters in private education, and Sophie was living in a flat with a part-time boyfriend. But she was still my closest friend.

Marlow: And one of these high-end clubs was where your husband and Miles Morgan used to drink?

Janie: (nods) Harry wasn't there the night she called me though, when she was crying on the phone for me to pick her up. I left him at home with the girls when I went to get her. I had to meet her on a street corner. I won't ever forget the sight of her: mascara streaked down her cheeks, this bright pink wrap tightly pulled around her as people staggered past. I knew. As soon as I saw her I knew what had happened.

Marlow: Go on.

Janie: She wouldn't tell me at first, just begged me to take her home. It was two days before she finally admitted she had been raped in the club while she was working. Sophie was embarrassed. But then I understood that. I saw enough women in court to recognize the shame, even when everyone tells them they had nothing to feel that way about. What I hated was that Sophie was used to men ogling her and she thought she wasn't worthy of being treated with respect. Just because they were sitting on these plush velvet chairs in their Savile Row suits, buying drinks that cost more than her hourly wages, they thought they could treat her like they had bought her too. But that night he had taken it too far and followed her into the toilets, pressing himself against her, telling her he knew it was what she wanted.

Marlow: Miles Morgan?

Janie: Yes. I asked her if anyone else had seen, and she laughed and said of course not. She was so bitter. I just wanted to take it all away from her.

Marlow: What did you do?

Janie: I told her we would do something about it. We'd go to the police there and then, that it wasn't too late. We wouldn't let him get away with it. Do you know what she said to me? She said, "You haven't been listening to me, Janie. Of course he will get away with it. You of all people know that all he needs is to find himself an expensive female defense barrister and he'll walk free."

Marlow: You think your friend was aiming that at you?

Janie: Of course she was. (laughs) Of course she was, because I had just won my last case. The one everyone was talking about, and so *I'd* done exactly what Sophie was worried about. She told me she wouldn't put herself through a trial to risk everything and not be believed. She wouldn't allow her life to be destroyed like other women's were . . .

Marlow: Let me get you a tissue.

Janie: (nods)

Marlow: Janie, did you see either your husband or Miles Morgan again on Monday after you left them at lunchtime?

Janie: No.

Marlow: What about Laura Denning? Did she tell you she had seen him in the office when you met her at the quay on Monday night?

Janie: No.

Marlow: So what did Laura tell you she was doing there?

Janie: Honestly? She didn't tell me a thing.

Marlow: (pauses) Janie, what I still can't get my head around is what you aren't telling me. You appear to be covering up something. Or for someone. And I really don't know why, when things are very serious for you, that you're still doing that.

chapter thirty-four

On Monday night Janie didn't go to yoga. She'd called Anna to babysit the girls on the pretense that she was going, but the truth was she had known the minute she started the car that she couldn't face an hour and a half of relaxation. Not when her head was spinning at a hundred miles an hour. What Janie needed was just to get away. Out of the house, because she couldn't spend another minute there, pretending everything was okay in front of her girls when it was anything but. She had been doing that all weekend and now she was exhausted. So exhausted, but at the same time so bloody wired.

———

On Friday night Harry had come home half an hour later, by which time Janie was in bed. The party was still going on downstairs, laughter and music weaving its way up both the stairs and the outside walls and in through her window like creeping ivy. She'd tossed around the idea of staying with the guests, drinking her way through it, but in the end Janie realized she didn't have it in her to pretend any longer. Escaping to her bedroom was suddenly the only option. She couldn't care less what any of them thought. Harry could deal with that once he'd figured out she was no longer downstairs. She wondered how long that would take him.

At some point he came up to the bedroom and poked his head in. "You're in here," he'd stated.

She feigned sleep as he padded in farther, patting the duvet that covered her as if he really had no idea anything was wrong. "Are you all right?" he'd asked.

Janie shuffled, pretending to stir, looked up at him. "I have a headache," she'd lied, dropping her head back onto the pillow. She no longer cared to argue, despite the fact she was burning inside. She considered there was no point listening to him telling her he'd done the right thing by taking Laura home, because possibly, in his self-centered brain, he believed he had.

Janie had no desire to tell her husband he was a thoughtless bastard, because she didn't want to give him the satisfaction of thinking she cared enough to argue.

So she had drifted through the weekend as if she were part of a still-perfect family. Her first priority was of course the girls, so it was easier to paper over the deep ridges that for years had been cracking her marriage apart rather than address them. She was actually pretty adept at it now.

Harry, in his wisdom, had seen fit to disregard the fact he had fled his own party to drive Laura home. His infatuation with the woman sickened her. Janie had always known that given a nod of encouragement Harry would jump into bed with Laura, so in a way did it really matter if he had or not?

They played Scrabble with their daughters. Janie drove the girls to their respective events—ballet and drama classes on Saturday afternoon, two different parties on Sunday.

By Monday morning she was relieved to hear the click of the front door as Harry left for work. By the time she dropped the girls at school, her day ahead was supposed to give her the time to get her thoughts together, a clear space to think. But then, just as she was walking out the school gate, Ella came running up behind her yelling that she had forgotten her sports bag.

"It wasn't at home," Janie said.

"No, it's in the boot of Daddy's car. Mummy, you have to get it, please," her daughter pleaded. "I need it for cricket this afternoon."

"I've got a hair appointment," she argued. "I can't do it—"

"You have to. Please. I don't need it until two o'clock; you can get it by then."

"Fine," Janie sighed. "I'll see what I can do."

"Thanks, Mummy." Her daughter beamed and ran off, leaving Janie wishing she'd told Ella that it was her responsibility to remember, because now it meant she would have to see Harry.

It was late morning when she walked out of the hairdressers and called her husband, leaving him a message to call her back, but by the time she reached the Morris and Wood offices, she wasn't surprised she hadn't heard from him.

Harry must have picked up the message only moments before she stepped out of the lift, because he swept across the floor as soon as he saw her. "I'll go and get the bag," he said, grabbing her arm and steering her around as he jabbed a finger on a button to call back the lift that was already descending to the ground floor.

If he wanted to get her away quick he was too late, because the voice boomed out, calling her name and forcing her to turn back. "Janie Wood! I was wondering if I'd get to see you."

The hairs on her arms pricked on end at the sound of the deep, gravelly voice that when she'd first heard it had sounded so soothing, so calm and assured. So sexy, she had even thought.

Beside her, Harry's face was creased into a frown, his hands fidgeted nervously at his sides.

"Miles," she said. She was surprised by how calm she sounded. "I didn't know you were coming."

"You didn't?" He grinned, his head cocked, his brows furrowed as he nudged Harry. "You didn't tell your wife, when you knew I'd want to see her? Well, no matter, you're here just in time. I'm taking you both out to lunch."

"I can't," she said quickly. "I've got to go, I'm afraid."

"Nonsense. Janie Wood, I haven't seen you in five years. I insist," he said, and before she had time to refuse, the lift door was pinging open and Miles was gesturing her into it, Harry sloping behind.

Like Janie would later tell the detective, she had managed to escape lunch with Miles, eventually begging off because she really had to get back to the school. She glanced in Harry's direction as she left the two men, but her husband could barely return her gaze. That she had once loved Harry, she thought as she walked away, was a notion that now seemed impossible. His pathetic cowardice made her feel nothing more than sick with anger.

She didn't see Harry again that day. Her mind was barely on the children as she picked them up from school, swept them home, fed them beans on toast because doing so didn't require headspace.

That night, the fire was already ravaging the offices when she saw the other women. Mia first, and then Laura Denning. It had all happened so quickly after that.

chapter thirty-five

At just after seven thirty p.m., Laura stepped onto the pavement outside the offices of Morris and Wood. Rage was coursing through her, racing through her veins, feeding her body until the tips of her fingers were tingling and didn't feel like they were a part of her anymore.

Moments before, she had wanted nothing more than to be back at home with the two people who mattered to her, but now that she was out of there, she found she didn't go straight to her car. Instead she stood on the pavement, her jaw so tense that her whole face throbbed with pain as her mind ticked. Back and forth like a metronome went her thoughts. Miles Morgan. Harry Wood. Despite everything that had happened in the office over the last two months, it was what had happened in the last half hour that was tipping her over the edge.

Two days previously, on Saturday morning, Laura had woken to Bobby crying at six thirty. A piercing yell of an alarm call that shot through Laura's sore head like a blade. She'd grabbed a cold flannel on her way to her son's room and pressed it against her throbbing temple, ignoring the urge to stop and be sick, telling herself that it really was the last time she would ever drink so much, as wine regurgitated in her mouth.

Pulling her son out of his crib, Laura pressed his warm body against her chest, taking him to the rocking chair in the corner of his room, where she sat down and placed him on her lap, smiling through tears that had sprung from nowhere as he lifted chubby fingers and pressed them against her mouth. "Hello, my gorgeous boy," she said. "I love you so much. Do you know that? I love you more than anything in the entire world."

It was the truth. The love she had for Bobby had expanded her heart in ways she could never have imagined possible before giving birth to him. He was her everything. So why was she so intent on wanting more? Why did it feel like she didn't have enough?

These thoughts had continued to plague her over the next two days.

What did it make Laura when she admitted that the thought of giving up everything she had worked for her entire adult life left her empty? That to be all those things for Bobby, she would have to say goodbye to the career she'd always loved?

It made her think that maybe she still wasn't loving him enough.

While she sat motionless in the rocking chair, paralyzed by the fear that any slight movement would make her feel worse, Nate poked his head around Bobby's door and asked if she wanted a coffee.

"No. I'm fine, thanks," she told him. The thought of coffee made her want to retch, and she knew that to get through the day she would need to pretend. Keep pretending she was coping when she was doing anything but.

Laura peered at Nate over the top of Bobby's head. He rubbed one hand through his ruffled hair as he scratched his leg with the other. His mouth was set rigid, his eyes didn't mask the anger he must feel toward her.

She'd wanted to cry at him that she knew he was right. Nothing was working as it was supposed to be. She had screwed up. She was still continuing to, and maybe she needed to accept that she couldn't have it all, or at least she couldn't without falling apart. Without eventually losing something. Or everything.

Laura knew all this, and yet she still hadn't said anything to Nate. Why was that? she thought as she stood outside the offices on Monday night, wrapping her arms across her chest. Maybe it was because she hadn't wanted to hear him say it was time to cut back her hours. To say goodbye to her career as she knew it. Maybe it was because Laura still wasn't ready to do anything about it when she hadn't found out the truth about Mia Anderson.

How far away any thoughts of Mia now seemed as she stood outside in the warm May night air. Others had tangled themselves around those thoughts, strangling them so they could no longer breathe. Right now it was Harry who filled her head; Harry who was filling Laura was such anger.

———————

It had, however, been thoughts of Mia that eventually forced Laura to go into the office that morning. When she had woken late, her stomach still felt queasy, even though it was three days after the party, and so Laura had texted Harry and told him she would be working from home.

But by midday she couldn't concentrate when her unfinished conversation with Mia was spread like spare pieces of a jigsaw in her brain. Laura had needed to put an end to it, and so she had forced herself in to work, head down to avoid the inevitable patronizing glances as she searched out Mia, who was nowhere to be seen.

As she dumped her bag at her desk, she caught sight of Miles in Harry's office and briefly wondered what he was doing there when she didn't realize they had a meeting. Harry's face was impassive, but Laura could tell he was tense by the way he stood, one hand leaning rigidly on the desk in front of him. But she hadn't hung around long, Mia had been her main concern, and so she'd continued to search the floor, peering into meeting rooms, stopping to ask Henrietta James if she had seen her.

But no one had, and neither did it seem Mia had called in. How much all the staff must have hoped she and Mia would have some kind of showdown in the office, Laura had thought as she'd checked her watch. It was strange that Mia hadn't turned up. There hadn't been a morning yet when she hadn't been there before Laura. For some weird reason it was oddly unsettling.

By late afternoon Laura had given up hope of talking to Mia and had instead waited for Harry and Miles to return. They had been out of the office since lunchtime, and she didn't want to leave before they'd caught up. She didn't want to admit that she had been put out they hadn't invited her to lunch, but she had been.

At six p.m. Laura texted Nate and lied that she was meeting Coopers and therefore would be back a little later than usual. Laura didn't entirely know why she hadn't told him the truth. Maybe it was that she didn't want to say she was waiting for Harry.

At seven p.m. Harry and Miles eventually appeared. A faint smell of beer wafted toward her as the pair wandered into Harry's office. Harry was sorry they were so late, he'd said, did she want to come in now? His face was set even harder than it had been that morning.

Laura nodded. Bobby would be in bed by now, she thought as she gathered her notepad and a pen. Nate would already be annoyed with her.

She followed the men into Harry's office. If Harry had been drinking he hid it well. He rifled through papers on his desk, his hands moving deftly as he found what he was looking for. He didn't look up when she walked in.

Miles, however, was casually leaning against the doorframe, arms folded across his broad chest. His words had an edge to them when he spoke, tumbling out of his mouth in a slur. "Laura, good to see you again."

She didn't feel comfortable with the way he was looking at her, his deep brown eyes holding such a steady gaze as he raised his eyebrows.

Laura gave him a thin smile and turned back to Harry. Now all she wanted was to get out of there and go home.

Suddenly Harry's mobile rang. "Odd," he muttered as he pulled it toward him across the desk. "Sorry, guys, I'm going to have to take this call. Anna's a friend; she's looking after the girls. Excuse me a minute," he added as he answered the phone, Miles gesturing as if to give his approval.

"Hi, Anna, everything okay?" Harry asked as he left the office, shutting the door behind him.

"Take a seat, Laura," Miles said, indicating one of the armchairs as if it were his office, and despite this Laura found herself feeling for the armchair and backing into it. Miles beamed at her as he perched on the edge of Harry's desk in front of her, crossing his legs at the ankles and folding his hands in his lap. She could feel the edge of his trousers brushing against her bare calf and automatically shifted out of the way.

"I can see why Harry has you working for him," he said. His eyebrows were pinched into a point again, his mouth skewed. The closer he leaned, the more she could smell the beer on his breath, and she wished he wouldn't sit so near.

"Sorry?"

"I mean, I'm sure you'd do a good job and all, but . . ." He drifted off, grinning.

Laura fidgeted nervously in the chair. "I'm not following." She glanced out to where she could see Harry wandering back and forth as he continued to talk into the phone, slightly too far out of reach for comfort.

"Oh, come on," Miles said, edging closer again until she could feel him against her leg once more. "You and Harry."

"There's absolutely nothing going on between me and Harry," Laura replied, contorting herself so she was out of his reach again. How she could have thought him attractive she now had no idea, as he raised his eyebrows in a smug grin that clearly told her he wasn't having any of it.

"Really?" Miles grinned. "You may want to tell him that." He cocked his head in Harry's direction.

"Harry knows there's nothing between us," she hissed firmly, making a move to stand.

"Oh-ho, he also told me you could be a feisty one." Miles laughed, leaning back on the desk, splaying his hands to either side of him. "That's fine by me too. I like girls who can handle themselves."

Laura opened her mouth to speak, but to her confusion found tears pricking at her eyes, which in turn made her throat tighten. Unexpectedly she thought of Bobby, and suddenly she felt ashamed. To be sitting there, spoken to like that by a man she didn't know. She shouldn't be here at all. She should be at home with her husband and her son.

Laura got up, pushing the chair back. She wanted to tell him he was disgusting. That men like him made her sick. But if she did that she would lose the account in a shot, and maybe, for now, it was better for her to slip out of the office quickly.

"What are you still doing here so late then, Laura? The only one left in the office, waiting for Harry. I see it with you girls all the time. You make out you don't want anything, but if you ask me, it's all an act."

"Oh my God," she muttered. She couldn't hold her tongue much longer. Her heart thumped. She had to be careful. Her entire reputation could be damaged by a man like Miles Morgan, especially if Harry didn't believe her. "I was waiting to catch up with you," she said.

"Well, here I am." He opened his arms wide.

Laura shook her head, her hands trembling at her sides as she made her way to the door and reached for its handle, hoping she would make it out, that he didn't lunge for her, though Miles was still sitting on Harry's desk and didn't appear to be going anywhere.

"Harry's probably waiting for you somewhere," he said, peering out the window, making a meal of looking for Harry, who was now nowhere to be seen. "Better let your husband know you might be a bit late getting home." Miles grinned as he winked.

"Don't you dare," Laura suddenly spat. "Don't you dare insinuate I would cheat on my husband. Men like you disgust me," she blurted. To think of everything she had sacrificed for him, for Harry, and this was how she was repaid. Having to listen to crap, to be made to feel like she was nothing.

Miles pursed his lips, straightening himself on top of Harry's desk. The smile rapidly slid off his face.

"I won't be doing any more work for you," she said calmly. Already Laura wondered if she'd later regret her words, but what other option was there? She wouldn't spend another minute in that man's company.

"You're right about that," Miles sung out as she opened the door. "There is no job, Laura."

She paused and turned, cocking her head questioningly as Miles's eyes flared in triumph.

"The job's already gone to someone else. Which Harry knows," he added, raising his brows, goading her.

"I don't understand—" she said, despite her need to get out of the office.

"The work you've been doing for our tender—" Miles broke off, blowing out his cheeks and throwing up his hands to indicate it had just evaporated. "He's not broken the news to you yet, then? No. I know he hasn't. He told me that this afternoon. He said he was worried how you'd react, that you were getting your knickers in a twist over some other girl in the office—"

"What?" she gasped, sickened by his choice of words.

"Maybe I'm paraphrasing, but you get the gist."

"I don't believe you," she said defiantly. "He wouldn't let me carry on working on something that wasn't going anywhere. That's ridiculous."

"I agree." Miles chuckled. "He thought he could twist my arm, still try and play for something that wasn't up for grabs. Your boss is too desperate to let go of some things. I guess it was too attractive a proposition." He broke off, smiling.

Laura turned her back on him, her heart pounding as she released the door handle and paced to her desk, picking up her bag. She scoured the office for signs of her boss, who was no longer anywhere to be seen. Miles was following her out of the office, the scent of his aftershave preceding him. Grabbing her bag from the floor, she walked, as quickly as she could, to the lifts, stabbing her finger against the button until one arrived.

Harry had lied to her. He had told her he was looking out for her but he wasn't. He had made her put her heart and soul and hours into a job he already knew wasn't coming to anything, and for what? Because he was too greedy to let it go, only he couldn't be honest with her.

Ever since she'd come back two months ago, Harry hadn't been there for her, or at least not in any way she wanted. He hadn't accepted he should never have given her job to the replacement. He'd been looking out for himself while he pressured her into doing work for that man.

As Laura stepped out into the cool air, she stared up at the building through unblinking eyes, rage flooding her veins. Maybe it was a build-up of everything that had happened over the last two months— the guilt from her own sacrifices, the fear of what came next—but in that moment there was only one person who Laura blamed. Harry Wood. And she knew she should have gone straight home to the two people she loved, but right then she couldn't move.

chapter thirty-six

M ia cupped her hands around the glass as she leaned over the bar. She had watched women do this in films and always wondered how it would feel. To be distraught enough to go to a bar on her own and ask for a neat gin. To knock it back and slide the glass to the barman and ask for another and then another until her mind was blank. Until every memory that had gotten her to this point had been wiped out, if only temporarily.

It was seven thirty p.m. and still light outside, but the bar she had chosen was particularly dingy and empty. And instead of her memories being erased, they were floating around her head like they were perfectly content where they were, knowing they'd be able to taunt her for the rest of her life.

She took another swig of gin and felt the burn as it slid down her throat, wondering how many more it would take to obliterate her mind. Erase what had happened that day.

It had been late morning by the time Mia arrived at the office earlier that day. Jess had needed her, but Mia didn't bother telling anyone she was going to be late. She didn't answer to anyone but Harry, and after his party she hadn't particularly cared about that either. Harry had driven Laura home, leaving Mia to call a taxi. She had said too much to Janie. The night couldn't have gone much worse.

Mia was beginning to think she wouldn't be able to hold the job down for much longer. Someone would be on to her soon, find out who she really was. Probably that would be Laura, who was like a dog with a bone. Mia actually admired that in her. Under different circumstances, they might have been friends.

Lately nothing had been going the way she planned, though as she rode the lift to the third floor she hadn't imagined it could get much worse. But it did the moment she stepped out.

As soon as she saw him she had doubled over, gripping a nearby empty desk to steady herself. If only she had been prepared to see him again one day, she might have been able to handle it. But she hadn't. And so Mia had run back out of the office.

Now she tapped the side of her empty glass and allowed the barman to refill it. He was eyeing her carefully, no doubt wondering if he thought she might be a problem. He had every right to be suspicious, but whatever problems she might cause that night, they weren't going to be in his bar.

Mia hadn't gone far when she'd fled the offices that morning. She had only run to the quay. She wasn't sure how long she had been there, pacing up and down the cobbled path, knowing she needed to go back to work but not willing to return while *he* was in the office.

She had been biding her time when she saw them all together, walking down the street: Harry, Janie, and Miles—and had shot into a doorway before any of them saw her.

Mia had felt sick as she cowered by the bright pink door, an entrance to someone's flat. Her fingers trembled as they gripped the edge of the frame to steady herself, praying they didn't walk past and see her.

Would Miles recognize her if they did? Mia doubted it. It had been a few years and she had changed since then, cut her hair much shorter, lost weight, but she wasn't taking any chances. She waited as they passed, thankfully unaware she was lurking nearby, and only after they'd gone did she step out onto the street.

Her legs felt like liquid as she watched them retreat. At her sides her hands clenched into fists.

Miles might not recognize her, but he would recognize Jess. Despite the fact she was now in a wheelchair and a shell of the woman she once was, he'd have surely known her face.

Mia's teeth clenched, her jaw aching where she held it so tight. There they all were. Together again. Miles Morgan and his awesome defense barrister who had gotten him off, even though she knew exactly what that man had done to Mia's sister. The woman who had defamed Jess, crushing every ounce of confidence her sister once had, until Jess told herself she wasn't good enough to work anymore. Until she gradually became less and less of a living person; until one day she drank far too much and drove her car too fast on treacherous roads because she couldn't live with what Miles had done to her, and what he had gotten away with.

Her sister had lost everything. In turn, so had Mia and their mum. And meanwhile there was Janie Wood, walking down the road with that vile man, and she still had everything. Money. Family. Pride in that god-awful building that shone out like a blinding beacon across their beautiful town like they owned every one of them who lived there.

Janie was the one who really needed to pay.

"You all right?" the barman asked. His gaze drifted to her empty glass.

"No." She laughed. "Not at all."

But he didn't want to know about her worries. And his gin hadn't helped, it had only served to make Mia even more certain that whatever she had thought she might be able to do, working inside Morris and Wood wasn't working. It was revenge she was after, and she needed to up her game.

chapter thirty-seven

By eight thirty p.m. the fire was devouring the building. Janie stumbled down the path and toward the edge of the quay. The reflection of the flames licked the surface of the water as if they were dancing on it, while above them plumes of gray smoke billowed in the air.

There was a crowd of people gathered, spilling out of the Star pub and the other nearby restaurants, all of them captivated and bewildered by the sight across the river.

Mia was running down the cobbled path, her face a ghostly shade of white, her mouth hung open as she clutched a hand to the stitch in her side. She stopped abruptly when she saw the crowd.

Laura was hanging on the outskirts of it, immobile, her hands over her mouth, pressed into her face, slightly distorting her view as if this somehow took away the depth of the horror unfurling in front of her.

It seemed to happen so quickly after that. A hand on Laura's shoulder, making her spin round and nearly lose her balance. Mia clutching onto her, her face blank. Janie inching closer to the two women, step by tentative step.

When each of them noticed the other two, they glanced from one to the other, searching for an explanation as to what *they* were doing here. Each of them mirrored the others' panic in their own faces, and it felt clear by now that at least one of them must know what had caused the fire.

Mia spoke first. "Who did this?" She waved a hand in the air toward the building, as if her question needed explanation. "Was it you?" Her gaze darted to Janie, her chin jutting defiantly, her finger now pointing in Janie's direction. All of it could, of course, have been an act. No one was sure.

Janie shook her head, her mouth agape as Mia's finger now swung toward Laura.

"No!" Laura shouted, a little too aggressively, then she said it again, this time softer. "No."

The truth was they all looked frightened. Something had happened to each one of them that day and in the days leading up to it, and even if they hadn't lit the match that burned down Harry's office, the thought had been present in all of them that maybe they could have. Maybe they had wanted to.

"It was you." A shaking finger prodded at Janie again. "You." Mia laughed. "You did it, didn't you? You bloody well burned down that building. Oh, I can't believe you did it. Because of her?" Now the same finger was thrust in Laura's direction. "Because you thought they were having an affair? They weren't, you know, she never would have, for what it's worth. Any fool can see that."

Janie's eyes flicked toward Laura, scanning the woman's face for signs of either denial or confirmation. She no longer knew if she cared what the answer was, it would just be nice to know the truth.

Laura shook her head, glaring at Mia. Everything she had told Tess Wills had all been part of her act. "You think I was having an affair with Harry?" she said to Janie.

"Weren't you?" Janie replied, her voice toneless.

"No!" she cried. "Absolutely not. I love my husband, my family—" Laura broke off. Nate had no idea where she was. He thought she was in a meeting with Coopers but he must have expected her home by now. She hated that she had been lying to the one person she loved the most. "I would never have an affair with your husband," she said to Janie.

For some reason, Janie believed her.

"So what are you still doing here?" Mia turned on Laura now. Somehow she had assumed the role of detective, tossing questions at the two women, deflecting attention from herself, her body soaked with alcohol, her head hazy.

"I was still in the office and then—" Laura broke off and turned to look over the river, to where flames lapped at the sky, the smoke swelling in great puffs of dark gray. Even in that moment she knew not to tell them more than that. Even then she realized she might have been the last person to have seen them, and that if she told the women her story, she would have motive.

Janie was shouting. "Was he in there?" she asked Laura. "When you were in the office, was he in there with you?"

"Harry?" Laura breathed, and turned to Janie. Of course she had to admit he was. They would all know soon enough. "He was, but that was—it was over an hour ago . . ."

Janie looked across at the building sharply. What was he doing in there? He wasn't supposed to be. Harry and Miles had been drinking, he had texted her that earlier. That was why he hadn't been home in time and why she'd called Anna and asked if she could sit with the girls. She'd been angry with Harry, that he could have let her down for that man, and yet—

"Could he still be in there?" Janie asked eventually, as Mia was also asking, "Was he alone?"

"No—he was with . . ." Laura's voice trailed off. How she didn't want to be the one with the answers, for suddenly it felt like the more she knew, the more guilty she must seem.

"Miles Morgan," Mia finished for her. It wasn't a question.

"Yes," Laura confirmed, as she glanced at her watch. "But like I said, that was over an hour ago. I left an hour ago," she repeated, drumming this into them.

For a moment the three women were silent. It was Janie who eventually spoke as she took a step closer to the edge of the quay. "They were still in there," she said, and neither Laura or Mia knew if this was a question or a statement, so they didn't reply.

chapter thirty-eight

friday, may 17
four days after the fire

Janie was given a short break. She curled her fingers around her cup of water, pressing them in and then releasing them, listening to the satisfying pop of the polystyrene cup as she did so.

Her daughters were at the forefront of her mind. She wondered what they were doing while their mother was arrested and their father was in hospital, barely conscious as he drifted in and out of sleep. She wondered what Anna had told her girls, how much they knew about what was happening to her, whether they thought she was actually capable of burning down their father's office.

She had told Detective Marlow her story. At least up to a point. "We met by coincidence," she said. "I saw Mia first, then noticed her grabbing someone's shoulder. When she spun around I saw it was Laura."

The detective had wanted to know what the three of them were all doing there if they hadn't arranged to meet, and Janie continued to press they most certainly hadn't planned to be there together. This part had been the truth.

She told the detective that Laura had been in the office late, working, Janie assumed. By now it was believed that Laura had been the last person to have seen Harry and Miles Morgan before the fire. The last person to see Miles alive.

But there was a gap, Marlow kept insisting, between Laura leaving the office and the point when Janie saw her. "What was she still doing at the quay? Why hadn't she gone home?"

Janie never had found out why. She couldn't even remember if the question had been asked. Possibly Mia had asked at some point—she'd been the one demanding answers—but what Janie was certain of was that Laura hadn't told them. "I don't know," she kept replying, though she knew how doubtful that sounded.

And Mia? Yes, Janie knew Mia's explanation for that had all come out. It had momentarily distracted her attention from the fact her husband may have still been in the building.

By now the detective had been able to build up a very clear connection between Mia and Janie. But what Emily Marlow had been demanding to know was why the three women weren't telling her everything. Because she knew they weren't, and yet it made no sense that one of them, at least, wasn't speaking.

———————

What Janie hadn't accounted for, following the night of the fire, was that four days later she'd be sitting in an interview room yet again, only this time under a threat of prison. Marlow was right when she told Janie she couldn't let it get that far; of course her girls were her priority and she would not jeopardize anything for them.

Marlow was offering her a way out; Janie was sure of it. All she needed to do was tell the truth. *Start talking, for God's sake.* The detective had said it enough times.

Janie drew in her breath, pressing harder into the cup, crushing it between her fingers.

She would not be charged with the murder of Miles Morgan, she would not give up her life for that man, but at the same time how could she tell the truth?

Janie looked up at the sound of the door opening. Emily Marlow walked in, her face pinched, eyebrows knitted tightly together. She didn't take her gaze away from Janie as she strode purposefully to her chair. Even when she slid onto it, she didn't once look away.

Janie shuffled on the plastic seat. She wanted to turn away from Marlow's gaze, but it was quickly apparent something had happened. Emily Marlow was clearly walking back into the room with knowledge she didn't have earlier, and Janie had a feeling that the detective might know exactly what had happened on Monday night.

chapter thirty-nine

monday, may 13
the night of the fire

Here's the question you know Miles Morgan?" Laura was asking. "You said his name when you asked if Harry was in there alone, like you expected him to be there."

Mia's eyes danced as she turned to Janie. She had a gut full of gin, and the headiness of the night was overwhelming. "Six years ago he raped my sister," she said, her eyes fixed on the woman she had come for. She waited for a reaction.

Janie blinked, momentarily confused, before closing her eyes and shaking her head with sinking realization. "Oh God, no."

"You set him free. You stood in the courtroom," Mia went on, taking a step closer to Janie, "and told the jury and everyone sitting in it that my sister was 'asking for it,' because she was the type of girl to sleep with someone different every week. Only, you knew that wasn't really the case, didn't you?" She pressed forward until her face was only inches from Janie's. "You *knew* what he had done."

"I was doing my job." Janie's words were uttered in a whisper. Tears rolled down her face. When they reached her lips she dragged them away with her thumb. Mia must have been in the courtroom during the trial, watching it play out. There was a glimmer of something she recognized in the younger woman's high cheekbones, the deep brown eyes, but her hair had been longer then. That was it, Janie thought, she'd had highlighted hair that came down to her waist, and after the case Janie hadn't given her any thought because she was only a face in the crowd.

"Did you believe him?" Mia was asking. "Did you actually believe his lies, or did you know deep down what my sister had gone through?"

"I was defending him," Janie went on. "I had to—"

"Do your job, yes I know, but did you *believe* him?"

Janie had, at first. When he'd told her about the woman in his office who worked two levels below him, speaking of her with respect. How it had started with flirty comments in the pub one night, and Miles had told Janie that maybe he knew it was wrong at the time, and perhaps his fault, that he should have stopped it.

He'd told her Jess Anderson was needy, often asking for approval of the work she was doing. Miles had buried his head in his hands and said, "I think maybe I should have known to stay away from her. God, I wish I had now."

He'd discovered that Jess had slept with another man in the office only the weekend before, following a night out at work. Just like the one they were having the night Jess "suddenly decided Miles had raped her."

He'd said that maybe Jess liked men with power, and had gone on to say, "That sounds really awful when I say it out loud. Not that I *am* powerful." He had laughed and looked sheepish, but Janie had sensed he most definitely was.

As a barrister, what she could have said to Mia right then was that Jess's guilt or innocence in the proceedings was immaterial. Miles had the right to be defended to the best of her ability and that was what she had done.

But she couldn't say that. Because she felt sick with herself, like she had when Sophie told her why she could never put herself through a trial.

And so instead Janie said, "I believed him at first. But no, by the time it got to court . . ." She trailed off, shaking her head.

"Yet you stood in court and told everyone how my sister didn't think twice about having a one-night stand because it had happened the week before. As if that was enough to justify what that man did to her. You said that now her job was being threatened because Miles was her boss's boss, and so she was crying rape to protect herself. You skipped over the fact that the other man was her own age and someone she'd been having a casual relationship with, because that didn't suit your case, did it?

"Did you forget about my sister after that?" Mia went on. "As soon as you *won*, did you walk away pleased with yourself for doing a good job?"

"No," Janie said firmly, though she didn't expect Mia to believe her.

"You have everything!" Mia yelled. "Everything. You want for nothing."

"I never forgot about your sister," Janie pleaded. "I didn't." But what could she tell her? That the guilt of getting Miles Morgan acquitted had draped over her like a black cloud, though it wasn't because of what had happened to Jess. It was because of what subsequently had happened to Sophie.

The day she'd told Harry about her best friend she had broken down in front of him, hysterical that if it hadn't been for her, Sophie wouldn't have gone through what she did.

"You must have known what he was like," Janie had said to Harry, though she wasn't sure what she expected from him—maybe that he would tell her he had no idea, or that he was trying to protect her job by not telling her the truth. All she had *wanted* was for Harry to support her, but what he had said was, "So must you." In that moment she'd seen a flash in his eyes of something ugly, something that looked like: *Don't put this on me.*

Janie wanted to tell Mia she didn't have everything, because from that moment something had broken between her and her husband, something they had never been able to get back.

But she also knew it would make no difference to Mia.

"My sister's life is ruined because of you." Mia was prodding her finger at Janie's chest. "She lost her job, she lost her confidence. She doesn't leave the house," she cried, her voice rising. "She has no friends anymore, she does nothing. She's in a bloody *wheelchair* because she couldn't face living anymore."

"What?" Laura murmured, stepping forward. "What happened?"

"She drove herself into a tree. Only it didn't go according to her plan. She survived."

"I'm so sorry," Laura said. "I can't even imagine how hard that is." She paused. "But it's Miles you should be blaming. He's the one that did this, not Janie."

"No. She's right," Janie said. "If I hadn't defended him he would have been locked up. He would have gotten what he deserved, and he wouldn't have been able to assault anyone else."

Laura hesitated. The scene in Harry's office only hours ago hit her again, and she wondered if somehow Janie knew. But she couldn't have known, could she? There was no way. And as much as Laura had a sudden urge to share with these two women what Miles had just been like with her, she knew that if she did, she would effectively be giving them a reason for her to have lit the fire.

In the end she simply said, "But if you didn't defend him, someone else would have."

**Second interview between Detective Emily Marlow and Mia
Anderson staff of Morris and Wood following the fire at Morris and
Wood offices on Monday, May 13.**

**Mia Anderson, Account Director, on Friday, May 17, at Lymington
Police Headquarters.**

Marlow:	This interview is taking place at 1100 hours on Friday, May 17. Mia Anderson, please can you tell me what has brought you into the station this morning?
Mia:	I want to tell you what happened.
Marlow:	Okay. Go ahead.
Mia:	(pauses)
Marlow:	Ms. Anderson, you're doing the right thing. Coming here today, it's taking a lot of guts. I can see that.
Mia:	(nods) What's she saying?
Marlow:	What's who saying?
Mia:	Janie Wood. I know she's in there still. She hasn't told you what happened?
Marlow:	Janie is currently talking to us.
Mia:	I'm going to tell you the truth, but before I do I need to know something.
Marlow:	Yes?
Mia:	My mum and my sister—will they—I just need to know they'll be okay.
Marlow:	How do you mean? Ms. Anderson, how do you mean you need to know they'll be okay?
Mia:	It's just that I'm everything they've got. I know what's going to happen to me and—I've just always been there for both of them, after my sister's accident, and I don't even know how they'll cope. I don't know that they will. I just don't know. God, this is a mess. This is such a mess.
Marlow:	Can I call you Mia?
Mia:	That's fine.

Marlow: Okay, Mia, listen to me. The more you tell me, the more I can help you. Do you understand that?

Mia: (nods)

Marlow: For the record, the interviewee has nodded. So, Mia, can you tell me what happened Monday night?

Mia: (pauses) I set fire to the offices of Morris and Wood.

Marlow: And did you know anyone was in the building when you did it?

Mia: No.

Marlow: You didn't realize Harry Wood was in his office?

Mia: No, I didn't have a clue.

Marlow: Or that Miles Morgan was with him?

Mia: No. I didn't know anyone was in there.

Marlow: Laura, can you tell me why you did it?

Mia: I wanted to make them all pay.

Marlow: By all, who do you mean?

Mia: Laura. Miles. Janie.

Marlow: Only now you're confessing because—

Mia: Now I'm confessing because . . . You know, I'm not actually a bad person. I never actually wanted anything that bad to happen to anyone, not like this. Now I'm confessing because I just want it to end.

chapter forty

Mia wanted Janie to know she was to blame. That if it hadn't been for her defending Miles Morgan, her sister's life would not have been ruined. She would still be the same exuberant, clever, confident woman she had been before. She would still be able to run and walk out of the house when she damn well pleased.

It surprised her when Janie said Mia was right. That she was agreeing it was her fault.

"But if you didn't defend him, someone else would have," Laura had said, but Mia didn't want to think about that, because all these years her anger had been directed at Janie, and she couldn't begin to imagine it was in any way misplaced.

"Listen," Laura said, "whatever happened, the offices are on fire and as far as we know—" She paused and glanced over her shoulder. "There could have been someone in there."

Mia felt a shiver running through her body at the thought. Her fear was mirrored in the other women's eyes.

"Did you do this?" one of them was asking her. She thought it was Janie, but her head was spinning and the air was thinning around her.

"It wasn't me," Laura said, "I can promise you that."

"Well, it wasn't me," Janie cried. "So was it you?" She was shouting now. "Mia, did you do this?"

"No," she said, her breath rapid and sharp. Almost in slow motion, she reached out a hand to stop herself from falling, grabbing on to Laura's arm to steady herself. Mia's legs buckled, unable to hold her.

"Mia, what is it?" one of them asked, and then, "Who— Mia, who is that? Mia, is that your sister? What the hell—" The words cut off sharply as realization dawned on each one of them.

"Oh God, Jess," Mia muttered under her breath, hoping the women didn't hear her. "What have you done?"

———————

Mia, of course, thought she knew exactly what her sister had done, but she also knew it was entirely her own fault. That afternoon, when Mia had seen Miles, Harry, and Janie walking down the cobbled path toward the quay, she hadn't gone straight to the bar, like she now wished she had. Instead she had driven home, anger creeping through her veins. She had wanted to get out of town, away from the view of the office, somewhere she wouldn't have a chance of seeing that man again.

Her heart thumped hard as she crashed through the door, tossing her handbag across the kitchen. Mia stood by the table and silently slammed her fists onto it, fighting every urge to scream. Now what the hell was she going to do?

None of it had gone the way she'd hoped. All the plans she'd been carefully laying were being thrown up in the air. First Sarah Clifton leaving, then Laura and her doggedness, and now—how would she ever be able to walk back into the office again, knowing Harry was working with Miles Morgan? Each morning wondering if she'd come face-to-face with him again.?

"What's happened?"

Jess's voice had startled Mia. She'd turned to find her sister in the doorway.

"And don't tell me nothing, because I can see something has."

"I saw him," Mia blurted. "I saw him. Today."

Jess opened her mouth as if to ask who her sister meant, but she didn't say a word.

"That man. That—" Mia stopped briefly. "Miles Morgan. He was in the office today."

Jess's mouth widened, every muscle in her face tightening. "What?" she said in disbelief.

"He was there. With Harry Wood, discussing business, laughing with his bloody wife like they had no cares in the world."

If Mia were thinking straight she might have known she shouldn't be sharing this story with Jess, but her stomach was churning so tightly, and her pulse was racing so wildly, that her head wasn't straight in the slightest.

"His wife?"

"Janie Wood," Mia clarified. "That's her married name. You knew her as Janie Birch."

She watched her sister's face drop in horror. "You knew this?" she said. "You knew who she was and yet—" Jess broke off, shaking her head. "You still went to work there?"

"That's *why* I worked for them," Mia cried. "That's why I took the job—"

"No!" Jess yelled. "Stop! Don't you dare. Don't you try and justify it."

"Jess?" Mia gasped, taking a step toward her. "I'm doing this for you."

"For me?" she cried. "No you're not. No you bloody well aren't. If you were doing it for me, you would *never* have gone to work for them. You would have told me who she was. You wouldn't have treated me like a child. How dare you!" she'd shouted. "How *dare* you bring them back into our lives, his name into this house." Her sister's hands were shaking as she clutched hard to her chair.

"Jess, I'm sorry, but you're not listening to me. I was going to get back at her. I was going to—"

"Stop!" Jess screamed, bringing her hands to her head, digging into her scalp with her fingers. "*You're* not listening to *me*. I never wanted to know what that man was doing, where he was. I never wanted to know any of it because if I did, then I had no clue what I would do about it. I wanted to *forget*, Mia."

"None of us are forgetting—"

"And now we can't, can we? You've made sure of that. Get out," she cried. "Please, just go, Mia. Get out. Leave me alone."

"I'm not leaving you in this state."

"Yes you are," she hissed. "For once just do what I'm asking of you."

———

Slowly Mia walked across the quay toward her sister. Jess's hands were balled in her lap, her body shivering. Mia crouched down beside her and took one of Jess's hands in her own. "Don't say a word," she whispered to her sister as the other two women approached. "Don't say anything."

Jess glanced over Mia's shoulder. "What have I done?" she said eventually. "Mia, what the hell have I done?"

"Shush," Mia told her, squeezing her hand tighter. "Stop now," she urged, but she already knew it was too late.

"I have to go to the police." A single tear rolled down Jess's cheek. Mia lifted the hand that still gripped her sister's and wiped the tear away, her heart thumping.

"No you don't." A voice behind them made both sisters turn. "None of us do." It was Janie. "You can't—" She hesitated. "You tell them what you've done and you'll be locked up for certain, and you don't deserve that. Not one bit, and yet there'll be nothing you can do about it."

For a moment everyone stared silently at Janie.

"I, for one, haven't seen you here tonight," she went on.

Mia blinked, and Janie turned to Laura, who took a breath before eventually adding, "Nor I."

Mia held a hand over her mouth as she looked from one to the other and then back at her sister. Her thoughts whirled, but there was something she was becoming sure about. She was not going to let anything happen to her sister, and if these two women were prepared to help, then maybe they stood a small chance of getting away with it.

But if they didn't, if something happened to make one of them break—which she knew was the more likely scenario—then Mia would take the blame. Because if it weren't for her, this would never have happened.

"There was someone in there," Jess said. "I saw them being pulled out."

Janie suddenly turned to the building, fishing in her back pocket for her mobile. "Shit," she murmured, tapping her phone, pressing it to her ear. "Was it Harry? Was it my husband?"

Mia couldn't deny that her own concerns weren't what might have happened to Harry, but that she might not be able to rely on Janie to keep quiet if Harry Wood was dead.

"It might not be him," Laura was calling after Janie as she began running off. And all Mia could do was pray it wasn't, that Harry wasn't dead, because Janie and Laura were the only chance they had.

chapter forty-one

three months after the fire

Laura hung up her mobile and placed it on her bedside table. Beside her, Bobby lay flat on his back, arms splayed on either side of his head. The curtains were drawn and the window open, but still the summer sun flooded the bedroom with warmth and light. It had taken him a while to drift off for his afternoon nap, but Laura hadn't minded. She had waited until he fell asleep before she called Patrick back, knowing that even if she didn't get hold of him until later, it wouldn't matter.

In the last couple of months her bedroom had become a makeshift office. Two plastic crates were stacked by the wardrobe, filled with folders and client information. It wasn't ideal: she would have to decide what to do long-term if she were going to carry on working. She had wondered about building an office at the end of the garden, or changing the spare room, but that would mean selling the double bed and squeezing in a sofa bed, and right now Laura wasn't happy to commit even to that. Just in case one day soon she decided she didn't want to work at all.

Beside her, Bobby flung an arm out to one side, his tiny balled fist knocking her thigh. Laura slid down the bed, propping herself on her elbow so she could curl gently around her son. She watched his eyelids flutter, wondering what he could be dreaming about, what was filling his head. Gradually her mind drifted to the conversation she'd just had with Patrick. They needed to make a decision about recruiting, and sooner rather than later.

It was funny how the two of them had managed to pull together in the aftermath of the fire. She hadn't imagined it possible when Patrick first called her, a week after that night, and said he needed her to help him keep the business running. "Just until Harry is up to coming back," he had said, as if he somehow knew she might not want to be there longer.

Laura's first reaction was to tell him she wasn't interested. She hadn't been. She hadn't wanted anything more to do with Morris and Wood; she'd wanted to walk away and forget everything about it that had led her to this point.

Nate had found her a few days later, sitting in a darkened living room. "Talk to me," he said as he sat down beside her. He had been tentatively stepping around her since the fire, as if he didn't know if he trusted her or not. It wasn't until four days later, when Mia walked into the police station and gave her confession, that she saw a glimmer of relief on his face.

Laura had longed for Nate to believe her when she told him there was no way she had anything to do with it. She'd told him she'd walked out of the building at seven thirty p.m. and not looked back. That much was true. Laura could never be capable of burning down an office, as angry as she was.

But she also couldn't expect her husband to believe her when she hadn't told the whole truth from the start. When she'd later had to admit that she had been there—on the quay—and had known about the fire before the call the following morning, but had been too scared to admit it, when there was a chance she could get away with pretending she hadn't.

Nate had been furious with her for lying, but eventually accepted her fear.

She *was* afraid. She'd been afraid for her part, her silence, and even now the events of the night still ate away at her. How she'd found out that Mia had been at Morris and Wood for Janie all along, and that taking Laura's job had never had anything to do with her. Laura had been in the wrong place at the wrong time—her job had come up, and Mia was right there waiting for it.

Laura had been in the wrong place on Monday night too. How she wished she'd never been at the quay, that she hadn't learned the truth about the fire and hadn't been willing to keep quiet.

The day Nate had asked her to talk to him he was no longer worried that she'd done it, but he was still worried about her.

"What do you want me to say?" she'd replied.

"I want you to say whatever it is that's going on in your head. I want you to stop shutting me out," he had told her.

"I'm not doing that." Laura had shaken her head, folding her knees up and wrapping her arms around them. Gently Nate had pried her hands apart and taken hold of them in his own. "I have been talking to you," she'd said. "You know how I feel."

"I know you think the answer is to close yourself off to the job you once loved."

Laura had laughed softly. "I can't believe you're saying that after everything. Now you're suggesting I carry on? I'd have thought you'd be pleased I don't want to."

"I'm not pleased about anything if you're not happy," he'd said. "You know I never wanted you to give up your career."

"No," she had said quietly. "I do know that."

"I think you need to listen to what Patrick is suggesting, and between us we'll see if we can make it work. You can work from home, do the hours around caring for Bobby, and then I can start working part-time again."

Laura had squeezed her husband's hands in response. She didn't deserve Nate. Not one bit—and yet here he was, springing back into the loyal husband he had always been.

In the days after, they had talked about many things. Laura listened to how he really felt about the hours she'd been working, and in return she told him how she'd been feeling about Mia and what it had done to her confidence.

But Mia was out of the picture now, as Nate pointed out to her. Mia was currently in the remand wing of prison, awaiting trial. And Harry wasn't in a position to run his company. He was still in hospital. And maybe, Nate had said to her, maybe she *could* make a freelance career work.

Laura had mulled over the idea for a few days before finally picking up the phone to Patrick and listening properly to what he was proposing. There were going to be some tough months ahead in the wake of the fire, Mia's upcoming trial, decisions to be made as to what was going to happen to Morris and Wood, but between them they had enough contacts and experience to set up on their own.

In a moment of surprising honesty, Patrick had admitted he needed Laura, and her heart had beat a little faster when he told her how he couldn't make it work without her. "I've talked it through with Harry and he's happy," Patrick had said. "In fact, he wants you there. I think you should do it for him." Though those were the words that could have swung her the other way.

Harry. She hadn't been able to sift through her feelings toward the man she had trusted as her boss. Laura had always looked up to him, had never imagined he was anything but on her side, and yet he had let her down. But then the guilt of what had happened to him would creep in until, some days, it overwhelmed her.

She'd told herself she wasn't taking up Patrick's offer for Harry, she was doing it for herself. Laura didn't know which was true. Instead she focused on how she could make it work and now, three months down the line, she realized she had.

She and Patrick had kept on a majority of their clients as they worked remotely, keeping in touch with each other as regularly as needed. In the last few weeks Patrick had even rented office space, though he hadn't pushed her when she told him she wasn't ready to join him, that she wanted to keep working from home so she could be with her son.

Laura knew things might change soon, and when they did, she would have to tackle how best to adapt to them, but for now the situation was working. And if she were honest, the last three months had in some ways been a blessing. They had given her the chance to see that she could be a mum and have a career, and she could be good at both.

Nate tapped lightly on the bedroom door as he pushed it open. "I didn't know if you were still on a call," he said, sliding onto the bed beside her and Bobby, resting a hand on her leg. "All going okay?"

"Yes," she said. "Yeah, I think it is." She smiled at her husband and reached for his hand, squeezing it in her own. "Thank you," she murmured.

"What for?"

"For everything. For still being here."

Nate laughed as he lay down alongside her and wrapped an arm across her chest. "Where the hell else would I be?" he murmured.

She closed her eyes, enjoying the comfort of her husband and son next to her, though every time she was lulled into this security, her heart would jolt at the thought of the trial looming closer. Of Mia. Of the fact they had all lied.

As far as Nate was concerned, there were still patches of her story missing, and every day since that night, Laura had told herself she would come clean. But each night she promised to do it the next, and then the next, until she was caught in a vicious trap she no longer knew how to escape from.

Once the trial was over, she now told herself, she would tell her husband the truth. And she would pray that when that time came, he continued to understand.

chapter forty-two

Janie placed a cup of tea on the dining table in front of her husband and pulled out a chair to join him. She curled her fingers around her own cup as her gaze wandered out to the garden to some far distant spot, beyond where the girls were playing on the trampoline. She had promised them both they would go out for the day, and although the August rain had subsided, as yet they hadn't made it out of the house. There were still another three weeks of the summer holiday, yet somehow the days had passed them by. She regretted they hadn't made enough of them.

Of course it couldn't be helped when Harry was still recuperating, but she couldn't stop herself selfishly thinking it would be nice just to get a week away, like they had planned, before Ella started secondary school.

She watched her daughter, long limbs flying into the air as she landed on her back and bounced straight back up onto her feet. "What are you reading?" she murmured to Harry, lips pressed against her cup as she took a small sip of the too-hot tea.

"Just an email. From Patrick." He closed his phone, snapping the case shut and pushing it across the table.

"Everything all right?"

Harry nodded. "They seem to be doing a good job."

"Which is good," she prompted.

"Yeah. Yeah it is."

She knew Harry struggled with what was happening to his business. They'd needed to discuss it often enough over the last couple of months. Harry's lawyers were all over it, but there was a mountain of paperwork, decisions, conversations that sometimes got too much for him to handle on his own when he was only two months out of hospital.

On top of that, Janie had listened patiently as Harry dissected his feelings about working, oscillating between one extreme and the other. On the one hand, he would tell her, he had no desire to go back, not when the place had nearly killed him. "Maybe this is a chance for me to do something completely different," he would say. "We can use the money to do whatever we want. We could go traveling." In these moments Harry would be in a brighter mood as he focused on the positives of the situation that had befallen them.

"We can't go traveling," she had told him more than once. "Ella's at senior school now—"

"Yeah we can, of course we can," Harry would insist. "We've got nothing stopping us. Nothing keeping us in Lymington if I sell the business."

They had last had this conversation a week ago. Harry didn't want to go back to work at this point, though Janie knew his opinion would change again soon and they would start the circle again. And when they did, Harry would be unsettled, feeling worthless, like there was no point to his life.

"You wouldn't understand, Janie," he had said to her. "I was running that company for most my working life and now look at me." He had gestured at his face, scarred, still raw from burns.

Janie had wanted to tell him that of course she understood, but she had bitten her tongue. What did he actually think she had been through over the last five years? Janie had been completing this same circle since the moment they decided to leave London.

But Harry clearly didn't realize this, and maybe that was partly her fault because she had never told him. Now they had drifted so far out of reach from each other that she considered there was no longer any point mentioning it.

Instead Janie had continued to do what she always did and carried on, furiously paddling beneath the surface, but above it pretending everything was all right. She was mainly doing this for the girls, because it had been hard for them with their dad hitting rock bottom in the early weeks after the fire, refusing to leave the house. Janie had plastered on a cheery smile and continued to tell them this was a perfectly understandable and temporary reaction, and all the while had pushed any of her own feelings to one side. They could be addressed later down the line.

But she had come to a point, just after that last conversation, when she needed to speak to someone. And eventually she had picked up the phone and called Sophie. "I was going to leave him," she admitted in a burst. "Only now I can't."

Sophie had listened as Janie talked and finally told her she didn't have to feel guilty about whatever decision she made. She just had to make the right one for her.

Only it wasn't that simple. Because what was right for her might not be right for the girls, and anyway, despite all that, how could she? "What would everyone say?" she had cried on the phone to her friend.

Of course Sophie told her what Janie would tell any of her own friends—that it didn't matter what anyone said, her true friends would be there for her no matter what. But the platitudes didn't help.

And so Janie carried on watching Harry scurry around in circles, listening to him debate what he was going to do.

The funny thing was, she realized, as they sat in the kitchen that morning and the girls continued to play on the trampoline in the sun, he hadn't once asked her what it was she wanted.

In fact, since Ella was born, she couldn't actually remember a time when it had been about her. It had always been about Harry.

Finally she turned to her husband and said, "We need to talk."

His gaze flicked up from the phone he'd dragged back to himself.

"I don't think I've been totally honest with you," she said. Her hands shook against the cup that was still poised at her mouth, and eventually she put it down on the table and held it there.

"Okay," he said cautiously.

Janie opened her mouth, still not entirely sure what she was going to say. Because until that moment she hadn't known she was going to bring up the details again of Sophie's rape at the hands of Miles Morgan.

To his credit her husband listened, and as the girls continued to play outside for another hour, Janie managed to tell her husband exactly what had been going on in her life for the past five years, from the moment she'd told him about Sophie to the point she knew she was being followed.

When she finally finished, she picked up her cup and drank the cold tea while waiting for him to speak. She didn't miss the tears that had appeared in the corner of his eyes or the hand she no longer recognized as he wiped them away with the tip of his thumb. He no longer wore his wedding band. He had been tearful then, too, when he'd told her he couldn't, a week after the fire, though at the time Janie had coldly stared at him, thinking that was surely the least of their problems.

"Why are you only telling me all this now?" Harry had said.

She wondered what was going through his mind as he asked her. If she'd told him when it first happened, they might not be sitting here now in their current situation. If she had told him, he might never have brought Miles back into their lives. The fire might never have been set.

Is that what Harry thought? That this was her fault? He wasn't accusing her, but she couldn't get the thought out of her head, because Miles's actions had been the catalyst for the fire. Of that she was certain.

"I don't know why," she replied eventually. "I was angry with you. I think I blamed your attitude because I didn't want to carry on blaming myself for what happened to Sophie."

"I thought you wanted to leave your job; I thought you weren't happy," he went on. "I *thought*," he said, "that I was doing the right thing for you by moving down to Lymington because you didn't want to work anymore after . . ."

Janie didn't answer.

"Why weren't you honest with me?" Harry asked.

"I don't know," she said in a much quieter voice this time. "I just didn't talk to you, and then it kind of snowballed."

Harry's head sank into his hands. "You never told me you were being followed," he said. "I mean, why wouldn't you ever tell me that? It affects the girls too." When he looked up at her, his eyes shone with fear. Everything could have been so much worse.

"We know who it was now," she said. "And I believe Mia when she says she never intended to hurt me or the girls."

Harry gave a short laugh as he shook his head, dropping his hands to the table with a thud. "That's ridiculous. You clearly can't believe a word that woman says," he said, his scarred face contorting with anger.

"No, you're right," Janie said quickly, to defuse the situation before it blew up. "You're right, I don't."

Though the truth was she did actually believe Mia. Even though Mia had wanted to avenge her sister, Janie knew she would never have hurt her or the girls because she had seen it in her eyes when they spoke during one of Janie's visits to prison to see her.

But of course she could never tell Harry about that, either. And at some point Janie also knew she would have to stop visiting Mia, but not yet. Not just yet. For now it was something she still needed to do.

"So what do you want to do?" Harry asked. His expression had changed again, no longer angry, now more worried.

"I want to go back to work," she said. "I've been thinking for some time that I want to help women, encourage them to speak out about harassment in the workplace." It felt such a far contrast to her previous job, but in many ways so similar. "I want to show Ella and Lottie it's important to stand up for themselves," Janie went on. She wanted to show them that this was far more important than defending the men who took away their rights.

Harry nodded slowly. "Okay," he replied. "I get that."

"I don't want to work full-time because of the girls . . ."

"I understand."

Janie nodded too.

"But what do you want—" He broke off, his eyes on her. "What about us? Are you ever going to get back what you think you've lost?"

Janie turned away and watched Lottie clambering down the steps of the trampoline. Behind her Ella stood, clutching a netball, shouting something at her sister that Janie couldn't hear. All of a sudden the ball left her hands and landed with a thump on the top of Lottie's head.

Janie winced as she waited for tears from her youngest that to her surprise didn't come.

"Janie." Harry reached over and took hold of her hand, and by instinct she pulled it away. For a moment they were both silent as they looked at the table, their hands only inches apart, though it felt like an interminable gap between them.

It was easier when they weren't talking so honestly, Janie thought. When there were no questions from him that she had to answer, when she could drift through the days, pretending.

"I don't know," she said.

Harry held a hand over his mouth, rubbing his lips with his fingertips. His eyes searched hers. "Do you want to try?" he asked eventually.

"I don't know," she said again, quieter, with a small flick of her head.

Beside her Harry stilled. The air between them was deathly silent. Janie closed her eyes. She knew this was going to be a long stretch ahead. If she left him now, how would he cope? Would he lay that on her? Would he beg her to stay because he wouldn't be able to do this without her? In many ways she could imagine her husband doing just that, and yet to his credit he eventually said, "I love you, Janie. I just want you to be happy, and if that's not with me—" His voice broke with emotion, and she felt her own sorrow balling tightly in her throat as her mind flooded with too many thoughts than she could bear. "I just think we need to be honest with each other."

Janie nodded. She would be honest with him. Not about everything, maybe. Not about the fact she was seeing Mia, and that she'd been giving Mia's family money to help with Jess. But she would finally be honest about what she wanted.

chapter forty-three

Mia glanced up as the visitors rolled in. She had begun to recognize most of them now and always had to watch every one of them enter the room before her mum finally appeared at the end of the line.

She looked older than ever today. Her frail body even more stooped than usual, and her face was pale, deep eye sockets shadowed with dark circles, but then Mia supposed she looked no better herself. Her hair was growing out, shapeless strands touching her shoulders now, the roots showing, her nails were bitten low and ragged.

"How are you, love?" her mum said as she sat down.

"I'm good," Mia told her, though they both knew this was a lie. "How are you?"

Her mother looked at her, and Mia saw a flash of something in her eyes, though she couldn't identify it at first. "Keeping going. The traffic wasn't as bad today, took less than two hours," she said as if this was in some ways a bonus.

"I don't like you doing so much driving."

"Nonsense," her mum tutted. "I'm getting used to it anyway."

"How's Jess?" Mia asked hopefully.

"She still wants to come and see you."

Mia turned away, studying the other visitors intently.

"She doesn't understand why you won't let her," her mum persisted, the words spoken a little more sharply, enough to make Mia glance back. "I don't understand it either. You two, you were always so close. So close, and now—" She broke off, leaving the unfinished sentence hanging.

"Do you blame Jess for your being in here?" her mum asked, not for the first time. "You can tell me the truth, love. I will understand."

All her mum had tried to be was understanding, and it was breaking Mia's heart.

"You know, because you would never have been seeking revenge in the first place, would you?" she went on. "It would never have gotten as far as it did."

"Do *you* blame Jess?" Mia's words came out more abruptly than she'd intended. She hadn't even meant them, but she'd wanted to shut the conversation down.

"Mia!" Her mum pulled back, holding a hand over her mouth.

Mia wanted to reach across and hug her, tell her she didn't mean it, yet she stayed stubbornly rooted to the seat, her gaze drifting away and across the room. "That's not the reason I don't want to see her," she said eventually.

"Then please, love, tell me what I can say to her."

Mia gave a small flick of her head and her mum sat back, exhaling deeply. "You think she can't handle it?" she asked. "Is that it? You think she won't be able to deal with seeing you like this. Well, she will. After all, I can," her mum said, her voice cracking as she laid a hand over her heart.

"She's only just started going out again," Mia said quietly.

"That's what this is? You're scared it will put her off?" Her mum leaned forward again, grappling for something to grab on to that would make her understand Mia's obstinate refusal to see her sister. "It's not going to do that. She's doing so well; this wouldn't . . ." Her sentence fizzled out as if she wasn't sure she believed it.

Mia straightened herself and splayed her hands on the table between them. "Tell me what you've been up to this week?"

Her mum pursed her lips and took a moment, as if she were trying to recall what they'd been doing. In reality, Mia knew she was wondering how much to say.

"Go on. Please," Mia urged, because she *did* want to know.

"Well, last week we took a picnic to the beach. We went all the way to Sandbanks, over on that ferry you both used to love when you were kids." For a moment she was caught in the memory and her eyes sparkled as she spoke of it.

Mia nodded encouragement.

"Jess loved it there, but then it started raining so we came back and went to the cinema. Oh, and then Thursday she got us tickets to the theatre. Can you believe that? They had one of those London shows come to the Mayflower. Jess spotted it online; she said it was one she'd wanted to see for ages."

Mia smiled. "That's brilliant."

But the light drained from her mum's eyes as she said, "It doesn't feel right."

"Yes it does. You should be thrilled that Jess wants to do all this."

"How can I be thrilled? How can I be happy about any of it when you're here? I don't seem to be able to live my life without one of my daughters in a prison, do I?" As soon as the words were out of her mouth, her mum's face dropped. "Oh dear God, I shouldn't have said that. I'm sorry, love, I'm so sorry."

"It's fine." Mia murmured.

"No. It isn't fine at all. Why on earth do you want to hear all these things we've been up to when you can't—you can't even . . ."

"I *do* want to hear them. I love knowing what you and Jess are doing. I want to know that she's beginning to live her life again."

Don't you think that's why I'm in here, she thought, though she didn't say this.

"So you need to make sure she carries on," Mia urged her. "Show her how much there is to live for. This is no more than she deserves, you know that. She deserves a bloody life at last." Mia's eyes welled with tears as her mum closed her own.

"What's the point of it all?" she said so quietly.

"What do you mean, Mum?"

"I've gained one daughter and lost another, so what's the bloody point?"

"Mum, you can't talk like that."

"This is what I don't get." She shook her head, opening her eyes and searching Mia's. "I don't get it at all. How you can talk about your sister with all this love but then refuse to see her?"

Mia flattened her mouth and dipped her head. She didn't want to get into this again.

"Are you still letting those other women visit?"

Mia shook her head. "I only saw Laura twice."

Laura had visited near the beginning, and Mia had been grateful for the chance to talk about what had happened that night. To tell her again how indebted she was for Laura's silence during those first few days of questioning.

She'd also thought Laura had come because she'd wanted to hear Mia explain to her again how she'd never been out for her. There was something so fragile about the woman who Mia had always been led to believe was so strong.

After two visits it was clear they had little left to talk about.

"And what about Janie Wood?" her mum asked.

"I've seen her a few times," she said. "The barrister she put me in touch with is amazing. Are you still okay, you know, you're still getting the payments?" Mia asked.

Her mum nodded. "It isn't right though, her paying us."

"She wants to. And while she does, take the money, Mum. You know you need it, and they don't."

"That doesn't matter." Her mother laughed. "It doesn't make a difference if they need it or not. She shouldn't be paying us, especially not after what happened to her husband."

"Mum," Mia urged, "Janie wants to do this, and it's for Jess, for her to get help. It's only for a few months, so please, just promise me you'll use it."

Mia had been grateful for Janie's money and contacts, though she couldn't deny she'd been playing on the woman's guilt. Janie had finally realized who Mia was, but that realization had been superseded by everything else that unfurled the night of the fire. Still, it had become clear during later visits how heavily her part in Jess's unraveling weighed on her.

It wasn't until the third visit that Janie had admitted to Mia that Miles had done the same thing to her best friend, and Mia wondered if they would have been in the same position if that hadn't happened. If Janie had learned that Mia had been trying to exact revenge on her one night while her husband's offices were burning to the ground, would she have been so supportive if she didn't have Sophie preying on her conscience? Somehow Mia doubted it.

Janie had wanted to know why Mia had been watching her. "What were you trying to do to me?" she had asked. "When you were outside my house—the girls?" She hadn't been able to get the sentence out.

"No, no, I'd never have hurt them," Mia had promised her. "I never wanted to hurt any of your family, not like that."

Janie had nodded slowly, her head hung questioningly. "Then why?"

"I wanted to know something about you—anything at all that could help me make you pay. You were never at the office, you had nothing to do with the business, no one knew the first thing about you, really.

"But there was just nothing about your life that wasn't driven by money, and so all I could do was work out a way to destroy that if I could . . ." Mia shrugged. It all sounded so childish and amateur now, so unlikely to work, and yet all those months earlier, when she had seen the advert for Laura's job, Mia had convinced herself it was the opportunity she'd needed.

"You and Harry were so—" She waved an arm. "You had everything. Your lives were so glossy, and ours—" Mia broke off and laughed. "They couldn't be more different. I wanted to bring down Harry's company, including his reputation. I had no idea how at first, but then when Sarah told me she was being bullied . . . It was only a glimmer of opportunity, but it was enough."

"You could have ruined Mike's life too." Janie had said it plainly, like she wasn't trying to admonish her, just state a fact.

"I know. There were always going to be some casualties along the way," Mia said, and she knew she had sounded heartless as she looked away. "The fact was I didn't think of any of that, I just wanted to get you back. Women *are* treated differently there, you know," she'd added, as if this was some way of justifying her actions. "They're not promoted. Harry and his boys; it's all mates doing favors for each other."

Janie had nodded.

"I wanted to tarnish his reputation and lose him important clients. I figured that if Coopers believed me—" Mia shook her head. "I thought that if you lost your income, you'd be losing the most important thing. But despite all that, I am sorry for what happened to Harry. I never wanted . . . " She drifted off again. "Things spiraled."

Now Mia turned to her mum and said, "Please just take the money."

"Okay." Her mum held her hands up. "Fine."

Mia sat back in her seat and studied her mother. She couldn't bear to think how much of a toll the last three months had taken on her, and it was only going to get worse when the trial began.

Eventually her mum spread her hands across the table and Mia reached out for them, feeling the pressure of her mum's fingers as they wrapped around hers. "I wish there was something I could do; I don't want you here, Mia." Tears bubbled in the corners of her eyes until they slid down her cheeks. Mia watched them roll off the end of her mother's chin, dripping onto the table. "I wish I was here instead of you."

"You can't do that, Mum."

"No. There's nothing I *can* do," she said. "That's what breaks my heart. I would swap places with you in a heartbeat if I could."

"I know you would."

"I know you never intended to kill that man," she said, as she'd said in every one of her visits. "I know you would never have done that. It was just pure impulse." She smiled ruefully. "You always did have a quick temper."

"I know, Mum," Mia replied.

"Please, darling, please just let Jess come and see you. As soon as you see her you'll know she can cope. Please. Do it for me. Then I can close it off."

Mia closed her eyes, shaking her head a fraction. "Okay," she said eventually. "Okay, let Jess come."

But as soon as the words were out of her mouth, she already wondered if she'd done the right thing.

chapter forty-four

Mia had been refusing to see Jess, but not because she blamed her sister for her being in prison like her mum had suggested. She had made that decision herself. Rather, Mia worried that any day Jess would decide to tell the truth. And that if her sister saw her here, there was a greater chance of that happening.

Mia had often wondered if deep down her mum knew the truth, or at least suspected it. She had seen a flash of something in her eyes that she hadn't understood at first, but later realized it was the same look her mum used to give them as children. When she knew one of her daughters was lying.

It broke Mia's heart that her mum thought she could do something like this, but at the same time it would break her heart to think Jess had. It was a no-win situation.

Mia glanced around the room, at every other woman waiting for her visitor to arrive.

She had no idea what to expect when she saw her sister. She didn't want to talk about the night of the fire, though; she wanted Jess to tell her more about her life now: what she was doing, how much she was enjoying living again. Mia wanted to see the life back in her sister's eyes.

Still, she knew it was a lot to ask as she watched the first three visitors making their way in, catching her breath when she caught sight of Jess, a security guard holding open the double doors for her.

Mia lifted her hand in a wave, but when Jess turned it wasn't just life she saw in her eyes.

Jess paused when she saw her, her face open, a small smile on the edge of her lips. She blinked once and took a deep breath before she began moving again. All the time she didn't look away from Mia.

As Mia followed her movement, her head was filled with all the things her mum had been telling her about—Jess's desire to throw herself back into the world again. Picnics on the beach, a trip on the Sandbanks ferry, the cinema, theatre—suddenly it all dawned on her.

Mia wanted to leap up, run over, push her sister back out of the room, but instead she froze, her breaths shallow. Jess hadn't been doing it because of what Mia had given up for her. She had been doing it to make the most of the freedom she had left, a last hurrah.

Mia knew why her sister had wanted to visit so desperately. She now knew exactly what Jess was going to tell her today, and she also knew there was nothing she could do about it.

Jess never had any intention of letting Mia go to trial, or to take the blame for something she hadn't done. There was no way she was going to let Mia get sent down. All she was doing was giving Mia what she wanted first—showing her that she was living her life. And Jess hadn't done that for herself. She'd done it for the two people in the world who meant everything to her.

acknowledgments

To all the many, many wonderful mums I know, and those in particular who I greatly admire but who don't always realize what an amazing job they're doing—this book is for all of you.

My thanks go to my two wonderful friends Deb Dorman and Donna Cross, who have helped me shape the stories of Laura, Mia, and Janie. And to all my other friends who continue to be such a huge support. I am so lucky to have you all.

To my lovely readers, reviewers, and book bloggers, and everyone who has been generous with their time and comments, thank you, as without you I wouldn't be able to do what I love. And I really do love doing it.

And to the amazing and talented people I work with both at home and over the seas: my ever fantastic super-agent Nelle Andrew, who I would genuinely be lost without, and my two editors, who continually amaze me with their ability to turn the book around for the better at each edit. Emily Griffin and Jackie Cantor, you have both made my experience of writing this book an absolute pleasure.

The teams at both Century in the UK and Gallery in the US— thank you all for your support in marketing, PR, proofreading, designing brilliant covers, and getting the book into stores. I have to pinch myself that I have such great support working behind my books, and I know that any success is a massive team effort.

And finally to my family, this time with the added support of Pickle and Toffee the cats who help me by sitting on my laptop and biting the end of my pen.

To my mum, for picking up the phone and crying when she'd finished reading because she is so proud of me.

And to my amazing husband, for continuing to be my other biggest supporter, who never doubts me and loves to think that the characters are written around him. (Harry isn't you, John!)

And as always, my two precious children, Bethany and Joseph, you are my world. Words will never be enough to tell you how much I love you and how proud I am of you, but I am, every single day. Thank you for allowing me the time to work on my book when I need to and for basically being the two kind, loving, and generous little people you are.